SUMMER

OF

STORM

&

STRIFE

COPYRIGHT

TABLE OF CONTENTS

MAPS

LINDBARROW
AVAREE
PORT GALAN
Imbaelic Sea
CLIFF HALLOWS
Tebarian Mountains
Tatoch Forest
TARON
DANVERY PRISON
Caprianth Sea
EILBAST
BRAMBLEHALL
EVERNESS
To Njorske
SOUTHPORT
To the mainland
Strait of Celeroa

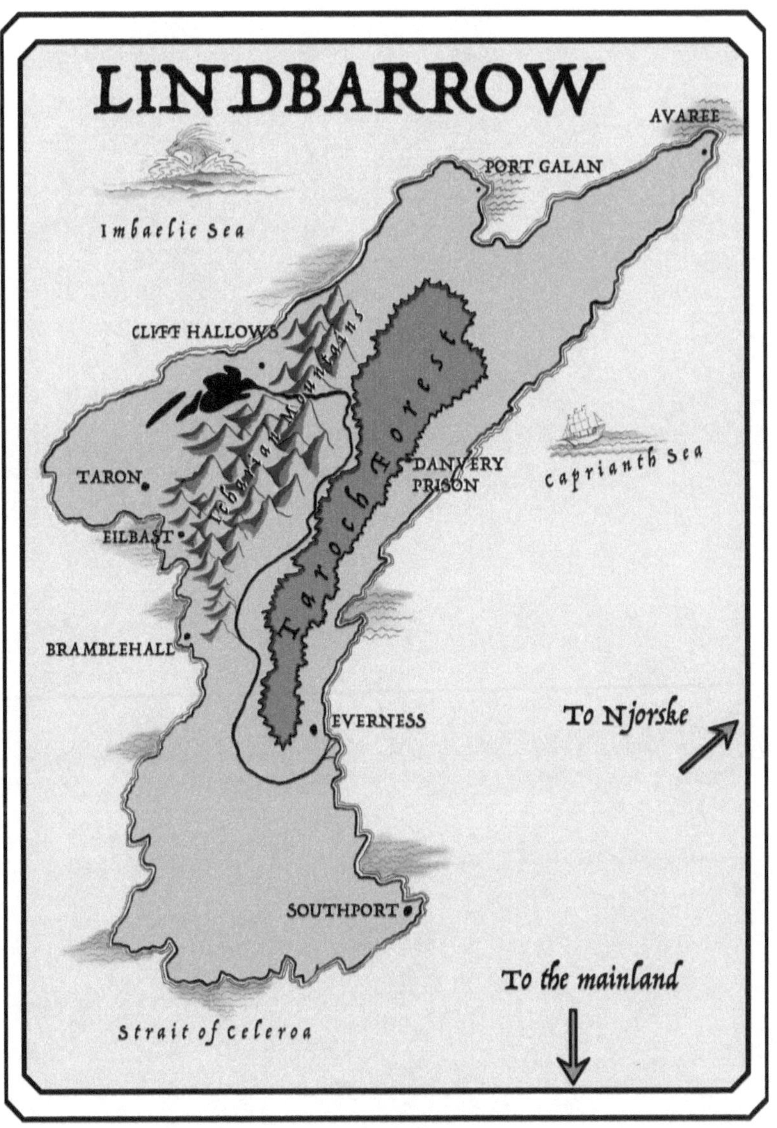

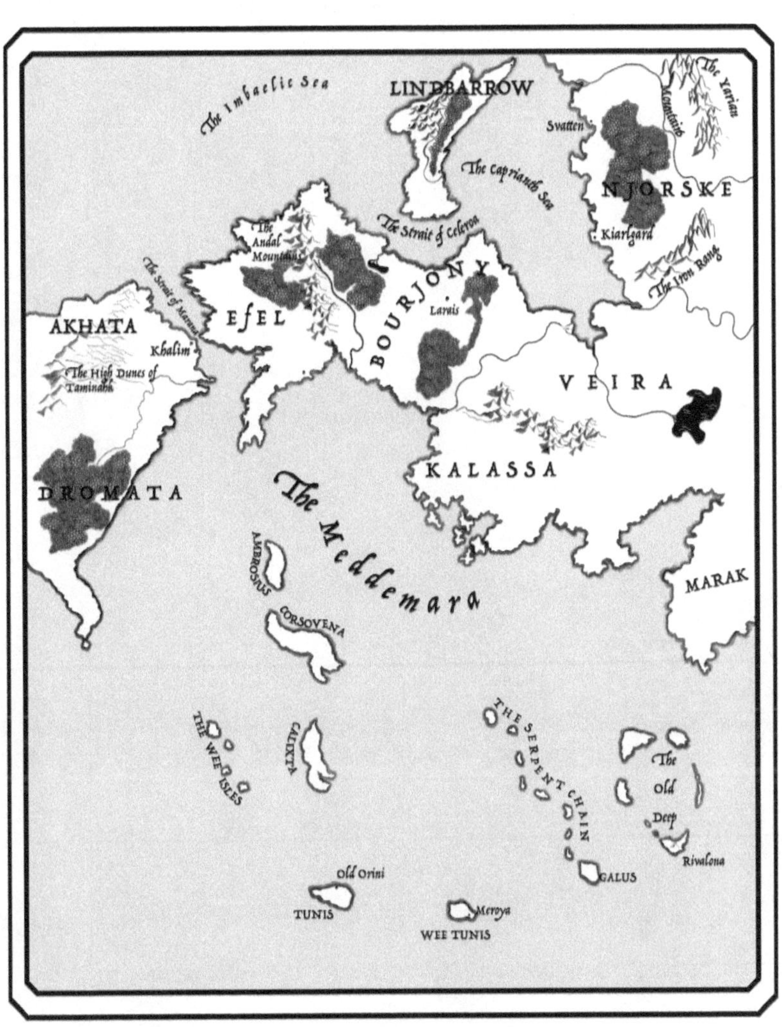

The Imbaelic Sea
LINDBARROW
The Caprianch Sea
Svatten
The Yarian Mountains
NJORSKE
The Strait of Celeron
Kiarlgard
The Andal Mountains
The Iron Rang
BOURJONY
Larais
The Strait of Meronal
EFEL
VEIRA
AKHATA
Khalim'
The High Dunes of Taminahh
KALASSA
DROMATA
The Meddemara
MARAK
AMBROSIUS
CORSOVENA
CALIXTA
THE WEE ISLES
THE SERPENT CHAIN
The Old Deep
Rivalona
GALUS
Old Orini
TUNIS
Meroya
WEE TUNIS

PROLOGUE

Adrienne Leone was not a woman of delicate constitution. She'd spent decades elbow-deep in entrails, splattered in blood, and stitching flesh. She'd reattached limbs, broken and set bones. She'd even spent two weeks in the bowels of a rather nasty Bourjon prison, and lived to claw her way out and escape across a war-torn countryside.

All that being said, she was not as spry as she'd once been. The days of hiking through Taroch Forest, the foothills, and into the Icharian mountains were taking their toll upon her, and despite summer's approach, the nights remained chilly. By her estimate, she would make it to the sacred ruins by nightfall. If she didn't, she would have to spend another night half-asleep, shivering, and praying no wolf, or worse, saw fit to make her his meal. She'd been out here for eight nights, and she didn't want to make it nine.

Nine days ago, the worst had come to pass.

Bourjony had invaded Lindbarrow, which meant the beginning of the end was well underway.

She shuddered, remembering the night she'd fled Bourjony, leaving behind the only home she'd ever known. Thirty years ago, she'd trekked through the Andal Mountains in the cold autumn, with even less preparation than she had now.

She would have crawled across broken glass on her belly to escape that place, though.

If she was right, there was a long and difficult road ahead for everyone. *If* she was right…

There was no sense fretting about it now. All she could do was climb the mountain ahead of her, and hope she would find what she needed at its summit. She would call upon the others.

As she began her ascent, her mind ran through what was to come when she reached the top of the winding mountain. Perhaps no one would answer her call. Perhaps there was no one left of the sacred order. Perhaps the sacred hearth had been destroyed.

At last, after many stops to rest against a tree, or sip from a stream, and with aching knees and back, she came to the crest where the hollow sat. The temple far above the world, on the Barrian Isle's tallest peak.

The temple was ancient, long predating the centuries-old conflict between the Lundi and Caelish sects. Its white stone was covered in moss and lichen and delicate alpine vegetation. Little cairns of pale stone flecked in opalescent deposits marked the overgrown path up to the structure, and even in the near-dusk light, the peak was shrouded in soft, cool mist.

The sky was bleeding a deep twilight violet above the clouds. One by one, stars winked out of hiding and into view as the sky darkened. Seven thousand feet above the land below, the view of the night sky was transformative. As the stars bloomed in the sky, so too did the flowers that had spread feral around the temple's ruins.

The blossoms began to glow blue and open in the night air, casting a soft and lovely radiance all about the mountainside.

Adrienne's face broke out in a smile as she beheld what must surely be the isle's variant of the sweet-ivy she'd come to know in Bourjony's countryside so many decades ago.

After allowing herself and her knees a few brief, glorious moments of rest, she stood and set about gathering a few small bundles of the sacred crop. When she had enough to fill the hearth, she pulled up a log and sat down. She used the corner of her cloak to sweep the dust from the stones before spreading the flowers in the trench, and letting them light.

The flowers ignited in a gentle, sweet blue. It was the blue of clouds on a calm day, of chilly autumn winds through the cliffs, and over the sea. After a moment, the flame faded to its usual warm orange.

The fire had begun to flicker down to embers when they came.

The first figure to arrive stepped cloaked and hooded out of the shadows and into the dim firelight. Beneath his cloak, he was short, broad-shouldered and not absent a considerable paunch that hinted at a fondness for ale and sweets.

"Good eve, *Mistra*," he said, removing his hood and dipping his chin in respect.

"Greetings, *Mistre*," Adrienne replied, standing.

"I am Nostrus Alvarian, Seer," the man said, approaching the hearth circle.

"Adrienne Leone, Life-Witch and Healer."

Nostrus was perhaps ten years her junior, halfway to bald, but making up for it with his impressive, well-groomed facial hair.

"Will any others be joining?" she asked.

Nostrus nodded with a grim expression. "We can only hope. Each city on this isle has faced much bloodshed these past days."

Almost as if on cue, a third figure stepped into the circle cast by the fading fire.

"It has been many years since the north's sacred hearth was lit with the windblossom." The speaker was tall, absent the traditional cloak, but hooded nonetheless. "Greetings, *Mistris*."

When he removed his hood, Adrienne's eyebrows twitched up in recognition. "You are the stable-master."

"Aye," he conceded. "Alick MacVale, at your service."

"How did you escape slaughter during the invasion?" she asked, a little breathless. She'd been sure she was the only grounds staff to have made it out after the attack.

"I fled with a small group of rebel operatives. Halfway to Galan, I circled back to see if I could find any survivors."

"Did you?" Hope took root in her chest, digging in its claws.

"Several small groups, all scattered in the foothills and the forest. I was leading a few to the cliff-pass when I felt the call." He reached into his shirt and pulled forth a pendant on a leather cord, the tiny gemstone at its center pulsing with silver light.

"I see," Madame Leone nodded.

And so, the three practitioners of the ancient order sat around the fire waning in the hearth, and began to discuss what was to come.

PART

ONE

CHAPTER ONE

T his is becoming ridiculous," Rhi muttered to himself.
"What is?" Ferrin asked from where she perched—rather precariously, but Rhi supposed that didn't matter for her—cross-legged on the balcony railing, peeling a fat orange.

"These complaints," Rhi let out a long-suffering sigh. "The skirmishes. The tussles. The general contempt."

"I suppose we shouldn't be *too* surprised," she mused. "It's not as if centuries of conflicts were going to resolve overnight. You said as much when you volunteered for this position."

He shot her an unamused look. She popped a section of the orange into her mouth with an innocent lift of her brows.

"Despite the common enemy, the Caelish and Lundi people have been fighting over this island forever. *Everyone* knows someone who was slighted by the opposite side. Or killed, or stolen from, or shamed, or—"

"Right, Ferr. I know that." He closed his journal abruptly. "It's still ridiculous. These are fully-grown adults. Trained soldiers, most of them. Not petulant children. I have one report here of an altercation that was started over one missing boiled egg."

"Well, I suppose…"

"It turned into a twenty person brawl! Eight soldiers were injured down in the barracks. Twenty people!"

"Perhaps if it had been a *fried* egg," she mumbled.

"Thank you, you're terribly helpful," he sighed. "The strict rations on food aren't helping ease tensions, either."

"No, no one is happy about that," she agreed, extending half of her orange to him. It was part of their allotted daily fruit serving as per the commissary. No scurvy was to be had among the ranks.

Rhi took the half-orange in one hand and rubbed his jaw with the other. He'd been too busy to shave that day, and a fine layer of scruff was sneaking its way in. He'd vowed to do better than his father. Even though he had no throne or crown here. The day after they'd arrived, he'd marched down to the barracks and asked how he could be of service. That had been three weeks ago. He was starting to wonder if he was making any difference at all.

He couldn't be sure, but the alternative to his cooperation might well end with his head on a chopping block in an attempt to rid the land of a relic from the old regime. He supposed Arabella's old connections to the resistance were a saving grace on his part, but too much fuss just might land him back at the noose.

After the invasion, half of the Lindbarrian soldiers had defected to the Caelish lines, having nowhere else to go now that Bourjony had claimed so much of the island. Both the barracks and the manor were over-crowded, and there was no shortage of friction and tension between the new arrivals and the Caelish rebels.

Someone always needed something.

"Here, give me that." Ferrin swiped for the leather-bound journal. "Go take a peaceful walk or something. I'll sort through these."

Rhi decided not to mention the two identical journals stuffed to the snapping with complaints, potential court martial appeals, and reports that he hadn't even touched yet.

When Bourjony had begun its infiltration of Lindbarrow's major cities and towns a year ago, and finally their assault and annexation of most of the island just three weeks ago, they'd created a new rift within the Lindbarrian Royal Army. It had started as a small crack, but in the wake of the invasion, the splitting of loyalties had been stark and decisive.

Many Lundi soldiers and nobility had either already been in on Bourjony's plan, or had defected shortly after. Some of the Caelish, out of resentment toward Rhi's father, had defected to Bourjony's lines as well.

The other half of the former Lindbarrian Army had defected to Port Galan, filling the barracks with disgruntled Lundi soldiers, none of whom were overly enthusiastic about joining up with the Caelish army, but who certainly weren't about to bow to the Bourjons.

That left the barracks in Port Galan filled with Caelish rebels, and defectors of the former Lindbarrian Army.

Those two groups did not mix well, and the encampment seemed to be in near constant tumult.

Rhi sighed again and passed Ferrin the journal. "Thanks."

Now, just as it had been long ago, before he was born, the island was divided north and south. Port Galan and Avaree were the last two free-standing cities on the isle, while the south was crawling with the Bourjonaise-Lundi-what-have-you occupation. There was no easy solution to smooth over the relations of people who'd been at each others throats for generations on end. Their common enemy was likely the only thing keeping the camp from breaking out into a full-scale battlefield.

Rhi chewed his lip as he paced along the hall leading back to the main level of the manor.

It had to be some sort of personal advantage, for there was no other reason for Bourjony to pour so many of their resources into conquering the island.

Bourjony had long claimed its ruler, King Avent II, was of godly heritage. Had proclaimed his divine right to rule all land.

From a strategic standpoint, it made no sense to prioritize taking Lindbarrow.

The Efelians had the superior navy. Kalassa was rife with temples and holy land, as well as its convenient location between the peninsula and the bulk of the continent, and both seas. Akhata was at the most strategic position for land and sea trade. Veira was rich with farmlands. Dromata had its gem mines. Even Njorske, with its wide ice passes and iron mines, seemed a more optimal place to start.

Something was missing from the equation that he couldn't quite put his finger on.

He dismissed the thought for the time being. He'd be better off dealing with the matter at hand rather than worrying over Bourjony's hidden motives. If he could find passage to Avaree, he could find out more about what exactly Bourjony might be seeking here.

As for the matter at hand, one name seemed to recur in a pattern most consistently among complaints.

Lieutenant Lachlan Tarrish.

Once she'd delivered several answers, sentences and approvals to the various reports, complaints, and generally abrasive bits of information from the barracks, Ferrin found herself worn out and more restless than usual.

It had been three weeks since she'd taken a musket ball to the thigh. Three weeks since lead had ground against bone for an entire night, sealed in by an enemy healer just so she wouldn't bleed out before they could publicly execute her. Three weeks since Soviel had split her flesh open to dig out the invasive piece of metal.

Though Soviel had healed her injuries, she was still on the mend. A soak in the sea might do her some good, she decided.

When she was satisfied with the distance between her and the ever-reeking outer fish pier at the harbor's mouth, she shucked off her boots and coat and plowed into the water in her base layer. The coolness of the ocean, even at the beginning of summer, was biting. At last, when her body had adjusted, the soothing feel of the sea washed over her bones. Her knee had been complaining almost as much as the soldiers in the barracks.

She floated awhile, letting the gentle waves ebb and flow beneath her as she paddled aimlessly into the surf. From beyond the breakers, she could see the clifftop manor and the fort in its entirety.

Port Galan's central seat of power was nestled atop the rocky cliffside, facing northeast, out to the sea. A winding stair was carved into the face of the cliff, a quick and precarious egress down to a small inlet and sea cave (there was no shortage of those around these parts). The perfect way to make a clandestine exit out of the manor in case of an attack.

Though it sat right on the sea, it was nearly impossible to launch a successful naval attack on Port Galan. With the manor itself fully outfitted with a fifty-gun complement and the fort a half-mile to the east at the mouth of the harbor, only a fool would attack from the sea. The cannons would take them out before they could get close enough from the east, and from the west, there was a rocky wall rising high enough to block the true location of the barracks and the town from view.

The only safe way to approach was through the harbor, with the explicit say-so of the stone fort.

As summer waxed toward its zenith, the days grew longer, warmer. Ferrin tipped her head up, floating on her back as she soaked up the sun's warmth. Even exhausted, she could feel the wind calling her out to play.

With a small smile, she ducked underwater, sinking as far down as she could before shooting out and into the sky.

The refugee center, recently erected in the wake of the invasion, was little more than a tossed-together shanty that stood between the barracks and the docks. It was run by soldiers and volunteer civilians alike, and over the past few weeks, Lukas had found himself checking the lists nailed to its walls every morning.

When Ryder never resurfaced after the prison break, a gnawing feeling in Lukas's chest had begun to eat away at him. Little by little, day by day. Ryder had not returned to the capital as planned following the prison break, nor had he shown up in Galan since then. Tolline, Ryder's wife, had been gone from their little apartment by the Pit when Lukas went to check, and considering that their belongings and their dog had also been neatly removed, he suspected she had cleared out of the city before the invasion. Ryder had once said she had distant family in one of the northern cities.

He was sure if he did run into her, she'd beat him over the head with a shoe for dragging her husband into 'another one of his schemes'.

Lists of names went up every morning, though as the invasion moved further and further into the past, they grew shorter and shorter. But there was still hope.

"Back again, are ye?" the stout, older lady who was here most mornings asked from the table-turned-desk. Her name was Agneath. "She must be a lovely to have you down here checking those names every day."

"*He's* just a friend, actually," Lukas said as his eyes skimmed the page.

No Ryder Berry.

Might he have given a false name? Ryder had had more than a few run-ins with the law, and might not have wanted to advertise his presence.

"Any luck?" Agneath asked.

He gave a grim shake of his head.

Had he led yet another friend to his death?

Itching for something to do, something to distract him from memories of a hot day in the desert, and the sound of gunfire, deafening and maddening, he headed down to the barracks.

In the weeks since they'd arrived from Everness, some even cruder, more shabby version of the Pit had sprung up on the edge of the encampment. Many of the soldiers and castle guards who'd once frequented the Pit had arrived in Galan along with the refugees, so he could always count on there being a modest pool placed on a few dust-ups.

It wasn't the same as the abandoned warehouse-arena, and it was far less organized. The large tent held a big enough space for a crowd to gather beneath. The ring had no ropes, no boundaries, just the wall of onlookers to shove you back to the center if you lost your footing. Standing in the front row guaranteed catching an elbow or a fist every once in a while.

Unlike the constant brawling throughout the barracks, these fights went unreported, and generally ended in good spirits and a few coins made.

Lukas was just about to approach the sign-up stand to put down his name when a quick blur and a high, boisterous laugh turned his head. He inched through the crowd, angling to get a better look, though he had an inkling of who he was about to see.

Ash ducked the next punch, barely missing having her teeth knocked out right along with her senses.

Her breathing was hard and fast as she danced out of the way, slipping a right hook from Dreszen. His nose was still bleeding from where she'd caught him in the first round. While the momentum from his swing still carried him, she weaved under his guard and hooked her ankle around his before punching him in the gut. He went down hard.

The crowd went wild, filling the tent with roars of approval. From the corner of her eye, she spotted Soviel and gave her a wink.

The scheme they'd hatched to pull extra coin was going well. More than well. Each day she'd entered, the two of them had made more than the average brawler might make in a week. After each fight, Soviel would fix the inevitable little injuries that kept most fighters from entering the ring for so many days in a row.

All for a good cause, of course.

Between the five of them, they'd arrived in Port Galan with the clothes on their backs, a few tired horses stolen from the capital, and little else. Two throneless royals, a smuggler, a low-level spy and a previously imprisoned pirate.

The round finally finished when Dreszen declined to get back up.

"Sorry, lad," Ash said under her breath. She paced across the ring, catching a towel someone tossed her way, before dropping onto the rickety, precarious bench beside Soviel.

"Well? How did we do?" she asked, her blood still high and pumping.

"Not as excellently as last night—from a fiscal standpoint, that is—but the crowd is still really into it. Just fewer people in the crowd at one in the afternoon, I suppose."

"Nice." Ash flipped her hair out of her eyes, and ran her fingers through it to keep it pushed back. "Do we have our total yet?"

"One… minute…" Soviel said, flipping to her previous page, face pinched in concentration. She reached into her skirt pockets and pulled out a graphite stick to begin tallying the numbers.

"So. *This* is what you two get up to during the day," her brother said as he materialized behind them.

"Shit…"

"No, no, by all means. You know, I had wondered where the two of you scraped up the funds to buy us all new shirts. I suppose thanks are in order," Lukas said with his usual smirk.

"We're up a good portion compared to last week," Soviel said into her book.

"Why are you here?" Ash stood, crossing her arms.

"Well, dearest little sister," he said, removing his coat. "I come here to blow off a little steam every so often."

"So… no luck in finding your friend?"

Lukas's expression fell, hardened into stone. He didn't answer, but began wrapping his hands with a strip of linen from the bag slung across his shoulder.

"Right… well… keep looking. I'm sure he'll turn up," Ash said sheepishly. "He's a sturdy fellow."

"You've never even met the man, Ash."

"Alright, that's true. But he's probably with the rest of the ex-prisoners in Njorske, having the time of his life and slugging back Deathwater. He's *probably* better off than we all are here."

"His wife was still in the capital when we left for the prison," Lukas gritted his teeth. "He wouldn't have just left her."

"Well, maybe he *did*, maybe she's—"

"He would have come back."

"I'm just saying, things were hectic all over the island during those last few weeks. He might be hiding out any number of places. Maybe he's in Avaree, or laying low somewhere south."

"You don't know what you're talking about."

She could tell he was starting to get frustrated. "I'm sorry, look, this clearly has you in a bind—"

"I'm *not* in a bind!"

"Sor-*ry*, I just think—"

"Alright!" Soviel stood abruptly between them, halting their bickering. She patted Ash on the shoulder. "Let's go collect our winnings, shall we?"

"Fine," Ash grumbled. "Have fun, Luk. Be careful."

CHAPTER TWO

Lachlan Tarrish, now *Lieutenant* Tarrish, was almost exactly as Rhi remembered him. It had been nearly a decade since the brief time of their shared schooling, but Rhi had dredged his image from the recesses of his memory. He was the red-gold of molten metal, all freckles and hot temper. His copper hair was too short to be tied back, but just long enough to fall into his face.

Lachlan, even when they were boys, had a brazen attitude and a stubborn unwillingness to let what anybody thought of him slow him down. It was no wonder he'd been at the center of so many brawls since the army's melding.

At twelve, he'd had a short fuse, always ready to spark. At twenty-two, he burned with an ever-present fire. Everything about him screamed competitive, brash, unfaltering.

It made him Rhi's opposite in many ways, and it made him envious of him. How freeing it must be to act without considering how it looked to every single person, ever. To not agonize over every interaction, and wonder what the consequences might be. To not fear pissing anyone off. Lachlan seemed to make enemies as quickly as Rhi made allies, if the reports were even half-accurate.

"You look grim," Lachlan's voice pulled Rhi from his thoughts.

"Sorry," Rhi said, straightening his posture. He was seated on an overturned barrel in Lachlan's tent in the encampment. "So does Ashwife shove all of his lieutenants into little tents like this?"

"No… just the ones who weren't lucky enough to be stationed in Galan prior to the shift of power," Lachlan said carefully as he finished shaving in the tiny mirror hung from the tentpole. The straight razor scraped against his chin, taking the last bit of ruddy scruff and soap with it.

Rhi nodded, about to use this opportunity to segue into his purpose for being there.

"So," Lachlan swished the razor in a cup of water. "What did you say you came down here for?" He turned from the mirror, toweling off his neck and chiseled jaw.

"Well… like I said, there's been a great deal of unrest here in the encampment. I've been sorting out some of the less serious infractions, under General Ashwife's direction."

Lachlan snorted. "Yeah."

"Your name has come up a few times."

Lachlan turned slowly, eyebrows raised expectantly. "Just a few?"

"Fine, about a dozen times."

Lachlan let out a low laugh as he dried his hands. "So… what? They've sent you down here to scold me? Court martial me? I got in a few scraps. It's not as if I'm the only one."

"For the time being, with everything being so hectic, they've actually put me in charge of the more minor complaints made within the encampment."

"Oh, so my fate rests in your hands?" Lachlan looked Rhi up and down before slinging the towel over his shoulder. He crossed his arms. His forearms were muscled and freckled, visible where his sleeves were rolled up to the elbows.

"I'd like us to work together. And maybe, while we're at it, fix the rift that's growing within this encampment."

"Why?"

Rhi bristled. "Why… try to depolarize the army?" He couldn't help the raw sarcasm that crept into his tone.

"No. Why me?" Lachlan quirked one eyebrow, staring Rhi down. "Work together on what?"

"Well, from the reports I've read, you led the rescue mission into Danvery Prison earlier in the month. I want to know what you saw."

"And you think that will help mend the rift," Lachlan said, sounding unconvinced.

Rhi stood. "Well, the way I see it is this; Ashwife says you're one of the more promising young soldiers in this army. Old Caelish family, formidable battlefield reputation, well-educated." Rhi ticked each item off on his fingers like a list. "He thinks you have what it takes to climb the ranks. But you keep landing in trouble. He thinks you're volatile. Loose cannon."

"That doesn't tell me *your* motives."

"I think you want what's best for the army. For the nation." Rhi stood. "Half the incident reports with your name on it have quoted that fights broke out regarding the use of resources on the victims from Danvery. You care about this issue."

Lachlan considered for a moment, before stepping around to face him. They were just about eye to eye in height, though Lachlan had more bulk to him.

"Perhaps if you direct some of that drive toward unraveling what was happening in that prison and preventing it from happening elsewhere, instead of wasting time picking fights with the newcomers, we could actually accomplish something here," Rhi said smoothly.

"You may have forgotten, Prince," Lachlan said pointedly, eyes flaring, "but some of us have more reason to distrust the Lundi defectors than others."

"Be that as it may," Rhi continued, his voice steady and light. "We can't afford to keep squabbling amongst ourselves. Not if we have any hope of surviving the year."

"*Hm,*" Lachlan snorted a derisive laugh. "Yeah, alright. I'll help you."

Rhi didn't bother to tell him that the other option was hard labor and potential court martial, according to Ashwife.

"Great."

"Well? Was there anything else you needed?" Lachlan asked, turning to pluck his coat off its hook. He shrugged it on and adjusted the lapels.

"Yes," Rhi said, crossing his arms. "I want to hear your account of what went down in Danvery."

"Was my report not sufficient?" The words were just shy of venomous.

Rhi tilted his head, eyes coolly narrowed, and let the silence drag out for a second longer than was comfortable. "Your report was fine. But I want to hear the full description. Even any details you think unnecessary."

"What exactly do you want to know?" Lachlan asked.

"Anything you can tell me," Rhi said.

Something flashed in Lachlan's eyes, briefly guttering their flame.

"That place," he sighed, shaking his head. "That place was foul. There was something truly despicable happening within those walls. By the time we made it in, the apparent rogue mission had come and gone," his upper lip curled in distaste. "But still, the evidence…" he shook his head again, as if he could be rid of the memories. "Unaccounted-for prisoners of all origins, the door that leads to nowhere, the bodies that had been discarded from whatever that room was."

"The lab?" Rhi asked.

"They bring people in. Healthy, strong. We managed to get ahold of one of the guards who monitored it. He didn't know much, but he told us they experiment on them. Most of them die. We still don't know what purpose it serves, what they're testing."

"That's a terrible waste," Rhi chewed his lip.

Lachlan's pained sidelong-glance confirmed it. "There is some other motive, yes. But what we've learned isn't enough to determine it. Yet."

Rhi shuddered.

"We got there a few days after your lot pulled that prison break, so I can't speak for the conditions beforehand. But what we saw after was despicable. Inhuman."

Rhi grimaced.

Lachlan ran his fingers through his hair, pushing the strands out of his face. "Walk with me."

Rhi followed Lachlan down the main thoroughfare of the barracks. The sky beyond the cliff wall grew darker and darker ahead of the encroaching storm, bleeding into a midnight blue far earlier than seemed proper.

Eventually, they reached a wide tent, set off to the side.

Just outside, Lachlan stopped short, halting Rhi.

"What you're about to see, you're not going to like."

"I can manage," Rhi said.

"Don't say I didn't warn you." He swept through the tent flap, and Rhi followed.

It was dark in the tent; no lanterns had yet been lit for the night. As far as Rhi could see, there were a few cots similar to those in the infirmary, all unoccupied save for two. In those two beds…

Rhi felt his stomach churn at the sight of them. Two figures, each on their backs, lay strapped down to their cots with restraints secured on their ankles, wrists and across their chests. Deep, bright blue veins punched through their waxy skin, eyes shut, faces hollow with sickness or starvation.

"Are they—"

"Dead?" Lachlan shook his head. "No. Just heavily, *heavily* sedated. They've proven to be extremely unpredictable in their strength. And when they wake up hallucinating, or unsure where they are…" he trailed off.

"Dear Gods," Rhi whispered.

"We pulled three of them out of the lab when we stormed it," Lachlan continued. "The first died about a week in. The other two haven't made much progress. It's… hard to treat them for an ailment no one knows anything about."

"When they're awake - when you say…" Rhi winced, "*unpredictable*, what do you mean?"

"See that attendant?" Lachlan gestured to the woman stirring a large pot broth. She had one arm in a sling, and a jagged, stitched-up cut running down the left side of her face. "About a week ago, she was feeding that one there." He pointed to the patient on the left. "He snapped his restraints in a blind panic, swept at her and knocked her back, hard enough to break her arm."

"*Sweet Bastara*," Rhi hissed. "And… the cut on her face?"

"That's the other thing," Lachlan said glumly. "About what they've had done to them. He just…" he shook his head, "grew these fucking *claws*, out of nowhere."

"Claws?" Rhi whipped his head around.

"And once he was sedated again, nothing."

"Interesting."

"I had half a mind to put a bullet in both their skulls. Put them out of their misery. But the higher-ups want to know what's going on in there, how they're being altered."

"I think I'd take the bullet," Rhi said without meaning to. "What hope is there of survival, for undoing this torment?"

"No one knows yet, and if they do, they haven't deigned to tell me." As he said it, the corner of his nose twitched up in annoyance.

"Who's in charge of this whole thing?"

Lachlan opened his mouth to answer, but was interrupted by a loud, roaring cough. A spout of flame erupted from the mouth of the woman on the right side cot, her chest heaving with effort, the orange of the flame reflected in the sheen of sweat covering her skin.

"Time to go," Lachlan said, pushing Rhi out by the shoulder as chaos erupted in the tent.

Once they were outside, and Rhi's eyes adjusted to the light, it struck him. "What are they using to sedate them?"

"I have no idea."

"Can you find out?"

"Maybe," Lachlan ran his fingers through his hair again. "General Alemont isn't terribly forthcoming with these things."

"I might have a friend who can help," Rhi said. "She's got a way with…" he wiggled his fingers for emphasis. "Healing."

Lachlan arched one eyebrow, crinkling his freckled forehead. In the distance, thunder rumbled.

"When are you available to meet again? I'll bring her."

"I've been on leave," Lachlan said. "Mashed up my wrist in Danvery, so I have a few more days of freedom."

"Oh," Rhi frowned. "Is it getting better?"

Lachlan nodded. "Tomorrow evening?"

"Yes," Rhi agreed. "I'll meet you back here then."

As he turned and walked back up to the manor, Rhi wondered why, if Lachlan had been on medical leave for so many weeks, he had stuck around the encampment instead of going home.

The cliff face along the northern coast was studded with all manner of caves, caverns, and holes. With the ease of a slow sigh, Ferrin coasted into the one she'd spotted from the surf. It was low, flat, and probably covered by the swollen sea when the tide was high.

The walls were slick with algae, and crusted with barnacles. The rock around her was smooth with ages of slow wearing-down by the sea. Mollusks clung in desperate clusters to the damp, dark rock. Waves lapped at her ankles, gentle and insistent as she stepped further into the cave. Brine and sea spray slicked the floor by the entrance as she moved further into the cave, peering into the dark with apprehensive curiosity.

The echo of the sea was melancholy, and left her on edge as she ventured further into the dark. By the time she neared the limits of the entrance's illumination, it was almost too dark to see the carvings on the walls. Almost too dark to make out the story, so worn and old, and smoothed over by decades, perhaps centuries, of changing tides.

A woman walked alone on a path of stars. Then came a boy, crafted by her hand from the space between night and day, from stardust and tears and loneliness.

He rose small and gleaming from the void of the stars, greeting his mother with open arms.

Those carvings were simple. Crude, worn down, barely legible.

As Ferrin moved along the wall, deeper into the cave, she had to squint to see the rest. Figures carved with a more detailed hand, delicate edges still clear on the rock. She recognized some of the stories. Gwelie leaping into flight. An enormous horse-shaped sea creature carrying a maiden to safety. Ancient wellsprings gifted to the human race by the gods.

Then there were more, all stories she didn't recognize. A king in chains beneath a giant tree, his crown sundered in two. Two identical figures, dueling with an axe and a sword. She squinted closer, it was nearly impossible to make out some of the shapes. There were symbols she didn't recognize, their curves and notches familiar, only she couldn't remember where from.

Just as she leaned in, eyes adjusting, a cold blast of water roared through the mouth of the cave, sloshing up her legs. She yelped. The sea was beginning to surge, spilling into the cave.

"Right, then, time to go," she muttered to herself as she launched into the oncoming tide.

Ash and Soviel were halfway between the barracks and the manor on the path through the marsh and dunes when the rain doubled down.

The summer storms had been on and off all week, the remains of the previous shower still evident, puddling in the wet sand, in the divots between scrub pines and beach grass. Ash's boots were still wet from their trek across the path earlier in the day. The second-hand boots never seemed to be dry. If it wasn't so bloody cold half the time, she'd have gone barefoot everywhere, but even with summer finally beginning, the chill hung in the air on the rainy days.

As she took her next step, there was a loud squelch and she felt a fresh stream of brackish marsh water and sand flood into the toe of her boot.

"Oh, that's just great," she grunted. "Shit."

"Go on, we're almost there," Soviel said behind her. "That storm is only a few minutes off."

"It's pouring out here. I think it's safe to say the storm has arrived."

"True, but those look like thunderheads rolling in."

"Uch. This isle is far too cold and rainy."

"It's still spring," Soviel chided. "Most places north of the Meddemara are like this. Rainy in the spring, lovely in the summer—which is almost here, so don't fret."

"I never realized how much I would miss sweating my ass off down south," Ash grumbled, stepping over another puddle.

A crack of lightning split the sky to the north, out on the sea.

"Ah, shit."

"Time to go," Soviel nodded. Thunder sounded a few seconds later.

"It's pretty far off, still. We have a few min—" she cut off as she realized Soviel had stopped several paces back, her gaze downcast and transfixed on something small in her path.

At first glance, it looked like a little stone, or the smallest, most waterlogged bit of detritus.

Soviel's gaze was unflinching as she sank into a crouch, the fabric of her dress falling into a nearby puddle.

"Soviel… what is it?" Ash's words fell flat as she stepped closer.

A tiny marshmouse lay in the path, sodden and limp, curled over itself in a wet lump.

"The burrows must have flooded," Soviel said, her words punctuated by the not-so-distant rumble of thunder.

Another crack of lightning bit the sky to the east, briefly illuminating the darkening sky. The rose-hips swayed in the breeze.

Ash started forward, halting as Soviel leaned onto her knees, examining the little creature.

"This one isn't even fully grown yet," she said softly.

"He's so small," Ash said, unsure of what to do or say.

She perched, hesitant as she watched Soviel reach out a tentative hand to the little mouse.

"Sov… I think he's dead," she said, gently reaching out her hand to help Soviel up.

"He's just so tiny," Soviel breathed absently, laying her fingertip on the mouse, entranced.

"I know. It's the way of the world, though. Sometimes… things… die," Ash said awkwardly. She didn't always know how to blunt the hard edges she'd acquired growing up in the slums of Khalim.

Soviel swallowed, and Ash could swear she felt some charge rip through the air that had nothing to do with the approaching storm, like every chaotic particle of every living thing in a one mile radius had halted in it's path and begun orbiting around Soviel and where her touch met the dead mouse. Like a hinge, an axis, all pulled into play by what was about to happen.

The storm became a distant thing, and all Ash could do was watch. Watch, and hold her breath along with the rest of the world.

One second the mouse was limp, broken, lifeless in the wet sand.

The next, his tiny ears perked up, and he tensed, fur ruffling as his legs unbent from their curled position. His eyes popped open, and he scurried off the path and into the bushes.

Ash was so focused on the little beast running off that she almost didn't catch Soviel as she slumped over in the dirt.

"*Shit!* Are you alright?" she asked, scrambling to pull Soviel upright against a nearby boulder. She'd gone pale.

"I suppose… he wasn't… dead," Soviel panted.

"I guess not," Ash said, not at all convinced. Something told her that what she had just witnessed went far beyond the scope of a healer's power. "Hey, aren't you supposed to use some special medicinal plant or something when you do that?" she asked gently.

"It's fine, I've done it before," she said, her eyes closing slowly as she took deep breath. "Besides," she spread one hand wide at the clusters of rose-hips and scrub pines, "the environment allows it."

"You don't seem fine," Ash frowned. "That storm is rolling in fast. We need to get inside. Do you think you can stand?"

"Just need another minute."

Ash pursed her lips, nodding. She flipped her wet hair out of her eyes and sat back on her heels, eyeing the horizon. A crack of lightning pierced a scrub pine not fifty feet from the path, and it erupted into a bonfire, the hot, harsh flame eating away at the green.

"Alright, minute's up." Ash stood, grabbing Soviel by the hand and yanking her up. She stumbled, barely staying upright as her knees buckled. Apparently, more drained than Ash had initially thought.

"What did you *do*?" She looped Soviel's arm over her shoulder to support her weight. She'd never seen her like this, even after healing Ferrin's gruesome bullet-wound a few weeks back.

"It'll pass," Soviel squeezed her eyes shut against the flaring wind. More thunder echoed, this time much closer.

"We're going to get fried if we stay out here, Sov. Come on, you can lean on me," Ash grunted, as they lurched forward.

Soviel obliged, her hand gripping Ash's opposite shoulder.

"You're heavier than you look!" Ash laughed as they rushed towards the cellar-entrance of the manor. Her boots squelched with every waterlogged step.

Lightning cracked again, closer this time.

"Shit!"

"Definitely not good," Soviel said, her voice faint.

"We have to hurry!"

They hobbled down the sandy path, but not fast enough. Soviel's strength was still flagging, and the storm had raced in fast. Too fast. As if some force had pulled the gale inland on purpose. There was a quarter mile to go till safety, and they were moving too slowly.

The ground shook beneath them, and Ash waited for the prickling sensation on the back of her neck to come to fruition and smite them.

"What are you two doing out in this storm?" Ferrin appeared on Soviel's other side, looping her other arm over her shoulders as she yelled over the wind.

She had blown in out of nowhere, hair slicked to her scalp with sea and storm.

"Coming back from the barracks!" Ash shouted.

"What's happened to her?" she asked, jerking her chin at Soviel as they rushed along the path.

"Long story! We need to get inside!"

With Ferrin's help, they made it the rest of the way to the manor with hardly a second to spare, as the full might of the storm bore down on the coast. By the time they burst through the scullery door to the manor's lower level, the sky had blackened with thunderheads, and the three of them were soaked to the bone. They deposited Soviel on the wooden bench by the hearth in the small atrium.

"Damn this constant rain," Ash swore, again flipping her awkward-length hair out of her eyes. It was too short to be tied up, and just long enough to always be in the way.

"It won't last long, the summers really are nice," Ferrin promised, panting.

"I second that, not too hot, not too cold," Soviel said weakly.

Ash whirled on her. "You scared the *shite* out of me! What in the true hell was that?"

Soviel blanched, somehow going paler still.

"What happened?" Ferrin asked, looking back and forth between the two of them.

Ash gave a nervous, humorless laugh as she shucked off her outer shirt and hung it over the hearth-screen. "Oh, first we're rushing across the damn marsh, trying to outrun the storm that's barreling off the sea. Then, this one," she gestured at Soviel, "stops in the middle of the path, and drops to the ground to revive a drowned mouse."

"I only healed him, he wasn't d—"

"That's horseshit. He *was* dead. Drowned. And then *you* passed out on the path, just as the damn lightning storm rolled in."

"You *what?*" Ferrin asked, also whirling on Soviel.

"She nearly got herself—and me—killed," Ash said, and though her words were harsh, it wasn't anger she felt, but panic.

"You're meant to be the practical one," Ferrin said, squinting at Soviel.

"Please, I am very tired. Can you not chastise me later?"

"Sov, I love small animals as much as the next fairytale maiden, but that does sound quite odd. Are you feeling alright? I mean, before all that?" Ferrin asked.

"I know it was stupid," Soviel said, squeezing her eyes shut for a moment before standing to move nearer to the fire. She braced one palm on the brick, and leaned on the wall. "Something just came over me. I couldn't leave him there like that."

Ash bit back her comment that the incoming storm had probably already undone whatever Soviel had conjured to save the mouse. Now that they were inside and the rush of imminent danger had left her body, Ash's hands had begun to shake.

She eyed Soviel. Her blonde hair was limp and slicked back as she stared into the fire, arms wrapped over her chest as the golden light flickered across her face. Whatever had happened on that marsh, it was something new. And she could see on Soviel's face, it had shaken her more than she was willing to let on.

CHAPTER THREE

O nce Ferrin and Ash had forced some hot bone broth down Soviel's throat, some color at last returned to her cheeks.

The storm had taken Ferrin by surprise when it came racing in off the sea in a fury. If she hadn't cut across the marsh, she'd have been smashed on the rocks with the spindrift. The strange cave and its contents were still on her mind as she paced quickly down the hallway to her room, eager to get out of her rain-soaked clothes.

Upon arrival to Galan, she and Rhi had been welcomed and given two modest rooms, which they'd packed into with Lukas, Soviel and Ash.

Considering the overcrowding in the whole of the city, their small shared rooms were downright luxurious. Ferrin knew the only reason the five of them had been allowed rooms in the manor rather than being directed to a boarding house in town or to the encampment was her mother. Arabella had spent her much of her youth here in Galan, before the Unification had forced her into a marriage to an enemy prince and tossed a crown atop her head.

When she arrived at the pair of adjoining rooms, Ferrin pulled up short, surprised to find Lukas standing shirtless by the mirror just inside the doorway, wrapping a thin bandage of linen around his ribs.

Or, rather, trying to.

"Sweet storm steeds," she cursed. "Sorry." She stepped back awkwardly.

"You know, there's something to be said for watching where you're going," he said with a wry smile.

"Well, there's also something to be said for lighting a lamp," she cut back at him, walking to the center of the room where an oil lamp sat on a small table. She turned the nob and struck a match to light it. "It's pitch black in here, no wonder you're doing a terrible job of bandaging yourself." As the lantern sprung to life, she shook out the match and crossed her arms, hoping he couldn't see her reddened face. His skin blazed dark gold in the lamplight, the shadows casting the ridges and planes of his stomach and chest in deep contrast.

"It probably doesn't really need to be wrapped anyway. I was going to see if Soviel could take a look at it…"

"She's all tapped out," Ferrin sighed, setting the lantern on the table beside Lukas. "We need to clean it. Sit."

"As you say, Highness." He bent into the chair and handed her the bandage as he leaned back to look down at the wound on his side.

"I'm not sure you can technically call me that anymore, you know," she said as she pulled up a chair.

He smirked at her. "You'll always be a royal pain in my ass, though."

"Piss off," she said, not fighting the grin already forming on her lips.

He winced as she brought a rum-soaked cloth to the wound.

She was glad their easy bantering had resumed, that they were back to constantly teasing each other again.

After she'd kissed him in order to execute her admittedly half-baked plan, and he'd carried her unconscious and wounded body halfway across the countryside, everything had been a little awkward for a few days. Now she didn't know where they stood.

It wasn't as if things hadn't been escalating for weeks before that point, but she was worried she might have soured whatever was growing between them when she'd used that kiss to trap him, deceive him. Even though it had been for the purpose of rescuing Rhi, that fear had been gnawing at her since they'd arrived here.

"So," she said, dabbing at the wound. "Did you win?"

He hissed through his teeth, tensing as the liquor-soaked cloth touched the open wound. "Yeah."

"Good."

"What had you in such a hurry just now?" he asked, watching her intently.

"Oh. Needed dry clothes," she paused in her task, remembering that she was still soaked through every layer with sea and rain water. "I found something out in the cliffs."

"What?"

She let out a long exhale as she reached for a clean strip of linen, her knuckles brushing against his bare side. She felt his breath hitch just the slightest bit.

"A cave," she said in her cheeriest, lightest voice.

"A cave," he repeated with far less enthusiasm.

"Yes."

He studied her as she leaned in close, wrapping the bandage across his broad chest. His skin was hot against her icy hands, and her heart lurched into a sprint as she pulled the linen over his side. She swallowed, her mouth dry. Could he hear how loud she was breathing? Did she *always* breathe this loudly?

"A cave full of carvings and paintings. And maybe more," she answered quickly, her eyes darting up to his, then back down to the task at hand. "It was too dark to tell."

He raised one incredulous eyebrow as she finished the bandage with a double-knot.

She sat back to check her work, then looked up. He was watching her. "Is that too tight?"

He shook his head slowly. Their faces were close, she could feel a whisper of his breath on her cheek.

"Well," she leaned back in her chair, tamping down on the thumping of her heart. "You're going to regret doubting me. As soon as this storm clears out, we're heading out there with lanterns. You'll see."

The storm didn't cease until the next morning, but as soon as the sun rolled its way out of the sea, orange and pink on the edge of the horizon, Ferrin slipped out of the bed she was sharing with Soviel and Ash. She pulled on her clothes, dry and warm from the hearth, and padded to the door that adjoined their room to the one the boys' shared.

She knocked softly, and Lukas opened it almost immediately.

He looked exhausted, disheveled, like he'd been up half the night tossing and turning.

"Been up long?" she asked.

"Couldn't sleep."

Her brow crinkled. Since they'd been free of the imminent danger in the capital, he'd been restless. Something about Ryder's continued absence seemed to be bothering him more than he let on. He hadn't said anything, but on more than one occasion she'd stumbled across him making rounds to the refugee center, seeming a bit frantic as he checked the lists.

"Are you sure you're feeling alright? We can go later in the morning. High tide isn't until this afternoon."

He shot her a sidelong glance and shrugged on his coat. "Let's go."

They stopped at the groundskeeper's shack by the gardens to borrow some lanterns and oil, greeting the groundskeeper.

When they arrived at the cliffs, day was breaking gold into blue, painting everything it touched with bright, buttery-gold light. Below, the ocean churned easily, lapping at the rocks.

"Oh." Ferrin halted suddenly, halfway through taking off her coat. She frowned as she peered over the side at the far drop.

"What is it?"

"I just realized… there's really no way down. I flew in and out." She chided herself internally. How had she not thought of that?

Lukas stepped closer to the edge, eyeing the water below, where it met the base of the rocky cliff. "Check the depth for me?" he asked.

With a nod, she dropped her coat and pulled off her boots. She toppled over the side of the cliff, falling for an instant before letting the updraft catch her, and settling gently into the water. Taking a deep breath, she plunged to the bottom, ignoring the bracing cold.

Her feet hit the bottom only a second after her head went under, and she popped back to the surface. "Don't jump! Too shallow!"

She flitted up the cliffside again to figure out a way down that made sense.

"I know a spot a little ways down. You fly the gear in, and I'll swim over," Lukas said, passing her the oilcloth-wrapped lanterns.

She took two trips, carefully moving the dry goods down into the sea cave. The north-facing mouth of the cave made it hard to get much light, particularly so early in the day, but the tide was low enough for her to safely place the lanterns on a raised bit of the cave floor while she lit them and waited for Lukas.

He swam up to the cave mouth a moment later and climbed out, his hair slicked back, and the taupe fabric of his breeches dark with seawater. He'd left his shirt above, along with their coats and boots—all hindrances in the water. The white bandages, still around his ribs, offered a stark contrast to his golden brown skin. Since arriving in Galan, his already rich skin tone had deepened into a beautiful bronze, making his sea-green eyes even more salient. Bits of his dark brown hair had lightened to gold with the days of sun and salt.

Ferrin bit her lip, hoping the lack of light hid her blush. He'd grown even more handsome over the last few weeks.

"Well," he said, slicking his hair back, oblivious to her gaze, "that was refreshing."

He seemed invigorated, more awake and alive with the touch of the sea. She wondered if he'd always been that way, if the waves called him home the way the wind called her.

The sea echoed through the cavern, and Ferrin had to dodge the backsplash when a particularly large wave crashed against the rocks below.

"Shall we?" She handed him a dry linen and a lit lantern.

He wiped his hands and forearms off before taking the lantern and stepping further into the cave. "Looks slippery," he said.

"Yeah, well, better watch your step," she countered.

"You slipped on algae down here yesterday, didn't you?"

She narrowed her eyes. "You know nothing."

He chuckled as she shot him a vexed look, despite the warmth in her chest.

They slunk deeper into the cavern, blackness swallowing any daylight from the entrance behind them. The only light was the flickering fire of their lanterns, wobbling in the damp, drafty air. When at last they reached the wall of carvings, Lukas exhaled a deep breath. "Oh."

Ferrin hummed in agreement.

"They're stories," he said. "Old stories. That's Larakhe and Ioran dueling—and that must be Gwelie taking flight."

Ferrin nodded. "Do you know this one?" she asked, gesturing to the one before her. It was the one of the king beneath the tree.

Lukas looked it over and gave a dismissive shake of his head. "Doesn't look familiar."

She chewed her lip.

They scanned the walls further, lanterns shedding light on things that had been too vague for her to make out the day before.

"Ferrin," Lukas's voice echoed slightly in the deep cave.

She turned toward the sound of his voice, deeper in the room.

"You need to see this," he said, illuminated in a circle of light. He set the lantern down on a stone.

No—on an altar.

How had she missed that the day before? It seemed like something she ought to have noticed, or at least bashed her shin on in the dark. When she got closer, she could see more carvings, dozens of them crowding on the carved stone.

Strangest of all was the small, wooden chest tucked beneath the stone altar. It was covered with a thick layer of algae and barnacles. The hinges were crusted over with sea-moss and rust, and the latch seemed to have been sealed shut with salt water. It had been claimed so fully by the sea, she almost couldn't tell what it was.

After trying a few times to pry it open, it was clear they were going to need some tools.

"We'll take it with us," Lukas suggested, holding up one of the oil-cloth-lined canvas bags they'd brought.

The chest remained unopened for the better part of a day, until driven by frustration, Lukas jammed a knife into the seam and twisted it, cracking the top with a little hiss of air.

"I don't know why you two didn't try that from the start," Rhi said, not looking up from the army ledger he was skimming through.

"Didn't want to completely destroy it," Ferrin shot back.

The lock was completely rusted into one piece, though, and the hinges pulled apart. It would be impossible to repair, but it seemed the contents had remained dry.

There was a pile of folded papers, a handful of coins, a scrap of fabric.

She picked up the little scrap of fabric and ran her thumb over its woven texture. It was a faded shred of checked wool in a green, yellow and red pattern.

When she looked up, Lukas was gingerly unfolding one of the thick pieces of paper.

"It's a map," he announced.

"Of what?" Ferrin leaned over to see, their shoulders brushing.

"I'm not sure, it's sort of hard to read."

"Let me see." She scooted closer, frowning. "That looks like the coastline between here and Avaree, almost, but that island isn't usually there…"

"I've never seen it," Lukas agreed.

"Let me see," Rhi said, setting down his book and coming around the table.

"Look, that," Ferrin pointed to the tiny dot above the coast, perhaps ten, twenty miles north, and circled in blue ink.

Rhi looked over the map for a moment, turning the paper in his hand a few times.

"The ink that drew it on there is different from the rest. And the ink that circled it..." He crossed his arms.

"Was added later," Lukas finished, peering closer at the drawing. "Do you think this is real?"

Rhi shrugged. "It must have some significance. Maybe it's like Rochmere, an outpost for smugglers and traders to use when they don't want to deal with harbor patrol."

"I would have heard of it by now, then," Lukas said. "Unless it's no longer in use."

"Oh, really, there's *no* way something could escape your all-knowing ears?" Ferrin asked.

"Well, it's not *likely*. Besides, that's a rather inconvenient spot for that type of rendezvous."

"How so?" Rhi asked, measuring an approximation of the distance using his thumb.

"Well, it's too far north to be useful for any major trade routes. The only thing it might be convenient for is sneaking goods between Avaree and here, and maybe, *maybe* one of Njorske's northern cities." Lukas crossed his arms.

"Then what is it?" Ferrin tilted her head, as if she could find the right angle to see the answer.

Lukas shrugged. "What else is in there?"

CHAPTER FOUR

T he next day, an hour or so before dusk rolled around, Rhi found himself hesitating outside Lachlan's tent. The sun was gilding everything in soft, warm, buttery light as he crossed and uncrossed his arms a few times, earning him a few odd looks from Soviel.

"Lll…ieutenant Tarrish?" he called uncertainly.

"Just a minute," came the muffled response. Moments later, Lachlan emerged, waistcoat unbuttoned, coat slung over his shoulder. His hair was a rumpled mess.

"Rough day?" Rhi raised a perplexed eyebrow.

"You have *no* idea," said Lachlan, rubbing his jaw. The cut on his forehead from the previous day had closed, and a red-gold shadow of scruff caught the light as he turned his head.

"Well," Rhi said, "this is Soviel. She's very talented."

"Hi." She extended her hand in greeting.

Lachlan shook it briskly, giving her no more than a cursory glance.

Well, he is in disarray today.

Soviel shot Rhi a concerned, questioning look. Rhi shrugged in response before the two of them followed Lachlan to the tent at the fringe of the barracks.

"So, Lieutenant, you saw the inside of the prison, the laboratory?" Soviel asked.

"Yes ma'am."

"I myself didn't see it, but friends of ours were involved in the prison break that took place just before the excursion you led."

"Yes, and it would have been splendid if someone had warned us about that," Lachlan snapped.

"It was unauthorized," Soviel seethed, "and it was done in haste."

"Well, what did your friends tell you about the place?"

"The experiments in the lab, the pit-creature, the guards sent by the Duke," she said.

"Two of the *experiments* we were able to save," Lachlan said. "They're under sedation in here." He motioned to the tent. "Things are… rough."

"They're ill?" Soviel asked.

"Something like that," Lachlan continued. "They've been kept heavily sedated for the last few weeks."

"Sedated? With what?" Soviel asked.

"You'll have to ask the healer on duty."

"Fine then. Can I go in and take a look?" Soviel asked.

"Under supervision." Lachlan crossed his arms.

"She's not going to harm them," Rhi said.

Lachlan shifted his attention to Rhi for a moment, studying him, then turned back to Soviel.

"Well, in you go then. Esher is on duty for another half-hour."

"Got it," Soviel nodded, narrowing her eyes.

"Aren't we going in?" Rhi asked as Soviel disappeared through the flaps.

Lachlan shook his head, his expression bitter. "Overcrowding makes them restless."

Rhi grimaced.

"I gave some thought to what you said, by the way."

"Oh?" Rhi arched an eyebrow. In the soft afternoon light, Lachlan's amber-hazel eyes were gilded by the sun, level with Rhi's own.

"There's unrest in the army. Too much. If we don't patch it up, we're going to have far bigger problems." He dragged a hand through his copper hair, the longer strands in the front falling back into his face.

"So?" Rhi asked hesitantly.

"Well," Lachlan pushed off the post he was leaning on with a sigh. He paced a few steps before turning back to Rhi. "Human nature can only account for so much of it. Finding answers about what happened three weeks ago might be a good place to start. Clearing up the conspiracy of it all."

"You think so?" Rhi chewed his lip.

"Starting with that damned laboratory, and how it's all connected to the attacks on the capital and the rest of the cities."

CHAPTER FIVE

Ash was out roaming the docks that morning as usual. After cramming breakfast into her face with Ferrin and Soviel, she'd come down the cliff to sniff out *some* kind of work. For the last two weeks, she'd been trying, and failing, to talk her way onto a crew. Be it seafaring militia, privateer, or even a damned fishing skiff, all she'd been given were emphatic '*nos*'. She needed something to do, something that would contribute to getting back at the sick bastards who'd run the prison. This was the way she knew, only no one seemed to be hiring.

She'd resigned herself to another day of being dry-docked after another handful of captains had rejected her offer of service. Regardless of experience, nobody wanted to take on a stranger no one could vouch for. After all, she'd practically washed up from of the sea with only the clothes on her back.

So, there she sat, killing time atop one of the pier's pylons, watching, waiting, and flipping a small oyster knife between her knuckles as she did so. Today she'd brought along another philosophy book from the archives. She'd only picked the first one up because of the bright coloring on the cover, but had found herself increasingly interested in what Eronylous Roths had to say about the concept of the self and whether it was possible to be anything *but* self-serving. It was hard to get through; some of the words she couldn't even pronounce, or had never heard before. Her education at the neighborhood school while growing up in Khalim had been cut short by the arrival of the Veirans, and after that she had tried to learn bits and pieces of words and letters in the common tongue. It had been hard—especially on a pirate ship, or on the run from the law, but she knew the best way to learn was to just keep at it.

She thumbed it closed after finishing the mind-spinning chapter on primal motivation versus secondary motivation, and dropped it back into the canvas sack she'd packed her lunch into, making a show of sitting up straight as a pair of important-looking sailors walked by, deep in conversation.

They didn't pay her any mind.

From what she had gathered, the Caelish resistance had no formal naval presence, only privateers, some well-armed patrol ships, and a few very gun-happy fishermen.

She sighed as she watched a small sloop cast off. She missed the swell of the sea beneath her, the creak of the ship, the spray on her face. She thought back to the days of her childhood spent watching ships come and go as they rolled out of Khalim's vast harbor, and wishing she could be on them while she hid in the closet of their tiny apartment. Later, after the dive wardens had spotted her, she watched from the rafts as she rested between dives.

Growing up in Khalim during the peak of the bloody but short-lived Veiran occupation had been nothing short of traumatic for any kid on those streets or in the slums. The bottom of Khalim's harbor was rife with treasure of all kinds. Throughout its long history, hundreds upon hundreds of shipwrecks had accrued in the harbor's depths, and in the mineral-rich reefs surrounding the bay. The bottom of Khalim harbor held a bounty fit for a king. She'd spent months conscripted by the Veiran sailors, diving with little more than a knife at her hip, collecting riches from the sea floor.

Lukas had done it, too. And Damijan, and Indira, and Larisa, even Eman. All of the slum kids had, even though the pay was dirt compared to the danger.

If you weren't willing to dive for pay, you dove at gunpoint until your lungs gave out.

Ash was ripped back to the present when a shout went up, followed immediately by the frantic ringing of an alarm bell somewhere high up on the cliff above.

She turned her gaze to the horizon. There, at the mouth of the bay, two ships were at full sail, making a run into the harbor. Their masts loomed tall, not a flag in sight to identify who they sailed under, or what their intentions were.

"All hands! All hands to stations!"

Ash didn't think. She sheathed her oyster knife and launched into the stream of sailors boarding the nearest ship, keeping her head down as they flooded over the gangplank. Chaos roiled around her as all stations readied to go out and meet the two mysterious ships nearing the harbor. Her heart began to race and she assimilated herself into the throng, keeping her collar high.

"Oi! Why aren't you in the riggings yet, eh?" snapped an accented voice on her right. A blond man shoved a coil of rope and a long rifle into her arms with a reprimanding *tsk*.

"Good question," she mumbled to herself as he passed her by.

She double-checked for the familiar weight of a knife and pistol at her waist, happy to have them, and headed for the Jacob's ladder. She looped the rope across her torso, slung the rifle's strap over her shoulder, and climbed the ropes, just as she had done a thousand times on the *Gravedigger*, until she reached the crow's nest.

"You new?" a voice called from just above her.

"Ah… yeah!" she called back. *Acting confident is usually the best way to sell a bald-faced lie. Pretending you're supposed to be there usually works,* Soviel had told her some weeks ago. "Just took me on last week," she elaborated.

They were closing in on the nearer of the two ships, close enough that Ash could make out the colors of the crew members' hair.

"Shit," the man above her cursed as he collapsed his spy scope.

"Well?" she asked, expecting him to move aside so she could clamber up beside him.

"Well, what? Do you have it?"

"Have…?"

"Oh for *shit's* sake. Are you not the runner who's supposed to have my second rifle?"

"Oh! Of course," she said. Bracing herself on the ladder with one hand, she reached over her neck and pulled the strap of the rifle over her head, handing it to him. When he took it, she scrambled up onto the platform.

"Hah! See how these bastards like messing with Port Galan," he laughed drily. "Hope you can reload fast!"

Ash returned his laugh nervously and took out her own pistol. She had a few spare powder cartridges and balls in the satchel at her hip.

The approaching ship was not military; its crew were in plainclothes, and still no flag flew to give any indication of where they might be from, what their intentions might be. Perhaps it was only a mishap—

The first shot fired across the bow below Ash, nearly putting a hole in the starboard rail.

"Start picking off their gunners. Before they punch a hole in our hull!"

Ash took aim with her pistol while her nest-mate did the same with the rifle. "And be ready to reload!" he yelled, taking a shot and slamming the gun down between them.

Ash ripped furiously into a powder cartridge, reloading the rifle as quickly as she could while her new comrade took aim with his second rifle. She was already low on shot, as she hadn't expected to be in this position when she'd readied her effects for the day.

"Bilge-rat's kneecaps!" the man spat as an explosion below rocked the mast, causing his shot to miss. "They're going to board us."

"Shouldn't the fort be trying to take them out?"

He bit his lip and shook his head, glancing back at where the fort was perched high on the cliffs near the harbor mouth. "They must've lured out harbor patrol intentionally, to keep the fort from firing on them."

"Should we not be turning tail? Getting out of the way?"

"They'd put us at the bottom of the harbor before we could clear the fort's sight line," he grunted.

She reloaded the rifles and her pistol with the few shots that remained in her satchel and waited as the ships converged. In what was perhaps her most reckless decision of the day— and that was saying something—Ash jumped from the crow's nest onto the boom, and leapt across the gap, catching in the riggings of the enemy ship.

"What the hell are you doing?" the sharpshooter cried after her.

"Taking out the gunners!"

"We don't even know what's on the bloody ship yet!"

"One way to find out," Ash said under her breath. She shimmied her way across the boom, keeping low as she approached the enemy crow's nest. When she was in slapping distance, she popped up and slammed the enemy rifleman in the face with her pistol. He stumbled back, going slack as consciousness left him. She just managed to grab a fistful of his shirt before he tumbled over the side to the decks below.

"Don't need anyone knowing I'm here *just* yet," she said as she propped him against the mast. With her weapon primed, she peered over the side, trying to make out any identifier. Coastal raiders left Port Galan alone, because it was near impossible to approach the shore on account of the cliffs. It simply wasn't worth it for thieves. Invaders left the port alone on account of the clifftop battery and the well-armed manor. From what she'd gathered by unintentionally eavesdropping on the docks each day, Njorske left it alone because they were trade partners. The Bourjons had already failed to take the city by land, and it seemed unlikely that they'd be fool enough to try and take it by sea.

Whoever this ship sailed under, they weren't foreign navy, but they weren't petty thieves either. They had to be backed by someone with intel, and with enough means to entice them into range of the fort.

A cry came from below just as the smash of wood pierced the air.

"Prepare for boarding!"

With the two ships interlocked, the enemy crew below swarmed over the planks onto the sloop Ash had just come from, leaving the deck below her sparse. With a sharp laugh through her nose, she grabbed a rope and rappelled down the mast, ready to explore.

Her feet hit the deck, and she was met first by a knife flying past her head, embedding itself in the wooden mast behind her. The second knife followed before the first had finished its *thwang* sound. The knife thrower came at her with a savage grunt, her blonde hair two shades darker than Soviel's coming loose from its knot. Ash ducked again, throwing a fist in the direction of her face. The girl stepped back, the blow only glancing off her cheek.

She slashed at Ash with a third knife, the steel singing as it cut through the air. Ash leaned back, narrowly missing losing an eye to the woman's next swipe. A thin line of blood bloomed on her cheekbone. They were too close for her pistol to be of much use. The enemy sentinel tackled her to the ground.

"No one to help you here," she hissed, pinning Ash with her knees.

"Get—off—me!" Ash grunted, bucking her weight up and to the side. They scrapped on the floor, hands on throats, elbows landing in guts, a tangle with too many knees.

A knife clattered onto the ground. With deft swiftness, Ash grasped it by the hilt and plunged it into the sailor's ribs, blood painting her hand red. The woman keeled over with a grunt, freeing Ash. With a gasp, she pulled herself up from the deck, cleaned the knife off, and tucked it into her belt. Out of the corner of her eye, she noticed the door leading below decks was ajar. She approached it with caution as the sounds of battle behind her roared into the background.

She slipped into the hallway, light and quiet on her feet.

A damp and eery feeling crept over her as she descended into the depths of the ship. It seemed empty.

Too empty.

She swallowed her nerves and kept going, edging silently into the beckoning dark down, down, down, until she came to what had to be the brig. As her eyes adjusted to the darkness around her, she took in her surroundings.

Her heart did a swan dive into her stomach.

She scrambled back the way she'd come, rushing up the stairs and bursting onto the deck as the men from her own ship began filtering on, victory cries on their lips. She had scarcely managed to catch her breath.

"Get off! Get off! Cut us loose!" she screamed, waving her arms. Her eyes darted to the stern, where she saw a rope tying off the ship's wheel at an angle, but to steer it where?

"Who the hell—"

"She's rigged to blow! Go! Get us out of range!"

Without thinking, she ran towards the ship's wheel, pulling the knife embedded in the mast free as she went. In two clean strokes, she severed the rope holding the steering wheel hard to port, and the wheel spun furiously back to center as the harbor patrol ship pulled it toward the east.

All she could hope was for someone to recognize her from the docks and take her warning seriously so they could cut loose and let the fort take the ship out before it dragged them all to the depths.

Neb, one of the main harbor patrol officers, locked eyes on her. She narrowed her gaze in recognition and shot Ash a scolding look that said *we'll talk later,* before turning to repeat her order to the rest of patrol. There was a mad scramble to pull off of the enemy ship. The second enemy ship, Ash noticed, had been tacking back and forth a little ways away.

Ash spun, running over the gangplank back onto the patrol ship.

At last, everyone was off, and the patrol ship was a riot of orders and curses as they scrambled to get underway while contending with the enemy sailors still aboard.

The blast went off, tearing apart the ship, and they escaped without a moment to spare. The pressure wave threw her—threw all of them—backwards with its force. Had the patrol sloop been any closer, they'd have been kindling. The heat seared Ash's skin and she lifted a hand to shield her eyes. Whether it was triggered from beneath, or by the fort's well-placed cannon ball, she wasn't sure. At last, the smoldering remains of the enemy ship began to sink beneath the waves. In the distance, a few enemy sailors were swimming towards the other ship. The second patrol ship made haste towards the sinking ship, but was warned off by the unfavorable wind, and the warning shot fired from its leeward side.

Ash watched, breathless as the fort fired after the second ship, tearing a hole in its main sail, and eventually managing to crack the timber of the stern as the ship ran for it. She didn't see if the ship sank or not before she was being pulled to the side by the harbormaster.

"Kid, you have some explaining to do."

CHAPTER SIX

The explosion had been loud enough for Rhi to have been woken up from where he'd dozed off with his head on a desk in one of the manor's several studies. The very air around him seemed to shift and shudder with the force of whatever had blown up. He jerked upright, eyes foggy and dry as he looked around. Was that faint screaming, or just the gulls calling in the wind?

He launched out of his chair and ran from the room. He was already in the lower levels of the manor, so he hardly passed a soul on his way out, but a general sense of panic did seem to be in the air. He didn't think he'd imagined the sound of the blast.

He made it down the winding stair that led to the beach, and when he came out of the door of the stairwell, he drew up short.

A smoldering wreck sat sinking in the center of the bay, smoke curling out of the enormous flames. A second explosion went off, somewhere close to the ship's stern, sending timber flaking and flying about like pine needles. Two harbor patrol ships were on the run, making haste toward the docks, away from the flames. Far off, beyond the harbor mouth, a ship was retreating into the distance, harried by the fort. He could just make out a dent in its side.

Rhi ran down to the docks, ready to offer his help. From across the marsh, soldiers were emptying out of the barracks to come down to the beach.

"What's going on?" Rhi asked as he pulled up beside Lachlan. The beach and the pier were teeming with people.

Worried, scared people. They needed to break this up, before it escalated into another brawl.

"Strange ship appeared, lured out harbor patrol and then blew itself up, by the looks of it," Lachlan explained.

"Anyone hurt?"

Lachlan shook his head. "Don't know yet."

A few people shoved against him in their haste. An indignant bark went up from somewhere in the crowd.

"We need to disperse this crowd," Rhi muttered.

"You're not wrong, but how?" Lachlan grimaced, surveying the mass.

"Here." Rhi jerked his chin at one of the closer pier pylons. It was tall, but he stepped onto a crate beside it and climbed up on its flat top.

"Listen up!" he shouted, cupping his hands around his mouth as he used his deepest, loudest voice. "There could be wounded people on those boats. We're all going to be in their way. Anyone with medic experience get to the dry patch of grass just up past the beach for a preliminary triage. Everyone else, go back to the barracks and resume your duties. I'm sure most of you have assignments you're neglecting right now," he surmised. "I need ten volunteers to stay here to carry the wounded, and help with the boats."

He caught Lachlan's expression in the crowd. One eyebrow raised as he watched Rhi's pronouncement. A dozen or so hands went up, and Rhi chose the closest cluster.

"Now *clear out!*"

He was surprised when the crowd actually dispersed.

He jumped down from the pylon and approached Lachlan.

"What was *that* voice?" Lachlan asked, mimicking Rhi's deep affectation.

"A crowd of panicking people are more likely to listen to a deep commanding voice," shrugged Rhi.

"Interesting," Lachlan said with narrowed eyes. His gaze flickered over Rhi's shoulder towards the beach. "There's a very furious young woman marching over here. Kind of looks like you."

Rhi spun on his heel to see Ferrin jogging down the path, wearing her usual resting expression.

"That would be my sister."

"I figured as much," Lachlan grunted as she approached.

Ferrin slammed into Rhi and threw her arms around him, then pulled back and smacked him in the chest. "You had me worried *sick* when I couldn't find you. What happened?"

He gave her the few details he knew just as the first of the launches pulled up to the pier.

"Alright," Rhi barked to the crowd of volunteers. "Let's get these sailors in."

"Who put you in charge here?" one voice asked from the knot of volunteers. It was a middle-aged woman in a soldier's uniform.

"Rhiach Valcara, Administrative Ambassador for the Allied Resistance." He stuck his hand out in greeting, hoping the Caelish last name would garner him some favor.

She shook it reluctantly, a hint of apprehension still in her eyes.

He felt Lachlan's skeptical gaze on him. "*Administrative Ambassador?*"

"Just go along with it," Rhi said pleasantly through his teeth.

"If there's one thing this one is capable of, it's lying his ass off to avoid trouble," Ferrin said quietly to Lachlan. "Hi. Ferrin, sister to the Ambassador of Bullshit here."

Lachlan shook her hand.

"I resent that," Rhi fired back.

She shot him a saccharine smile.

The remaining launches crowded onto the side of the docks, and it was all hands to tying off the bowlines and helping any injured sailors onto the pier. To Rhi's surprise, Ash stumbled off the second lifeboat, covered in soot and peppered with tiny cuts.

"Ash!" Ferrin exclaimed.

"Sweet mother of pearl, do I have a tale for you," the girl said, bracing a hand on Ferrin's shoulder. She turned and looked around. "What are you all doing down here?"

"We heard the explosion, obviously," Rhi heard Ferrin say from where he coiled one of the ropes at the side of the first boat before looping it over one of the knobs at the side. He didn't know if that was where it was supposed to be, but it was how the other respective ropes and knobs were laid out.

He finished and joined them.

"It was a trap. These two ships showed up, unmarked, and lured out harbor patrol to use as a shield against the fort. I got on there—"

"You got on *where*?"

"On the enemy ship, after they boarded us."

Lachlan came back over from where he'd been helping tie off the stern. "Doesn't look like there's too many casualties," he said, standing beside Rhi.

"Lachlan, Ash, Ash, Lachlan. Actually…" Rhi considered for a moment. "Ash, you and Lachlan should talk. Perhaps not at this exact second," he amended. "But you saw more of the inside of Danvery prison than anyone, yeah?"

She nodded with a grimace.

Lachlan turned and furrowed his brow at her. "You were a part of the prison break?"

"Uh… yes? I was broken out."

Lachlan slid his eyes to Rhi. "You know half the reason Wilcoe was so pissed about that is that there were prisoners locked up in Danvery that *we'd* put there."

Ash paled. Rhi was still unclear on how Ash had wound up in Danvery, but it wasn't as if she was a war criminal. At least, he was pretty sure she wasn't.

"I assure you, Wilcoe knows my situation," Ash said. Rhi wasn't sure that was true, but decided not to question it.

"Well, fine then. I'd like to hear what you saw while you were there. How long?"

She shrugged. "A few weeks? A month? I was sicker than a dog, it's hard to say."

"Right," Lachlan nodded, his voice rumbling and strained. He looked from Ash to Rhi and back. "So, later then? I need to go and check in with Ashwife."

Ashwife, one of Port Galan's two resident generals, was a broad, stout man, fond of ale and meat, with sanguine skin and yellow hair going gray in most places.

"Yeah," Rhi said. "We'll stop by later."

"Good, I'll see you then," Lachlan said gruffly, hands in his pockets. He turned to leave.

"Bye, Lachlan," Ferrin said in a too-sweet voice, her eyes cutting to Rhi with a mischievous glint.

Shut up! He glared at her without words.

HA. You think he's handsome, she returned with her expression.

And? So what?

Ash cleared her throat, interrupting the silent, unproductive conversation.

"You should probably go check in with the healers. They're setting up on the grass over there," Rhi gestured to Ash.

"I'm fine," she said, shaking her head.

"*Ash,*" Ferrin said, giving her a pointed once-over.

"All *right,*" Ash conceded. "I'm going."

The morning's attack on the harbor had left everyone in the manor, town, and barracks rattled. There were enough injured for a field hospital to spring to life on the grassy patch down by the beach. Soviel was there lending a hand to the healers and nurses. The latest patient was a man with a scalp avulsion caused by a broken timber launched by the blast. The injured man, despite his partially peeled off skin, was lucky. Had he been standing a few inches to the right, the piece of wood might have impaled him through the skull.

Soviel had just finished closing over the wound when she caught Ash watching her. She waved her over.

Ever since the mouse incident, she'd been careful not to exert her abilities too far. She didn't need anyone fussing over her. Still, that edge, that stopping point in her magic was feeling further and further away lately.

The temptation to find out just how far she could go was dark and glittering as a forbidden gem, ever in her mind's periphery.

"Need a patch-up?" she said lightly as Ash stopped in front of her.

Ash was sporting a shallow slice beneath one eye, and a myriad of nicks and bruises elsewhere from the explosion.

"I can manage. Looks like you've got worse to attend to." She lifted a shoulder toward the wounded. "Just wanted to see if you could use a hand," she said pointedly.

Soviel sighed. "I'm not raising the dead."

"Didn't say you were."

"Right, well, if you're going to stay, you might as well tear some bandages. Four-inch wide strips, if you please," she instructed, pointing to the pile of clean donated linen.

"Yes ma'am." Ash gave a mock salute.

"What were you doing out there, anyway? I thought you couldn't find a position."

Ash shrugged. "Once the alarm was raised, everything happened so fast, I just jumped on one of the outbound ships and got in the riggings."

"Of course you did," Soviel said with a smirk as another patient arrived at her station.

They fell into an easy rhythm, Soviel patching wounds and setting bones as Ash dutifully handed her bandages, medicinal herbs and all manner of makeshift equipment. Working side by side with Ash felt so natural that she didn't immediately notice who had deposited himself in her chair.

"Hi, Sov," Grey said in his usual monotone.

Her eyes widened when she looked up. "Grey, what seems to be the problem?" She gave him a once-over. He didn't appear to be injured.

"No problem. I'm here to fetch you for a conference. One hour. You know where."

"I'm a little busy, there's still a dozen wounded—"

"There are other healers. Be there," he said stonily before standing and stalking away.

"Who is that?" Ash asked with surprise.

"An… associate. From my other occupation."

"He seems like a real sunbeam."

"He's almost always a sour grouch these days," Soviel agreed, for some reason unwilling to divulge the previous romantic nature of her relationship with Grey. She sighed. "I guess I had better get ready for that."

After Soviel had departed for the meeting, Ash meandered back to the beach, where Rhi and Lachlan, easy enough to spot by Lachlan's red hair, were shifting debris out of the tideline. Already, timber and bits of sail and rope were washing ashore with the noon tide.

"Find anything good yet?" she asked as she came up beside Rhi.

He straightened up, a broken, charred piece of wood in his hand. "Not particularly."

"Hmph. If you find anything of value, I call claim to it as a spoil."

He tossed the wood into the pile and glanced skeptically at her. "Isn't that a little 'old ages'?"

"Maybe it is," she said, pretending to be offended. "Perhaps those were the good old days."

"I'm hardly about to start raiding villages and drinking out of cow horns, if that's what you're referencing. I prefer my modern comforts." He looked around at the mess around them and lifted a shoulder. "Usually."

"Oh, *pish*. Anyway, I'm here to talk about Danvery. If the two of you aren't too busy moving wood."

Rhi narrowed his eyes at her. "Just a minute." He turned, tossed the timber up the bank, and cupped his hands over his mouth to yell, "Tarrish!"

Lachlan stood from where he'd been hauling a bit of debris out of the water and swiveled around, catching sight of them. He jogged over, the swoopy front of his hair bouncing.

"Ready to go?" Rhi asked.

"Yeah."

They made their way across the marsh, only the small, raised sandy path was dry now that the tide was coming in. Ash shoved her hands in her pockets and shivered as they passed by the charred tree that had been struck in the lightning storm only a week ago. When they reached the barracks, a bit further inland and behind a rocky promontory, Lachlan led them down a row of canvas tents to an opening where a circle of turned over logs were arranged around a small fire pit meant for cooking.

Ready to be off her feet, Ash plopped onto one without waiting to be invited. She was exhausted.

"Well, ask away, I suppose. Can I also please get something to drink?" she added.

"We have water, or watered down ale. Take your pick," Lachlan said, sitting down on the nearest log. He angled himself to face her.

"Water is fine."

"Care to fetch some refreshment?" Lachlan asked Rhi, who had not yet sat down.

"Certainly. Anything else, Red?"

Lachlan glared in response to the nickname.

"Thank you, kind prince," Ash said with a too-bright smile, earning an eye-roll from Rhi.

"So," Lachlan returned his attention to her. "Danvery. You were there for how long?"

"A few weeks. They moved us around a bunch, but fortunately for *me* I became ill within the first week. I was never well enough to be considered for the workshop."

"The workshop," he repeated.

"Yes—" Ash said, pausing as Rhi returned, water in hand. She took the cup, swigged from it, and set it down. "That's what most of the guards called it. They'd come around each week or so and round up prisoners, usually healthy, hearty ones. As far as I could tell, that seemed to be the determining factor."

"Interesting," Lachlan puzzled.

"But, they did bring me and a few other prisoners in to clean some of the chambers in the lab. Sometimes there was blood on the floor, sometimes not." A somberness came over her as she let herself remember those long, terrible weeks. "Always corpses to be moved. They had a trap door that led out into a large cart, and when it filled, it was hauled away. I assumed they burned the bodies somewhere off-site."

"How do you know?"

"It filled up at least twice in the time I was there. And…" she gulped in revulsion. "We escaped through that door. We landed in the cart; it was full of dead bodies."

Lachlan's face paled, darkening his freckles.

"There was a lot of technical equipment, I really don't know what any of it was. I'm not even sure I could describe it. By the end of my time there, I was in a bad way."

"We were able to see a bit of the laboratory when we went in," Lachlan said, his voice gruff. "But they locked the door and set fire to the room before we could really get a good look. Anything you remember could be helpful."

Ash swallowed and nodded slowly. She could feel Rhi watching her. "There were chemicals, too. Once when I was cleaning the floor, they had spilled some, and I was wiping it up. It burned me," she trailed off as the memory flooded back. She'd nearly forgotten it. "It burned the skin off entirely," she said, incredulous. That couldn't be right. She didn't even have a scar on that hand.

And yet, she remembered the pain, the sight of her hand ruined by this chemical, steaming and bubbling as she screamed in agony. She lifted her hand—the left one—to look at it, turning it over and over. It was completely unmarred.

"That's the strangest thing," she said to herself.

"What?" Lachlan asked.

"It's like it grew a new skin entirely. I've not had a life of leisure, I had marks and scars and the like on my skin here… I must have. But now…"

"So what does that mean?"

"Whatever burned you must have changed the skin it came into contact with, right?" Rhi interjected, pulling a log around to close their circle.

Ash shook her head, bewildered. "How?"

Rhi cut a glance to Lachlan. "That's part of what we're trying to figure out. What happened in that lab, and what they were trying to achieve. Why all those people died."

"That reminds me—" Lachlan turned to Ash. "Why *were* you in there? Were you one of the ones rounded up in the capital?"

"What? No," Ash said, aware far too late of the face Rhi was making at her that seemed to be saying *keep your mouth shut*.

Lachlan crossed his arms. "Well, what were you in for? The less you say, the worse it sounds."

Ash paused and looked at him. "I had never set foot on this isle until I was dropped here, unconscious and with my pockets full of incriminating documents, put there by someone who wanted to be rid of me."

"Have you proof of that?" Lachlan asked. "There were prisoners in Danvery who Resistance officials put there— people who committed actual crimes. Why should I not have you arrested?"

"Because you know what's good for you." Rhi turned to fix Lachlan with a stony glare. "Trust me, she isn't your enemy."

Lachlan held Rhi's hard gaze for a moment longer, then sighed begrudgingly. "Carry on."

She frowned from Lachlan to Rhi before continuing. "They had different chemicals. Blue ones in jars, milky purple ones, red-brown ones. I don't know what they were. Some of them steamed, some were thick like sugar-syrup, some were thin as water. Sometimes there was a smell."

"A smell."

"It was earthy and tangy only before we started cleaning."

"Earthy how?"

Ash squinted as she tried to place the memory of the smell. "Now that I'm thinking of it, maybe like raw *popava*."

Rhi's inhale was sharp, and she winced. She didn't know exactly what the story was, but Rhi had a complicated history with the drug. She hadn't wanted to pry when Ferrin mentioned it some weeks ago.

"Like *popava*," Lachlan nodded, his brow crinkling.

"Maybe, yes."

"Well, which is it, maybe or yes?"

Rhi shot Lachlan a pointed look. "Lay off."

"As I *said*," Ash breathed out. "It was a long, delirious few weeks."

"Right, um. Sorry," Lachlan said, frowning slightly. "Can you… remember anything else?"

Ferrin sat with her knees tucked up to her chest beside Soviel in Helene's office. Since the evacuation in the capital, Helene Wilcoe had been promoted to Major. Grey, stiff as always, stood behind the desk while Helene chewed her cheek, waiting for the small crowded room to settle. She placed her palms down on the desk. "Today's attack on the harbor has shown us that the conflict brewing on the continent is far from over, and we are *not* so far north as to be left out of it. Now, I know the tension in the barracks has grown worse of late, and I know the lack of answers about this attack is not likely to *help* that." She let out a deep, long-suffering sigh. "We have some of the sailors from the enemy ships in custody. They will be questioned, and we will get answers. But I need time to let my people work, so I need you to keep your folk in line. We can't afford any more slip-ups."

"How many were captured?" asked a man with dark skin and an old, wicked scar cutting down the side of his face. Ferrin didn't recognize him, but she supposed that made sense, given she'd only ever met plainclothes intelligence operatives, aside from Helene and Grey.

"Major Cavenn." Helene nodded. "Three were captured out of the water, and seven are in recovery in the infirmary."

"You can't be serious, Major," asked a middle-aged woman in what looked like a tattered Lindbarrian Regular uniform. "We hardly have resources to keep our own soldiers in good health. Surely we should not be diverting healers to the enemy."

"Captan Morgaine," Helene said. "Your commanding officer and I *both* agreed that extracting all relevant information from the captives was paramount, no matter the resources."

Ferrin squinted. Captain Morgaine was one of the defected former Lundi soldiers. When had the Caelish intelligence branch elected to join forces with its counterpart? Ferrin noticed that a few details of her uniform had been altered—some of the gold stitching had been ripped out, and the typically-cream epaulets had been swapped for a gray pair. A freshly embroidered crest was emblazoned on the left breast and sleeve of the coat.

"The three we have in custody, are they Bourjon?" Morgaine countered.

"That remains to be determined," Helene said, looking at Ferrin for the first time since she'd arrived.

The hours she'd spent in Bourjon captivity only a few weeks prior were fresh in her mind, and her heart jackrabbited in her chest. "Why don't we know?"

"They don't have Bourjon accents, if that was what your next question was going to be," Grey said, his tone dripping with condescension.

"It *wasn't*," she lied, feeling a touch foolish.

"Then are they mercenaries?" Soviel chimed in.

"Most likely," Grey said, his tone far softer when he addressed Soviel.

Ferrin frowned. "Ash made it onto the first ship before it blew. She's why the rest of you aren't shredded to bits at the bottom of the harbor right now. You should ask her about what she saw."

"Who?" Grey asked.

"Ash. Ash Mazrihn."

"A civilian?" Grey puzzled.

"Yes, you met her not an hour ago," Soviel quipped back flatly.

"Why ever was she *on* that ship?"

"Half the people who just defended the harbor are civilians, Lieutenant."

"This is *not* protocol—"

"In case you hadn't noticed, Lieutenant," Helene's voice rose sharply. "Very few things are going according to protocol. You'd better adopt a more flexible attitude." She drew in a long breath. "Now could one of you please bring me this Ash person?"

"Yes ma'am," Soviel said, beginning to stand.

"No, not you." Helene shook her head. "Ferrin, you go. Soviel, we need to speak. The rest of you are dismissed."

Once the room had emptied out, Soviel slid into the seat across the desk from Major Wilcoe. "You wanted to speak with me?"

"Yes. Tea?" offered Wilcoe.

"No, thanks."

"Right. Well, I may have that assignment ready for you."

Right to the point, as always.

"Go on," Soviel said, leaning back in her chair.

"As you know, we left you behind in the capital for the purpose of preserving your cover."

"Yes." Soviel crossed her arms, still perturbed at being abandoned to the wolves just before the invasion.

"This assignment is contingent on the continued handling of that cover."

"Well, what is it?"

"It is not unlike your previous assignment," Major Wilcoe said. "You'd be a lady-in-waiting to a wealthy woman in a prominent household. Part of her entourage."

"And?"

"It would be *strictly* observational. Unlike your last post, you would not be trying to recruit her. Only gathering intelligence and reporting back on the goings-on in the household. Particularly, her husband's doings."

"Who is it?" Soviel asked hesitantly.

"The Duke and Duchess Hadringston of Bramblehall."

"Bramblehall? On the southwest coast?"

Wilcoe nodded. "The very one. There are yet some logistics to work out."

"I see, and when would this assignment begin?"

"By midsummer, I reckon. There will be an opening in her retinue soon; I have it on good authority that one of her ladies is with child."

"I see," Soviel pondered.

The major frowned as she eyed Soviel. She looked like she was deciding whether or not to say her next piece. "It is a dangerous assignment, Soviel. You'd be far away from any ally, in a place where one slip might send you to prison, or worse."

"I know that—"

"These jobs, they can take a toll on you."

"But the information we could gather would be *invaluable*, Major. Hadringston was involved in the prison fiasco this spring. I'm sure he's the one heading up that entire operation." She recalled the message she and Rhi had intercepted.

"Besides, if today is any indication, someone is letting slip information of *our* defenses. How else would those ships have known to draw out harbor patrol as a shield?"

"You are very young, Soviel," Helene sighed.

"There're plenty of soldiers my age or younger," she countered, trying not to bristle.

"Sending you into these sorts of situations—" Helene broke off. "Well, it is against my better judgment."

"What was the purpose of leaving me behind to fend for myself if not for this?"

"I only wish to make certain you know what you're getting yourself into. It is no reflection on your skill."

Soviel crossed her arms and chewed her bottom lip, then stopped herself, feeling petulant.

"You'd have no one to confide in, no one to rely on besides yourself. Your contact with a courier would be extremely limited."

Soviel swallowed. Being that deep undercover, so far behind enemy lines, it could take its toll on the mind. She knew that. "We were completely blind to the invasion of the capital until it was almost too late. It's thrown us into a disastrous situation, one we've had to adapt to rapidly. Things here are untenable as it is. It can't happen again, Major, we won't survive it. Not if there's another way. If you can make the transition happen smoothly, I will do it." She paused, thinking. "But there's something I'd like in return."

"And what would that be?"

"I know new positions are opening up with harbor patrol. Give one to Ash Mazrihn."

"You know I can't—"

"Can't give away positions, I know. But pull some strings if you can. She's been trying to find work down at the docks for a while now, and she's more than qualified to be on a harbor patrol ship."

Helene pursed her lips and considered Soviel with her gaze. "Well, if what I heard about her role in today is true, it shouldn't be too difficult to persuade the right people," she said. "I'll see what I can do."

"Thank you. And, no need to tell anyone I asked you to do this. I don't want—" she broke off, unsure of where she was going with the sentence. "I'd rather my name be left out of this favor."

Ferrin had walked Ash to Helene's tent and been promptly —and a bit coldly—dismissed while Soviel and Helene debriefed Ash on the attack. Soviel had looked pale, and deep in thought at whatever she and Helene had discussed.

The army may not have prioritized investigating the prison break, but that didn't stop Helene from holding it against Ferrin.

She almost didn't see Lukas shuffle past her on the path as she approached the stair up the cliff to the manor.

"Hey!" she called after him. He halted below her and turned around.

"Ferrin," he said. The tension in his expression deflated. "I was looking for you all over after the—"

"The explosion?"

"Yeah, I heard. I've been," he paused and shook his head, his eyes clearing. Something seemed off, the way his breath hitched, the frantic set to his shoulders only just beginning to ease. "I've been trying to find you and Ash and—"

"Ash was out there. She's fine, just being debriefed."

"*Ash was out there?*" The color drained from his face.

"She's fine," Ferrin repeated. She'd been about to joke about how she and Ash had been through *far* closer calls, but the pale tang of panic on his face had her swallowing those words. "Just a few little scrapes."

"Good. Good."

"Rhi is fine too," she said slowly, waiting for relief to cross his features. It didn't. She hesitated, wondering if he was alright, and wondering if he'd give her a straight answer if she asked. "Actually, I wanted to show you something, if you're not busy."

"What is it?" he asked, still wound tight as a trebuchet.

She studied him a moment longer. "It's about the map we found," she said, rummaging in her coat pocket as she descended the stairs between them.

"What is it?"

"I cross-referenced it with some other maps of the area from different times. Ten, twenty, fifty years ago. You know, to see if it might be an island lost to changing coastlines." She paused, letting him take a look. "Well, it wasn't. But I noticed this same mark here—" she pointed to a spot in the east of the Meddemara, "and here, on the map *we* found." She pointed to the spot in the Imbaelic Sea. "It's faded, but they're the same."

Lukas peered closer, his brow knitting as he focused. He froze suddenly.

"What is it?"

"That symbol. I know it."

"What? Where from?"

"Look," he said as he reached into his breast pocket. "It's here." He pulled out that odd little pocket watch he was always fidgeting with, and popped it open. Sure enough, inscribed inside the tarnished metal of the lid, was the very same symbol.

CHAPTER SEVEN

T he discovery of the mysterious symbol had led to a frantic rush to the library in town, where Ferrin and Lukas had spent a few afternoons searching for proof of that symbol on any other maps. Three days had gone by, and they now sat side by side at the study table by the fire with a mess of maps, books and journals spread before them.

"This is a depth-map from seventy years ago, just for charting shoals and rocks and things for fishermen. It's got that same symbol inked on it." She pointed to the little mark, in a different shade of ink than the rest of the map. "How far out is that, do you reckon?"

"Not sure, can't you tell with your seafaring ways and whatnot?"

"Hard to tell," she hummed as she peered at the map. "The coast is always changing. That trench might be a sandbar now, or those rocks? They might be covered over."

"There is one way to find out." He set down the map he was holding and leaned back in his chair, raising an eyebrow at her.

"What—go out there? The Imbaelic is cruel, Lukas. It isn't like shooting across the strait by moonlight."

"I know," he said mildly, all traces of his previous tension erased. "But don't you want to find out what's out there?" he asked with a glimmer in his eye.

She chewed her cheek and held his gaze thoughtfully. It was like he'd glimpsed that ever-echoing line that had been rattling around in her mind for nearly a decade, and plucked it right out of her skull.

There is just so much out there.

"Of course I do." She crossed her arms. "I just don't know how we'd manage it. It's a fair few miles from the coast, and we don't even *really* know what we're looking for. What if it's just some little rock pile and we miss it?" She shook her head, pondering. "And we don't have a ship. We'd need something big enough to get us out there safely, and enough people on board to crew it."

"How big of a ship?" he asked.

She tipped her head from side to side, calculating. "This time of year? Bigger is better with all the storms rolling up from the south. The last thing we need is *Strata*'s wrath coming down on us in open water."

"Maybe someone will be willing to make the trip," Lukas suggested.

"I doubt it. Rhi and I have no money to offer them, and we're probably close to wearing out our welcome as it is."

"I'll see if I can rustle up any old connections," Lukas said, reaching up to twine a loose strand of her hair around his finger.

She met his eye with half a grin, appreciating the comfort of his closeness.

He returned her smile and began folding up the depth chart.

"Wait—" Ferrin caught him by the wrist before he could tuck the chart away again. "There's something on the back."

Sure enough, a few lines of script were written across the back of the chart. The writing was in the same color of ink as the symbol drawn on the other side.

"Let me see the other maps again?" she asked.

He set them on the table. They leaned into each other's space as they pored over the backs of the maps.

"It looks like they were *all* marked later. Look at this, what does it—"

"My mother marked these," Ferrin felt the air rush out of her lungs as she dropped her hand from the page.

"How can you tell?" Lukas asked.

"I'd recognize her handwriting anywhere. See how she does her 'G's in that strange way?"

"Does that mean you can make out the notes?"

"Sort of…" she leaned in, her face inches from the map. The indigo ink had faded and bled into the page.

"Something about an entrance through a wall—no—a veil," she said.

"What do you think *that* means?" He picked up the map to squint at where she was reading.

She shook her head. "You're right, we have to get out there."

"Get out where?" came Ash's voice, startling them both.

Ferrin and Lukas flew apart as if poked with a branding iron. Ash grinned as she stood on the opposite side of the table and bit into an apple.

"Here," Ferrin turned the map around to show Ash and placed her finger on the spot.

Ash let out a long whistle. "It just might be your lucky day, Gil."

"And why is that?"

"Because I just got recruited into the privateering effort, even have my own small commission. And the harbormaster said she 'owes me a favor personally.'"

CHAPTER EIGHT

T he hour was late when Rhi finally got around to the notes
Soviel had left him. Apparently, she'd swiped one of the
vials used to sedate the victims, and had done a few tests of
her own. As Rhi had suspected, it was largely comprised of a
unique strain of *popava*, one meant to have a mellowing effect.
Also detailed in her missive: all other common sedatives had
sent the patients into a riot of sickness, agitation, and fury.

He rubbed his eyes and read over the notes again. The
strangest part was the newfound abilities the victims of the
laboratory had exhibited—was it possible that the purpose of
the lab was to study magic?

The work seemed far too destructive for such a vague end
goal. Lukas had mentioned the pile of cooling bodies, cast out
of the prison in a heap. Ash had said the same—dozens upon
dozens dead, skin covered in raised blue veins, eyes bloodshot
and unblinking. All aged in their prime. Strong.

He scanned to the bottom of the page where Soviel had
scribbled a little asterisk and a note. *They may have been
testing Gerreway's theories on magical origins. I'm not overly
familiar with it. Check the library for his work.*

Rhi frowned. He'd never heard of Gerreway, but granted,
he didn't spend much time researching healers or magic theory
or whatever it was Soviel knew this from.

He headed down to the manor library, determined to puzzle
out exactly what was going on in that prison, only to be
thwarted by a short, frazzled woman with wild gold hair.

"Can't go through there," she said, stepping in front of him. "The storm flooded the floor. Water damage on everything."

"I only need one particular book, I'm happy to help tidy —"

"Everything is a mess. Destroyed." She adjusted her brown spectacles, which sat unevenly on the bridge of her nose.

"Well, can you at least tell me if you've heard of it?" he asked, peering over her shoulder through the door frame. Several stacks sat empty, surrounded by bins of wet books and pulp.

She narrowed her eyes. "What is it?"

"It's ahh… Gerreway. Gerreway's theories."

She scrunched up her nose. "We don't have those. These are historic archives. We have chronicles of the Lords of Galan through the ages, Scrolls of the Caelish tribes, and the like. All of it priceless," she bemoaned, wringing her hands. "So much history lost."

"Oh, err - I'm very sorry." Rhi thought a moment. "Well, do you know where I might find such writings? In town, perhaps?"

She shook her head forcefully. "No, no. You'd need to head inland, to the archives in Eilbast. Their collection is vast."

"Eilbast… at the university?" Rhi squinted.

"Yes," she nodded nervously. "I studied there. Many years ago. They have what you're looking for."

"Is Eilbast not… occupied territory now?"

She looked left and right, the motion jerky and nervous. "Think so."

"Right," Rhi said. "Well, thanks for your help." He let out a deep sigh, turning from the library door as she closed it in his face. A strange woman indeed.

That left him with exactly nothing to go on about this theory. How was he to find out anything if he couldn't get to the university archives?

The next morning, Rhi forced himself out of bed despite the nagging headache that had taken up residence between his eyes. He hadn't experienced these withdrawal symptoms as persistently as he had weeks ago, but every time he thought they were over with, he'd wake up with some form of malaise. He pinched the bridge of his nose and splashed cool water on his face, though it did little to stop the ache. A few bites of food and a bit of coffee helped the throbbing to cease at last, and he made his way down to the barracks to share his findings from the library, or lack thereof, with Lachlan, who, it turned out, was *not* a morning person.

That fact did not surprise Rhi in the least.

"Anything useful come from the tests?" Lachlan asked, squinting at the brightness of the breaking day as he picked up a steaming tin cup of hot coffee. He barked a curse and dropped it immediately, the hot metal burning his hand.

"Well, yes and no—are you alright?" Rhi frowned at the steaming puddle of coffee mud.

"Fine, fine," Lachlan muttered irritably, shaking the spilled coffee off of his hands. "Let me see what Soviel found."

"Here," Rhi said, passing over the folded pages. "She's indicated that they may be testing Gerreway's theories. Do you know what that is?"

"Not an inkling. You?" Lachlan asked, raking a hand through his hair as he squinted at the notes.

"Beats me."

"And she didn't elaborate?"

"She says she's not very familiar with the works. Just knows the gist, about magical origins."

"So that's another dead end," Lachlan said with an exasperated sigh. He sat down on the edge of his cot and placed the papers on his knee, resigned.

"Well, maybe not. I went down to the library in the manor and the woman said there might be something about it in the archives at Eilbast."

"Eilbast? That is deep in occupied territory. Who knows what's even become of the archives," Lachlan said with a huff.

"Right," Rhi said, sitting down on the latched chest across from Lachlan.

Lachlan picked up the papers, skimmed the notes, and set them down again with another sigh. He stared out into the distance, frowning.

"What is it?"

"I studied at Eilbast for three years."

"Oh? Only three?"

"Despite what you *may* believe, I left of my own accord. Anyway, I do know the layout of the grounds."

"Interesting," Rhi said.

"I also know a few covert ways in and out of the library," Lachlan added after a second, giving Rhi a sidelong glance.

"*Very* interesting." Rhi cocked his head to the side. "You think they're still there?"

"Maybe. Hopefully." Lachlan stood, shrugging on his coat. "Get your things in order, pretty boy. We leave at dawn in two days."

CHAPTER NINE

When the weather cleared a few days later, Ferrin, Lukas, Ash and Soviel boarded a small ship on loan from Captain Brock of the Thanaseia.

With Ash at the helm and Ferrin overhead on the mast, they set off. Lukas stood by the bow, and Soviel readied a little healing station amidships, just in case. They had a few hired crew who Ash had recruited for the day, making ten of them altogether.

Rhi had been otherwise occupied. According to Soviel, he was deep in an investigation regarding the two rescued people from the lab. He'd looked deeply torn when Ferrin told him that she was going after answers about their mother.

She wished he could be here. The closer they came to their strange destination, the more wary she became, the more nervous. What if this map was just some stupid scribbling? What if it only provided more confusion? What if there was nothing there at all? She crossed her arms against the wind and stared out at the horizon, waiting for something definitive to come into view.

Somehow, she had managed to cobble together enough funds to hire the necessary crew to get them underway. This was a must, since she and Ash were the only ones with any real sailing experience.

Once they were clear of the harbor, Ferrin slipped down from the riggings, landed in a crouch, and approached the navigator's table to go over the map with Ash once more.

"Just like old times?" Ash said, sliding a paperweight in place over the map.

"Just like old times," Ferrin replied with a grin.

She had copied the map's details over the top of a current one that detailed all the dangers of the ever-changing coast. She wouldn't risk losing or damaging the original, and besides, they needed to be sure they wouldn't run aground on a new sandbar or exposed bit of rock if they planned to make it back in one piece.

She knew in her bones that it was all part of the same puzzle. The map, the cave, the ring. Her mother had been caught up in something big, and she was *meant* to follow the trail. A trail that, at the very least, might finally give her some answers after five long years. Perhaps, it would even lead her to Arabella herself.

"So," she said, turning to Ash. "How does it feel to be at the helm?"

"Better than ever," Ash said, returning her grin.

Ferrin chuckled and smoothed over the edge of the map.

"So, with updated shorelines, shoals, bars… we think this is the spot we need to find," she said as she tapped the spot, "here."

"What exactly do we think this is going to look like?" Ash frowned.

Ferrin lifted a shoulder. "Not sure, could be a small island, could be a pile of rocks. Or it could be nothing."

Ash nodded, eyes narrowed at the spot on the map. "Give it an hour, maybe two. Unless the winds start acting up."

Ferrin glanced skyward, checking the tells on the main sail. They were heading north, with a solid breeze coming in from the west-northwest. If it shifted any further towards the north, they'd be stuck adding countless tacks trying to climb upwind, and slowing their journey. "Och, now that you've said that, it will. Curse-speaker."

"That is *not* true!" Ash smacked Ferrin on the shoulder.

"Wouldn't be the first time you've doomed us with one of your 'unlesses'," Ferrin grumbled. "'*Of course we'll make it through Marana before low tide. Unless customs decides to board us.'"*

"Oh, please. Zare steered us *right* into that boarding. I had nothing to do with it."

"Whatever you say, Captain." Ferrin mock-saluted and immediately regretted it when Ash's smile faltered.

They hadn't spoken much about Pierre in recent weeks. Sweet and kind Pierre who couldn't seem to shake his rigid habits from his time in the Bourjon Navy. Zare had always berated him for his overly formal, stiff addresses, salutes, and posturing. All Ferrin knew was that he'd stood alongside Ash when they'd discovered Zare's plans of betrayal. Ash had ended up in prison. Pierre had ended up at the bottom of the sea with his throat cut.

They were quiet for a moment, both stewing in the memory of their murdered friend. And how things had turned so quickly.

"Say… would you go fish the bowline out of the drink? It doesn't appear that Lukas realized it has to come *out* of the water after we cast off."

"Yes," Ferrin said, squinting towards the bow.

Lukas was studying one of the other map copies they'd brought aboard as he absently played with the chain of his pocket watch. He'd sat himself on a wooden crate, and propped his feet up on the rail with an air of casual ease.

The bowline was, indeed, trailing over the bow and dragging in the water.

"You know," she grunted as she bent down to pull the rope out, "this is supposed to stay *out* of the sea when we cast off."

He started, as if he'd been lost in a maelstrom of his own thoughts, and swung his feet off the rail and back onto the deck as he turned to her. "Come look at this," he gestured with the map.

She stepped up beside him, his skin radiating warmth despite the chill breeze sweeping over the bow. He handed over the map and used his thumbnail to flip open the watch.

"It's running backwards," Ferrin frowned.

"It does that sometimes," he nodded as the minute hand slowly wound it's way back from the fifty-seventh minute.

"Not all the time, though?"

He shook his head.

"You don't find it odd that your mysterious, symbol-marked pocket watch sometimes counts backwards of its own accord?"

"Of course I find it odd." He snapped the watch shut and turned to her.

"Well, when else has it done this?"

"A few times."

"Specifically?" she pressed.

"Awfully demanding today, princess." He curled up a corner of his mouth.

"I am used to getting what I want," she said primly, leaning over him with a sly smirk.

He cleared his throat and averted his gaze back out to the sea. "Well, once when I was standing guard for Rhi. Another time when I was ambushed by bandits while moving product down the coast road last summer…" he trailed off, his brow furrowing.

"And then it started running forward again? All by itself?"

"Well… yes."

"It's a countdown," she said under her breath to herself, then, louder: "It's counting down. To something important."

"But that can't be, because the other time it did it, nothing happened. It was—" his eyes narrowed as he looked at her, his expression bordering on suspicious.

"What?"

He shook his head, eyes still on her, expression unreadable. "Nothing."

She returned his suspicious expression.

"It was the same day the suitors arrived, this spring."

"That seems an odd event to count towards."

He shrugged, flipping the watch open again.

"Fine, if you insist on being so dodgy about it. Has it happened any other times?" She reached out and touched the metal in his hand.

"In the three years I've had the thing?" He thought for a moment, inhaling slowly as she ran her finger and thumb past the watch and over the skin of his wrist. "Yeah. Right around the time the first blockade went up down south."

"Well, that confirms it," she said softly. "It's a forewarning of important events, it must be."

He hesitated before nodding in agreement. There was something he wasn't telling her. Something about the time coinciding with Havian's visit.

"Well, let's hope that whatever is going to happen in," she squinted down at the watch, "fifty-four minutes isn't some unspeakable atrocity."

The next half-hour or so went by with relative smoothness. Ash was steady at the wheel, Soviel lingered nearby, the two of them chatting easily over something Ferrin couldn't quite make out from where she was perched on the rail. The wind had shifted further west, speeding them closer and closer to that spot on the map.

"Ferrin!" Ash called across the deck. "Get up in the nest and see if you can see anything yet!"

They must have been getting close. She flitted up to the nest, weightless on the breeze, and hooked one hand around the timber to survey the ocean around them. There was nothing to be seen—no island, no treacherous whirlpool, no floating castle. Nothing.

"Nothing yet!" she called, swiveling just in time to see Ash flip open her compass and shake her head at the map.

"Keep looking!" Ash shouted over the wind, now whipping faster through the sky.

Ferrin sighed and pulled out her scope, squinting against the brightness of the afternoon sun on the water. She saw it at the same time as Lukas, who shouted from below.

"Look out!"

Something *big* brushed against the side of the ship with a thud, sending it listing to the side. Ferrin nearly lost her grip on the mast. She swore as she looked below, catching a glimpse of a silvery tail slipping over the rail and beneath the waves.

"What the hell is that?" she yelled.

"You're the lookout!" Ash fired back, followed by a string of unintelligible curses as she tried to right the course.

Ferrin swore as she watched the dark shape pass beneath the ship. It was huge, more than half the length of their hull, and thick and fast. "Shit," she cursed. "Starboard side! MOVE!"

Soviel only hopped out of the way a second before the huge, scaled and taloned arm cracked into the rail, and the creature climbed up onto the side, sending the ship heeling dangerously.

It was not quite a dragon, and not quite a serpent, and not quite a water-horse.

Several shouts went up from the hired crew.

"Only one can pass," it rasped through sharp teeth the length of a human hand. Its scales were silver and keeled, glinting in the sun as it flexed its long, arched neck. The creature's mane was coarse like a catfish's whiskers, and the color of burnt copper. Its eyes were gems of the hottest blue fire as it stared them down.

Ash gripped Soviel's arm in wide eyed disbelief, and the two of them backed away inch by inch as the creature glared at them, heaving mighty breaths as its claws sank deeper into the wooden rails.

"We are searching for the meaning of this symbol," Lukas stepped up, strangely calm, the pocket watch open in his hand as he moved towards the creature.

The sound of a gun being cocked sent the tension snapping.

"Hold your fire!" Ash commanded the hired crewman who'd drawn the gun.

The creature gave a short, amused snort as it looked them all over. "You are not who I was expecting," it said with another great sigh.

Ferrin took this opportunity to drop down from above, landing beside Lukas.

"What do you know of that symbol?" she asked. "Of its marking on these maps?"

The creature looked her up and down. "I've been waiting for you." Its eyes flared brighter.

She resisted the urge to step back.

"Come, I can transport you to where you must go to begin."

"Begin *what*?" At that, she did step back.

"I see…" the creature bristled, preening its shoulder once. Its scales rippled with the motion. "You do not yet know." It seemed to ponder for a few moments. "Very well, I will show you. You need not carry out the task today, but time runs short, and you have much to learn, Sky-Blessed."

He angled himself to bare his back, inviting her to climb upon his scaled hide.

"Where?" Ferrin asked, apprehensive.

"I can only show you."

"I am *not* riding into the unknown on the back of a… a…"

"A Portal Guardian, darling."

"Oh, that makes it better," Ash snorted behind her.

"Bring the Timekeeper, if it will ease your mind," the creature drawled. "You both have much to learn."

"What about our friends, the ship?" she asked, crossing her arms.

"I will return the both of you to them in one hour, unharmed."

After Ferrin climbed up onto the beast Lukas settled in behind her. He could feel her hands shaking.

At any other time, he'd have been pleased to be in this position with her, her back pressed to his chest, his arms around her waist. However, at that moment, he was far more preoccupied with the enormous beast on which they sat. The creature, whose name was apparently Norhi, skimmed over the waves as easily as a hound bounding through the fields and forests of a hunt. Though he had no wings, Norhi seemed to fly over the surface, skimming the waves unburdened by anything so commonplace as gravity.

The late afternoon sunlight glinted off Norhi's silver scales as he whisked them away so fast Lukas didn't have time to worry about how horrible an idea it was to have agreed to this. But there was no way any of them were going to let Ferrin go alone. Especially after what happened in the spring.

He tightened his grip on the strands of Norhi's mane, the inside of his arms flush against Ferrin's waist. She turned her head to glance back at him, a mixture of fear and wonder in her eyes as she held fast to the mane of the Portal Guardian. Beneath his hands, the whiskers were tough and fleshy, thick as reeds.

At last, Norhi slowed, spindrift falling around them as he skimmed to a halt. They had reached an island—no, not an island. A rocky shoal about twice the size of Rochmere, surrounding two slim boulders the height of a house, leaning against each other in an inverted-V.

Norhi neared the rocks, weaving in and out from them as the waves frothed below.

Then Lukas saw it, between the two boulders was another sea-cave.

"This is a Door."

"A door to what?" Ferrin asked.

Norhi gave a light, hissing chuckle. "Not just any door. A Door to nearly anywhere, girl."

She tensed.

"But for you, I suspect it will lead to one place above all others," the creature continued.

Flecks of something brassy and metallic shimmered within the black rock.

"Where?" Ferrin asked with trepidation.

Norhi sighed again. "Far away, there is an island that can be found on no map. On that island is a temple that is unlike any other."

Ferrin shifted nervously in front of Lukas, and he reached out and grasped her hand, weaving his fingers through hers. She squeezed his hand, her knuckles going white.

"If you passed through that door today, you would come to the temple of Vaiorka, and they would guide you to the secrets of all magic and divinity. They would show you exactly what you need to know in order to defeat what is to come, to protect the equilibrium of the natural world."

"To stop Bourjony, you mean?" she breathed.

"My dear girl, there are worse things on the horizon than gunfire and political disputes," Norhi said, shaking his mane.

"And you will need what they can offer you there long before the end."

"Can't you just tell her what it is without speaking so cryptically?" Lukas interjected.

"I am afraid even I cannot see who is coming. Only that a terrible presence stirs beneath the earth. Something that should have stayed asleep, and yet, someone strives to waken it."

"*Rasernemaud*?" Ferrin asked.

Lukas tensed, remembering the horrible feeling of standing over the pit, the hot breath and the stench of death exhaling from the earth itself. He remembered how it had drained the energy out of Soviel when they'd sought to blow it up.

"While the Great Destroyers may be agents of the conflict to come, they are not its key instigator. What stirs is unclear, but it is something far older than a mere monster. It will be some time yet before whatever ancient bonds hold this great power at bay finally crack, but make no mistake, someone works to break them."

"You called me Timekeeper," Lukas said. "What did you mean?"

The beast grunted a dry laugh.

"Is it because of this?" He held up his pocket watch from its chain, as it swayed in the wind.

"It is not the only artifact of its kind. Forged from the ore that springs up within the very rocks making up the Doors all over our world."

"What does it do?"

"They are all different, my dear boy," Norhi crowed. "Perhaps it allows time to be frozen temporarily, perhaps it allows one to jump through space and time like skipping through puddles. Perhaps it slows time, perhaps it reverses it."

Lukas waited, anxious for answers on the old watch he and Damijan had won off a fur trader years ago back home.

"Like I said, this Door can lead anywhere. Mostly, to other Doors, other folds. But I would hazard a guess that anyone in possession of a timepiece like that would have a little more control over where in the world he ends up."

Ferrin met his eye over her shoulder again, then turned back towards the island.

"Is my mother alive?" she asked the Guardian.

"Arabella is alive and well," Norhi responded.

Ferrin's shuddering gasp was audible even over the crashing waves.

"She waits for you to contact her, by way of moon and shadow."

"What the hell does that mean?" Ferrin demanded.

Lukas could sense her losing her patience with Norhi's ambiguous answers.

"When you dream, leave a way open. She will tell you all you need to know."

"But—"

"It is not time for your journey yet, my child," Norhi explained, suddenly sounding almost kind. "I will return you to your companions."

Scales shimmering, Norhi dove beneath the waves. Lukas braced himself for the frozen plunge, but it never came. Silver flashed and they broke the surface just as the sun dipped below the horizon. They were not twenty feet away from their waiting ship.

The sun had not begun to bleach the dark sky when Rhi rolled out of bed that morning. Though the hour was early, he'd grown used to starting his day before the sun. He'd come to rely on the constant business—it kept away any lingering urges to seek out a bundle of *popava* down by the docks, or in the lower levels of the manor where he'd seen a kitchen maid selling *something* in twine-wrapped bundles.

He'd taken to sparring with some of the soldiers in the training room in the barracks, and while he was out of practice, it helped steady his mind. The soreness it caused seemed to anchor him to his body in a way that surprised him.

Very few people knew it, but before Rhi had turned twelve, there had already been four assassination attempts on him.

His parents had added more guards to his retinue, more tasters for his meals, and insisted he learn to defend himself. He'd spent five afternoons a week, and early mornings, too, learning to fight with swords and knives and fists and pistols. He'd been trained by a fellow from the continent, Guntar Morrain. He had a bald head, a sharp accent and no patience for tomfoolery.

It had been years since Rhi had done any sort of consistent combat training, but to his surprise, he'd found it easy to remember the movements.

Hefting his bag onto his shoulder and pulling his newly-mended coat tight around the lingering soreness in his shoulders, he hoped he would not have need for that training upon sneaking into the university library.

Ducking through the kitchens, which were also already awake and abuzz with cooks and workers, he swiped two ceramic mugs of coffee, careful not to spill them as he made his way down the cliff stairs and across the marsh to the barracks. The mugs were still hot when he arrived outside of Lachlan's tent.

"Lach, are you up?" he called into the tent.

No answer.

"*Strata* above," Rhi huffed to himself before pushing into the tent.

The pre-dawn light illuminated the space in a muted gold, showing Lachlan still very much asleep, blanket tucked around his waist, shirt off, lips slightly parted.

"Wake up." Rhi gave the leg of the cot a kick, prompting Lachlan to sit bolt-upright, frantically reaching for the knife sheathed beside the cot.

"Oh," he said, relaxing visibly when he laid eyes on Rhi. "It's morning already?" He rubbed his eyes and stretched his back before climbing out of bed.

"Close enough. I brought you a coffee," Rhi said, offering one of the mugs.

"Thanks." Lachlan squinted, his fingers brushing Rhi's as he took the mug.

"It's still—" Rhi paused, wincing as Lachlan knocked back the steaming coffee, "—hot."

"Well, let's get a move on." Lachlan smacked his lips once before throwing his shirt over his head and pulling on his jacket.

"Are we taking horses?"

"For a portion," Lachlan said. "We have to go through the mountains on foot, though. I hope you packed light."

"More or less," Rhi hefted his pack higher onto his shoulder.

"This journey will take us a few days. Maybe a week. Anything you need to do before we set out? Anyone to let know where you're off to?"

"I told my sister. Is this expedition, ah, approved?"

Lachlan's expression was unreadable. "More or less," he shrugged after a moment, and pushed past Rhi through the tent and out into the breaking dawn.

The two travelers kept to the road on horseback for the majority of the day, the Icharian mountains looming ever closer on the southwest horizon. Dressed in civilian garb and moving towards enemy lines, Rhi's nerves had gone taut. He wasn't sure of the current rules, but from his few years of schooling on military protocol, he knew it was standard to interrogate, torture or execute any soldier caught behind enemy territory in civilian clothing, with no further questioning or trial. It was not a fate he particularly relished, considering how recently he'd slipped the noose with only hours to spare.

"We'll stop for the night soon," Lachlan said. "In the morning, we'll ride till we hit Aigley Town, and leave off the horses before we head into the Tarrifaire Pass."

"Alright," Rhi agreed. "I know these woods well. Used to hunt in them."

Lachlan cut him a sidelong glance. "A bit far from Everness for a hunting trip, no?"

"I happen to enjoy long days on the road."

"Interesting," Lachlan mused.

They continued on the road for another hour before stopping to find a stream to cook beside, about a hundred feet from the road.

"Know much about trapping?" Lachlan asked as he used a stick to dig a hole for the fire. His sleeves were rolled up, revealing his forearms. They were dappled with freckles.

"Some." Rhi shucked off his jacket and hung it on the tree branch nearest to their little campsite. "Better at shooting, though."

Lachlan straightened at the waist and craned his neck to look back toward the road they'd just come from. "Better not, I don't want us attracting unnecessary attention. Save the rifles for bears. Or worse."

Rhi sighed and scratched his head. There were many bears and wolves and other large beasts that roamed these woods.

"Right, I'll go rig up a few snares. Did you pack anything else to eat?"

"Got some dried beef and half a loaf of bread," Lachlan said, holding up a linen sack.

When Rhi returned to the campsite, the fire was blazing. Lachlan had dragged up two stumps for them to sit on, and was currently using a dagger to carve up some spare tinder from the dry wood. Night had nearly fallen, and Rhi's snares had managed to catch one fat rabbit. He set to skinning it, reminded of the many nights he'd spent out in the woods under the stars with his hunting party.

He wondered if he'd spent more time outside the castle walls whether he'd still have fallen so hard last year. Being in the woods seemed to ease his entire soul. The sound of the crackling fire, the chirp of insects, the rustling of wind through the leaves and needles above.

When he'd finished skinning and gutting the rabbit, he took the offal and skin fifty paces downstream and buried them, lest bears come sniffing. He returned to find Lachlan rubbing a bit of seasoning on the rabbit.

Rhi stifled a chuckle a few paces from the fire. Lachlan's head snapped up, his face glowing in the firelight.

"What?"

"You brought seasonings?"

"I can't stand plain food. I'd rather starve," he said defensively.

"Interesting," Rhi mused.

Lachlan quirked an eyebrow. "You have an opinion you'd like to offer on that?"

"No, I just didn't take you to be a… culinary enthusiast."

"Well, you'll thank me when our dinner doesn't taste like raw dirt."

"Can't say I've ever known game to taste like *raw* dirt," Rhi pondered.

Lachlan glowered at him over the fire before returning to his seasoning. "How about you go ahead and slice up some of the bread? Better eat it before the bears get a whiff."

Rhi chuckled. "Sure."

CHAPTER TEN

Ferrin tossed and turned that night, doing her best not to kick Soviel in the shin as she tried to get comfortable. It was no use.

She was too hot. Too cold. Too crowded.

Her mind was too full of thoughts as she tried to fall asleep. She was too far in her own head about what 'leave the door open' could possibly mean. It was past midnight when she gave up on falling asleep altogether and eased out from beneath the covers. She wrapped a shawl tight around her shoulders to stave off the cold of the night as she headed out onto the manor roof.

Really, it was far too cold for this time of year.

She could even see her breath in the wind. With a deep sigh, she dropped her shawl on the roof's edge and stepped off into the air.

Her mind cleared, despite the cold, and the wind on her face calmed her as she shot skyward. The air pressing against her skin was both a comfort and a thrill. When she was so high that the cliffs below her looked like pebbles, she stopped and hovered mid-air. A few clouds ambled by, lazing in the distance, and the moonless night was lit with dancing stars.

"Why don't you take a rest for a little while?"

She froze.

That *voice*. That voice she hadn't heard in years, that had frequented her dreams and nightmares alike.

"I suppose I must have managed to fall asleep after all," she guessed, turning around to face her mother. "Last I checked, clouds haven't enough substance to sit on."

Arabella gestured to the cloud upon which she was indeed seated cross-legged. She was dressed in simple gray breeches and a white shirt. Extending a hand, she reached out and patted the buoyant mass, inviting Ferrin to sit with her as if it were a feather bed.

"I've missed you, my little bird," she said, smoothing the strands of hair out of Ferrin's face as she climbed onto the cloud.

It was like a dam breaking, the relief of seeing her mother. The words began tumbling out. "I've missed *you,* you have no idea. When you vanished, when father—"

"Shh, I know sweetheart. Henrik was attempting to have me killed, so I had to disappear."

Ferrin sagged. She had suspected as much. "Well, if it makes you feel any better, his new wife turned out to be a Bourjon spy who got him killed, probably."

Her mother's laugh was a short, bell-like sound. "I see you haven't lost your spark in all this strife, darling."

"I'm in Galan. Everness fell to the Bourjons. I don't think Father survived the attack. Everything is such a mess, and I don't know what to do," she admitted.

"I know it's been hard on you," Arabella looked pained. "But there isn't a lot of time, and I have so much to tell you."

Ferrin nodded, swallowing down everything else she needed to say.

"If I can reach you here now, then that means you have been shown the Door, and therefore know where it leads."

"More or less," Ferrin nodded.

"Before you were born," Arabella began, "just before the Unification, I went to that island beyond the door. To the temple there."

Ferrin waited for her to continue.

"But… I was too early. It wasn't time yet, and I could not acquire what they guard there. Magic still slumbered too deeply. Even bearing the ring of Gwelie, it was not enough."

"What is it they have?"

"It is knowledge, and it is something else."

"I don't understand what it has to do with winning back the isle. The Caelish Army is—"

"This is about far more than winning back the Barrian Isle, my little bird. I didn't know it when I went twenty-four years ago, but the Caelish struggle is only one small part of the larger picture. Its exacerbation is little more than an orchestrated distraction. Bourjony's king seeks something dark, dangerous. By weakening us, he gained a foothold here into the Storm Lands." Arabella's eyes fluttered, and she gave a strained sigh. "He is grasping at unimaginable power."

"So this is where you've been this whole time?" Ferrin could feel herself becoming frustrated. "This island no one seems to have a straight answer about?"

"No, Ferrin. I'm afraid I cannot return there. It was never *meant* to be me, only my offspring."

"I'm sure Father just *loved* that," she scoffed. "Caelish magical lore being bred into his bloodline.

Arabella tensed, the ghost of a sad smile crossing her lips. "You still don't know."

"What else don't I know?" Ferrin asked, shifting nervously on the cloud. *Shouldn't clouds be more comfortable?*

"Henrik… he isn't your father."

Ferrin froze.

"Alick MacVale is."

Her heart was hammering in her throat—if that was possible in this strange dreamscape. Her head felt light, dizzy.

"When I was unable to complete the trials, we realized what it meant. We were one generation too early, that it would fall to our children to lead the Caels out of their struggle. So, we had you."

"And Rhiach? Is he…" she trailed off, swallowing around the sore lump in her throat.

"Most likely, yes. It is nearly impossible that Henrik shares any blood with your brother, either."

Ferrin gave a hollow, humorless laugh. Every ounce of joy she'd had at finally reuniting with her mother evaporated into mist.

"So Rhi and I are just some part of your political agenda."

"All royal children are that in some way." Arabella crossed her arms. "And this goes far beyond politics, Ferrin."

"You don't even deny it?" Ferrin shook her head.

"It's more complicated than that."

"Why two of us? You had Rhi, so why bother at all with me?" she asked hoarsely.

Arabella hesitated.

"Why?" She clenched her hands into fists.

"Whoever can pass the trials, whoever can go on to claim the power… they cannot sit on the throne, too. Rhi passes as Henrik's heir without question. He has a rapport with both sides of our homeland. It's just the way it worked out."

"Why not? Why can't they do both?" Ferrin asked, her voice dangerously close to breaking.

"It was never specified to me. Perhaps something to do with balance of power."

"So you *made* me just so I could finish a task that you couldn't do." Ferrin's voice was raw, her vision foggy.

"It is so much more complicated than that, I promise you."

"How can you just drop this on me? After vanishing for *five years?*"

Her mother sighed again, her expression sad and tense.

"I needed you, Rhi needed you!"

"We're running out of time. I'm sorry you had to find out like this. I'll find you here again, and explain more—"

And suddenly she was falling, plummeting through vapor and tumbling through open air perilously fast and with no way to stop or slow down or—

Ferrin jerked violently awake, panting and covered in sweat, the night air cool and still as she sat up in bed.

"Are you alright?" Soviel asked beside her, rubbing her eyes.

Ferrin sucked in a breath. Then a second, unable to get out the words.

Soviel, immediately aware that something was not right, sat up. "Hey, breathe," she coaxed. "You're safe."

She must have been working some sort of healing magic, because Ferrin felt her racing heart slow and her lungs ease with every circle Soviel rubbed on her back. When at last she could speak, she gulped, "I'm fine. Nightmare."

"Do you want to go for a walk? Talk about it?"

Ferrin took a shuddering breath and squeezed her eyes shut before shaking her head.

"I'm fine." *Alick is my father.* "Go back to sleep."

Soviel eyed her for another second before resigning her head back to the pillow. Ash was still sleeping soundly as a stone on the other side of the bed, completely unbothered.

Ferrin climbed out of bed on shaky legs, careful not to disturb either of them as she padded across the dark room. The cold water from the wash basin did little to calm her. Tumbling out of the dream world had been nauseating, like putting her mind in a jar and shaking it to a pulp. Coupled with the load of life-altering information she'd had dumped on her… her stomach twisted.

Did she even truly have free will if she had been created for the sole purpose of carrying on the work of her ancestors?

The thought of processing any of it right at that moment was too much.

She eyed the crack in the door that adjoined their room to the one Rhi and Lukas shared. She knew she wouldn't be falling back asleep any time soon, so with a deep breath, she tip-toed across the room and pushed the door open.

She found Lukas alone, his chest rising and falling evenly, gold-streaked dark hair spilling across the pillow, his face relaxed in the light of the wee hours.

Right, Rhi is on a trip inland to some library. She'd nearly forgotten.

Sucking in a breath, she took a step into the room. *Gods*, he was beautiful. A storied kind of beautiful, with rough hands and mischievous eyes, a gentle heart. She crossed the room and his eyes fluttered open.

He squinted up at her sleepily. "You're not my usual roomfellow."

"No," she said, her voice coming out far huskier than she meant it to. "Rhi won't be back for a few days."

"He certainly has been busy," Lukas said quietly, propping up on one elbow.

"Sorry for waking you, I'll just—" She shook her head and turned to leave, not sure why she'd thought this was a wise idea in the first place, until he caught her fingers in his.

"Wait," he said, his voice low as he pulled her closer.

Her breath caught in her throat, and she found herself turning, closing the rest of the distance between them. Her thighs hit the bed, and she was easing onto the mattress beside him, onto his lap.

Warmth flooded through her, and her heart set to racing again, albeit for a far different reason. She snaked her free hand up his bare chest, over the divots and valleys of his warm brown skin. The sun he'd gotten in the recent weeks had deepened his complexion, painting him a dark gold. She cupped her palm around the side of his jaw, and felt his breath hitch, neither daring to take their eyes off the other. She raked her fingers into his hair—shorter now than it had been in the capital—just behind his ear, and he leaned into her touch, eyes dipping shut in pleasure. He curled his fingers tighter around her other hand.

His eyes slid partway open, and for a moment, he was still, his eyes locked on hers in the low light of the room.

Then the moment ended, and he surged into the kiss. They were push and pull, give and take, exhaling and inhaling each other in matched hunger. His hands were lost and tangled up in the fabric of her sleeping shift as he pulled her across his lap. Her fingers wreathed into his hair, pulling his head close as she kissed him. Covers were kicked aside, legs wound around each other. In one breath, she felt his arm wrap around her waist, the other still tangled in her own as he flipped them so he could hover over her. His lips made a silent murmur against her neck, and her teeth found the sensitive lobe of his ear, teasing and toying, gentle and sharp.

Abruptly, she felt his absence on her body like an icy wind as he pulled back, suspended above her. Both of them were panting as he looked down at her.

"What is it?" she gasped.

"Why did you come over here?"

"Couldn't sleep," she said.

"Because of what happened today?" he asked, his shoulders relaxing.

She nodded and saw as it dawned on him.

"She visited you, didn't she? In your… dreams."

She bit her lip and lowered her eyes.

"What happened?"

"Nothing."

"You're clearly rattled. What did she say?" he asked, running his thumb in a distractingly slow circle over her palm.

"Please, Lukas," she breathed. "I can't—I can't think about it right now—I just…"

Something like hurt crossed his face. "You came over here for a distraction."

"What? Oh. No. Please don't think that's what this is," she squeezed his hand for emphasis, closing her eyes. "I'm just not ready to talk about it. And what I have to say… it's only right that Rhi is the first to hear it."

His expression softened in understanding as he rolled off her, still holding on to her hand. "Then you should at least try to get some sleep," he sighed.

She swallowed, her heart still pounding in her throat. He sidled up next to her, pulling the covers back over them. Her skin pebbled when he pressed a kiss to the sensitive skin just under her ear. "Get some sleep."

High noon was passing Eilbast University by when Rhi and Lachlan arrived at the campus. Buildings of cream-colored stone stood solid and resolute against sprawling green lawns, sporadically placed trees, and a small pond where a family of ducks had made their home. Young people in fine but disheveled clothing lounged on blankets in the grass, reading poetry and sketching. A few scholars waded amongst the reeds in the pond, breeches or skirts hiked up to their knees as they collected samples of water and muck. Some rosy-cheeked students played a leisurely game of field sticks, one player running while balancing the point stick in his mitt as the rest of them chased him down with their mallets, laughing.

Lachlan appeared uncomfortable as he surveyed the green, and Rhi tried to imagine him among these people, reading poetry on a lazy afternoon or playing a casual game, barefoot in the grass. *He is probably viciously competitive,* Rhi thought. Pulling the collar of his coat up higher, Lachlan stalked onto the grass towards the building at the head of the lawn. Rhi followed, trusting Lachlan to remember how to navigate the place.

"I'm trying to picture you among these scholars," he said with a laugh. "I'm having trouble."

Lachlan smirked. "You certainly wouldn't see *me* wading through the muck like those fools. That pond is a cesspool."

Rhi grimaced. "How about reciting poetry with a bottle of summer wine? Was that more your persuasion?"

"Only in certain company," Lachlan grudgingly admitted.

"I see." Rhi nodded, glancing back at a couple sharing a kiss, book splayed face-down between them.

"You'd better hope we're lucky enough to find one of my old schoolmates here, otherwise we're going to have to break into the library after dark."

"Why?" Rhi balked. "It's only a library, can we not just… walk right in?"

"Not anymore," Lachlan said as he shifted his gaze to the squad of soldiers drilling further down the lawn.

"Damn it. I'd hoped they would leave places like this alone."

"They check everyone's information at all building entrances. Student identification papers, military papers, all the like. Given this place's proximity to the new border… well, they must expect rebel agents to come sniffing around here."

"How then are we to get in?" Rhi asked as they neared the library.

"Like I said, I have a way. Probably," said Lachlan, before taking a sharp left turn down the path.

"You don't sound terribly confident," Rhi noted. "What if your friend is no longer here?"

"He's still here. But the… club we were both a part of may have been dissolved in light of the new management," he explained, jerking his chin at the soldiers.

"*Club*? Oh don't tell me you were in one of those secret university societies I've read so much about," Rhi laughed.

"Keep your voice down," Lachlan ordered, voice gravelly as he glared straight ahead at the building they were approaching.

Rhi bit back the rest of his laugh, composing himself as they went around the side of the building, where a staircase led down to what looked like a cellar door in the building's foundation.

"Wait out here." Lachlan glanced around before descending the steps and knocking in a two-four-three pattern. A few moments later, the door cracked open and Lachlan exchanged a few words with whomever was behind the door. Rhi couldn't make out a voice or face. Another moment passed and Lachlan beckoned Rhi forward with a wave of two fingers.

Rhi glanced back at the lawn, then popped down the stairs after Lachlan, following him through the mysterious door. They reached a long, dark hallway that led to another staircase, and then another dark hallway, as they blindly followed Lachlan's contact. At last they came to another door.

"He's not going to be pleased to see you," said the woman.

"It's been *years* Mabel," Lachlan grunted.

She shot him a pointed glare before returning the way they'd come.

Lachlan let out an exasperated breath and turned to knock on the door.

A few moments later, the door opened, and a man in gold-rimmed glasses looked out at them, one eyebrow raised skeptically. His sleeves were rolled up, his mahogany hair was disheveled, and he had traces of a chalky, white dust on his light brown skin.

The man's face contorted in surprise, and then bitter amusement as he let out a long, low laugh before dusting his palms off. "Lachlan Tarrish," he dragged out the words slowly, his voice deep.

"Hassan," Lachlan greeted. "You seem to be doing well."

"Oh, indeed," Hassan laughed again. "No thanks to you, that is."

"Please," Lachlan replied, "that had nothing to do with me, and you know it."

"You nearly caved in the dig site on my head!"

"That's *not* what happened," Lachlan scoffed. "There was a small mistake in scaffolding placements, it was out of my hands!"

"Oh, right, completely out of your hands. I see you're still incapable of accepting responsibility." Hassan crossed his arms.

"It looks like they upgraded your facilities in light of that instability, so really, I did you a favor."

"You've never been good at sweet-talk, Tarrish. Don't start now."

Rhi watched them bicker back and forth and tried to figure out the exact nature of their relationship.

Hassan shifted his gaze to where Rhi was waiting uncomfortably.

"Who's this one?" he asked with a nod.

"Hi. I'm Rhi," he said cheerily, sticking his hand out in greeting.

Hassan narrowed his eyes and glanced back at Lachlan. "You brought a *hunted royal to my doorstep?* This ought to be interesting."

"That's a touch extreme," Rhi said. "We were hoping you could help with something."

Hassan sighed and rolled his eyes. He stepped to the side of the door, gesturing for them to enter. "You'd better not make me regret this," he said as he shut the door behind him.

The room was lit by lanterns along the walls, and one in the center of a very large table, which was covered in drafting paper, rocks, and the same dust that seemed to cling to Hassan.

"You study rocks?" Rhi asked, peering at the samples, particularly intrigued by the big hunk of crystal pillars the same blue-green shade as the sea.

"Gems, fossils, artifacts. If it comes out of the ground, it's in my field of study," Hassan explained, walking around the side of the table. "University grant landed me this lab space after *someone* nearly destroyed the last one. I give a few lectures each week on the subject as well."

"Neat," Rhi nodded, his eye catching on a lump of dirty, brass-colored ore.

"What brings you back here?" Hassan asked, easing into his desk chair. He leaned back and clasped his hands behind his head, crossing one ankle over his knee.

"We need someone to take us to the library," Rhi spoke for Lachlan, taking a seat adjacent to Hassan. "This one," he jerked a thumb at Lachlan, "seems to think you're the man for the job."

Hassan eyed Lachlan before shifting his gaze back to Rhi. "Sure, I can get you into the library."

"Perfect." Rhi flashed him a dazzling grin.

Lachlan sulked in the corner.

"And when precisely does this need to happen?" Hassan asked, the question directed at Rhi.

"Today, ideally," Lachlan interjected.

Hassan whistled. "I've got a lot of work today, and a mountain of papers to grade."

"We would really appreciate it," Rhi said, angling his head to the side, brows raised.

"Alright," he said after a moment's hesitation. "I can sneak you in. What section are you looking for?"

"Wherever Gerreway's theories might be housed," Lachlan supplied.

Hassan nodded slowly. "I can get you there."

Navigating the vast library while remaining undetected was about as hard as it sounded. Proctors circled like hawks, soldiers on and off duty were everywhere. Watching Lachlan try to blend in was like watching a sunset fill with clouds—all it did was reflect more colors across the sky. Whenever he ducked behind his collar or peeked over his shoulder, he looked far more shady than usual.

They'd split up to find the specific volume they were searching for, as apparently the cataloging system was a mess in the wake of exams. Every time Rhi caught a flash of Lachlan's red hair, he was sure someone would notice him and demand to see his identification papers. They'd had to leave most of their weaponry behind in Hassan's studio, so if things went awry, there would be little they could do against an onslaught of soldiers.

Rhi was stalking through a section labeled 'MAGICAL HISTORIES', which was riddled with gaps more plentiful than a boxer's teeth, and books with spines more bent than a crone's. It was hard to say if the book in question was housed here but merely checked out, or if it had never been here to begin with. He huffed and pulled his collar closer, trying to hide his stupid, handsome, recognizable face.

He thumbed through a few books on magical theory and chronicles of historic figures, one detailing the life and legend of a witch-warrior, another of a war-band of magic-wielding soldiers over a thousand years ago.

He continued down the aisle to a cart where a young, sharply dressed intern was re-shelving volumes in the biological studies section, when his eyes snagged on the title. *Sources of Energy* by *Nathenium Gerreway.*

With a quick glance back to the intern to check that he wasn't looking, Rhi snatched the book up and strode down the aisle towards Lachlan, doing his best impression of someone who absolutely *was* allowed to be here, thank you very much.

He lightly grabbed Lachlan's elbow, and was greeted by a blitz of curses as he whirled around.

"Don't sneak up on me like that!" Lachlan hissed, the words sharpened and hard.

Rhi put his finger to his lips in the universal symbol for *shut up and pay attention to what I'm about to say in this precarious situation we've landed ourselves in,* and held up the book in his other hand, eyebrows raised expectantly. Lachlan's eyes flitted between him and the book. He gave a nod.

Hassan had given them a one-hour window to get in, find the book, and get out. According to the wind-up pocket watch that Lachlan often forgot to wind, they had twenty minutes to discern if it was the correct book.

"We have to work fast," Rhi said under his breath. "I took it off the re-shelving cart, it'll need to be slip—"

"No," Lachlan said quickly. "We're taking it with us."

Rhi sighed with exasperation. "You don't think that's going to cause a problem? Them going through the catalogue and realizing exactly *which* book is missing?"

Lachlan shook his head stubbornly. "We need this. We need the information. What the hell are you going to do? Copy the entire book and bring it back?"

Rhi narrowed his eyes. "This," he tapped the cover of the book, "makes us being here *traceable*. If Soviel's hunch is right, then they'll know we're looking into what they're doing. They'll change their behavior."

Lachlan swiped the book from Rhi's hand and thumbed it open, dropping his gaze to the page without another word.

"This is the one," he said a minute later. "Time to go."

Rhi took a second to check his irritation and pursed his lips before following after Lachlan.

"Well?" Hassan asked when they all filed back into his underground office.

"We got it." Lachlan leaned back against the counter, arms crossed, narrowly avoiding knocking a sample of reddish ore off the surface.

Rhi held up the copy and wiggled it.

"I can arrange to get you off campus this evening, after dark," Hassan said. "New guards have arrived from the south, and it may not be as simple as waltzing off the way you came in."

Night fell with little ceremony once the bank of clouds rolled in from the east, bringing with it a severe chill that could only be attributed to the university's proximity to the Icharian mountains. Rhi, Lachlan and Hassan sat around the table in Hassan's office, sipping black coffee and thumbing through the stolen book.

"So, Hassan," Rhi began, not sure where he was going with this particular thread, but nonetheless sure it was one he needed to tug. "How did you manage to keep your research grant when the occupation rolled through?"

Hassan shrugged. "Honestly? I'm still trying to work that out. Most of the university's funds were diverted to more… shall we say… 'productive' efforts? Crop engineering to feed the army, battlefield medicine, the like. Even in my own department, most people were ah… *asked* to shift their focus to testing different iron and steel alloys, in the interest of weaponry."

"You don't find it odd that they let you continue your research on… what exactly is it?" Rhi asked, looking around.

Lachlan sat up a little straighter and shifted his gaze to Rhi, studying him.

"Metals and minerals and their properties in relation to magic," Hassan said slowly. "Still workshopping the title for my thesis, though." He gave an uncomfortable chuckle.

"And you don't think it's suspicious that such a niche, interest-based level of research is still being fully funded by the violent war-hungry occupation now controlling this university?" Rhi asked politely.

Hassan hesitated, his shoulders tensing.

"What aren't you telling us?" Lachlan asked in a barely-restrained even tone.

Hassan twitched, his eyes flitting to the filing cabinet beneath his desk.

Lachlan surged out of his seat. In a flash, he'd hauled Hassan out of his chair and pressed him against the wall, his forearm poised to crush Hassan's throat.

"Yes, I *do* find it odd, but I also find it's best not to ask too many questions of those who might decide to shoot me in the head and drop me in the river," he wheezed frantically.

"Why are they letting you continue your studies?" Lachlan growled, easing off just enough so Hassan could speak.

"*Aesterium*."

"*What*?" Lachlan demanded.

"Aesterium," Hassan repeated. "They're very interested in my findings on Aesterium. They agreed to finance a dig if I can locate a vein of Aesterium ore on the isle."

Lachlan released Hassan and stepped back.

"Gods," Hassan gasped, a hand clutched to his chest. "You'd better learn to temper him," he barked at Rhi.

"*That* seems like something that is not my business," Rhi raised both hands in surrender. "But back to the metal.

Aesterium, you called it? What makes it so special?" he asked, his tone still casual.

"I'm still early in the research process. Throughout the centuries, scholars have noted unusual energy fields surrounding it, but little else. No one has documented much about it at all, in fact. I found a lump of it a few years back and noticed that strange things seemed to happen in its presence."

"Such as?"

"I don't know." Hassan threw up his hands in exasperation. "Little things! Visions, time slowing down, objects moving of their own accord. I tripped on my way to my desk with a pot of scalding coffee and a pile of papers, and it all just…" he shook his head as if still in disbelief, "hung in the air for a moment… suspended. Like it was floating in the sea."

"That's impossible," Lachlan snarled.

"No," Hassan shook his head, "that's magic."

"As I said, impossible. You probably breathed in gases from one of your mines. Or didn't get enough sleep from too many nights in the library."

"What were the visions of?" Rhi cut in.

"They were vague, but," Hassan swallowed, "they shook me to my core. Snippets. Flashes. Falling from the sky and careening from so high it was like looking at a map. A man… no, a king… in chains. Surrounded by angry figures. Trees and roots growing around him, *through* him, impossibly fast."

"You don't happen to take *popava*, do you?" Rhi tilted his head questioningly.

"This was *not* that," Hassan insisted, before turning his attention back to Lachlan, who'd cooled off enough to lean back against the wall, arms crossed. "And you don't think the Bourjon Army would be financing my research if they thought I was a crazed, exhausted madman, do you?"

Lachlan shook his head begrudgingly.

"Well," Rhi said, inclined to break the unpleasant silence he seemed to be incapable of sitting with, "this trip has been a fucking revelation."

Lachlan pushed off the wall, heat again rolling off him in waves. "Any other tidbits you'd like to let slip before you hand it over to Bourjony and they engineer it into some kind of weapon to kill us all?"

"I'm just a scholar," Hassan said weakly.

"Yeah, so was I. But I left when I realized what little help it was when our people were being rounded up and shoved in holes in the ground. What's your excuse?"

Hassan gulped, surveying Lachlan like he was an uncontrolled wildfire. "They already have copies of all my notes," he said. "There's little else for me to do."

"You could stop helping them. This is pathetic. You're doing all this for them, and for what, money?" Lachlan gestured around the room. "Pull up your stakes and come to Galan before it's too late."

"I can't do that," Hassan said quietly.

"What do they have on you?"

"Nothing, it isn't that."

"What, then? The man I knew in school would never do this. Not for payment so trivial as coin."

Rhi watched their exchange, still trying to imagine Lachlan as an academic, trying to imagine what Lachlan and Hassan's lives might have looked like all those years ago.

"My family," Hassan said, defeated. "They have my family."

Lachlan's hands fell to his side as he cursed.

"Where?" Rhi asked.

"They're in their home, but… under watch. With soldiers on standby to do horrible things to them should I step out of line."

"Then why did you agree to help us?" Rhi wondered.

Hassan shook his head and then Rhi understood.

"No," Lachlan's voice was a violent rip through the ether. "You wouldn't."

"Not everyone has your knack for brutal honesty, I'm afraid," Hassan said slowly, dropping his gaze to his lap.

"Fuck. Fuck!" Lachlan roared, kicking over a side table and sending rock samples crashing to the floor.

"We need to go." Rhi lurched out of his chair, grabbing Lachlan around the waist as he launched himself at Hassan. He was nearly pulled down by the force of Lachlan's wrath. The scent of betrayal hung bitter in the air. "Lach, we need to *go, now!*"

Rhi was more concerned with whatever trap was about to come crashing down around them than whatever sense of betrayal and subsequent rage that Lachlan was experiencing towards Hassan at the moment. He had gone completely feral, snarling a colorful string of curse words both in the common tongue, and in Old Caelish as he struggled against Rhi to get at Hassan.

"Come on, Lach, let it go! He isn't worth it!"

"You fucking bastard!" he spat at Hassan, who had backed away, hands in his pockets as he eyed the door.

Hassan looked terrible. Torn, guilty, terrified.

"Is there another way out of here?" Rhi wasn't sure which of them he was asking, and wasn't sure Lachlan would be able to hear him over his own thundering rage.

Hassan squeezed his eyes shut and gestured at the floor, to a worn-out throw rug. Not a second later came a loud banging on the door.

Lachlan went silent, still, which was almost worse.

"I'm going to let go of you," Rhi said quietly into Lachlan's ear. "Are you going to control yourself?"

"For now," he seethed, shaking his jacket straight.

Rhi released his grip on Lachlan and knelt at the rug. He peeled it back and found a trap door.

"Where will it lead us?" he whispered to Hassan as he wrenched it open.

"A quarter mile. Just past the main kitchens," Hassan said, a pained look contorting his face as his eyes darted from Lachlan to the door of his office. "Hurry, I can't buy you much time."

"You're fucking dead if I see you again," Lachlan said low under his breath, eyes locked on Hassan.

"I'm sorry."

"Save your fucking groveling for your new masters," Lachlan shook off Rhi's hand as he climbed down the trap door steps.

Rhi shot Hassan one last look before he climbed in after Lachlan and pulled the door shut behind him. A second later, he heard footsteps echoing above as Hassan crossed the room to the staircase up to the front door.

They hurried through the dirt-floor tunnel, completely blind.

"Are you going to be alright?" Rhi asked quietly when he was sure they were far enough away.

"Yeah," Lachlan answered without conviction.

There was no light to see by, but Rhi was sure if there had been, he'd see Lachlan's shoulders tense with agony and barely-bridled rage. A lot could be said about Lachlan and his temperament, but if there was one thing Rhi had come to appreciate about him, it was that he didn't have it in him to be duplicitous. He was honest to a fault. So when betrayal came from an old friend, perhaps someone who'd once been more than a friend, it hit him hard.

They carried on through the dark, and Rhi allowed the silence to engulf them.

CHAPTER ELEVEN

The hour was early, and the air still pleasantly cool as Soviel trekked out into the woods. Just as she had done many a time during her tenure at Everness, she'd readied a basket and a list of herbs she required for the infirmary, and for her own purposes. As the sun slanted over the grassy hillside, she was reminded of the days she and Nimhe had picnicked out around Everness, taking their time gathering up roots and berries for special remedies, leaves and plants for healing resources. Nimhe had never had magic, but early on in their friendship, she'd accompanied Soviel out into the woods just for the enjoyment of nature. Perhaps when she'd begun withdrawing, Soviel should have taken it as a sign something was amiss.

The little edge patches of Taroch's northern borders were only a mile or so from the clifftop manor, a bit further than the closest forest access in Everness had been, but she didn't mind the walk. She could use a little solitude, time alone with her thoughts without anyone watching her.

Her power had been changing—growing. She could feel it inside her, like it was alive, a second little beating heart. The idea of it thrilled her as well as scared her. Her ability to heal others and work with life energy was what made her feel most connected to herself. At the same time, she had no one to guide her as her power changed, no one to set a precedent. She wished Madame Leone had made it to Galan.

The tall grass swished golden-green in the wind as she crested the hill, the sun at her back. Across the field, the tall trees of Taroch rose—dark and green and whispering for her.

She picked through the underbrush, searching for what she'd need to complete the amulets as the sun swelled overhead.

A curious red fox trotted up and nuzzled her calf.

"I don't have any treats for you," she said apologetically.

He plopped down on his hind quarters, tail wagging expectantly.

With a sigh, she reached down and scratched between his ears. All her life she'd been chided for petting strange animals in the woods. And all her life, all manner of creatures had sought her out. Birds, squirrels, salamanders, foxes. Even a bear had once approached her with curiosity when she was playing in the woods back home. She'd been only ten years old. Her mother had howled at her in fear after the fact, and sent her to bed without any sweets. Because of that, she'd never told *anyone* about the wolves.

The curious little fox trotted after her as she went about plucking up various stones and herbs. "Know where I might find any cedar trees around here, friend?"

He blinked once, still staring at her with a goofy little grin.

She sighed. "Right, well. Off we go, come on then." She picked up her basket and made to march further into the forest. When at last she'd gathered all she needed from the woods, she turned to head back to the manor.

The fox followed her to the tree line, then halted, sniffing the wind.

"What is it?" She turned, searching the distance for some larger predator. Perhaps a wolf, or maybe an elk lurked in the tall grass.

"Well… I suppose I do need to gather a few more rocks. I'll skirt around by the cliffs," she said casually, redirecting her course slightly north, toward the path through the cliffs.

She'd only just begun winding through the rocky terrain when a prickling sensation caught her between the eyes.

"*Oh.*" She halted. Her sinuses went aflame. The fox loped off, back to the safety of the woods.

Her head was pounding—her brain turning to mush and trying to escape the confines of her skull. *"Sweet Lalana,"* she groaned. The pressure was *blinding*. She fell to her knees, letting out a cry as the basket thudded to the ground beside her. She had to get *out* of there, right away…

"Soviel?" the familiar monotone voice was barely audible over the skull-cracking pain.

"Sov— Are you alright?" Grey's voice was much closer now, right beside her.

"Help. Me," she hissed through clamped teeth.

"What's wrong?"

"Need to get—" she winced, bracing a palm on the ground. Every sensation was too much. The sand and gravel digging into her knees may as well have been knives. "Away from here," she croaked out.

"Um… alright," said Grey a little awkwardly.

In the distant corners of her screaming mind, it occurred to Soviel that this was the most they'd spoken outside of official matters since ending their courtship last winter.

He pressed the basket into her arms, and a second later she felt his arms under her back and knees as he lifted her.

"Where to?"

"Away. Anywhere." She squeezed her eyes shut once more before forcing them open. The sun was far too bright.

He walked her along the cliff path back down toward the manor. Finally, after what seemed like miles, her headache eased.

"I can walk on my own now," she said weakly. He set her down and stepped back one pace.

"Are you sure? At least let me escort you down to the barracks infirmary."

"Yes, fine," she nodded. Her head had cleared, but the exhaustion lingered. She took two steps and her knees gave out.

"Alright, that's it. I'm carrying you," Grey said, scooping her up once more.

"Fine." She took a deep breath. What in the deepest pits of Harrow-Hall was happening to her?

"Any chance you're going to give me an explanation?"

"If I had one, I would," she choked out.

"How long were you there like that?" he asked, his voice a shade gentler.

"What time is it?"

"Around noon."

"Not that long, then," she gulped.

A few confused glances turned their way as Grey elbowed into the infirmary, and more than ever, Soviel wished Madame Leone was there. Perhaps she would have a solution, or at least an explanation of what was happening to her.

"Heat exhaustion," Grey barked coldly at one of the young nurses who'd gawked a little too long, before depositing her onto an empty cot. "There," he said, adjusting the coverlet over her. His closeness was startlingly familiar, even after so many months of being apart. "I'll—uh—I'll go find a healer."

"That's not necessary," she blurted. "I'm fine now. Really!"

His usually stony face crinkled with what might have been concern. Out of all the people she'd courted, not that it was a long list, he had the thickest shell.

"Truly, Grey. Thank you for your assistance," she said more evenly. "I will be fine."

He nodded curtly before turning on his heel and leaving as quickly as he'd come in. The tent flaps hadn't stopped swaying before her eyes drooped shut and she fell asleep.

Later, Soviel awoke to screams.

Though disoriented and bleary-eyed, she was on her feet in seconds, the blanket of the cot tossed to the floor as she whirled around to find the entire hospital tent and barracks beyond in complete chaos. Soldiers rushed past half-dressed, screams of anguish bit through the air, and crashes melded with the whistling sound of projectiles in a terrible cacophony.

She burst out of the tent flap and only narrowly missed being pummeled by a bit of rock that flew her way. They were under attack. The shots were coming over the side of the cliff. The steep wall of rock that should have obscured them from any scouts or ships was being battered and cracked by cannonballs. There was no way it was a coincidence.

"Incoming!" a voice shouted.

A section of rock exploded into dust and detritus as a cannonball slammed into it, raining rubble down onto the encampment below as people scrambled for cover.

Soviel's heart jumped into her throat, hammering away as she took in the lay of the land. She ducked another projectile as she headed for the cover of an unhitched hay cart. A hideous cry of pain grabbed her attention, drawing her frantic gaze to the left. A soldier was trapped, his leg caught beneath a heavy, jagged stone. He cried out again, and the sound of it wrenched her gut. Abandoning any semblance of self-preservation, she ran out into the fray and skidded to her knees beside the soldier.

"Be still!" she commanded as she took stock of his injuries. Blood still flowed to the trapped extremity, but the rock was crushing into his shinbone, which was certainly broken, if not shattered.

Another cannon blast rang out, and it was all Soviel could do to throw her arms over her own head and cover the soldier with her body.

"Get this thing off me!" he pleaded as the dust cleared.

"I am trying!" she coughed, frantically searching for something, someone to help her shift the weight. At last, she spotted a figure darting back and forth from the biggest pile of rubble about five yards away, a cloth tied over his mouth and nose to ward off the dust. When he turned, she recognized him immediately.

"Lukas!" she screamed, tearing her dust-riddled lungs and throat raw with the effort.

His head whipped around and his eyes went wide when he saw her. Setting down the bit of rock he was moving, he sprinted over.

"What are you doing out here?"

"Help me shift this rock!"

"Lenson!" Lukas shouted at the soldier. "Stay with us! We're getting you out of here."

Soviel briefly registered that Lukas seemed to know this soldier. Lenson's face pinched in agony as he nodded back, lower lip trembling as he bit into it.

"Ready?" Lukas positioned himself on the other side of the rock. "One, two, *three!*"

Lenson groaned as they threw the rock off him. The spot it had punctured on his leg began to bleed, *fast*.

"Hold still!" she shouted at him as she went to work staunching the flow.

"Do you need anything?" Lukas asked.

Soviel looked up, maintaining pressure on Lenson's leg with her kerchief. Lukas's eyes were wide and his shirt was filthy with dust and flecks of blood.

"No! Go help the others!" Soviel shouted back at him. "Be careful."

He nodded and was off.

Soviel made quick, sloppy work of healing the soldier's leg, only expending enough time and energy to stop the threat, and allow him to limp to safety. He'd need an additional checkup later, but it would have to wait.

She heard Major Wilcoe's voice over the tumult, barking orders at a messenger. "Get to the manor! Tell them what's happened!"

She set to work searching for more wounded and trapped, dodging falling rocks and splintering wood from a cart smashed by another piece of debris. Another cannon shot sounded, and a moment later the rock wall of the cliff shuddered with the impact of the blast.

A human chain had formed to remove gunpowder by the barrel from a broken down cart close to the cliff that was fortunate enough to have not been smashed to bits just yet.

"How could they have known to fire here?" Soviel shouted, pulling up next to Major Wilcoe.

Helene shook her head, grim as she passed Soviel another barrel of gunpowder to be handed down the chain. "There's no way they could have scouted this spot from the harbor. There is a spy amongst us, mark my words."

Soviel's stomach soured and she thought of Nimhe, sneaking around beneath her nose all those weeks, causing problems at every turn. Nimhe poisoning Rhi, Nimhe trying to take the flight ring from Ferrin's rooms. She could *not* let that happen again.

Another cannon blast sounded, and they braced for impact.

"And they're out of range of the fort? What of the manor's guns?"

"Short of climbing up onto the promontory with a complement of guns, we are *completely* at their mercy!"

"Dammit," she cursed.

"We've got a leak!" a voice called from closer to the carriage. There was indeed a trail of gunpowder following the last barrel.

"We need to get everyone off this field," Wilcoe muttered with alarm, "Until they cease firing, we cannot stay here."

In the wake of the attack, Lukas stumbled back onto the ruined field.

The sun was too bright. Every sound was a keening roar, pitched too high in his ears. He squinted into the surreal scene and his eyes blurred with the dust and heat. He was a thousand miles away from each action as he combed through rubble, shifted timber and rock. He squinted and staggered across the steaming field to a broken pile of wood and smoldering canvas. He passed a severed arm, discarded on the ground.

Everything was too colorful, too saturated.

Dozens were still unaccounted for. The angle of the shots had been precise, aimed to hit this side of the encampment, cannonballs and bombs and stone debris arching over the cliff wall to land and destroy everything that should have been safe, well-hidden.

Lukas sunk to his knees by the pile of rubble and began sifting through it. His movements were machine-like. Blood rose in his palm where a loose nail caught his skin, but he barely noticed.

He had to find them.

His throat was tight. He had to find them. Everyone who was unaccounted for.

He blinked, and he was back in the desert, three years ago, outside of Khalim. Laying in the bottom of the gulley, choking on dust and sand and blood as the sun bore down with an unforgiving vengeance. Dead people and dead horses surrounded him. Agony. The surreal sight of white bone protruding from his forearm. *You aren't supposed to see your own bones*. His body twitching as he lay frozen in some stunned state, only a hair's-breadth from the sight of one of the

Veiran gunmen waiting to pick them all off one by one. Waiting. Waiting.

He'd have already been dead, shot through the chest, had Damijan not launched himself off his horse and knocked him out of the way, shoving them both to the ground and catching himself a bullet in the process.

He remembered Damijan's choked coughs as his lungs filled with blood. His hoarse, near-inaudible last words. They'd been fighting for freedom from the cruelty of the Veiran soldiers occupying their city, particularly the wardens who conscripted kids in their neighborhood to dive on impossibly dangerous wrecks. Damijan had ended up drowning anyway.

He remembered the cries of anguish from his friends, injured and dying where they lay in the wake of the ambush.

It had been his fault.

His fault. His fault. *His fault.*

His vision blurred again.

"Leave now, while you still can, Lukas. All of you could get out of the city with me tonight," Shani had said.

If only he'd listened to her.

"I said *do you need help with that*?" Ferrin asked from where the mirage of Shani had been hovering moments ago.

"Fine," he croaked.

Something in her expression changed, softened as she took in his face.

Her hands landed on his, and he realized he hadn't stopped digging through the ashes. His hands were filthy, bleeding, slightly singed. He let her quiet his movements as she knelt beside him.

"Hey, hey," she said, pulling his hands toward her. "What are you doing?"

He frowned as her touch pulled him back to the present.

"You looked about ready to murder that cart," she said softly. "Which is understandable, considering how it's torn up your hands. Are you alright?"

"How long were you standing there?"

She took a cloth from around her neck and wetted it with her water skin. "A minute or so. You seemed intensely lost in thought and I didn't want to disturb you."

"Oh," he blinked.

"What are you doing digging through the dirt out here?"

He hesitated. "I have to find… Rhi and Ash… They're both unaccounted for, and—"

"Luk, Rhi has been out of the city for days, and Ash is in the medic tent with Soviel. They're both fine," she said slowly, her brow furrowing in concern.

"They're both fine," he intoned, needing confirmation.

She nodded slowly. "But you don't look so well…"

"I'm fine," he said, swiping at his forehead. "There's still more people missing. We have to find them."

"You need to let me wrap your hands first," she said. He hadn't realized she was still holding him gingerly by the wrists. "Alright?"

He nodded, and let her lead him away from the ruins.

The sun was still blazing hot when Ferrin sat Lukas down in a quiet corner of the camp in a wide tent, probably meant for meetings of some sort. She hoped whoever it belonged to wouldn't mind.

He was looking at her a little funny, like he wasn't sure if he was awake or not. Like he was far, far away. With a sigh, she knelt before him and took his hands in hers, turning them over to survey the damage. She gasped. With his hands palm-up in her own, she could see it was far worse than what she had initially seen.

"Lukas, how long were your hands in there?" she asked quietly.

He stared back at her, numb and quiet for a moment too long to be excused as simple fatigue. "I don't know. Not long."

She grimaced as she looked down at his palms. They were torn up, bleeding, bits of jagged gravel and timber were lodged in some of the cuts, and furious red burns permeated the center of his palms and between the thumb and forefinger on both hands. The damage was extreme—the pain had to have been unimaginable.

And yet, when she'd found him, he hadn't even seemed to notice.

She leaned back on her heels, still cradling his hands, and looked up at his face. "This looks bad."

He looked down at his palms and something shifted in his countenance, as if he was finally back in the present. His expression sharpened, his eyes widened, he sat a little straighter.

"What the hell? I don't understand how—" he broke off, shaking his head.

"Does it hurt?"

"Yes," he said in a low, rough voice.

Though she was glad he finally seemed to notice the world around him, the sudden shift out of whatever trance he'd been in worried her. What had been going through his head that he could ignore such obvious pain?

"Alright," she nodded. "Stay here, I'll get supplies."

She darted out of the tent, unwilling to leave him for too long. Her heart was pounding. She ducked into a few tents, lifting various supplies. A flask of Deathwater. Linen strips. A pair of tweezers meant for cartography. When she returned, she found Lukas with a grimace on his face, rocking back and forth in his seat.

"Alright," she said, unloading her armful of supplies onto the bench beside him. "I'm back. First of all," she began, uncapping the flask, "take a drink."

He obliged. She had to hold it up for him to drink from, tipping his chin up with her fingers. He winced, whether at the taste or the pain, she couldn't say.

"This is going to hurt," she warned as she wet one of the rags with the liquor.

"I know," he said with a sharp inhale through his teeth. "Just do it."

With a grim nod, she wet the cloth and began to clean the cuts on his left hand. He winced in pain as the sting set in and Ferrin grimaced in sympathy. Next, she set the cloth down and took the cartographer's tweezers, rinsing them with the alcohol. Holding her own hands steady proved to be harder than expected. Piece by piece, she extracted the shrapnel, gravel and timber from his left hand. She wished she could hold his other hand, let him squeeze hers, take away some of his pain. But all that would do was hurt him more.

She set aside his left hand and moved on to the right. Every pull had him tensing and flinching.

"I'm sorry," she murmured after a particularly bad one. It oozed blood once she'd pulled out the jagged piece of green glass. She had to pat down the area with the liquor cloth again to keep it clean.

When she was done, she looked up at his face to gauge how he was faring. His jaw was clenched and his eyes were squeezed shut. When he opened them and met her eyes, he let out a long, shuddering breath, and swallowed thickly.

"That was the last piece," she said calmly. "I'm going to do my best to bandage the cuts. The burns probably shouldn't be covered too tightly, though." She was trying her best to remember what she'd learned in her few weeks of working in the infirmary back in Everness.

"Right," he nodded in understanding.

He held her gaze a moment longer, and something in her chest felt frail and vulnerable in a way that scared her. She reached past him to the bench where she'd laid out the supplies, and plucked up one of the rolls of linen, very aware of his eyes on her. She hoped whoever she'd taken these supplies from wouldn't need them urgently that night.

She didn't know what to say. *Are you alright* seemed a bit dim, given the circumstances. People who were 'alright' didn't mutilate their hands without noticing. But then again, none of them were 'alright'. Maybe never would be again.

The linen was soft, and she did as careful a job as she could to wind the strips around his palms, covering the cuts. He winced a few times when she doubled over the particularly deep ones.

"You need to have someone who knows what they're doing look at these," she said. "There could be real damage that I wouldn't know to look for."

"Yeah," he said distantly. "I will."

That far off sound of his voice set the hairs on the back of her neck prickling. Something was wrong. She didn't know what to do, didn't know how to bandage that kind of wound.

"Lukas," she said, sitting back on her heels. "I'm worried about you."

"It'll heal," he said.

She inhaled, ready to say more, but the look on his face told her not to push him. He looked inches away from cracking, and she didn't know why, didn't know what was haunting him.

"I just want you to be safe."

He looked at her and she could see his eyes were bloodshot, rimmed by dark circles.

"Lay down, get some rest. I'll wake you if someone needs to use this tent." She stood, and walked a few paces to the desk.

"Wait—" he said, his voice raw and startling.

She stopped and turned back to face him. He hadn't moved.

"Will you stay here for a while? With me?"

She smiled faintly and nodded, returning to the padded bench. This must have been a war tent meant for officers to meet in, given the finer amenities. She helped him onto his side, since his hands were virtually useless, and climbed onto the bench next to him. She wished she could sing for him, tell him a comforting story, anything. She wished she was better at this, but it was hard to heal someone else when she was hardly holding her own pieces together.

In the late evening after the attack, there was another meeting. This one was big. Ferrin had squeezed into the back of the war tent beside Soviel and Ash. Helene—Major Wilcoe —stood to the side of the large table presided over by Generals Alemont and Ashwife. There were a few other high-ranking officials Ferrin didn't recognize.

It was General Ashwife who spoke first. "Today's attack has made one thing abundantly clear. We cannot continue this passivity. Bourjony and its allies must be faced head-on."

Ash stiffened beside Ferrin. "What do you reckon this is going to mean?"

Ferrin shook her head, unsure of the answer herself.

"Over the next few weeks, we will begin the process of shipping troops south to the Efelian border. We will work with them to crack Bourjony's outer defenses in the Andal mountains. If we can harass them on their own front, we may be able to put a stop to this, or at the very least, shift their attentions from our own base," General Alemont said, flicking back her gray braid.

In her periphery, Ferrin caught a silent, split-second wordless conversation between Helene and Soviel. As if they'd already discussed this.

"All infantry will receive your unit's assignments first thing in the morning. Plainclothes units, see your superiors after this meeting. Special units and all fort and manor militia, you will remain here until further notice."

"Are we allied with Efel still?" Ferrin asked Soviel under her breath. "I thought that was with my—with the Lindbarrian crown."

Soviel lifted a shoulder. "Well, they're certainly not going to side with the Bourjons who have been openly attacking their borders for months now."

Ferrin nodded. "Good point."

At least her rejection of the Efelian prince in the spring hadn't burned that bridge entirely.

Helene quickly retreated from the room, and Ferrin followed Soviel as they made their way out the back to meet with the rest of the Southern Intelligence Unit at the unmarked safe house Helene kept in town. Ferrin released an anxious breath when she wasn't barred from entering. Ever since the prison break, the major had given her one-word answers whenever they interacted, with a business-only and cold demeanor. She hadn't yelled at her, hadn't screamed. That might have been better, for now only ice flowed from her words.

She'd never let herself admit it, but Ferrin looked up to Helene, and now it seemed that she'd done irreparable damage to their relationship. She'd looked up to Madame Leone, too, and now she was as good as gone. And what she'd just learned from her mother…

She'd be sick to her stomach if she dwelled too long on it.

"Before we go into the office… there's something I should tell you," Soviel grabbed her by the arm, hanging back.

"What is it?" Ferrin asked, glad to be pulled out of her own head.

"I've accepted an assignment," she said under her breath. "I'll be going south, but not so far as the rest of the army."

"Where?"

"…Bramblehall," Soviel said in a hushed voice.

"Bramble… is that not where that dreadful Duke running the horror-shop in the prison lives?" she hissed.

"Well, yes, Ferrin, that's the whole point."

"Does Ash know?"

Soviel shook her head. "I'll tell her later tonight, so keep it to yourself for now."

Ferrin looked alarmed but agreed to remain silent as they filed into the office.

"This is a strictly need-to-know meeting," Helene said, stopping her at the door. "You're an informant and you do not need to be here. Should we require your assistance again, we will send word."

Ferrin jerked to a halt.

"What?"

"This is a strictly—"

"I heard you. Again, am I not need-to-know?"

"No, Ferrin, you are not, at present."

"Major—" Soviel began, but was silenced quickly by Helene's raised palm.

"Understood." Ferrin backed away, the bitter sting of rejection sharp in her chest. "See you later, Sov."

Soviel gave an apologetic wince before she ducked into the office.

Ferrin turned on her heel. She supposed it was fitting. She'd only been of use to the army for her station in the castle, her title. Now those were both gone, and as it turned out, had been based on a lie anyway.

Her stomach twisted as her thoughts turned sour once more, returning to the volley of heavy information her mother had dropped on her.

CHAPTER TWELVE

*H*adringston?" Ash asked, incredulous. "He's a madman!"

"Well, I'd actually only be his *wife*'s lady in waiting," Soviel cringed.

"You realize he was the one heading the operation at the prison, where they were mutilating people by the dozen."

"Yes, Ash. That's why we need to keep a close eye on him."

Ash let out a deep sigh, closing her eyes tightly for a moment. "Alright, alright. How can I help?"

Soviel frowned. "Aren't you on assignment already?"

"Nothing official yet," she grumbled, crossing her arms. "I've just been accepted into the ranks is all."

"Well…" Soviel pondered. "I will need a courier between here and Bramblehall."

"Done."

"It's a touch more complicated than that," Soviel laughed. "You'll have to speak with Major."

"Cranky Helene?"

"You think *everyone* is cranky."

"True, but only because my sunny disposition is so superior."

Soviel rolled her eyes but allowed a smile nonetheless. "Well, speak with Helene, see if it'll work."

"When do you leave?" Ash asked, falling into step beside Soviel as they made their way from the manor down to the barracks to continue running their scheme for the evening.

"Two weeks."

Ash let out a low whistle.

"I won't be too far off." Soviel jostled her with her elbow.

"Everything is going to be changing soon." Ash grumbled. Since the attack, since the strange encounter with the Portal Guardian, things had been escalating. The barracks were in shambles and the encampment had moved closer to the marsh. The air in the manor had become charged and tense. Ferrin had been a walking ghost most of the week, and Lukas seemed to be unraveling at the edges over his missing friend.

"That's war, I suppose," Soviel said pensively, her gaze falling far away to the sea as they approached the stairway down to the barracks. The sun was near setting, and had deepened to a burnt gold, looming low on the horizon to their right.

"I wonder what more will come to pass before this entire thing is done with. If you'd told me a year ago I'd be sailing under any flag besides the black, I'd have laughed in your face. Now here I am, further north than I've been in my life, serving a country I only just arrived in."

"To be fair, the cause is far more than for this country. It's not as if I'm Caelish by blood, either," Soviel reminded her. "But Bourjony's reach grows long, and whatever it is they have planned, I doubt it will stop with the isle. Akhata could be next. Or Njorske. Or the free ports of the south."

Ash nodded with a sad smile of recognition. "I know, I'm only musing on it. Change makes time feel like it's moving too fast."

"It does," Soviel sighed. "It really does."

Nightmares chased Lukas from sleep that night, more vivid and rattling than they'd been in a long time. Flashes of hot sand and bullets all around burned into his mind like a brand.

His hands were still raw and throbbing beneath the bandages, the wounds still fresh. It had been only a few days since he'd injured them.

When midnight passed, he found himself shrugging into a coat and pacing down to the docks, content to let the sound of the waves calm him, let the chill air of the sea remind him he was not in that desert gorge anymore. Besides, he had business to attend to before dawn anyway. He didn't need to answer anyone's questions when he retrieved the package of rare elk hide he'd arranged to have brought in with an iron shipment from Kiarlgard. If all worked out, he'd turn a mighty profit on the tough furs. It was said that the hides of the strongest ice elk could turn a bullet.

Though the hour was late, the docks were not empty. A few fishermen were either preparing for an early morning, or just finishing up after a long night. Watchmen stood at their posts, looking bored as they spat wads of Arimopo into the harbor or played cards by torchlight. The lanterns that lined the pier flickered in the wind, hinting at yet another incoming gale.

"Night like this used to be called a 'witching night'," came an old rickety voice from an ancient man sitting on the rail of the pier, net spread on his lap and a ball of spare twine at his side.

"And why's that?" Lukas asked, turning to face the old man as he lit his pipe.

The old man hocked back and spat over the side of the pier. "Wind howling through the cliffs, dark sky, sea thrashing something fierce just beyond the bay…" He narrowed his pale brown eyes at Lukas. "You must not be from around here, if you've never heard of the Witch of Galan."

"Alas, I am not. What's the story?"

The old man grunted a *hmm*.

Lukas took a drag of his pipe and shoved his hands in his pockets before glancing around, unsure if the conversation was meant to be over.

"Why don't you sit down and help me mend these nets, and I'll tell you all about the weeping woman."

"Why not?" Lukas mumbled under his breath as he dragged up an empty barrel and sat it across from the old man.

"You got a name?"

"Lukas," he said. "And you?"

"Gerard Oakvul. Somewhat-retired captain of this fine vessel." He lifted a shoulder at the ancient fishing skiff moored behind him. Its paint was chipping, but still it bobbed happily on its mooring.

"What happened to the net?" Lukas asked, picking up the slack of the ruined twine in his bandaged hands. It looked like something had taken a bite out of it. Something with big teeth and a bigger mouth.

"Sharks, most likely," Oakvul replied, brown eyes narrowing. He ran a hand over his balding head, sun-weathered skin wrinkled and wrought. "Or somethin' else. A lot of somethin' else out there these days, if you ask me."

Lukas immediately thought of Norhi, the Portal Guardian with his enormous claws and teeth and cryptic words. "Like what?"

Oakvul shook his head, brow crinkling in apprehension. "As I said. The Witch of Galan. Lady Lachrymosa. The Weeping Woman," he ticked off.

Lukas noticed the man was missing a few of his front teeth.

"It's a tale perfect for a night like this one," he said, squinting as he stared off into the distance at the harbor mouth. "When the sea is remembering grudges long held. A storm's coming, you know," he sighed, looking back to his knotting. "As I was saying. Many years ago, some say fifty, some say five-hundred, there was a young woman who lived by the sea. Her family was respected here in Galan, well-off. She spent time at an old tavern by the docks, even though she was betrothed to a wealthy landowner further inland."

"And she was the witch, I presume?" Lukas tilted his head skeptically as he looped one knot through the tear in the net.

"Yes. Only, she did not know it. Not until much later. She was connected to the sea and sky, a witch of the winds. *Stormrider*."

"A Stormrider," Lukas repeated with clear skepticism. "So this had to have been hundreds of years ago, no?"

"Hush, I'm not done," the fisherman cast him a glower. "She met a sailor there, one day in the tavern. Very quickly, the two fell in love, even though she was betrothed to another. When her family learned of their plans to elope, her father cursed the sailor's name and swore his daughter would only marry a rich man. And so, the sailor went off to find his fortune in the south."

"Ah, he was a merchant, then?"

"He was a pirate," the old fisherman said with a wink. "First, though, he sailed south aboard a merchant vessel and made his way up in the ranks until he was quartermaster. One day, the ship was captured by a notorious pirate captain. The silver-tongued sailor convinced the pirates to make him captain of the very merchant vessel he was serving on, promising to give them twenty percent of the plunder he'd earn."

"Silver-tongued indeed." Lukas whistled. "That's quite the stroke of luck."

"So, the sailor traversed the Meddemara. He won and stole riches until he was wealthy beyond his wildest dreams. He turned and headed north, where his love waited for him."

"The witch?"

"Yes, lad." Oakvul shot Lukas an impatient look. "You see, after her sailor left her, she found she was with child. Her engagement to the landowner was broken off, and she was free to marry her sailor when he returned, though without her inheritance, most likely," he sniffed. "She had two rings crafted, set with jewels the color of the sea, and waited. The village cast her out. Shamed her. One day, to protect herself and her child, she tapped into those unknown powers of wind and sea.

"On a cold, spring night, she stood on the cliffs, betrayed, abandoned, alone. She realized the baby was coming, and she threw her power wide and far, her pain materializing into a hurricane of epic proportion to knock all those wishing her harm out to sea. Alas, what she did not realize was that her lover was just off the coast, on his way to sweep her away and shower her with riches."

Lukas frowned. "Hang on." He shook his head. "How could he possibly have done all he did in the span of nine months? It would have taken him weeks to get south, and weeks to come back, leaving little time in between for him to *become* so rich. Especially if this was before the dredging of Marana."

Oakvul scowled, his sallow skin tightening. "He was a man of wit—he knew precisely where to sail to end up where he needed to go."

Lukas paused in his net-knotting. "Is it not more likely the baby was simply not his?"

"The baby was his." Oakvul squinted menacingly.

"Right, yes, the baby was his," Lukas conceded, far too exhausted to argue with a stranger about a dubious folktale. "So, did he make it to shore?"

"Her storm wrecked his ship—tossing him, his crew, and their riches into the sea and scattering it up and down the coastline from here to Avaree. Some say he drowned," he sighed, "and some say he was captured and hung for theft when he washed up on shore. But, there are also those who say he simply dissolved into the sea, the creatures and weeds of the deep claiming him, changing him, binding him with some great force. They say they made him one of their own." He set down his netting with a huff. "And there are some who will tell you she sent a beast after him. Cursed him, intentionally, for leaving her."

"Well, then," Lukas cleared his throat, working the salt-crusted knot in his hands. "What happened to the lady?"

Oakvul shrugged. "People have long claimed to see her wandering the cliffs at night, *especially* when a storm is brewing. She cries out to the sea for her lost love. Wailing and howling into the wind with terrible screeches."

Lukas nodded slowly.

"Some say she controls the sea using a cursed gem that she plucked from her very own wedding ring, they call it the *cetamaris*. Some say she rides the wind even now. Screaming over the harbor in the night like a banshee." Oakvul shuddered, looking up at the sky. "There's been talk down the beach of people seeing her again. The dark shape of a woman screeching through the skies, waiting to curse men who've wronged their wives."

Lukas chuckled. "That sounds a bit like the sort of tale a man having bad luck with a tavern wench might come up with after a few too many drinks."

"Mark my words, boy, you don't want to see the Weeping Woman. It's bad luck, an ill omen."

Lukas decided it best not to mention that the figure hurtling through the skies at night was likely just Ferrin out for a midnight jaunt. "And the sailor? What ill omen has history turned him into?"

The man shrugged. "Could be bones at the bottom of the sea, could be in an unmarked grave out by the old jail. He could be haunting the deep in the form of some dreadful beast."

Lukas nodded thoughtfully and eased the net off his lap. The story, no matter how strange, had been a welcome distraction. "Well, Sir Oakvul, I thank you for your story, but I believe the person I'm looking for is arriving."

"Be watchful, boy. Strange times we're in," Oakvul warned. "Strange times indeed."

CHAPTER THIRTEEN

R hi awoke to the last embers of the campfire dying to a faint glow in the night. Something wasn't right. He blinked, raising himself onto his elbows, stiff from the hard forest floor beneath his bedroll.

The bedroll across the fire from him was empty, blanket thrown askance.

Lachlan was gone.

Rhi sat upright, now fully awake as he whipped his head around, searching for his traveling companion. The sounds of the forest had quieted into a deafening hush. He pulled on his boots and rose to a crouch, hand wrapped around the hilt of his knife as he crept out of the dim circle of light from the embers.

Perhaps he's gone off to take a leak, Rhi thought to himself, albeit unconvincingly.

Creeping toward the road, he kept close to the thick underbrush as he listened, waited. The sound of spur-clad footsteps had him ducking behind a bush. Hushed voices followed, and Rhi's breath caught as a group of soldiers came around the bend. His pulse quickened, and he gripped the sword in his hand hard enough to whiten his knuckles. Just as he was about to retreat back further from the campsite, a hand clamped over his mouth, and another around his wrist.

He inhaled sharply in surprise as his heart launched into his throat, and jammed an elbow back into his attacker, who loosened his grip immediately, allowing Rhi to turn.

Lachlan was inches behind him, eyes wide and frantic, shaking his head. He removed the hand from Rhi's face and held one finger to his lips: *shh*.

Rhi nodded back, silent. Lachlan released his wrist and jerked his head at the soldiers who were approaching the campsite, perhaps twenty feet away.

"*Bourjons*?" Rhi mouthed.

Lachlan nodded slowly.

"Captain!" one of the men called from beside the fire. "Two empty bedrolls, and the embers are still hot."

The captain approached the campsite, squatted beside Rhi's bag.

Shit.

"Confiscate everything, they won't make it long without supplies," he ordered his men with a laugh. "Fan out, they can't have gone far."

No, no, no.

Rhi glanced back and forth. There were more of them coming up the road from the east. They were going to have to backtrack to avoid being seen.

This way, Rhi mouthed to Lachlan, gesturing in the dim light to follow him. Keeping low, they slunk deeper into the forest, not daring to separate more than a foot, lest they lose each other in the dark. Things deadlier than Bourjon scouting parties lurked in this old forest.

The glow from the campsite dimmed as they crept into the woods. Brush creaked and branches snapped behind them as their pursuers closed in.

"Shit," Lachlan cursed. "Go, go, go!" he hissed as a torch flared to life behind them, its light only inches from giving them away.

Taking hold of Lachlan's wrist in a vise grip, Rhi broke into a blind stumble through the dark wood.

"Any plan?" Lachlan hissed.

"I know a place!" Rhi hissed. "Just a mile or two. Across the river."

"The river will be swollen! The mountain thaw came late this year!"

A shout went up just yards away—they'd been spotted.

"We ford it, or we die here," Rhi said, and they hastened.

Something thwanged behind them, and they had only a second to launch into a nearby bush as an arrow—no, a *flaming* arrow—whizzed past and thunked into a tree trunk.

Ignoring the cut of the thorns and brambles, they surged through the thicket as the trees behind them went up in flames.

"Oh, *shit*," Lachlan cursed again. "They're mad! They'll burn the entire damn forest down!"

Another arrow streaked past, catching the underbrush alight before lodging itself in the bark of another nearby tree. There was no time to stop and stare as the forest lit up like a bonfire.

"I really hope you have a plan, Rhi!" Lachlan yelled as another arrow set fire to a tree ahead of them.

"Just don't get hit," he called back as they ran through the forest, soldiers on their trail shouting through the blaze.

He hoped he was right. He hoped the little game cabin still stood down the river. He hoped the canoe he and his men had kept disguised under moss and bush was still propped and hidden in the rock pile. It had been months since he'd been out in these particular woods. Almost a year, in fact. If they couldn't find the canoe, they'd be torn between the mercy of the soldiers' flames and the mercy of the rushing river.

Just a few more steps, he thought to himself as his heart hammered in his chest. He could hear the roaring of the river ahead. *Gods, it's loud.*

Lachlan had been right—the late thaw of the mountains had swollen the usually calm river Rhainor to a torrent of rushing water. There was no chance they could swim across if the canoe was gone.

"Come on! This way!" Rhi grabbed Lachlan's wrist again and jerked him towards the rock formation. He dropped to his knees and began furiously shifting the moss covering from the hiding hole until finally his hands hit the smooth wood of the light-weight hull.

Rhi let out an unhinged laugh, "Oh, thank gods!"

"Don't thank them yet, we've still got a dozen of those bastards on our tail! Let's go!"

Without a second to spare, they managed to get the canoe out of the hole and into the river, Lachlan snatching the lone paddle off the forest floor. They waded into the turbulent water and jumped in, launching the boat just as the soldiers came around the bend.

As they cleared the bank, Rhi could see the entire section of forest going up in flames, illuminating the hunting party that had pursued them to the river.

"Oh no…" Lachlan's voice was uncharacteristically forlorn.

Rhi snapped his head around to see what the matter was. In Lachlan's hand was a short pole—no. It was the paddle. Broken with rot.

"Shit!"

"What are we going to do?"

They were careening downstream, and fast, but the problem of steering was quickly set aside as a huge wave rose up before them.

"Lean back!" he shouted over the roar of the river.

Rhi's heart leapt into his throat. The eddy of the wave's trough grabbed the bow of their boat, trapping them at its base. The wave grew taller, the water churning and spraying as he tried to jounce the boat free.

That's when he saw it—within the wave, the shape of a face had emerged. It was hard to make out with only the dim moon and fire light to reflect on the water, but a face it was indeed.

Who dares enter my home? the voice boomed with the force of rapids over rocks.

Rhi and Lachlan shared a petrified, confused glance. His heart was pounding in his chest; what was he *seeing?*

Who dares set fire to my woods? the commanding voice asked again.

"It wasn't us! It was the soldiers chasing us!" Rhi chanced answering as the wave molded into another shape. A vaguely *human* shape. Tall as the trees and wide as a boulder, Rhi stared aghast, wondering if he had somehow ingested bad *popava* again. Never had he seen something like this, this strange woman of water.

I grow weary of these trespasses, this disrespect!

"We respect you! We would never set the forest on fire!" Lachlan yelled, scooting as far back in the boat as he could to put distance between himself and the river-woman.

Rhi recalled how he'd begged and begged to know about magic as a child. He'd asked his parents both about magic incessantly. Where it came from, why it was gone, where was it now. His father had told him it was an important part of history, but no longer relevant. Like broadswords or leeching. A relic from a more savage time. It had faded for a reason. Man was civilized, and need not lean on such arcane arts.

His mother had told him cryptic stories and hoisted him into her lap when he was still small.

None of it prepared him for what happened next.

To Rhi's horror, the river-woman bent down and extended her watery hands—nearly the size of the boat—and plucked the canoe out of the current.

"Please," Rhi reasoned, though his voice shook.

I may have slept for an age, young prince. But I am no fool. I know when men seek to conquer my forest.

"We are only fleeing from those who would do us harm, those who harm this forest! We swear it," Rhi said, his voice catching in his throat as he watched the river-woman. A misplaced sturgeon swam through her torso, illuminated by the silver moonlight above and the molten gold light of the fire devouring the banks. "We are only travelers, it is the soldiers on the banks who seek to destroy."

She tilted her head, considering. *Very well. Do not trespass here again, Prince.*

And with that, she dropped the canoe back in the water, her form returning to the river quick as a loose fish off the dock. The water went wild, surging over the shore, further than before, as if the river-woman had pulled the tides to her, swelling the river to wash out the flames.

The canoe tilted in the turbulence and went over before either of them could do anything about it.

"Lach!" Rhi shouted. He saw Lachlan's head go under the chop of the furious river just before the fire's light on the bank went out, quenched by the vengeful river-woman.

Rhi fought to keep his head above water as the currents ripped at him. He couldn't see, could barely think over the roar of the river that grew louder and louder as the current carried him downstream. The water was impossibly strong and insistent as it tried to force its way down his throat, into his ears, up his nose.

He needed to get to the shore—to the far side of the river. There, he could make a plan.

The roaring ahead became louder, and in the back of his mind it registered that they were still in the mountains, that there would be rapids.

Swim, Rhi!

The roaring grew louder still and he sucked down as deep a breath as he could manage before putting his head down and swimming a few strokes to the side. When he popped up again, he could see something ahead. *The canoe!*

He put his head down again and began to swim for the boat. When he raised his head to breathe again, he was met with a wave of cold water to the face as he tumbled down a rocky step in the river. He choked and coughed, losing his grip on the current just long enough to be sent sprawling. His head went under and he lost all sense of up and down, turning over and over in the tumbling of the river. He brushed past something tough, a log or a rock or some other huge creature of the river. It was all he could do to put his arms up and protect his head.

The rapids roared closer, and when he finally righted himself, the boat was no longer in sight. The light of the moon illuminated the river ahead, until it dropped away into nothing, only a veil of mist shimmering off the surface. Lachlan was nowhere in sight. Perhaps he'd gotten out. Perhaps he'd drowned.

Rhi coughed and sputtered again as he tried to kick to the side, fighting the current as little as possible as he swam perpendicular to the bank. Any bank would do, at this point.

"*Hey!*" Lachlan's voice was raw and faint beneath the roaring of the rapids, but it was him nonetheless.

Wasting precious seconds, Rhi whipped around to see Lachlan bobbing down the river behind him. He snapped one arm out and caught him by the forearm.

"Rapids!" Rhi shouted, the effort of getting words out almost too much. He fought for purchase on the bed of the river, but it was too deep.

They weren't going to make it to the bank—there was no way.

"Cover your head and take a deep breath when I say!" Rhi shouted, squeezing Lachlan's wrist. "Keep your feet ahead of you!"

The edge loomed closer, closer. The current was violent as it herded them to the drop.

"Now!" He released Lachlan's arm and took a deep breath as he folded his arms over his skull, protecting his head.

The water around him pressed in so hard he thought it might crush him. He slammed his elbow into a rock and flinched, nearly uncovering his head. The pressure was all around him as he fought to keep his feet ahead of him, and suddenly, with the roaring near deafening in his ears, he dropped. It struck Rhi as quite funny, how violent the water could be when all it was doing was falling.

He pressed his lips together, determined to keep his breath in as he plummeted down the falls. Hitting the water below was like hitting a brick wall, and he was shoved under once more. Still with his lips shut tight, he swam furiously away from the impossible heaviness of the falling water, fighting for the surface.

At last, his head broke the surface of a much calmer stretch of river. He panted and gasped, taking breath after hoarse breath as he paddled to the side, away from the falls. Where was Lachlan? He swiveled his head, searching for him. At last, he saw a soaked head break the surface, a little closer to the falls, and begin to take labored strokes toward him.

When at last they managed to drag themselves out of the river, Lachlan turned over and coughed up a mouthful of river water. Neither had the energy for words as they caught their breath.

How far downriver had they been swept? Had any of the enemy hunting party survived the river-woman's wrath? And most importantly, how were they going to make it through a cold night in the mountains, soaking wet, with no supplies? These were the questions that began to flood Rhi's mind as the urgent rush of survival left him and the impossible soreness seeped into every inch of his being. His arm ached, his lungs burned and his heart pounded. The cold was starting to settle in.

"Come on," Lachlan panted. "If we don't start moving we'll be dead within the hour." He stood and offered Rhi a hand.

They trudged through the woods for an hour, barely moving fast enough to stave off the cold. Though it was summer, the nights in the mountains still dropped to perilous temperatures. Dawn wouldn't come for hours, and they were far from the game cabin that Rhi had been banking on for salvation. They had no dry clothes, nothing to start a fire with, no provisions. On top of all that, the book they'd made the whole journey to retrieve had been lost when they fled the camp site.

"We need to find shelter somewhere," Lachlan said. Though the light was dim, Rhi could see his lips were tinged blue.

"I know," he replied. "We will."

After another mile or so, light appeared in the distance. Small, and faint. *A quaint little mountain town?* Rhi hoped.

"Come on, there's—" Rhi tried to speak through chattering teeth.

"M-maybe they h-have a tavern—" Lachlan stuttered.

They continued through the hills for what seemed like years before at last approaching the little outpost.

Rhi stumbled and caught himself on a tree, halting with shaking hands.

"Don't stop. Can't s-stop," Lachlan nudged him with a shoulder as he continued past.

Rhi took a deep, shaky breath and followed after. The outpost was small—only a few buildings, the largest being the barn.

"Come on," Lachlan said, grabbing Rhi by the elbow.

"W-wait. S-still in enemy territory—"

"Keep your mouth sh-shut, then," Lachlan said. It looked like he was trying for a smirk, but lacked the control of his facial muscles to pull it off.

Lachlan poked his head around the door before ducking into the barn and picking up a torch. The interior of the barn was warmer than the outside, but their clothes were still soaked through and cold.

"Horse blankets," Rhi jerked his chin at the tack room.

Lachlan nodded and carried on into the room. A lone stable hand snoozed in a chair outside.

"Here," Rhi whispered, looping two horse blankets over his arm. They were dusty and dirty, but warm nonetheless. They felt heavy as rocks in his exhausted arms.

Stolen torch in hand, they trekked back out of the settlement on stiff legs. When they could go no further, they set to building a fire. Rhi stripped off his soaked coat and shirt, hoping they'd gone far enough from the town to not draw attention. He laid the clothing over a fat log near the fire, and drew one of the horse blankets around himself. Lachlan did the same, the firelight highlighting the ridges and valleys of his freckle-dappled chest and stomach.

"Share heat," Rhi suggested, standing to sit beside Lachlan. "Too tired to get warm f-fast enough."

Lachlan nodded, his lower lip still quivering with chill. His red hair was plastered to his forehead.

They combined the blankets and sat shoulder to shoulder as close to the fire as they could without catching it on their blankets.

"Don't fall asleep," Lachlan said. "Have to stay awake."

Some of the color seemed to be eking back into his face as the fire warmed them.

"What are we going to do?" Rhi huffed, turning to face Lachlan. He started when he realized how close their faces were. Lachlan's eyes were heavy and lidded with exhaustion.

Rhi swallowed. The cold must have been slowing his brain.

"About what?" Lachlan breathed, his throat bobbing.

"All of it. We lost everything. Our supplies. The book."

"Oh," Lachlan said with a small mischievous smile. "The book may be gone, but…"

Rhi waited with anticipation. This close, he could make out every fleck of gold and green and amber in Lachlan's irises.

"The important pages… I used to be a scout, and it's standard procedure to put important documents in a messenger capsule, sealed with tree sap. If I did it right, it's watertight." He jerked his chin at his coat, drying by the fire.

Rhi barked a laugh. "You sweet bastard!"

"That's what I was doing when I heard the party coming. Talk about perfect timing," he said with a breathless laugh.

"So it wasn't all for naught!" Rhi looked at Lachlan and grinned. "Well, that's a relief."

"Yeah, well now we just need to make it back to Galan in one piece," Lachlan reminded him, rubbing his hands together to warm them. Beside him, Rhi was keenly aware of the side of his leg pressing into Lachlan's.

"Any idea how far we are?"

Lachlan squinted into the middle-distance, puzzling. "The river took us a long way. That outpost was right on the outskirts of occupied territory."

"So we still have a long way to get out of the borderlands," Rhi said, removing one of his water-logged boots and propping a heel up on one of the stones near the fire.

"Yeah. With no supplies, no weapons and no food."

Rhi looked around. "We could hike up there," he pointed to a tiny dot of light in the distance. "Get food, maybe some gear.

Circle back into the mountains and find Hassan's old dig site. Maybe there's someone there willing to t—"

"No. Absolutely not," Lachlan shook his head. "We're not going back there."

"Lach," Rhi said. "He knows a *lot*. What if his research is related to the prison experiments? If the occupation is funding it, it must be important."

Lachlan stood, his blanket sweeping like a cape about him. "Next you'll be suggesting we go back to the university to *talk* to him."

"It's not a bad idea," Rhi considered. "Better prepared, of course. And with a more solid plan."

"*Dear suffering gods!*" Lachlan grunted, pinching the bridge of his nose.

Rhi bristled.

"You cannot be serious. He tried to have us captured. Do you know what they do to captured soldiers? Particularly ones out of uniform?" He broke off with a derisive, humorless laugh. "You can't go through life expecting people to cooperate with you because you throw a few pretty words at them."

"That's hardly what I'm suggesting," said Rhi, feeling heat rise in his face, despite the chill. "You can't deny that it's mighty suspicious that his research is being so well funded by the occupation. We need to get ahead of this before it turns out to be our downfall!"

"Oh, and how do you suggest we do that? March back to the university where—mind you—we just *fled* from, after the man *you* want to negotiate with sold us out? Or should we just write him a letter?" Lachlan's voice rose. "No. Rhi, you can't always talk people into doing what you want them to do. Perhaps this concept is new to you, but the world outside of your palace does not work that way."

Rhi balked, his heart ratcheting up to speed as his stomach clenched. A fermented mix of guilt and fury roiled in his gut. "I know that. I wasn't saying—" he broke off, cursing. "I'm not suggesting anything like that. I think he *wants* to do what's right, but he's scared."

Lachlan scoffed bitterly. "If he wanted to do the right thing, he would have done it."

"That's not true, he's obviously terrified for his family, Lachlan. Sweet gods, why can't you understand that?"

Lachlan grit his teeth, his expression unyielding. "He's a fool if he thinks they'll spare his family in exchange for being the army's dog."

"You have *no* idea," Rhi said, standing. His voice sounded gravelly and rough even to his own ears. "What it's like to have to do something you don't want, something *awful* just to survive."

"Oh, and you do? Tell me, besides running from the capital a few weeks ago, when has your life been difficult? Don't lecture me about survival."

Rhi held back the explosion building in his chest. "I know I can't just blow up at every person I disagree with like some childish beast," he said icily. "My father, who had me drugged, beaten on more than one occasion, who likely had my mother killed, was not someone who took kindly to acting out. I learned early on to play along, or face the consequences."

Lachlan stiffened almost imperceptibly. He looked like he was about to say something, but Rhi turned away. "I'm exhausted. Wake me in an hour for watch," he said, still seething.

CHAPTER FOURTEEN

I t was early in the morning when Ash set off to the docks to see if there was work for her that day. Through cloud cover, the sun peeked silver and muted over the dark and rolling sea. A storm was surely coming. The glimpse of the sun's rising light that she'd peeped through a gap in the overcast sky had been blood red and scalding to the eye. An ill portent for sure.

She slung her knapsack higher on her shoulder and huffed a sigh into the cool air. Despite the inclement weather, the pier was abustle with fisherman and folk trading for first pick of the early catch. She spotted Neb, one of harbor-patrol's lead officials and came up alongside her.

"Got anything for me today?" She rubbed her hands together anxiously.

"Yeah, I might," Neb nodded, assessing Ash. "How do you feel about gutting fish?"

Ash grimaced. "Anything that might actually land me on a *ship*?"

"Only joking," Neb said, her kohl-lined eyes twinkling as the skin around them crinkled with her smile. She pointed to a small ship at the end of the pier. "You're to be on *The Brisk* today."

"Oh? Who's skippering?"

"You are."

Ash balked. "Me?"

Neb nodded sagely, and Ash had an epiphany. *Ah, this craft is experimental. They must want someone competent, but expendable.*

"It's… very lightweight for this weather, is it not?"

"Aye, you're not wrong there. It's a new design, one of the army's engineers has made it: a high-speed skiff. You'll be the first one to take it out."

"Oh," Ash said, her voice shooting up an octave. She was unsure whether to be unnerved or honored by the prospect.

"You'll take a small crew. No more than five, including yourself," Neb continued as they strode down to the end of the pier. "She's armed with two guns. One just ahead of the mast, another just behind the centerboard. Both are lightweight and rotatable. They shoot four-pound balls."

"That's *quite* lightweight," Ash said again with surprise. "Four-pounders won't do much against a twenty-gun bark. Or anything much, really."

"No, but it is not meant to be a battleship. It is meant to outrun."

"And what exactly am I to do on this maiden voyage?"

"You're to run a bundle of correspondence to Avaree." Neb crossed her arms, the brim of her tattered black hat lifting in the breeze. "If it goes well, the ship, and you, will be put to use carrying correspondence more widely."

"Right then. Can I pick my crew?"

"You may pick two, so long as they are cleared. One of the engineers will be aboard with you."

"Great," she chirped. "Well. When am I casting off?"

"Give it an hour." Neb gazed into the distance. "Traffic coming in the bay is congested this morning. A lot of fishermen looking to hit their quota for the week. Report back before eight bells."

Ash spent most of the hour she had to kill munching on a fried fish-on-a-stick that she'd purchased at the edge of the pier, looking out onto the waves. Once she'd gone up to grab

Ferrin from the manor and sent for the other sailor she had in mind, it was nearly time to go.

She hoped the fish-on-a-stick didn't turn out to be a mistake.

"That's something," Ferrin said, eyeing the small ship.

"It's some new innovation the army has been working on," Ash explained. "Built for speed and maneuverability."

"Are those… harnesses?" She squinted at the pile of ropes and straps beside the ship.

"She's quite prone to heeling," Toscan, the engineer Ash had been introduced to earlier, strode up, speaking in a level voice. He was a slight man, with wire-rimmed glasses that sat low on his nose. He wore a loose-fitting linen shirt with the sleeves rolled up, exposing his tawny, wiry forearms. "So the crew on the windward side can strap in and hike further out to prevent her tipping."

"Now that sounds like a thrill," Ash said, eyeing the harnesses intently.

"Unfortunately, the skipper does *not* do that."

Ash pouted. Toscan shrugged.

"We're just waiting on one other person," Ash said, scanning the docks.

"I'll man the bow gun, and monitor how she runs," Toscan said curtly as he tucked a notebook under his arm. Ash wasn't sure how he planned to keep it dry. Neb's courier had transferred the correspondence documents to a brass, watertight tube before handing them over to her.

"Oi! That's quite a vessel." Rorin had arrived.

Rorin was the sailor she'd followed into the crow's nest the day of the harbor attack.

"Indeed it is," Ash said by way of greeting. "Let's get moving, we've got a delivery to make. I want to be back by dark."

"Oh, that won't be a problem," Toscan said.

Once they were on their way out of the harbor, Ash relaxed a little. The ship was so damn quick, she felt like she was doing something wrong by sluicing through the harbor at such a speed.

It was a strange feeling to be so low on the water, but moving so smoothly through the waves. The ship's sleek length kept it steady even as it cut through the chop. Ferrin and Rorin had both donned harnesses, and it would only take one swift move to hook onto the trapeze, as Toscan had called it when he gave them the brief overview. The ship had a mainmast, carried close to the center, two small foresails meant for catching close to the wind, and a long tiller for steering. It was perhaps twenty-five feet in length.

"Assuming we're able to run all the way back," Toscan began, referring to the downwind stretch that should bring them back from Avaree, barring any changes to the wind, "I'd like to wing out the second jib to the windward side to increase our speed."

Ash paused, unused to being asked for her opinion, much less her *approval*, to do things. "Yes, that sounds like a good idea. Though… is there any risk of us pitch-pulling?"

Toscan grimaced. "If the wind were blowing ten knots faster, maybe. But we kept this in mind and put the mainmast further back. And if we need to, we can shift more of our bodyweight back toward the stern."

"Perfect," she said, flipping open her compass.

They left the harbor with no problems, and came about to head east to Avaree.

The *Brisk* moved like a dream over the waves. Even as it heeled with the wind, the ship cut like a hot knife through butter. Ferrin had never been aboard such a vessel, had never sped so close to the surface of the water, propelled only by sails.

Toscan perched beside the lightweight bow gun, scribbling away notes and calculations in his little journal as he assessed various components of the ship and how they were faring. In only an hour and a half, they'd made it to Avaree—a journey that might have taken a regular ship this length most of the day.

As instructed, they raised the signal flag once in view of the harbor's patrol tower to avoid being blown to bits upon arrival. The smaller of the two harbor patrol ships signaled them to pull up and drop sail.

A uniformed man thumped down onto the deck of the *Brisk*, jostling the entire vessel. One drawback to the ship's sleek profile—stability had been sacrificed in favor of speed. "So, little brother's big project has finally come to fruition?"

"Obviously," Toscan said, tensing as the burly patrolman clapped him on his slender shoulder.

The man who'd boarded the ship resembled Toscan in his beige skin and brown hair, but had half a foot in height on his brother, and was built like a brick wall.

"My brother, Colren," Toscan grumbled by way of introduction, much in the manner of an embarrassed child, as his brother looked around the ship.

"So, what's the real purpose of this test run?" Colren asked as two other patrolmen tossed tow lines over the sides. Rorin and Ferrin grabbed them and tied them off on the bow's cleats.

"We have a classified delivery," Ash said.

"Ah, and I take it you're the chosen sailor to head up this endeavor?"

"Asha Mazrihn." She extended her hand.

"*Captain* Asha Mazrihn," Ferrin amended from behind.

"Yes. Right." Ash straightened. "And we have explicit delivery instructions for the manor."

Colren slapped the patrol ship's hull. "Right then, lads! Let's drop them up at the Big House." He turned back to Ash and saluted her. "Captain."

Ash and Ferrin exchanged a look as Colren clambered back onto the patrol ship, and they were towed further into Avaree's inner harbor.

The manor of Avaree came into view: a symmetrical, mint-green and white building with columns and a wide grassy lawn between its entrance and the private dock. A few civilian vessels were tied off at the dock, with plenty of space left for a landing at its T-shaped end.

"We'll drop you here. Same signal on the way out if another patrol ship should flag you down," Colren called down to them.

Ash gave him a parting wave before turning her attention to making a smooth landing. It was a good thing they were only running on momentum from the tow, because at full-sail, the landing would have been treacherous. Yet another compromise in the ship's stability.

Even as they glided up to the dock, Ash nearly missed it and slipped past.

"Toscan, perhaps put in your wee log there that we could use some kind of chute-anchor for landings."

"It's already in the works," he said, pushing his glasses up his nose.

"Wonderful."

Once they'd tied off, they made their way up the dock to the manor. To Ferrin's surprise, they were greeted by an immaculately dressed butler.

"Isn't this the second rebel base?" she whispered to Rorin as Ash introduced their party.

Rorin only shrugged.

"Follow me, I'll alert the master of the house that you've arrived."

Once inside, the butler left them in a foyer that was nothing short of splendid. Natural light cascaded through a wall of windows. A chandelier of crystal and gilt caught the light in its prisms and scattered it into bright colors across the floor. A little rainbow caught in Ash's hair, spilling across her cheek as she spun around, no doubt taking in the lay of the land.

"Ah! Messengers from Galan, at last!" called a jovial voice. The man who appeared atop the leftmost of the twin sweeping staircases was clad in a burgundy and black velvet dressing robe. His face was round and ruddy, topped by thinning dark hair.

"Yes," Ash confirmed, clasping her hands behind her back as she studied the man striding down the stairs.

"General Kenrose, Commander of base Avaree," he introduced himself, extending a hand to Ash, who took it and gave it a good shake. "And whom do I have the pleasure of hosting today?"

"Captain Asha Mazrihn, currently of *The Brisk*."

"Have you the missives?"

"Yes, sir."

"Wonderful, wonderful, come to my study. The rest of you, make yourselves at home. Minnedall will bring you whatever you need." He picked up a little bell from beside a nearby fainting couch and gave it a brief ring. Seconds later, the butler appeared in the doorway as Ash followed the general up the stairs, casting a perplexed look back at her crew.

"Anything I can bring you?" Minnedall asked primly.

"Water," Ferrin and Toscan said at the same time Rorin said, "Whiskey."

"Right away, sirs."

"So, this is different from Galan," Rorin said, picking up a gilded candlestick.

"Certainly less crowded." Ferrin observed.

"I'd thought their situation was similar to ours."

"The General is not popular among the common soldiers," Toscan said quietly. "Believe me, I've heard no short list of complaints from my brother on the subject."

"Interesting." Ferrin absently picked up a vase that she had chipped over a decade ago, back when her family would visit this very manor every summer. The knick in the porcelain was still sharp beneath her thumb.

"Come in, come in! Please, sit down," General Kenrose said, ushering Ash into his study. The room was larger than the two bedrooms the five of them had been sharing back in Galan, combined. "Care for a smoke?" He clicked open a box of cigars and offered it to her.

"No, thank you," Ash said.

"Are you certain? Finest Corsovena has to offer. And it'd better be, considering what it costs to have it shipped up here," he chuckled. "Though it's utter shit compared to Calixtan."

She shook her head and hauled the satchel off her shoulder, removing the water-tight container. "Here's the letters, General."

"Excellent, excellent." He snatched the capsule from her and twisted it open.

"Do you have anything to send back?"

"Perhaps, dear, perhaps," he said absently, thumbing through the letters.

Briefly, it struck her that *dear* wasn't her proper address.

"Oh, yes, perfect! This is the one I've been waiting for." He broke the wax seal and tore open the envelope, eyes hungrily scanning the page. He slapped it down with an enthusiastic "*Ha!*"

Ash watched, perplexed as he swiftly penned a response.

"This is excellent news," he said as he stood, letter still in hand. He seemed in awfully high spirits.

She leaned over and snuck a peak at the initial letter while the general walked to a cupboard at the side of the room. She parsed a few of the sentences, though they were wordy and long, and the handwriting far too swoopy and curling. His excitement had her expecting good news about the movements of Bourjony, or progress in one of the southern blockades. She had to school her features into neutrality as she laid eyes on the approval letter to ship *Arimopo* into the mainland via Njorske. Not a scouting report, not a briefing, nothing to do with the war.

"Sir, do you have any other correspondence to send back to Port Galan?" she asked.

"Hm?" He looked up from the seal he was pressing into the hot wax. In front of him sat a box of multiple identical seal rings, each with his personal crest. He wore one on his neck on a cord, and yet another on his littlest finger. "Oh. I suppose. Why don't you read some of them out loud to me? You can *read*, girl, can't you?"

She cringed. "Some, sir, though my schooling was rather short, and mostly in the Akhatan language."

"Well, give it a try," he said, lifting his cigar to his lips as he dropped into the ornate desk chair across from her.

"Alright, sir," Ash said, frowning as she picked a letter out of the capsule. She scanned over the addressing on the front. "This one is from the former Lindbarrian naval outpost on… Ambrosius by way of Efel."

She popped the seal open and unfolded the letter, skimming over it as she cleared her throat.

"*Request for additional provisions to be sent—*"

"Send that one down to Major Schilling. That's an issue for the commissary to worry about. Damn Lundi bastards, eating this army out of business," he muttered.

"Yes, sir," she refolded the letter and set it aside, picking up another. "This one comes from the Efelian border.

'Scouting report from the last week before summer. Bourjony has pulled several companies back from the mountains. Sightings of Kalassan officials confirmed to be meeting with the army. Intelligence operatives needed in Kalassa to discern their motives.'"

"I take it your people have already seen to that?"

Ash shook her head. "That's above my pay grade," she said, "sir."

"Well, bring that back around to Galan. Alemont will be wanting to stick her pointy nose into that." He gestured dismissively with his lit cigar, and stood from the chair, pacing back to the wide window.

Ash grimaced. "Will do. Sir."

"What's next?"

"Oh, the ah—" she squinted at the sloppy handwriting. "the western outpost in the Icharian Mountains needs medical supplies badly. They sustained an attack last week that left half their number wounded and three scouts dead."

"Send it down to commissary." He waved a dismissive wrist as he paced back to the window.

"Should I read any more?" Ash asked, eyeing the box of seal rings. She was positive that there was some rule against copying those, lest they fall into the wrong hands.

"I'll get to them later, I suppose," he huffed, as if the lack of any more exciting news had deflated him. "Now, what news do you have of Galan's harbor? How are the repairs to the patrol ship coming along? I'd lent them one of my trade ships and was hoping to see it returned by now."

"I believe they expect to be done by week's end," Ash hedged.

"Very well, very well," Kenrose clasped his hands behind his back as he gazed out the window. "You're dismissed, then."

Ash stood, her eyes darting back to the pile of rings in the box. Before she could think better of it, she reached out and snatched one of the silver seal rings and pocketed it. She strode out of the room before she could begin panicking.

"So, that was… interesting," Rorin said as they got underway.

"He was most concerned with correspondence regarding his *Arimopo* trade with Njorske," Ash said, eyes focused on the horizon. "He didn't even have an immediate response for the actual important information on the war."

"Colren says he hoards the wealth of the manor to himself, and neglects his duties, but not enough for him to be relieved of his administrative command."

The stolen ring sat heavy in Ash's pocket and she wondered just how stupid she really was.

"If Avaree has even half the number of refugees that came into Galan, they must be shoved elsewhere."

"There's a shantytown outside the barracks. It's not very nice," Toscan scrunched his nose.

Ferrin pulled a face of distaste. "I grew up spending summers in that manor, and trust me, there is no shortage of spare rooms."

"Wilcoe is not going to be pleased that we only have a few little messages returning. This whole thing was a bust."

"Not so," Toscan said, offended. "Our test-voyage of *the Brisk* has greater purposes beyond message-running between Avaree and Galan."

"Care to share?" Ash asked with no small bit of annoyance.

"The details are still being kept quiet, but there is a mission in which fast, undetectable correspondence will be paramount."

"Interesting," Ferrin nodded.

"And how do you determine this test-voyage to be proceeding, Toscan?" Ash asked with a sigh.

The engineer pushed his glasses up his nose. "So far, so good."

"Well, that's something, I suppose."

He set his notebook down and faced Ash squarely. "You realize we made that run, straight upwind, mind you, in record time for a ship this size?" He pulled out his pocket watch, holding it up for emphasis.

"True, you've built a brilliant ship," Ash conceded.

"And once we head back toward Port Galan, we should start absolutely flying. We should beat our own record by a landslide."

"And the stability?" Ferrin asked. "When your brother thumped down onto the deck it jostled us a fair bit. How's the ship going to take to a quick jibe?"

"The crew on the leeward side will be there to counteract it —whether or not the skipper can switch sides fast enough to offset the weight of the boom," Toscan explained, picking up his notes.

"I hope so. I also hope I don't have to take another boom to the face."

Ash snorted. Ferrin's crooked nose was thanks to an event that had taken place two years ago coming into the harbor on Meroya. One minute they'd all been snickering at something stupid Pierre had said. Then the wind had abruptly crossed their stern, causing the boom of their skiff to rapidly swing across and smack her in the face, hard enough that she went over the side. Pierre and Tabka had laughed themselves hoarse before they realized she was unconscious and bleeding out of her face in the water. Zare had dived in and pulled her out, and then made himself out to be some humble hero for it. As if it hadn't been his lack of warning before taking the jibe that caused the accident in the first place.

"Perhaps you should ready your harnesses. If the wind picks up on the way back, you'll want to be prepared," Toscan advised, peering over the top of his notebook at Ferrin and Rorin.

CHAPTER FIFTEEN

Lukas had been restless all day. Maybe it had something to do with his lack of proper sleep, though that was nothing new. Maybe it had to do with the new list of influx refugees that had been posted, still absent Ryder's name. Maybe it had to do with Ferrin and Ash being out on an experimental sea craft, or Rhi trekking across the countryside on some secretive mission.

He flipped open his pocket watch, the metal familiar and smooth under his fingers. It did little to quiet the nerves buzzing beneath his skin. The action, once an absentminded habit, now seemed to bring with it a host of new worries and questions.

When he'd exhausted all of his usual tasks, he made his way down to the barracks, hoping to burn off some restless energy in the scrapping ring. He found it empty.

With a sigh, he paced back through the encampment before he glimpsed Soviel, working in one of the open medic tents.

There was no patient seated before her, no wounded soldier or ill child to tend to, just a table full of… well, all kinds of things. Stones, bark, sticks, dried herbs, fresh herbs, a jar of honey, a vial of what he thought might have been blood.

She was so absorbed in her work, she didn't look up until he was standing right beside the table.

"What's all this?"

She blinked, drawn back into the real world. "Protective amulets."

"Aren't those a scam?" he frowned, sitting down across from her.

"Perhaps the one's *you've* seen," she shot back, "but the ones I am making are imbued with a touch of my own healing power, therefore *not* a scam. The wearer may even skirt death if they are wearing one at the right time."

"You can put magic into an object like that? Store it?" he asked, taking a closer look at the stones set before her. Sea-smoothed rocks in shades of banded gray and earth tones, small enough to sit snugly in his palm, each surface worn smooth by the sea, were lined up on the table. A small, round hole was bored through each one.

"People have put magic into objects for a long time," she said, almost defensively. "It's an old practice."

"How does it work?" He thought of his pocket watch, sitting heavy inside his coat.

"Well," she began, "it's a sort of generalized spell. Rather than focusing on a specific tissue, or cut, or bruise in the way I would with an actual body in front of me, I focus on the energy and molding it into something usable, the same way I do when I draw it from a plant. Then it settles into the stone, unused, to be accessed later. Hagstones, like these, work best."

"Does it deplete you? What's to stop you from making and selling off a huge batch of these?"

She rolled her eyes and shook her head, gesturing to the table. "Yes, it depletes me. It's careful work, and it doesn't last forever. Once the magic is used up, the hagstone will break. And no, I will not make a dozen for you to sell to the highest bidder."

"I wasn't going to ask," he said, holding up his hands in a gesture of innocence. One was still bandaged, but the other had healed enough to be freed of its wrappings.

She cracked a wry smile. "I still need *all* of these ingredients just to make four. How are your hands?"

"Better," he said, looking down at his palms. "Starting to get a little itchy."

"Care for some help?" She looked down at his unwrapped palm, tilting her head. "I could hasten things along."

He shook his head brusquely. "What's the occasion, then?" he touched the nearest stone, one of dark gray banded with soft white lines.

Soviel eyed him with a touch of wariness before refocusing on the stones. "I'm leaving. In a few days. On a mission."

"You… really?"

She nodded. "I'm making four of these. For you and Ash and Rhi and Ferrin."

"Oh," he said, surprised. He wasn't sure what else to say. "Thanks."

She continued her work, a little smile on her face.

"Where are you off to? Or can I not ask?"

"South of here. An estate. I can't say much else."

"When do you leave?"

"Ten days."

Another three-quarters of an hour passed and they were already closing in on Port Galan.

"Does it seem to be getting a bit colder?" Ferrin asked with a yawn as she rubbed the back of her neck.

Ash nodded her agreement, glad someone else had said something and that she wasn't the only one with a vague sense of unease. For the last twenty minutes as they'd made a graceful, fast run to the west, she couldn't help looking over her shoulder. And once she started, she couldn't stop.

"It can be like that this time of year," Rorin said lightly, though he didn't seem convinced either. No, a blanket of tense discontent had settled over the four of them.

It was then that Toscan stood bolt upright from his seat by the bow. "Storm," he mumbled, clutching at his glasses as he pulled them from his face. "Storm!"

Ash whipped her attention back to the horizon to the north, and found nothing. When she looked back to Toscan, she found him pointing one clammy hand to the southwest, overland. With the main sail blocking her view, she hadn't seen the dark stain on the horizon, bleeding black-gray into the light cloud cover that had inched its way over the sky since mid-afternoon.

"What the—"

Ash gasped lightly as the wind picked up, the rope of the main sail bit into her hand as she untied it from its cleat. She pushed the tiller away from herself, toward the sail, to head up into the wind a few degrees before they started heeling. She didn't want to take this opportunity to find out if Toscan had included any measures to prevent *The Brisk* from capsizing in open water.

"Ferrin, get on the windward side," Ash directed.

Ferrin hopped over the centerboard casing with deft ease, and sidled onto the gunwale beside Rorin.

"Rorin, hook into the trapeze," Ash instructed, feeling the ship begin to heel.

Rorin looked far too overjoyed at the prospect of this, and immediately reached up to grab the line that Toscan had indicated earlier that day. He fastened the hook to the ring on the front of his harness and braced his feet on the gunwale before leaning all the way backwards, over the water as it raced by beneath them.

The storm was pulling them in fast, the fort coming into view in the distance, squatting and stern atop the promontory.

With both Ferrin and Ash hiking out and Rorin on the wire, the speeding ship had leveled out significantly, though it still heeled as it cut through the chop.

"Toscan, I'm going to have to take a jibe at some point to get us into the harbor!" Ash called to the engineer. "How much of a problem is that going to be in these winds?"

He'd carefully stowed his notebook in the watertight container amidships, and looked ready to hop sides at a second's notice.

"This is the maiden voyage!" he cried with a shrug. His panicked expression did *not* give her hope. "Just give us all a fair warning and let Rorin off the trap so we can all swap sides as quickly as possible!"

When the wind crossed a ship's stern, it could be quick and violent. The boom might swing unpredictably fast, dangerous to all in its path, and in some cases, with enough speed to capsize the ship. Especially in a smaller craft like *The Brisk*.

She tensed her body. She was already planning on doing that. She'd been hoping he'd pull some nifty contraption that would counter the swift momentum of the boom, but such was the way of things.

They were nearing the promontory that marked the entrance to the harbor with startling speed, and the chop from the wind had become frantic and chaotic as hungry teeth. *I don't like this*, Ash thought. Something about this storm was wrong.

They hit a gust, and the mast creaked. "Oh, I don't like that!" Rorin shouted.

Despite the weight of all four of them, the ship was still heeling dangerously, leaning far to its port side as it sliced through the sea. They were close to the harbor. She'd have to jibe soon, or decide on another course of action. The dark of the storm blanketed overhead now, tearing them toward its center.

She could spin in a circle, do a safety-tack, but she'd have to head all the way up into the wind and through it. She didn't trust that method at the mouth of the harbor in such winds.

"I'm going to go past the harbor and head up, circle around and head straight into it from further out!" she called over the wind.

"Let us know when we need to move!" Ferrin yelled back, still hiking over the edge with all her might.

Ash leaned her own weight as far over the side as she could while still holding the tiller steady.

They shot past the fort. The sky had gone entirely dark. Ash sucked in a breath, feeling the wind intensifying. Rain whipped sideways through the air, pelting her cheek. She saw no lightning in the storm clouds, but it was only a matter of time before the storm turned deadly.

The beach was a tiny strip at the bottom of the cliffs at the far side of the harbor. She blinked once. They'd sped past the harbor mouth, and were even with the channel that bracketed the promontory to the harbor.

"Everybody ready!" she called, giving Rorin a second to remove himself from the wire. "Coming about!"

With decisive force, she slammed the tiller as far away from her as she could, steering the nose of the ship up, through the wind, spinning from west, to north, to east, until the boom swung to the starboard side. Her crew ducked under the sail as it crossed, and situated themselves on the port rail, their weight settling the ship.

Ash had switched sides with alacrity as she tacked. As she headed off, back towards the harbor, she felt a strange shift in the air.

Not in the *wind*, but in the atmosphere.

Hairs stood up on the back of her neck, and she locked eyes with Ferrin just as a bolt of lightning struck the cliffs.

Something about this storm was *wrong*.

As they sailed towards the harbor, the tension on the tiller grew, pulling against her grip.

"Something is wrong!" Ash called over the wind, which had grown to a deafening level.

Above her, the mast groaned.

"I don't like that," she muttered again. She reached forward and undid the cleat, taking the main sheet in her hand. She let some slack out. "Let the jibs free!"

Ferrin hurriedly unhooked both jib sheets from their cleats, and the sails began to flap furiously in the rogue breeze. The sound was almost unbearable.

We're not going to make it. If the wind shifts even a little, it'll dump us over in the channel, or worse, throw us into the rocks.

"Sorry, Tosc," Ash mumbled, and she jerked the tiller toward her, heading off toward the strip of sand at the base of the cliffs.

"Ferrin, the main halyard, get ready to drop sail! Rorin, get off the wire! Toscan, shift back!"

She fired her commands in rapid succession, and they all fell in, readying to beach *The Brisk* on the shore.

They were coming in fast, too fast. Beaching the ship on the sand was one thing, but if it plowed over the narrow strip of beach and crashed into the rocks, that was another thing entirely. That would be weeks of repairs and expensive resources that the army just could not spare. She needed to get this right.

The beach waited like bait before the teeth of the cliffs.

They hurtled closer, the wind screaming overhead. Far, far above, something exploded out of the cliff.

"What the hell is that!"

"Focus!" Ash barked back. "Drop the sail on my word!"

They were careening toward that spit of sand. Ash reached forward and yanked the centerboard up before it could break off on a rock in the shallow water. *Ready, and...*

"Now!" she screamed just before they hit the beach. Ash yanked the tiller toward herself, bringing them parallel to the shore just as the sand scraped the bottom of the ship, wedging the vessel onto the beach. She stumbled out of the hull onto the sand.

She'd only taken about two breaths of relief when her attention was ripped toward the cliffs high above. The sails flapped loudly in the gale. A funnel of wind had formed just at the cliff's edge above, and *everything* was being pulled towards it. An intense negative pressure demanded its presence be felt. Her sinuses throbbed. She searched the rocky bluff for answers, and saw the trees embedded in the cliff's side wither and die, as if passed by many seasons in only seconds. Every scrap of green evaporated from their leaves, their roots growing slack and feeble. One cracked and fell, taking with it a boulder from the cliff.

"Ash, look out!" Ferrin slammed into her side, tackling her out of the way as a huge boulder hurtled to the ground and buried itself in a crater where she'd been standing only a second before.

"Thanks," she gasped as they picked themselves up from the sand.

"We need to get *out* of here!" Ferrin yelled over the wind.

"Take cover!" Ash yelled, nodding in agreement as the made for the ship again. "It's a—" she couldn't remember the name, something with an 'R' "A pit creature!"

Ferrin swore as they all ducked behind the mast. Above, at the bottom of the funnel cloud that kept forming and un-forming, there was a small hold in the side of the cliff.

"How did you all manage to kill the one in the castle?" she shouted as she landed by Ash.

"Blew it up!" Ash answered. "But I think it's going to take more than a few cannonballs to do that!" She gestured at the ship's extremely small artillery.

"Oi!" Rorin's voice came from behind them. "Everyone get clear!"

When Ferrin turned, she saw him poised over the cannon, ready to light it in spite of their limited supplies.

As Ash and Ferrin were about to dive out of the way, there was a piercing, screeching roar out of the cliffs. It rippled through the air and threw them all back, snapping the mast of *The Brisk*, and putting Rorin's shot wide.

"Dammit!"

"Reload!"

"There's not much left!" Toscan protested, anguished at the state of his creation.

"Reload!" Rorin shouted again.

Another tendril of dust-filled hard air protruded from the cliff, carrying detritus and rock with it. It was all they could do to jump behind the ship to avoid the onslaught of falling debris.

Soviel's attention was not first caught by the twister, nor by the shaking earth beneath her feet, nor by the screaming in the distance.

It was the throbbing, pulsing pressure pounding through her skull she'd only felt twice before. It came on fast, as if she'd run head first into a brick wall. Over, and over, and over.

"Hey, are you alright?" Lukas's disquieted voice was faint and far away against the blood boiling in her skull.

"Not this again," she hissed weakly through gritted teeth.

"What again?"

"*Something* is feeding on my magic," she groaned, pressing her fingers to her temples and squeezing her eyes shut.

"*What?*"

"It's the same as before—in the tunnel. The-the pit."

She opened her eyes to see Lukas's face blanch. "We need to get everyone out of here. *We* need to get out of here." He spun, looking out at the unconcerned street.

"No—" she choked out, struggling to her feet.

"It isn't safe here, we need to evacuate so that the army can get in there and blow—"

"*No!*" Her hand shot out and grabbed his wrist. "I can *feel* it."

He looked askance at her.

"I can trace it," she argued. "Give me a second. Tell, I don't know, tell someone to empty out the northwest half of the barracks, then meet me back here, *fast*. I'll need your help."

Lukas nodded tersely and disappeared. Soviel, leaning heavily on the table in front of her and fighting to keep her breathing even, gathered up a bundle of strong plants that she'd been saving for a particularly grievous injury. Now seemed like the time to use them.

Lukas returned minutes later, and evidence of his message became apparent when uniformed soldiers began ushering people away, back towards town and out of the barracks.

"Are you sure about this?" Lukas gave her a dubious look.

"I can kill it." She didn't add, *if I can make it there.*

Soviel and Lukas trekked up the cliffside path from the barracks, which had been made even more perilous thanks to the recent attack. She was lagging behind, stopping every few minutes in a desperate attempt to catch her breath, her strength. It was slipping through her fingers like sand, and she leaned heavily on the rocks as they climbed. A trickle of dark blood had made its way out of one nostril, and had not ceased its slow flowing as they ascended.

"We're almost there," Lukas assured her, pausing for her to catch up. He helped her over one of the more treacherous spots. "Are you sure about this?"

"Yes," she panted, her breaths haggard and raw. "I'm sure."

She could feel it in her fingertips, in her toes and her tongue and her lungs and her head. Her skin was on fire with it. The more it hurt her, the more she knew what she had to do. The more she could feel what was at the center of that presence.

They continued on the narrow path, and her foot sent a bit of rock skittering, the ground beneath her shifting. Lukas caught her wrist before she could stumble off the edge.

"Careful," he said as he hefted her back onto the path.

"Thanks."

The pulsing throbbing was even more insistent now, drilling into her skull with the force of a battering ram. It demanded she feel its presence, its life-force.

"I can feel it, its heart," she said weakly as they crested the cliff. The wind was sucking, pulling, leeching them toward that cave.

"Are we close enough?" Lukas shouted over the gusts.

"Almost," she nodded, raising her bloodshot eyes to the swirling mass of air and energy ahead.

They clambered down the ocean-facing side of the cliff, onto the next ledge. The negative pressure was almost unbearable, pulling in any bit of living matter that came too close.

"Get back," she ordered Lukas, stumbling into the wall.

That's when she felt it, felt what the throbbing was. The heartbeat of a creature corrupted, a hole torn in the fabric of life itself, of the world, of space and time. This mangled, horrible *thing*, this beast of destruction and death—it wasn't a weapon, it was a wound.

And it was desperate. It was dying of starvation and taking what it could to survive.

So Soviel grasped it with her power and twisted, tugged with all her might.

She leaned into that awful throbbing that seemed to jar her very bones and squeezed.

She felt it falter, shiver, tug at her, begging to be fed. More, more, *more*. She felt it wither as she refused, felt the festering gash in the earth pull closed as she drained it of its malevolence, like poison from a wound.

She felt it die, felt the pounding in her head slow, ebb, and cease, going out with the tide, receding and fading with the angry storm the beast had drawn up. She felt the core of its energy and recognized it, for the very same spark of power was what lived in her own magic.

Then, she fainted.

If Lukas hadn't started forward a second before it happened, Soviel would have dropped over the side of the cliff. He caught her by the elbow and hoisted her into his arms, leaning away from the cliff edge as he re-balanced himself.

Overhead, the clouds were clearing, the sun peaking out from behind the cover like a shy child.

"Let's get down from this death trap," he suggested as he balanced her weight across his shoulders. Below, he could see a small, odd ship with several figures huddling behind it on the rocky shore.

"Hey!" one of the figures shouted distantly. "HEY!"

He turned back, and realized it was Ash. She'd clambered out from behind one of the boulders below.

"What the hell are you two doing up there?" she yelled.

He tried to shrug, but doing so while carrying the weight of an unconscious girl in layers of heavy fabric was nearly impossible, so instead he just turned to find a safe way back down the cliffs. A moment later, Ferrin landed beside him. She was easing Soviel to the narrow ground, taking half her weight, helping him carry her.

"What did she do?" Ferrin asked, tenderly pushing Soviel's hair out of her face.

"She," Lukas shook his head as he searched for the words, "she seemed to find a way to connect to the thing. Through her power. Then she killed it, I think."

"It seems to have desisted."

There was a loud gasp, and Soviel reeled upright.

"Soviel!" Ferrin cried, scrambling to keep both of their balances. "You're alright!"

"Oh my gods," she panted. "That was..." she shook her head clear.

"You're not still sick from it?" Lukas asked, surprised.

"No. No. I feel," Soviel exhaled once, her eyes fluttering shut. A healthy flush had bloomed on her cheeks. She was glowing like someone who'd just completed a running race, and won. "I feel perfect."

"Really? You passed out." Lukas tried to keep himself from looking too shocked. That level of magic, whatever it was she'd done, was unheard of.

"Yes, for a moment," she nodded, shifting out of their grasps. "Healing that rot out of the land was invigorating."

"You *are* glowing," Ferrin narrowed her eyes.

"I fixed it," she said with a small smile. "The *ras*. It's healed. Returned to its natural state."

"You saved our asses, that's for sure."

They descended towards the bottom of the cliff on shaky legs, and Ash, who had run partway up the cliff, slammed into Soviel and threw her arms around her, then Lukas.

"You killed it?" Ash exclaimed. "We would have been *dead* in that maelstrom. How did you do it?"

174

"Just had a hunch," Soviel laughed breathlessly.

CHAPTER SIXTEEN

Soviel awoke the next morning feeling oddly rested. Unlike when she'd pushed her limits in the past, she was not exhausted, not depleted. She was invigorated. The shift she had felt in her power a few weeks ago had deepened. As if she could feel its roots beneath her skin, growing and stretching. She didn't know what it meant, but she knew she was more than simply a healer now. If she were braver, she might venture out with the sole goal of testing her limits, seeing what she was capable of.

"You leave in nine days, just before the summer celebration," Helene said. "How are you doing?"

Truthfully, she'd been so preoccupied with her powers that she hadn't had time to think too hard about her new assignment, which was fast approaching.

"I know I'm ready. We need this," she affirmed.

Helene paced to the window of her office. "I know that you are smart and cunning, and emotionally intelligent beyond your years, but I have to admit, it weighs on me to send someone as young as you into this."

"Major, you cannot continue to fixate on that. I'm nearly twenty, I'll be alright. This is about more than just me."

The conversation had been brief. Now, Soviel sat out on the roof with Ash and Ferrin, whiskey bottle in hand, sun gently falling in the distance.

"So, there it is," Soviel said after giving them as many details as she was allowed. "Nine days from now, I leave for Bramblehall, the very belly of the beast."

Ash rested her head against Soviel's knee and propped her feet up on Ferrin's lap. Of the three of them, Ash was the most free with her affection. Soviel thought it brought out her own warmer side.

"You already know we're going to worry for you," Ash exhaled.

"Well, worry not, because Helene has tasked you with once-every-two-weeks treks down to the rendezvous point to retrieve my correspondence," she said lightly. "It's not set in stone, but someone should be along to brief you shortly."

"You know we'll worry for you anyway. Always," Ferrin said. "We need you."

It was true that the events of this spring had bonded the three of them. Even Ash, who Soviel had known for all of a few months, now felt like an irreplaceable part of her. An organ she could not do without.

After Nimhe's harsh betrayal, little moments like these were even more special and important to her. She had to cherish them, as if the rug might be ripped from beneath her at any moment.

"And that," Soviel said, "is why I made these." She set the hagstones down on Ash's middle.

"What are they?" Ash asked, craning her neck to squint down at her abdomen.

"Healing amulets. They'll protect their wearer until the power runs out. Even if I'm not here to heal you," she explained.

"That's not what I meant, Sov," Ferrin said quietly.

"I know," Soviel acknowledged. "But I wanted you all to have these anyway. Wear them *always*."

It was Ash who sat up and turned, gripping Soviel's hands in her own, amber eyes wide and shining in the evening light. "We will."

"I just can't believe it's so soon," Ferrin moaned. "I just… the three of us working together here feels so right. I know it sounds," she broke off, shaking her head with a laugh. "The two of you mean the world to me. I don't want anything to happen to either of you. Ever."

"Aw *Ferr*," Ash goofed, turning to face Ferrin. "We love you, too."

Soviel couldn't help the grin that broke over her face, warming her whole chest. "I'm going to miss this," she said.

"Well, at least we have a few more sunsets," Ash said, breaking the tension as she often did.

"Think they have those down in Bramblehall, too?" Ferrin jested, watching the changing colors wash over everything.

"The manor faces the western horizon." Soviel smiled slightly.

Ferrin laughed, and Ash took a perfunctory swig of the shared whiskey bottle before resuming her position of lounging between the two of them.

They were quiet for a while, steeped in the warm glow of the dying sun and each others' company.

"When this is all over, what do you suppose you'll both do?" Ash asked contemplatively.

There was a beat of silence as the weight of the question settled differently on all of them. For Ash, it was light as a breeze, her optimism casting her idea of the future to a wide scope of possibilities. For Ferrin, it was heavy with questions and unknown responsibilities, laden with fear of being trapped, fear of losing everything. For Soviel, though, it was blank. As the one who'd played this game the longest, she was the most uncertain of how it would end.

"I don't know," Ferrin was the first to speak. "I suppose the conclusion of this war could land me with a job." She said it with deceptive flippancy. With her mother still in the wind, and her father's traitorous fate unknown, Ferrin and Rhi would have a great deal of patching up within their country to do, come the end of the conflict. "But if it were up to me, all consequences aside, I'd head south for a while, see the world some more."

Ash nodded in agreement. "Once these bastards have been stopped, I want to go back to Khalim, see my family."

"How long has it been?" Soviel asked, shifting her focus from the red horizon to Ash's face.

"More than three years now," Ash admitted, with both guilt and longing heavy in her voice. "Lukas says our sister has two babies now, and our mother lives on her farm with her and her husband."

"I think I'd head home for a little while, too," Soviel added, needing to fill the silence, to do something to stop Ash's face from crumpling the way it did when she felt this sorrowful shame. "See my parents, see Callia, leave before we start ripping each other's hair out again."

"You don't get on well with your sister?" Ferrin asked.

Soviel gave a grim shake of her head. "Not in the slightest, I'm afraid."

"Well, Sov, what do you say, in the hypothetical future, once your sister has driven you mad, you come south with us? See the world?" Ash asked, her face lighting again.

Soviel laughed lightly and said, "I can't say no to that, can I?"

And for that moment, that delicate slice of time, there was a fragile happiness born of sisterhood that washed over them as the sun sank below the horizon and painted the sky a deep, wine red.

When Rhi and Lachlan at last stumbled into camp, half-frozen, travel-weary and exhausted to the bone, they split with hardly a word.

Rhi had been prepared to have it out again, for Lachlan to lose his temper and have to start the work of smoothing over the cracks between them before the dam blew out, but that hadn't happened.

"I'll see you later," Lachlan had mumbled, splitting off to go and report his findings to Wilcoe or Alemont or whoever it was that signed his checks.

Rhi had stood frozen for a handful of moments, watching Lachlan stalk down the main way of the encampment, eyes fixed on his back. His arms had been wrapped tight across his chest against the morning chill, pulling the wrinkled fabric of his shirt taut over his broad shoulders.

And that, more than the yelling and fighting, had been so much worse.

He felt eerily quiet. The hollow, icy bubble that had been growing in his chest for the last few weeks finally burst.

Something had solidified in his throat and dropped down to form a pit in his stomach that he couldn't explain as he walked numbly up the path to the manor. Something demanding and itchy had squatted in the back of his mind, and seemed intent on making its way forward. Something he hadn't felt in a while. Because what was the point of all this?

The marsh opened into emptiness on either side of him, what seemed like miles of flat beach grass and mild dunes stretching on forever. He was *exhausted.*

He was halfway across the marsh when he couldn't ignore the nagging, gnawing feeling anymore.

He wanted it to go away. *All* of it. He wanted to not feel this way.

The fight with Lachlan was only a small part of it all. The occupation, the war… what had happened to his father? Was he dead, or was he working alongside the Bourjons? Ferrin had been so busy with all the strange clues Arabella had left for her, Lukas was hung up on what had happened to Ryder…

Everything was going to shit.

He wanted it to stop.

He needed to *make* it stop.

Rhi halted on the stairwell. He released one shaky breath, and turned off on the lower levels, making his way toward the scullery. If he was careful, if it was only a little…

He walked on phantom legs as he neared the kitchens. Was he *doing* this? Was this happening?

"Hi," he said in a soft voice to the courier he'd seen days earlier. Money changing hands, pouch being passed from person to person, furtive looks thrown over cloaked shoulders.

"And who might you be looking for?" The woman looked at him askance.

"I was hoping you might be selling."

She laughed through her nose, a quick, sharp huff. Crossing her arms over her chest, she looked him up and down. "Don't you soldier types have your own supplier down in the barracks?" She arched a thin eyebrow.

He shook his head slowly. "If we do, I don't know about it."

She laughed again. "Alright then, fancy man. What can I interest you in?"

"Maraki blue, in powder, if you have it?"

She stared a moment before smiling. "I've got it in a liquid, if that suits your fancy tastes?"

"Fine." He dug into his pocket to draw out the stiff coin purse.

They settled up and Rhi was on his way, the thing in his hand practically pulsing as a heady mix of dread and anticipation surged through his veins.

He made it to the top floor of the manor and found a window overlooking the sea, leagues below.

The waves beat against the rocks, far beneath the manor walls. Sea on stone, and sea on stone. He let out a long, labored breath and unwrapped the vial of *popava*, the shining liquid glistening beneath the clear glass in his palm.

He drew in a sharp breath as conflicting parts of him screamed each other down.

Remember last time.

Don't you want it all to go away? What does it matter...

He gripped the vial in his fist and twisted the cork—

A shrill scream shot through the air from down the hall.

Without wasting a second, Rhi plunged the vial back into his pocket and took off toward the sound. There was a second scream, from further down the hall.

What was on this floor again? He couldn't remember. Living quarters?

He rounded a corner, and came upon two girls—

And a rat.

One girl was perched atop a chair in the middle of the hallway, eyes wide with terror, while the second clutched her stomach in a fit of laughter.

"Are the two of you," Rhi panted, bracing a hand on the wall to catch his breath, "quite alright?"

"Yes, Minnie has just had a fright from this *fearsome* creature," the second girl mocked.

"Shut *up,* Harrien!" the girl atop the chair whined, her face stricken. "Those things carry disease! And sharp teeth!"

Rhi balked. "It's only a rat, miss," he said, the hammering in his chest slowing. "Look, he's already scurrying back to wherever he came from, see?"

Minnie eyed the wall that the rat had disappeared into with suspicion. "I've heard a bite can give you a wretched sickness of the flesh."

"I suspect he's more afraid of you than you are of him."

"Listen to the gent, Min," Harrien rolled her eyes. "Come on. We've work to finish. Sorry for the disturbance, sir."

"No… no trouble at all," Rhi said, blinking. The vial of *popava* had gone leaden in his pocket.

The two girls, scullery maids perhaps, turned and hurried off to wherever they were expected next.

As soon as they were gone, Rhi let out a guttural gasp and leaned into the wall.

He'd been *so* close to doing something monumentally stupid.

With a shuddering sigh, he turned to the window at the end of the hall and stalked toward it like an automaton. He thrust his hand into his pocket and threw the vial into the sea with all the force he could muster, and turned to find his room and a hot bath.

Still bewildered and more than a little shaken from the near miss of a colossal mistake, Rhi dressed in his administrative assistant's jacket with still-trembling fingers. He'd been doing well. *So* well, all things considered. One cold bath later and his hands were still shaking. How had he come so close to throwing it all away? He was overtired, hungry. He'd been on the verge of freezing for days. And then there was the matter of the river, not to mention the hunting party.

He made his way down to the barracks, hoping to miraculously avoid running into Lachlan while finding Lukas or Ferrin or Ash or Soviel, or some combination thereof. It was a tall order.

His plans were immediately put on hold when he exited the manor—how had he not noticed on his way in? The cliffs were in shambles. The barracks themselves were half-packed up, as if readying to move out.

"Oi—" Rhi said, catching Edmin Flanerty by the wrist as he rushed by. "What's happened?"

Edmin looked Rhi over. "Where've you been?"

"On an assignment."

"Aren't you admin?" he squinted at Rhi's jacket lapel.

"Yes. Sort of. Don't worry about it." He shook his head and dropped Edmin's wrist. "What happened here? I've barely been gone a week."

"There've been two attacks in that time," Edmin snorted joylessly.

"*What*?"

"I don't have the time to give you a play-by-play, go check in with your c—"

Rhi didn't give him a chance to finish whatever vaguely condescending scrap of wit he'd planned to trot out next. He jogged down the main thoroughfare of the encampment, desperately searching for a familiar face. It seemed, though the area was in great disrepair, that there was no immediate danger. He slowed his pace until he found Lukas, one hand wrapped in white gauze, sweeping a pile of debris off of the path that led closest to the cliffs.

"Hey there, know where I could find some scrambled mountain goat gallbladders?" he asked, approaching. "They're supposed to be a delicacy in Njorske."

Lukas stopped sweeping and looked up, propping the broom up in his un-wrapped hand. "I might have a guy for that."

Rhi chuckled. "Splendid."

"Glad you're back, though you certainly picked the right week to be gone," he said, gesturing to the wreckage around him.

"Of course, I leave for one little week and all goes to complete shite in my absence!" he threw his hands up in mock exasperation before adding more soberly, "Though I was certainly not on a picnic stroll in the woods."

"Care to share?"

"You first," Rhi said, eyeing the charred remains of a wagon sitting below the rise of the promontory wall.

Lukas snickered. "First, there were cannonballs launched into and over this cliff, location chosen courtesy of a spy, or so says the general consensus. Though I'm not privy to what goes on in the war tent, so don't quote me. Then a few days later, a *rasernemaud* exploded from the cliffs further east," he recounted, pointing with his broom handle.

"Dear gods," Rhi gasped. "And now...?"

"Now nothing. Soviel choked it to death and then passed out."

Rhi's eyes bulged. "Is she well? What did—"

"She's fine. More than fine, actually, which we all agreed was rather strange."

"What? Why?"

Lukas grimaced. "She was practically glowing after she did it. And Ash thinks… well, Ash told some cracked off story that Soviel revived a dead mouse."

Rhi frowned, confused.

"I don't really understand either, but apparently she isn't supposed to be able to do that."

"Huh," Rhi pondered, again struck by how little they all understood of magic. "Well, wait until you hear about where *I've* been."

"By all means," Lukas said, and passed him the broom.

Rhi took it with a grin and began sweeping, happy to have a task to dull the whisper of panic that he had not yet managed to subdue. "So, we traveled to Eilbast to search for some book. We found it, but on the journey home, we were pursued by a hunting party of enemy soldiers."

"How many?"

"A dozen or so."

Lukas's eyes went wide. "And it was just you and Lachlan? Against that many?"

"Oh, there was no *against*. We ran."

"Likely the smart decision."

"We ran, and when we reached the river we got into the old rowboat from when I used to hunt in Taroch. We were floating down the Rhainor, which was *roiling*, mind you, and suddenly this great big woman emerged from the water, but she *was* water. Held up the boat, spoke at us like we were ill-behaved children, and then flooded the bank to put out the fire the soldiers had set."

"*What*?"

"I assume she was some long-asleep nature spirit."

Lukas shook his head in awe. "I've never heard of anything like that."

"Ha! So you can be surprised. No, nor have I, but it must mean something, right? And with Soviel's magic doing… whatever it is it's doing, and Bourjony's experiments—"

"—then magic coming into play in a more extreme way in this conflict is a very real possibility." Lukas sighed deeply, eyes settling on the distance, heavy with exhaustion.

"Precisely. Now, have you seen my sister?"

"Probably with mine," he said with a lazy shrug.

The five of them had gathered around the table in the shared rooms in the manor's northwest tower, and the light from their two lanterns danced among the shadows on the walls as they talked. Lukas listened as Rhi filled the rest of their little group in on what had happened on his journey from Eilbast.

"Where's Lachlan now?"

Rhi shrugged, the gesture far too nonchalant for it to go unnoticed.

Ferrin's eyes narrowed. "What happened?"

"Nothing happened. A minor disagreement." His tone was clipped.

She frowned, but apparently decided to drop the matter.

"As I was saying—magic is waking up. Slowly. Whether or not it is related to Bourjony's flying soldier remains to be seen, but…" he trailed off.

"Very curious," Soviel nodded thoughtfully. "I think you're right, though. Whatever is causing it, I couldn't say, but my own power feels different, more plentiful."

Lukas watched Ash watch Soviel with an expression that wasn't quite suspicion on her face.

"What does this mean then, for the rest of us? For the future of this conflict?" she asked.

There was a beat of loaded silence.

"I suspect," Rhi began slowly, steepling his fingers. "That we can expect to see it on the other side as well. We already know they had one soldier capable of flight and incredible strength, but how? And how much further will it go? I'll pass this on to General Alemont, but given our collective experience in the capital this spring, we need to find a way to get ahead of this. Together."

They all nodded somberly and looked at one another.

PART

TWO

INTERLUDE

Far, far off, in a part of the sea long forgotten, where long ago the gods had banished monsters of old, he churned and writhed.

He was no longer in his body. His *human* body. No, he had lost that long ago. When he'd become something else. Whether it was a curse or a salvation, he'd been changed, turned into something powerful, twisting, scaled.

The sea was deep, reaching down toward the gleaming pits of hell, and islands rose like teeth around him. Islands built to keep things far older than him contained, though somewhere along the way, he'd ended up among them, those monsters big as mountains, mouths vast enough to swallow worlds. Teeth and claws and spines fit for nightmares. Sea-ice flowed through their veins.

No, he did not belong here, but what was a man—a monster—to do?

Two ancient tugs kept him paralyzed in indecision. One called him far, far away, to a past long lost on a windswept isle where he'd… lost something. The other beckoned him south to the rich, cerulean waters of the middle-sea.

There was something else in those tugs, magnetic. Polar. Each equally as strong. There was something about them, something he couldn't remember, from another time, another world. Something that glowed silver-blue-green as the sea, mesmerizing.

He crested the surface, his body new and old all at once, stretching as he moved through the water with grace and ease. How smooth, how quick he'd become in this body.

Four hundred years since that fateful storm had landed him here, and it had passed in the blink of an eye. He no longer remembered his name, nor the face of his mother. He no longer remembered the feel of sand in his fingers, or sun on his face, nor wind in his hair. There was only the cool, quiet deep, and the sound of another voice, far away, buried beneath the earth, dreaming.

Free me, the voice said. *Please.*

"Who are you?" he'd sometimes asked.

I am lost, the voice would respond. Or, sometimes, *I'm just a boy. Please, free me. I can lead you to riches, to fame.*

This perturbed him. People who offered easy solutions to poverty and destitution were often conmen. Quacks.

He wouldn't fall for such trickery, but still, most times there was no one else to talk to.

CHAPTER SEVENTEEN

B ig storm washed all kinds of junk up," Neb spat over the side of the docks.

Ash shrugged. "If you could call it a storm."

"Harbinger of natural disasters, or just plain nature's wrath, it doesn't matter. Result's the same," Neb said with a shake of her head, eyes narrowed suspiciously at the calmly churning sea.

"So," Ash said in a deceptively light tone, "do we know the extent of the damage to *The Brisk*?"

"Toscan and a few of the inventors are hard at work on it, but it'll be a few days before we know more."

"Right then," she nodded, turning back to the bucket of paint she'd been stirring. "Anything interesting wash up, yet?"

Neb cut her a sidelong glance. "Hoping to get the best goods off the salvage run?"

"No. Yes. Just curious."

"Once the tide comes in this afternoon, I'm sure something interesting will crop up."

Ash looked at the horizon contemplatively. Her hands were restless. "I've got a strange feeling, Neb."

"You and me both, kid. Part of seafaring."

In the last week, the barracks, the manor and the town had been abustle with work. Reshaping the cliffside paths, restocking shot in the manor and fort, repairing the damaged ships and updating the defenses to account for the blind spots on the cliffs. Along with all that, Ashwife had begun bringing in soldiers and civilians alike for questioning, trying to discern who was leaking information to their enemies. None of it was easy work.

Soviel was finished packing, and had just made her way down to Helene's office for her final briefing before her departure.

"So, as you've requested, Asha Mazrihn will be your primary courier," Helene said, gesturing to Ash, who looked pale and nervous following her extensive briefing, "via the coast. You will leave your first message for us at *this* tavern," she tapped the map of the little town outside of Bramblehall's sprawling manor, "detailing your exact signal, and your designated drop-spot."

"Right," Soviel nodded. "Yes, ma'am."

"And you have the code committed to memory?"

"I do, and a spare cypher sewn into one of the boning channels in my stays." She patted her side for emphasis.

"Good."

"On the off-chance that we are not able to send Mazrihn, Eiran Faragh will approach via the road, and check for your message." Helene jerked her chin at the tall young man who'd been quietly seated in the corner since Soviel had arrived. "It will be slower, but better than flying blind."

"Understood," Soviel said, twisting in her chair to acknowledge the man.

"And remember, this is a strictly intel-only mission. Should things become volatile, should you even suspect you've been compromised, you *flee*."

"*Yes*, Major," Soviel nodded, trying to keep the annoyance at Wilcoe's motherly fretting out of her voice. "I'm not going to do anything foolish."

"Well," she clucked her tongue. "There is a first time for everything. Are you ready? The carriage awaits."

Soviel took a deep breath, committing the feeling of relative safety to memory. "Yes. I'm ready."

CHAPTER EIGHTEEN

Bramblehall, the Duke and Duchess Hadringston's manor, lay between a winding marsh, a long, flat coast, and the little village of Bragghly. The manor itself, perched high on the hill like a resting place for the gods, was a splendid and opulent building.

The main road leading up to a circular carriage-way was paved in shimmering pale stones, and lined by grand gardens and manicured lawns. The stone steps leading up to the front entrance were polished, white granite. The enormous front door, flanked by two smaller doors and covered by a row of towering marble columns, dwarfed the carriage Soviel had arrived in. The manor itself was hewn of elegant, cream-colored stone and clapboards, its black shutters thrown open to greet the day.

With a deep, calming breath, Soviel mustered her emotions and threw on her best attitude as she ascended the steps and raised one gloved hand to knock on the door. It felt good to stretch her legs after sitting in the carriage for so many days.

Moments later, the smaller door to Soviel's left swung open and a woman wearing a deep burgundy dress and a pinafore bowed her head in greeting. Beneath her sheer muslin cap, chestnut ringlets were neatly pinned around her peach colored face.

"Good morning, my name is Lady Soviel Larksen. I believe I am expected?" she said by way of greeting.

"Ah, yes!" Recognition lit the woman's face. "Mistress will be most pleased. Right this way."

Soviel obliged, picking up her lone traveling bag.

"Shall I have a servant come and fetch your bags?"

"I only have the one," Soviel admitted. "Most of my things were lost with Everness." Not a lie.

Her story was this: Soviel had left Everness a week before the coup. She had been visiting a companion in the north whom she'd hoped to secure a match through, but had been unsuccessful. When the fighting broke out in Avaree, where she was staying, she fled to the hills with a few other respectable nobles who were as yet unaccounted for. By the grace of fate, she made it to her distant cousin's farm. From there, she'd written to Bramblehall.

"Oh, dear," the woman said with sympathy. "Well, that's alright. Her Grace likes to have all of her ladies fitted and dressed by her own personal clothier anyway. My name is Bessa, by the way. I'm head of the maid staff here at Bramblehall," she said with obvious pride.

"Pleased to meet you, Bessa," Soviel replied meekly, already wiggling her toes, getting accustomed to this role.

"Hamesh!" Bessa called. Moments later, a well-dressed boy, perhaps fourteen, appeared in a blue waistcoat that brought out the orange undertones of his pale skin.

"Good morning, Madam," he bowed at the waist and picked up her single bag.

Though nothing strictly incriminating could be found in Soviel's bag, a flicker of anxiety went through her when it left her possession. One wrong move here could cost her her life.

"Right this way," Bessa said, turning to exit the foyer.

"I can't tell you how relieved I am to have made it here safely," Soviel gushed. "The last few weeks during the skirmishes have been harrowing."

"I'm sure you're exhausted, I'll call Maerie to draw you a bath."

"That would be lovely," she sighed with relief.

"You'll be staying in the north quarter of the house, in the room of one of Her Grace's previous ladies. It has the best view of the bay, after the Master Suite, of course."

"Oh, how lovely!" Soviel chirped. "I confess, anything where I have a bed and a room to myself will be better than my last lodging."

"Where were you before?"

"North of the capital, in a small estate of a distant relative. They were kind to shelter me, but had so little to spare themselves."

"Well, you'll want for nothing here. I wouldn't be surprised if you're engaged within the year. The duchess likes to keep lots of fancy folk around. Plenty of billeted soldiers and feasts thrown to honor the officers," Bessa explained.

"I just hope I can be of good service to the house, and make some connections," Soviel said demurely.

"Here you are," Bessa gestured, halting beside a painted white door. "Hamesh has brought your things up, and I'll give you a moment to settle in while I fetch Maerie."

"Thank you," Soviel said with gratitude that was not entirely false.

The door shut behind Bessa and Soviel exhaled deeply, letting herself relax. She was going to be here for a long time, there was no use in getting herself worked up *now*. She dropped onto the bed and stripped off her gloves.

She smoothed her hands over the light pink silk jacket and dark gray quilted petticoat. The rest of her clothing, packed into the suitcase, was rough and modest, fitting of someone who'd fled their home very quickly, and been nearly homeless for the last few weeks.

Helene had diverted valuable resources to find her proper attire to match her story. While it was true that she was born of a lesser Njorski Lord, and that she'd previously served as a lady-in-waiting to a woman of noble station, she certainly hadn't hidden out with a distant loyalist cousin after the conflict had erupted.

The idea was to show that she was desperate for this station, another foreign socialite looking to use the duchess's influence and money to find her way to a wealthy spouse with a good name and land to match. That she would save her one fine piece of clothing to make a good impression on arrival, but that the rest of her things were bordering on shabby.

She hoped it was working.

With a touch of vapidity and vanity, she would win them all over. Swallowing her pride had never been difficult for Soviel. Not in situations like these, not with the satisfaction that she would fool them all.

Perception was everything.

Moments later, a knock rattled the door. A very young woman—a girl, really—entered. Her thick, straight black hair was pulled back into a severe knot that made her look years older. She was thin, straight-figured and her light brown skin glowed in the afternoon light slanting through the windows.

"How do you take your bath, ma'am?" she asked.

"Just warm is fine, thank you," Soviel replied as she unbuckled the top of her bag.

Some twenty minutes later, the bath was ready. It was a welcome comfort to submerge herself beneath the warm water. She'd ordered the maid, Maerie away, protesting that she preferred to bathe in private. Though she could have used some help in detangling her hair, she wanted a bit of alone time to gather her thoughts. Who knew when she'd have the chance again? So she let mask she so often wore slip and rolled her shoulders, letting her face relax, relishing the idea of being solid and real for a moment before submerging again.

When she stepped out of the bath, she toweled off, pulled on her shift and replaced her mask, ringing Maerie to return and help her dress before she went off to meet her new mark.

With Maerie's help, Soviel dressed in the same silk-jacket ensemble, deeming it her most appropriate garment in which to meet the duchess, rather than the bedraggled gown that had been crumpled at the bottom of her bag since her departure from Galan.

After having her stays laced tight, her garters tied and her hair wrapped over what looked like a dead rodent, she followed Maerie down the center wing of the house. There, they ascended a smaller set of stairs to the grand suite.

The maid rapped sharply on the gold filigreed door, and another servant opened it.

"Mistress is expecting you," she curtsied.

"Come, come, I want to see her," the woman's voice was accented similarly to Soviel's father's. High and light and musical. "I do hope she isn't so strange looking as the last one, I don't want to be sick of her by the end of the month."

Soviel tried not to look taken aback as she walked into the room, shoulders back and hands folded elegantly in front of her. When she reached the dais, she curtsied.

"*Hialstet*, Mistress," she said in greeting.

"Oh, she is a pretty one. And she does speak Njorski! How happy I am," she clapped.

The woman lounging on the dais must have been about thirty. Her full brows were well groomed and soft brown, arched over large pale-blue eyes. Her skin was light and earthy, though clearly enhanced with a rosy rouge. Her light brown hair was braided in a coronet over her head, and adorned in little jeweled pins.

"Come, sit by me and tell me about yourself."

Obliging, Soviel crossed the room to the chair nearest the dais, where she adjusted her skirts and sat. "I am so grateful to have made it here," she said with a sweet sigh.

"We will have to have some new dresses made for you," the duchess said, looking Soviel over. "My maids tell me you arrived with only these travel clothes and a few extra rags."

"It has been a very trying few weeks, Your Grace."

"I'm certain it has been, but you're here now!" She clapped her hands onto Soviel's. "And you must tell me all about where in Njorske you come from, and how you miss it."

"Korolsk. Just outside of Karlgiard, Your Grace, a little ways north of the Veiran border."

"I see, I thought I detected some exotic features on you," she said, cupping Soviel's face between her hands. "Do you miss the old country?"

"Yes," Soviel nodded, brushing off the strange comment.

"As do I," the duchess sighed. "I come from Fairjold. My father is lord of all that land between the sea and Olssek Forest."

"I'm afraid I only visited there once, as a young child, but it is a lovely part of the country, Your Grace."

"Oh, please dear, call me Samia," she gushed. "Maerie, Evenna, you may go. Please send for the tailor."

The two maids curtsied and left.

"*Samia,* that means devoted to the gods, doesn't it?"

"You know your history," Samia raised her eyebrows. "Though, I can't say how accurate a name it is. My husband says I'd sooner worship a silk merchant than an altar. Ha! But what does he know?" she giggled. "I think this shade suits you well, but I'd like you to wear other pastel tones—yes, baby blue and lilac should be lovely with your complexion."

"Oh, a new dress would be wonderful," Soviel cooed. "But, I could never afford such things."

"Nonsense, I am the one who must look at you all day."

"You have a passion for clothing and fashions, Your Grace?" she asked, slipping in the title one last time.

"Yes. You'll have a whole new wardrobe to match my other ladies."

"Other ladies?"

"Yes, my dear," Samia said. "You'll meet them at supper tonight. And my husband, though he is not so charming as the rest of us. Always scowling so," she imitated a grouchy frown, complete with a pouting underbite.

"I see," Soviel said.

"And in time, you'll receive introductions to all the soldiers and household bachelors. You should find them quite appetizing." She wiggled her eyebrows mischievously.

"I'm sure I will," Soviel said, willing a blush to her face.

"Of course, I'm sure you're looking to eventually make an advantageous match, but in the mean time, you'll enjoy the beautiful things my home has to offer," Samia pronounced.

A knock on the door sounded, and Samia called them in.

It was a short, balding man in his fifties. Soviel wasn't sure which was rounder, his head or his belly. The sallow-toned skin on top of his head was shiny and spotted with age, but his suit looked like it had been cut, sewn and pressed only last night, the black waistcoat perfectly matte beneath the high shine of his silver buttons. This was the tailor, presumably.

"Hello, Your Grace," he bowed. "I see the latest addition to your entourage has arrived."

"She *has*, and look how pretty," Samia said, standing.

Not to be rude, Soviel stood as well.

"Allow me to present Lady Soviel Larksen of Njorske."

"Pleasure to make your acquaintance, sir," Soviel offered a shallow curtsy.

"The pleasure is all mine, Milady," he bowed, taking her hand and pressing a kiss to its back. "Theodilliam Marckrum, official clothier of His and Her Grace Hadringston of Bramblehall. At your service, Lady." He removed a pair of wire-rimmed spectacles from his breast pocket, and unfolded them before sliding them up the bridge of his nose. "Now, let's see about some new frocks for you, shall we?"

After having all of her measurements taken for every garment, shoe, and accessory possible, Soviel dressed once more with the help of Maerie, and walked arm in arm with Samia around the entire east wing of the manor. Behind them, Hamesh the footman trailed, in case they needed anything at all.

Even Everness had not supplied its royals with such excessive luxury. In the short time she'd been there, Ferrin had all but roamed the place completely unattended, dressing herself most days. Though, perhaps she wasn't the best comparison. The king and Rhi may have been accustomed to this level of ease. Soviel wasn't sure she minded it so much.

"And here is the way to the gardens. In the fall we have the most *wonderful* pears. Oh, and then the cherry trees bloom in the spring; that'll be soon, and it's just stunning," she rambled on. "In the mornings I prefer to walk through here with my ladies and watch the soldiers drill on the court field."

"Soldiers?" Soviel's ears perked up. Watching soldiers drill might give way to useful information.

"Oh, some are quite good-looking," Samia sighed. "Though I can't say I care much for those damned new uniforms the governor's issued. Too many obnoxious colors. But at least there're fresh faced Bourjon troops arriving at the end of the month."

"How many? Won't it become crowded?"

"We've an entire guest house just a ways down on our estate," Samia flipped her hand dismissively. "It can house a hundred men if we tighten up the chambers. The officers will have rooms in the west wing, since my husband's parents and their servants have left."

"Left to where?"

"Oh, they died," Samia chirped.

"Oh dear, I'm sorry to hear that," Soviel feigned sympathy.

"Don't be too sorry. The old bag had it coming, and he was a stinker too. Always going on about unreliability of foreign wives. Meanwhile my father's money all but financed the vineyard he insisted on planting."

"What happened to them?"

"Old age, I suppose. Or perhaps they nagged each other to death. Oh, blackberries! Let's eat some."

Soviel could have pulled a muscle in her neck from Samia's lightning-fast changes of subject.

"Are they safe?" she asked, peering over Samia's shoulder at the thicket.

"I eat them every spring!"

Perhaps it's damaged your brain, Soviel thought to herself.

They continued their stroll along the garden path, and Soviel made note of all the possible ways she could signal Ash. She could light a candle in her own window, but how difficult would it be to see from the sea? How would Ash be able to approach close enough without losing cover? There was much to put in order before she could start flowing information back to camp; the instructions she'd have to leave at a tavern in town, heavily coded, for Eiran to fetch. Then, the real work would begin.

The wooded area at the edge of the property was visible from the gardens, and one might take a walk in its direction to clear their head early one morning. That was where she'd already decided the drop-spot would be. If all went according to plan, Soviel would be able to glean information, scribe it into a code, hide it within her dress and then secure it in the drop-spot. Every other week, Ash or Eiran would collect.

The code used would disguise her messages on military, economic and political topics as gossip and love notes. Easy to dismiss, and easy to explain with feigned embarrassment if she was caught hiding a slip of paper down the front of her stays.

"This is where we have all of our festivals and garden parties. Just the other week we had the most stunning spring festival. We had pyres built high with flames of glorious blue and yellow and orange leaping about, our games master put a special sort of salt in them. Oh and then everyone smoked the most fragrant *arimopo*, and finally the finest *popava* was brought out."

Soviel frowned slightly. She had no intention of consuming *popava* after all that had happened over the spring at Everness. From what she knew, the toxic strain had not been limited to Everness. How were people so willing to keep taking the stuff after what had happened?

"Our cooks roasted pheasant and hens, oh and there was a pig slaughtering, a little like the winterly offering in Njorske. Although there was no pure white snow to spill the blood on, so the effect was rather dismal," Samia scrunched her nose.

"The estate is so large, I fear I may get lost on it," Soviel noted.

"You'll learn your way around in no time, especially when you're with the rest of the ladies. Now, let me tell you what you will be required for." Samia launched into her next subject. "You will be dressed by eight in the morning, and come to attend to me at half past eight. I may not be ready to dress then, but I will ask you to fetch a chambermaid, pick an outfit," she paused, "or fetch me something if I'm feeling ill from too much wine. That does seem to be happening more and more as I've gotten older," she added. "Once I am up and awake, you and the other ladies will help to dress me, apply my cosmetics and arrange my hair. You will be expected to learn my dress habits and fashion tastes, and to follow them. You will help me to ready for bed as well, and will accompany me in my entourage around the estate during the day."

"I can manage that," Soviel nodded and smiled.

"And in return, you are a part of my court, my circle. You have free rein of whatever resources you may need while living here, and I will make good introductions for you."

"It is more than I could ever ask for," Soviel curtsied.

"Oh, and I also ask that you only use my given name in familiar settings, and in any formal settings, balls, feasts, knightings, gatherings, you address me as Your Grace."

"Yes, of course."

"Shall we go and prepare for dinner? One of my ladies should have a dress close enough in size to lend you… yes, Tavara is about your height. I can't say her dresses will suit you in color, but it will do for now."

Soviel stifled a grimace as she bit into the third scallop on her plate. If anyone thought her actions at dinner suspicious she could surely blame it on her distaste for the chewy, leathery texture of the overcooked shellfish.

Along the table was a varied collection of men and women from all over the world, dressed in different sorts of clothing marking their various origins. Dishes from Veira and cutlery crafted in Bourjony, glassware from Efel and a tablecloth embroidered in Akhatan patterns were spread upon the table. It was clear that Samia liked to collect things from across the globe. The Duke and Duchess sat at either end of the long feasting table.

Samia had dressed in her third ensemble of the day, a powder-blue and lilac saque-back gown with little deer playing in a meadow embroidered on the bodice and skirts.

The duke, whom Soviel was still sizing up, sat stoic and handsome across the table of trinkets from his wife. He was well-built, with square shoulders and defined cheekbones. A prominent brow that gave him an air of constant sternness canopied his light gray eyes and Aquiline nose. His simple and luxurious frock coat was a shade of dark gray silk with a velvet lining and silver buttons that brought out his eyes. Beneath his powdered wig, she was sure she'd find dark brown curls to match the strong dark eyebrows hewn in his forehead.

Sat at the corner nearest to Samia, Soviel was too far to make conversation with the target of her intelligence interests. But it could wait. She could work this angle.

She shifted uncomfortably in the gown, a bright vermillion number that truly made her look pale as a ghost, and shifted her attention away from the duke and back to Samia, who was prattling on about the latest fashions coming out of Larais.

"Now that Bourjony is officially our ally, I'd like to start wearing more of their clothing," she said, pausing to take a sip of white wine from her crystal glass. "Lucelle, you came from Larais, tell me of their fashions."

"They're ever-changing, adapting with each season," said Lucelle, bedecked in a coral-colored gown with netted, sheer sleeves and lace flowers at its neckline. Her light beige skin was rosy and cool-toned beneath a pile of darkest brown hair. Her cheeks were full, and echoed her soft, voluptuous curves. A little black heart had been drawn in the corner of her eye - a beauty mark. "One year, wide skirts may be all the rage, only for the following season to favor a more streamlined silhouette."

Samia sat back in her chair, dazed, as if this were life-altering news. "Huh."

"Though, it is usually easy enough to have gowns altered to fit the new style each season," Lucelle amended. "I believe this year, metallic shades and two-toned fabrics are favored over prints and pastels."

"I see, I see," Samia said with all seriousness.

Soviel looked back to the duke, passing her eyes over him in a cursory glance as she reached for the butter plate. He seemed vaguely displeased with this entire affair, a man of few words, but many thoughts.

In fact, he hadn't said much throughout the entire dinner. Short of his formal greetings, he'd been near silent, repeatedly checking the clock over the mantle. He had somewhere to be.

But where? Where did the man of the house conduct his meetings, the ones he didn't want people listening in on? Who did he meet with, and what did they discuss?

Her primary goal for Helene was sussing out attacks before they could happen, finding ammunition storage, and bases of operations—particularly naval ones.

Her *own* primary goal was finding out more about Hadringston's involvement in the prison, the laboratory, and the *popava* strains, and how they all connected. Based on the missive she and Rhi had intercepted, the duke was high up on the chain of command, if not its ringleader. He was responsible for the horrors wrought in the village this spring, and for the horrors that had occurred in the laboratory within that prison. Though she hadn't seen it, Ash's descriptions and nightmares painted a chilling enough picture for Soviel.

She turned her attention back to the main course in front of her. Buttery white fish over lemon-rice, surrounded by a menagerie of asparagus, and *more* scallops.

The wine in her glass was paired perfectly with the meal, no doubt the Hadringstons had a specialist on duty at all times to attend to such luxuries. She'd limited herself to only one glass per night, as she needed to keep her wits about her. She'd been sipping and swirling it slowly.

Dessert was brought in and the duke curtly but politely excused himself before it was done, disappearing out the main entrance, his elegant coat swishing behind him. The ladies returned to talking amongst themselves as servants cleared away the duke's things.

Soviel made note of the time, just a quarter past eight.

Once she'd attended to her duties of dressing Samia for bed, gossiping about the day and dousing the lights in the duchess's room, Soviel wasted no time in taking to the manor for a stroll, unaccompanied.

She set her sights on the direction she'd seen His Grace stalk off to when he excused himself during dessert. The eastern portion of the square-shaped manor was off to the side of the in-gardens, the open, rectangular space that served to allow natural light into the more central rooms of the large building. It was quicker and more permissible to cut through the in-gardens, as if she were merely enjoying the summer evening, and then wander into the east wing before retiring to bed. Should anyone question her presence, she could easily play it off as being lost, given how recently she'd arrived.

She wound her way from the feasting hall through the library, to the tea parlor, then the greenhouse, and finally out into the atmospheric in-garden. The evening air was just beginning to cool off, and she could smell the sea on the breeze, wafting in from the west. The sky overhead was lit with stars, easy to see in the dim lighting of the garden. An alabaster fountain burbled cheerily at the center of the gravel pathway, and the manicured grass bordered stunning florals that were in full bloom. The entire place was reaching out for her, buzzing in a way that only she could feel—it wasn't something to be seen or heard or smelled, but rather a sixth sense, one only Soviel could understand, and had a great deal of trouble explaining to others. It was the buzz of life and growth and energy, tingling in her fingers and running up her spine in a comforting, familiar way. It exhilarated her. It made her awake.

The in-gardens, while much smaller than the orchards and botanical paths surrounding the estate, were no small courtyard. They stretched for perhaps forty yards in each direction, and she was halfway across when she realized she was not alone.

On the other side of a perfectly-pruned rhododendron bush, a thin column of smoke rose. It smelled earthy, *arimopo*.

She took a split second to weigh her options, and settled for waiting to see what she might overhear. It might only be a groundskeeper or a gardener seeing to the plants. Risking a few steps forward through the quiet grass, she strained to hear the conversation.

"This is going to become a massive headache if we don't get ahead of it now," a woman said. She didn't recognize the voice, but continued listening.

"I see your point, but I'm a little preoccupied with our other ventures in the south. Pushing this land buy-out through with speed is a far better use of our resources than chasing down a legend." It was Hadringston.

"If you could acquire this thing *before* the navy gets their hands on it, you would be untouchable. The power you'd hold —"

"I don't make it a habit to seek out fairy-stories, Roxen," he cut back disdainfully. "The acquisition of these *popava* fields will put us *years* ahead of where we were in the research. Bourjony will have no choice but to give us free reign."

"I'm not asking for much," Roxen sighed. "Only enough for a ship or two. I will *personally* see this through. Let us get ahead of them. We have been given a boon in learning this information so early. Take advantage of it, for gods' sake, Your Grace."

Hadringston was quiet for a moment. "And if it isn't real? If it's some charlatan's story meant to trick us out of coin?"

"According to my contact in Larais, they've managed to get eyes on the first half. Some rogue captain out of Tunis has apparently located and hidden it. The second half is still in the wind somewhere."

"And the first half? Where is it now?"

Roxen sighed. "He eluded all who gave chase. No one is sure where, but he stowed it somewhere between Karlgiard and Lindbarrow. It looked like he might have been heading for Port Galan."

Hadringston huffed. "Best it not fall into Galan's waiting hands."

"Precisely. And it won't be long before they send someone out looking for the second half."

"What is this thing called again?" Hadringston asked, his tone taking on an exasperated edge.

"The cetamaris, Your Grace. Named for the sea monster it is said to invoke," Roxen clarified.

"Very well. You may hire two ships. Find passage to Bourjony and head south to the coast, ask for Rienvald at the harbormaster's office in Frise. I'll draw up papers for you; head out in the morning."

"Yes, Your Grace."

"Oh, and Roxen," he said.

"Yes, Your Grace?"

"My sister-by-law is governor on Corsovena still. See that we loop her in early on this matter? I don't want the Efelians getting to her resources before we do."

"I wasn't aware of this."

"Distant relation. My youngest brother married her sister."

"Very well, sir."

Soviel held her breath and ducked around the rhododendron, nearly smacking her face into the branch of an artfully trimmed juniper before hiding behind its wide trunk.

She heard a ruffle of skirts and watched as Roxen passed, retreating from the gardens back into the house, her dark-gold hair tied up sensibly, and a dark leather folio tucked beneath one arm. She looked about forty, and her no-nonsense mannerisms reminded Soviel painfully of Madame Leone.

Running over in her mind everything that had been said, Soviel waited in the shadow of the juniper tree until she was sure the garden was empty. Finally, she emerged from her hiding place and made haste to her room, where she scribed down everything she'd heard, doing her best to keep the details accurate as she translated it into the code.

CHAPTER NINETEEN

Samia was sitting upright in bed when the ladies shuffled in a few mornings later. Her light brown hair was tousling out of a loose braid, and a cup of steaming tea already warmed her hands.

"Good morning, Samia," Soviel said lightly, adjusting the curtains.

"Ah, Soviel, the new gown is looking lovely! How does it fit?"

"Excellently, thank you," she said with a smile, smoothing a hand over the pale blue silk.

"I had dear Theo pull designs from an older Njorski style, but we brought it up to modern fashion standards. I had him add some embellishment for your Veiran heritage as well," she gestured to the designs at the wrists, hem, and neckline that were some distant cousin of the patterning she'd seen on one of her mother's dresses. Samia may have lacked perspective, but she could be thoughtful and generous.

"It's lovely," Soviel cooed. "The fabric is perfect, and so expertly finished."

"The color suits you," said Erina, one of the other ladies.

"And you're getting acquainted with my other lovely ladies?" Samia asked between sips of tea.

"Yes, we've been getting to know one another," Soviel said.

There were four other ladies in Samia's entourage, each dressed in what seemed to be some sort of contrived theme of their home country. There was Tavara, whose bright dress Soviel had borrowed her first evening here. Tavara was meant to play the desert maiden, dressed in lightweight fabrics that floated on a phantom breeze, the rich, saturated colors complemented by her bronze skin and dark glossy hair. She wore gold earrings and matching bracelets. Next was the Bourjon socialite, Lucelle, in her fashionable sacque-back gown. The little lilac-hued cape flowed into wide skirts, her raven hair was done up high in the latest of fashions, and her lips and cheeks were rouged with a shade of vibrant berry. She wore a strand of pearls at the lace neck of her gown. After Lucelle was Jorde, the Dromatan scholar, her deep brown skin shining in the mid-morning sunlight. She wore patterned dresses in a fashion similar to Tavara's, though they were more practical and simple in silhouette. Her hair was cropped short to reveal the rows of gold hoops in each ear. Then there was Erina, the Kalassan Nomad, Soviel supposed. Erina wore a mix of indigo and violet robes, wrapped and cinched at the waist. Her wild brown ringlets could be swept under a hood that completed the mystical image Samia had no doubt curated.

Truthfully, Soviel was starting to think she'd become part of some strange, living dollhouse of cliches collected from across the land.

"And how will we be spending our day today?" Tavara asked, pulling open the armoire.

"I think we will take tea and breakfast in the gardens, perhaps watch the soldiers do their little drills on the lawn," Samia said, tapping her lips with a finger as if she was considering how best to spend her time. "Then stroll the orchards for the afternoon."

"The duke has also asked that we remind you of the upcoming trip to Everness for the ball in honor of the capturing of the isle," Erina said.

"Everness, that's the rainy city, yes?"

"Extremely rainy," Soviel confirmed with a smirk she didn't need to fabricate.

A return to Everness. She bristled at the idea.

"Hmf," Samia pouted. "Well, we'll all need new party dresses for the ball. When do we leave?"

"A week from today."

"Lovely," Samia said, rolling her eyes with exasperation. "Well, time to dress for the day. Lucelle, send word to Theo that each of us will need a gown for the ball."

"Right away," Lucelle bobbed her head and exited the room.

"Now, what shall I wear? I'm feeling quite washed out." Samia held up her little silver-gilt hand mirror and turned her face side to side.

"Perhaps the ivory and gold gown?" Tavara suggested, throwing open the sizable armoire.

"Hmmmm," Samia smacked her lips. "I've not worn that one yet."

"It would suit you," Jorde chimed in, tilting her head as she looked at the dress. "And you can add that necklace His Grace gifted you last month."

"Yes, and perhaps it would make him less grumpy to see me wear it," Samia pondered. "Soviel, what do you think?"

"I think it's lovely. Though, perhaps you should hitch up the hem so it doesn't drag through the garden mud."

"Very well, my countrywoman," Samia said, hopping out of bed. She shrugged off her shift without a care and threw it on the ground.

"Your silk shift," Tavara said, handing Samia the luxurious garment.

"And which stays would you like to wear today?"

"The pale green set," she replied.

Breakfast in the garden consisted of a circus of cakes, crumpets, crostinis, pastries, puffs, pies, fresh fruits, and frosted slices of meats. Far more than the six of them could manage to eat in a day.

Samia sipped her cup of fine coffee. The sun was high in the sky as it crept toward mid-day, and the garden was bursting with summer blossoms all around them. It was a more luxurious breakfast than Soviel had ever seen in her life, and yet it was merely a casual morning for Samia and the others.

When they were finished, more than half the food untouched, the servants cleared it away without a word.

"So, we're to travel to Everness?" Soviel asked carefully.

"Yes, you'll be able to see your old home, though under the new rule, of course," Samia chirped. "My husband is good friends with the new governor."

"I wonder if I'll find the castle much changed," Soviel mused. "When I left, I had no idea it would be for the last time. I still feel I don't understand what truly happened there."

"The allied forces seized the capital, the rebels fled, the opposition was driven out, Loyalists now occupy the capital, and most cities, save Avaree and Galan," Jorde answered flatly.

"And what of the old king?" Samia asked.

"King Henrik? I heard he was executed."

Soviel had seen evidence of this. "Oh. He and the queen weren't a part of the shift?" she asked blandly.

"No, while Henrik had views that aligned closely with our new leaders, he was deemed too volatile. And unwilling to give up power." Jorde picked her nails, not deigning to look up at Soviel.

More like he was manipulated into causing the unrest until he was no longer useful and they did away with him, Soviel thought bitterly. She knew full well Nerena had been pulling his strings, going as far as sedating him into complacency, or using his angry outbursts to further alienate his people. Her technique as an insurgent was brutal, but effective. She had to wonder where Nerena was now. Was she on to a new task of manipulation, worming her way into the free cities? Had she been moved to the continent to sew new unrest there?

"Jorde is very wise on these matters. I consider her to be my political advisor," Samia explained, laying a hand on Jorde's shoulder.

"You seem very knowledgable in the politics of it all," Soviel said, taking a long sip of her coffee.

"I spent many years apprenticing under my uncle; he was a vizier to one of Dromata's Lord Governors."

"We should begin packing today. Do you know where we'll be spending the night on the journey?" Erina asked.

"At the Lofrell estate," Samia answered.

"Oh, *gods*, that reminds me," Lucelle perked up. "You won't believe what I've heard about Amery, the middle daughter of the Lofrells."

"What? Is she the blonde one?" Tavara narrowed her eyes.

"Yes, now listen to this," Lucelle shifted in her seat, facing inwards to the circle of ladies. "Amery is sixteen and unwed, and her parents are distant relations to the former royalty of this isle. Old Henrik's second cousin and his wife or something. Her family has no idea yet, based on what I saw the other week, but the poor thing is ten pounds heavier, and was green in the face all morning long, last I visited."

"And you suppose she's with child?" Samia asked, eager for the gossip as she wafted her face with a delicate lace fan. "Who's the father?"

"Well, that's the rub, isn't it?" Lucelle said, popping a dark cherry into her mouth. "She is unwed, unbetrothed, and the nearest town to the Lofrell estate is a few miles. Not nearly close enough for that sort of affair." She lifted a shoulder. "So that leaves a servant, of whom there are many, or even better: a soldier stationed on the property."

"And where exactly is it the Lofrells reside?" Soviel ventured casually.

"East of here, right in the center of the isle. They own miles of farm land surrounding the estate," Lucelle explained.

Soviel tucked that convenient bit of information away for later.

"Not to mention, they house a sizable number of soldiers there. Officers, too, from good, noble families," Tavara chimed in.

"It's true, a girl looking to marry well would certainly find adequate quarry there," Erina said, her tone disinterested as she examined her short nails.

"Well, that's good to know," Soviel said with a mischievous smile. "And the soldiers, are they Barrian, or Bourjon?"

"Both, it's a short ride from Southport, and there're shiploads of soldiers arriving every day since the change in leadership."

"Very interesting," Soviel said, the coy smile still on her lips.

An estate full of Bourjon soldiers, a farm providing the joint army with food, a visit to her old home.

There was work to do.

CHAPTER TWENTY

The waves beat the rocks in lazy thuds, frothing between the cracks of the jetty as Ferrin stared out at the sea. She felt Soviel's absence, perhaps more keenly than she'd expected to, and with Ash busy on missions running messages all over the coast, she found herself with idle time on her hands.

And that never boded well.

She'd spent the morning exploring in the cliffs, not finding much of interest other than the gaping hole in the rocks where the pit-creature had been. Then she'd gone over to the barracks, hoping someone might have something for her to do, but had no luck. Rhi had been in a mood unlike she'd ever seen him, so she'd wound up venturing out to the shore.

At least tonight there would be a celebration of summer. Likely just a small gathering on the green outside of the manor, but something to do nonetheless. Despite the sour events of the spring, she found herself missing her life back in the capital. At least then she'd had stable duties with Alick. She'd had purpose with the rebels.

Now, it seemed she had only one purpose. One for life. And she wasn't sure how much longer she could put it off, or what could even constitute being ready for it. She sighed heavily and rubbed at her face with her hands. She would go mad with this waiting, this idleness.

With a groan, she pushed off the jetty and stalked back up to town. With any luck, the order she'd put her last coin towards would be ready today.

The dress shop was modest, run by a small family who lived in a flat above the storefront. Isla, the matriarch of the family, had agreed to make Ferrin a new dress and a set of stays that wasn't tattered and that wouldn't stab her in the ribs. Because it was such a small shop—only one full-time tailor—the project took longer than it might have in Everness or Larais, where large, well-staffed cloth-houses abounded.

She rounded the corner onto the main street of Port Galan, and noticed Lukas on the other side of the street, right at the same time he noticed her.

He waved and jogged across the street, a few paper-wrapped parcels under his arms.

"I see you're back to your usual ways," she nodded at the packages. "Does Port Galan have its very own underground market as well?"

"Nothing quite like in Everness, I'm afraid." A shadow flickered across his face. "But yes, I have found somewhere to ply my finest trade skills."

"Anything interesting?" she asked as he fell into step beside her.

"For you? Certainly not." He snatched away the parcel she had been poking at. "Where are you headed?"

"To the dress-maker's shop to see if my order is ready."

"Ah, a dress? I almost forgot you used to wear such things," he teased, casting his gaze over her dirty breeches and raggedy shirt.

"Well, I have to look at least a little presentable for this evening's festivities," she countered.

"Ah yes, this evening's festivities… When shall I fetch you?"

"*Fetch me*? Am I a parcel of goods?" She put a hand on her hip, falling back into the banter that had always been their easiest rhythm. "We reside in adjoining rooms. Just knock when you're ready to go."

His answering look made her heart race.

"So, will Rhi be heading over with us, or is a certain red-haired soldier taking precedence?" she asked.

"He told me he'll be going with us. Though, after that, I can't say what he'll do. And Ash should make it back in time for the bonfires as well."

Ferrin's stomach flipped. She was still facing the consequences of her insubordination to Helene's orders a few weeks ago. She'd been shut out of meetings, barred from missions, and perhaps the worst, forbidden from accompanying Ash on her weekly runs down the coast on *The Brisk* to fetch Soviel's correspondence.

"Good," she nodded as they approached the dress-shop. "Well, here it is."

"I'll wait out here," Lukas said, eyeing the packages he was holding.

"Thanks," she said, wondering what he could possibly be carrying around in there.

The evening was clear and bright in the wake of the recent storms, and the wind had at last died down. In the cloudless sky, the moon hung half-ripe and bright as a silver coin. The gauzy curtains shifted at the open window in the insubstantial breeze, and Ferrin examined her reflection in the mirror.

The new set of stays fit like a dream compared to the old ones she'd scavenged. They even laced up the front, so she could put them on and take them off on her own without performing any acrobatics. Her new dress was a far cry from the fine luxury back in Everness, but nonetheless made her look fresh, clean and formal, if not extravagant. The cerulean linen was supple and finely stitched, and the spring-green bindings along the edge were accented with a hint of cream-colored lace. A borrowed necklace of silver and pearl gleamed at her throat.

She'd left her hair unbound, the brown-black mess of it curling in the heat as it dried. Her mother's ring glinted on her finger, now a bitter reminder of every secret that had been kept from her.

She self-consciously smoothed her hands over the fabric once more. The door swung open and Ash stalked in, muttering a brief greeting and a "*nice dress*," before flinging herself into the bathing room. She emerged five minuted later, scrubbed down with her short hair slicked back from the bathwater.

"Gods. *What* am I to wear to this thing?"

"I had something made for you," Ferrin said shyly, gesturing to the second parcel on the bed.

"You did?" Ash asked, perking up.

"I wasn't sure it would be ready on time, so I didn't say anything."

"Oh, Ferrin," Ash said, holding up the fine waistcoat of darkest teal. It was cut a little differently than a man's waistcoat, fit to accentuate her figure. There was a cream colored shirt that went beneath it, styled with gussets and a little rose-gold button at each wrist, and a matching coat of teal. "This is perfect."

"I hope it fits—I had to guess at your measurements."

There was a knock at the door and Ash retreated into the wash room to change.

Ferrin opened the door to find Lukas, holding a clear bottle of brown liquor in one hand.

His eyes widened nearly imperceptibly as he took her in, from her unbound hair to her roughed-up shoes that she couldn't quite hide beneath the dress.

"Hi," he breathed.

She looked him up and down and noted that he'd gone to the trouble of polishing his boots for the occasion. His sun-gilded hair was tugged back, and he'd found a fresh shirt and coat somewhere, the dark blue fabric much newer-looking than his typical get-up. He'd even shaved.

A blush rose to her cheeks when she looked up and found him grinning.

"Well, you certainly clean up nice," she said, a little more breathlessly than planned. "What's that?" She gestured at the unlabeled bottle.

"Ah," he glanced down at it before handing it to her. "Rhi mentioned it was a favorite."

"Is this," she began, pausing to squint at the amber liquid, "Meroyan Rum?" she asked, eyes widening as she looked from the bottle back to him.

He nodded with a little grin, his green eyes shining.

"How ever did you manage to track this down?" she asked, twining her free hand through his.

"I made a few new connections in town," he shrugged. "Old habits and all."

"I haven't had this since… a long time," she said quietly. "Thank you." Her gaze caught on his mouth, so near her own.

"This is the finest thing I've ever worn, I think," Ash said, emerging from the wash room.

"You look sharp," Lukas complimented, without stepping away from Ferrin.

"Thanks," she said, smoothing her palms over the new fabric.

"Oh, good! It all fits." Ferrin turned to survey Ash's ensemble as Ash spun around for her.

"Where's Rhi?" Ash asked.

"Likely still fussing about his appearance." Ferrin jerked a thumb at the adjoining door.

"I am not!" came Rhi's muffled voice.

"It's only a little bonfire, Rhiach!" Ferrin called back to him.

At last, he emerged from the other room in his fading rust-and-gold waistcoat done up over a clean white shirt, absent his usual cravat. He'd left a few buttons of the waistcoat undone near the top, and rolled up his shirtsleeves to ward off the heat, revealing the hint of a pleasant tan he'd gotten in the last few weeks.

"Oh, you look so handsome!" Ferrin clutched her hands in front of her chin. In the months since his bout of *popava* poisoning, his health had made a visible comeback. His cheeks were no longer hollow, his eyes not shadowed and sunken. He had a bit of a glow about him, despite the nervous energy present in his drumming fingers. Being in Port Galan, she'd thought, was good for him. Away from the court they'd grown up in, no longer under the thumb of their controlling father and their duplicitous stepmother.

"I look like an urchin," he said.

"Nonsense."

"Well, shall we have a little toast, before we head down to the field?" Lukas held up the bottle of Meroyan Rum.

"I'll find some glasses," Ash said.

"I'll help," Rhi nodded. "Nice coat, by the way. The color suits you."

"Thanks, your sister commissioned it for me."

"Ferr!" Rhi turned around, momentarily incensed. "You didn't think to have anything made for me?"

"Your diplomatic attire is no less formal than what we're all wearing! Stop your fretting."

Rhi grumbled a series of *hmphs* and pointed out that she was wearing a fully new dress. Ferrin rolled her eyes with exaggerated annoyance.

He's nervous, Lukas mouthed to her when he caught her eye.

I can tell, she widened her eyes for emphasis.

"Alright," Lukas poured them each a knuckle of the amber liquid in the wildly mismatched cups Ash had scrounged up.

"To… not dying at the hands of Bourjony's navy," Ash said, holding up her glass.

"To Soviel's mission and her eventual —hopefully soon— safe return," Ferrin added, meeting Ash's eye with a small nod.

The four of them clinked their glasses and tipped back the sweet rum.

Ferrin was hit with a barrage of pleasant memories. Warm sun, crisp waves on white beaches, palm fronds swaying in a gentle breeze.

"Well, what do you say, former frequenters of Meroya, how does it taste?"

"It's delicious, just as I remembered," Ash said, holding out her glass for a second shot.

"It is, sweet but with a pleasant burn," Ferrin agreed. "That's because the sugar is all stolen."

"What?" Rhi frowned.

"Yeah, and the amber color is because it's got the blood of sugar field owners in it."

Rhi tilted his head, eyes narrowed as he tried to decide if she was serious or not, while Ferrin tamped down on her laughter.

"It's true, you can ask anyone," Ash said, completely straight-faced.

Lukas shook his head and grabbed Rhi's shoulder. "Don't listen to Ash, she's got no idea what she's talking about."

"That is *not* true!" Ash whirled on him in mock indignation. "You've never even been there."

"She's right," Ferrin drawled to Rhi. "In fact, they mixed in some of the chemical they use to take barnacles off of anchors to give it an extra kick. You'll be feeling that right about now."

"You're horrible," he coughed.

She broke into a grin and looped her arm through his. "Come on then, let's go sweat beside some bonfires, eh?"

Rhi had been anxious and twitchy all day. He'd seen Lachlan only sparingly since their altercation, and it had been strictly-business and one word answers. After their harrowing experience with the river-woman, and then their fight by the life-saving fire they'd stolen, they'd journeyed on in near complete silence. It had been days of awkward and stilted exchanges since then.

He regretted the way he'd said what he'd said.

He hoped Lachlan would still come tonight, would still want to work together to find a way to shut down the laboratory in the prison.

The group walked out of the manor, Ash and Ferrin twittering animatedly about some inside joke relating to the last time they'd drunk Meroyan rum. Sometimes Rhi forgot about Ferrin's other life, the one she'd built and lived a world away as a completely different person. Ash was a reminder of that life, of that part of her he didn't know.

Ash was also a reminder that Ferrin couldn't have been *that* different in her years on the seas, based on the way they acted together.

It was a comforting thought.

"How're you faring?" Lukas asked him.

"Fine," Rhi nodded, not sounding at all convincing.

"Well, if you need anything… you know where to find me."

Rhi muttered a thanks before breaking off from the group toward the enormous silver bowl of spiced fruit-wine being stirred and served by the second pyre. He was still rattled from the near disaster of the *popava* he'd bought off the woman in the manor's lower levels. She'd caught his eye a few times after their initial transaction, always raising an expectant eyebrow in his direction. He'd shaken his head the first time and stalked away. The following three times, he'd ignored her.

He sniffed at the chilled cup of wine in his hand. It was heavily spiced, and sweetened with a load of dissolved brown sugar. He'd really only picked up a cup so he would have something to do with his hands, rather than to enjoy drinking it.

"Thanks," he said to the serving woman before ambling away aimlessly.

He stood by the edge of the clearing, taking in the growing crowd. When the torch-bearer came out onto the field, flames leaping red and gold from the torch, the crowd went silent. She approached the first pyre, the diaphanous white of her robe fluttering on the summer breeze around her bare ankles. The fire whooshed to life, glinting off the wreath of gilded ferns and flora crowning her black hair. The crowd whooped with glee.

It was at that moment that Rhi felt a presence beside him. The words of the priestess were drowned out as he glanced to his left and saw Lachlan had materialized there.

"Wasn't sure you'd be out here this early."

Rhi froze for a second before shoving away his nerves and, without turning to face Lachlan, said in a casual, confident tone, "I wasn't sure you'd come at all."

They stood with their heads angled toward each other, neither fully committed to turning and facing the other as the second pyre roared to life. The moment seemed to stretch on for a century. Red-gold light lapped at the side of Lachlan's face closest to the fire, shading him in stark relief, and capturing the sharp delicacy of his features. The arch of his brow, the sharp cut of his cheekbone, the amber spray of freckles across the bridge of his nose and cheeks.

"I wanted to tell you," Lachlan cleared his throat. Was he *blushing*? "That I'm sorry for insinuating that you always get your way, and that you're a spoiled brat."

"Thanks, although I'm not sure you ever said the 'spoiled brat' part," Rhi quipped.

"It was implied."

"Right," Rhi nodded slowly.

"I shouldn't have picked a fight with you over all of it," said Lachlan.

Rhi took a swig of the too-sweet wine. "I'm sorry, too," he said. "I was harsh, I shouldn't have called you a—"

"*A childish beast*?" Lachlan supplied.

"Yes, that," Rhi cringed.

Lachlan nodded. "It was fair, given the circumstances. I was angry about Hassan, and fucking terrified out of my wits by that river-woman." He shivered. "I was rash."

"You? Rash?"

Lachlan smirked. "I should not have goaded you into a fight." He added in a low mumble, "not after you saved my life."

"I'm sorry, I didn't quite catch that last part?" Rhi cupped his ear, leaning in to hear better.

Lachlan sighed and squared his shoulders. "You got us out of that mess. The boat, the rapids, all of it. Thank you," Lachlan said quickly.

Rhi chuckled, turned to the fire, sipped his wine, and then turned back to Lachlan and held his gaze for a long moment. Something intense flickered there, something that wasn't quite visible by firelight.

"So, did anything come of those pages we found?" he asked.

Lachlan shoved his hands into his jacket pockets. "Yes," he said with a nod.

"Oh?"

"There is *definitely* a correlation between the theories and the experiments they were running in Danvery." He extended his hand for Rhi's cup of wine. When Rhi passed it to him, their fingers brushed. Lachlan took a long gulp. "That is fantastic. What is it?"

"It's sugar-water with some wine dribbled in."

"Delicious," Lachlan marveled, handing the cup back. "Anyway, as I was saying. Gerreway's theories seem to primarily propose that magic is borne of necessity. Whether that be in a broad, 'we live in the desert and water is precious, so we have water-magic' way, or a much more specific way. I think the specificity is the major component of what they're testing."

"What do you mean?" Rhi asked, taking his cup back. He took a sip and absently thought of his own lips meeting the place where Lachlan's had just been.

"The druggings. You said the capital had an epidemic of people being dosed with bad *popava* this spring, yes?"

"Yes," Rhi nodded.

"Then, dozens of people get carted off to the prison in the middle of all of that, some get fed to the pit, others wind up in the lab. The bad *pop*," he said, "is the key. It sort of... unlocks any magical energy that might have been sleeping inside those affected."

Rhi froze.

"It's just a working theory, of course. I could be wrong, and I'm no magic expert. I even had to consult with—"

"I was dosed."

"You—what?" Lachlan stopped his summation to look at Rhi.

"Just before everything went down at the prison. My stepmother. She was a spy working for Bourjony. She dosed me with the bad strain of *popava* after I'd been clean off it for a month."

Lachlan went very quiet.

Desperate to fill the silence, Rhi added, "I hallucinated vividly for about an hour. It kicked in fast. Then I passed out on the floor of my sister's room and Soviel, she was Ferrin's lady-in-waiting at the time, if you didn't know, found me and doused me with cold water until I came to."

"What did you see?" Lachlan asked slowly.

Rhi shook his head, remembering far too vividly the things he'd seen and heard. Every horrible thing he'd ever thought about himself, every fear he'd ever projected onto those around him, all thrown back in his face with pinpoint accuracy. "First, a lot of bizarre visions. People turning corpselike, walls bleeding, the usual stuff of nightmares. Then it… changed."

"Changed how?"

He shook his head again, suddenly at a loss for words. "Things I prefer not to discuss."

"Was it," Lachlan paused, lips pulled back in distaste at some memory, brow furrowed as he searched for what to say, "deeply personal, specific fears?"

Rhi's entire body went cold.

"They got to you, too," he realized.

Lachlan's answering expression was grim, and he'd gone three shades paler. "No. But others in my unit. I thought they'd gotten some bad liquor," he admitted. "It was torment, watching them terrified of things I couldn't even see."

"Others in Port Galan were dosed? It was around midspring."

Lachlan shook his head. "I was on assignment. Further south."

"None of them ended up in the lab?"

"No." Lachlan snorted. "A small consolation, considering. A scout who got the worst of it slit his wrists before anyone could get to him."

Rhi shuddered, thinking of the terror that so many had experienced as a result of this poison. He remembered the cold voices of everyone he'd ever cared about airing his deepest fears and insecurities while the world decayed around him.

"We need to find out what this means, for those who were dosed. What kind of changes might be expected," Lachlan muttered, turning back to the fire and crossing his arms.

"Well," Rhi said, aiming for a light tone and missing by an inch. "I haven't begun shooting fire out of my eyeballs yet, so I suppose that's a good sign."

Lachlan laughed nervously, eyes flicking back to Rhi. "This is serious."

"Wasn't joking."

"Do you know anyone else?" Lachlan shifted from one foot to the other and back. "Who was dosed, I mean."

Rhi frowned. Everything had happened so quickly after his own experience that he'd never had the chance to ask. A memory surfaced in his mind. Lukas answering his door, pale and wan, smelling of puke. Ferrin passed out on his bed. Neither of them had seemed in good enough spirits to have spent the night doing what he'd initially *assumed* they were doing.

Had Lukas been dosed as well, maybe without realizing it?

"Perhaps," he pondered.

"Well, that's something to start with," Lachlan said, eyeing the fire a moment longer before looking back to Rhi. "We'll have to find out more."

Ferrin could feel the heat of the pyre on her face as she and Ash hopped around the fire, drinks sloshing in their hands while they sang in loud, off-key voices a bawdy drinking song they'd heard long ago and far away.

For a while, she forgot about the mess her life had become. And about the task that was to come. She was just dancing and moving and laughing among good company.

Ash excused herself after an hour or two, claiming exhaustion from her long day, leaving Ferrin and Lukas by the fireside.

Ferrin assessed Lukas, the blaze of the fire turning his bronze skin molten. Silently, she extended her hand, inviting him to dance. He took it, and they began to sway to the low and steady beat of the drum.

"Have you spoken to Rhi yet, about what you learned?"

The weight of the secret her mother had kept from everyone for two decades slammed into her. She hadn't told Lukas what it was yet, but he knew it was something big, something that impacted both her and Rhi.

She shook her head. "I haven't had the chance. Ever since he got back from the archives, he's been so busy or stressed out of his mind. I didn't want to add to it just yet."

"Have you decided when, or *if*, you're going to go back to the Door?" he asked.

She shook her head again, turning her gaze back to the fire.

"What exactly are you supposed to find there? Did she tell you?"

"I don't want to talk about it right now," she said, a little harsher than she intended.

"Sorry." Something flickered across his face that might have been pain.

"It's just—" she sighed with deep exasperation at the entire situation. "—it's all too complicated. Everything is," she broke off, feeling a lump build in her throat. She willed back the burning in her eyes and clenched her jaw.

"I didn't mean to—"

"It's fine," she said quickly, and in a desperate attempt to change the subject, asked, "have you had any word on Ryder yet?"

His face darkened. "No."

"I'm sorry," she said softly. "Maybe Ash can sneak a message to Avaree on one of her runs to see if he's there. Or —"

"I tried that already," he said, shutting down. "He's disappeared."

"Well—" she began.

"There isn't some clever solution," Lukas snapped. "He's gone. Because of something I dragged him into. *We* dragged him into."

His words hit her like a bucket of freezing water. She halted her swaying.

"He's a grown man, Lukas," she said evenly, feeling her temper rise.

He cut his glance away from her to the fire crackling beside them. "It doesn't matter."

She dropped her hands from his shoulders. "Is this just about Ryder, or is there something else you're upset with me about?"

He turned to her. "It's not about you."

"Well, clearly, it's about *something*," she said, feeling her calm slip away. "People make their own decisions. You can't act like every time someone close to you *might* be in danger, it's somehow your fault."

"Just drop it, alright? Don't you have enough to worry about with everything that creature dropped on you?"

"Tell me what this is really about."

"Nothing." His features iced over. Stone and shadow and unyielding rock.

"Fine, then," she said, stepping back, out of his orbit. "I'll see you in the morning." She turned on her heel and stalked away, making it halfway back to the manor before a guard, one of Helene's, came panting after her with a message.

"There is urgent news," he gasped, "down at the barracks. Major wants to speak with you immediately."

She was torn between being pissed that she'd been interrupted in her brooding, and grateful to have a distraction from it.

"What is it?"

"You need to come see it for yourself."

She followed the messenger back down the cliff path to the barracks, which were halfway repaired at this point. Soldiers and messengers were bustling about despite the odd hour. All the torches were burning, casting the encampment in a bright glow.

"What's happening?" she asked the messenger—Grandel, that was his name—as he led her towards Helene's office.

"Please, just hold your questions for the major," he pleaded, clearly displeased with having his sleep interrupted.

"Sorry," she said, trying to relax. "I hope you get to go back to bed after this."

A moment later they arrived at the large tent that served as Helene's office. The burnt panels of wood and canvas had been replaced with new ones.

"Wait here a moment," Grandel said, slipping through the flap.

Ferrin heard some muffled voices before he reemerged.

"In you go," he swept back one of the flaps for her before disappearing back into the night.

Ferrin swallowed, unsure of what she was about to walk into. Perhaps it was some sort of trap, some sort of—

"Good evening, Ferrin, you look well," Helene greeted from her desk. Her long braid was flicked over her shoulder, and as always, she looked clean and put-together in her lilac colored shirt and vest.

"Hi," she said, perplexed as she looked around the room. "What's going on? Did you need me for something?" she asked, almost hopefully.

"Not quite," Helene said, pressing her lips together.

"If this is about what happened in the prison…"

"When you put the entire operation at risk by bribing agents in transfer?" she scoffed. "No. It is not about that. Come with me."

Ferrin winced. "Where are we going?"

"To the brig." Helene stood.

Ferrin backed up one step, then another. "You can't mean to only *now* throw me in chains for what I did. It's been weeks."

Helene gave a hollow laugh. "It would not be worth the time and resources to bother with that. Don't worry."

Somehow, that stung even worse.

"Then what is this?"

"Earlier this morning, a strange ship washed up a few miles down the coast. Wrecked by one of the recent storms. Only one man was aboard, which was strange, considering the ship's size. One of our patrols picked him up for questioning. Protocol, given the recent attacks. Can't be too careful when spies may be afoot."

As she listened, a sense of foreboding crawled over Ferrin, prickling her skin.

"During questioning, he asked several times to speak with someone higher up. When I finally spoke with him, he refused to tell me *anything* until he was able to speak to you."

Ferrin choked. "He asked for me? By name?"

Helene stopped outside the heavy wooden door of the brig, shoulders squared.

"Who is it? Did he give a name?"

"He did not."

Ferrin's anxiety ramped up as Helene unlocked the main door of the building that served as the jail. She ducked in, Ferrin on her heels. Helene pulled one of the lanterns from beside the entrance and held it up.

"Come," she said, gesturing with the lantern.

They made their way to the back of the building where the cells were, and Helene paused to hang the lantern on a hook, using its flame to light a second, which she hung on the opposite hook.

"Well," a sickeningly familiar voice drawled. "It seems our time apart has been kind to you, Gillian. Ferrin. Or should I say, Your Highness?"

She froze as that voice, that face, hit her like a brick wall, her heart galloping into her throat as her stomach clenched in panic.

Zare was back. Zare was *here*.

And he'd come asking for her by name.

Lukas was still in a foul mood. He'd been in a foul mood for most of the week, trying and failing to pull himself out of it.

That mood was still with him when Rhi and the Caelish soldier he'd been spending all his time with—Lachlan— approached and sat adjacent to him on the logs around the bonfire.

"Lukas," Rhi greeted. "Where have Ferrin and Ash run off to?"

"Why should I know?" he snapped.

Lachlan raised his ruddy eyebrows in recoil, and Lukas caught the glance he flicked to Rhi.

"Right, then," Rhi said, rebounding. "We're doing some research into what exactly the end goal of the laboratory in the prison is, and we wanted to ask you something."

"Were you dosed with the hallucinogenic strain of *popava* this spring?" Lachlan launched right in, apparently deciding it not worth the effort to beat around the bush.

Lukas whipped around to look at Lachlan. He wore a blank, casual expression as if he'd just asked him what he'd eaten for lunch.

"Why?"

"Just answer the question."

Lukas took a long drink of the sweet wine. "Yeah. I think so."

Rhi cursed.

"And what exactly did you see?"

Lukas was quiet for a beat, running his fingertip absentmindedly along the lip of his tin cup. "Dead things."

Rhi frowned, as if that wasn't the answer he'd been expecting.

"Why?" Lukas repeated.

"Can you elaborate?" Lachlan asked, holding Lukas's stare without answering his question.

"Prefer not to."

"Please, it's important, Luk," Rhi urged. "The more we know, the more we can do to put an end to it."

"Alright, fine. What did *you* see?" he asked.

Lachlan wordlessly stared down at the fire. Rhi sighed and let his eyes drop shut for a moment.

"I saw…" he began, recalling the terrible memories. Lukas hadn't really expected an answer, but listened as Rhi recounted his experience. "First I saw grotesques—a dead sheep's face replacing my father's. Maggots crawling across Nerena's skull. Then I saw my mother, I saw Ferrin, I saw you," he gestured to Lukas with his half-empty cup. "I saw my first love, Willeem," he said, voice catching on the name like it was a jagged edge. "All launching terrible truths about me, about who I am, right in my face. They… pulled apart my entire psyche. Told me I would be better off dead. Told me I was completely worthless."

Lukas's stomach clenched as the words sunk in.

"It was so, so vivid," Rhi went on, staring into the flames as if in a trance. "Eventually, the voices just kept multiplying, growing louder and louder until I couldn't drown them out, or understand them at all. It was *maddening*," he stopped and rubbed his jaw. "I could barely move, barely stand. Probably for the best, considering. If I'd been in a position to do so, I'd have likely thrown myself off the roof to make it stop."

Lukas glanced at Lachlan, who'd gone stiff.

"I saw dead things. People who…" Lukas paused, trying to muster the strength to say the truth of what he had seen that night, "who were dead because of me. Indirectly. Mostly, they were people from my neighborhood in Khalim. People who died at the hands of the Veiran soldiers occupying our city. Either they drowned slowly, diving deeper and deeper on the wrecks in the harbor every day, or they followed me into a fight we were never going to win. My best friend, he—" his voice broke and he cut off, trying to maintain some of the composure he'd been fighting like hell to hold on to for these last weeks. "He died because of me. Because of my unwillingness to walk away from the fight. We could have left the city with one of the others who'd found a way out. I refused, so he stayed too. A day later he was bleeding out in the desert."

There was a beat of anticipatory silence.

"He was like a brother to me. And he's gone."

He leveled a gaze at Rhi, and didn't need to ask to know what he was thinking.

"Well, that makes sense," Lachlan nodded.

"Care to share?" Rhi asked.

"Fear. Terror. Panic. The *popava*, it must put your body and mind through enough horror to trigger some kind of—" he waved his hand as if he could catch the words from the smoke on the air, "emergency response. Opens the floodgates for magic to pour back in."

"How? How could that possibly work?" Lukas asked.

Lachlan shrugged. "I'm not sure. If I had a sample, I could try to do some tests on it, see what makes it different from the regular plant."

"You can do that?" Rhi asked with surprise.

Lachlan nodded slowly. "I studied plant sciences for a time at Eilbast. I know some basics, and there's a healer who works in the camp who can help."

"Well," Lukas quipped, "next time someone spikes my drink with it, I'll be sure to save you some."

*   *   *

Every word evaporated out of Ferrin's head, leaving her empty and brittle.

"Well? Do you know this man?" Helene asked impatiently.

"Really now, love, it's been four months, don't you have anything to say to me?"

She stared straight at him, not quite believing her eyes. Her dress was suddenly too tight, the room too small, the air too thick.

"Ferrin," Helene prompted. "Some answers would be appreciated."

"Hi," Zare turned his quicksilver gaze to Helene. "Captain Zare, of *The Gravedigger*."

Helene looked surprise. "The reports did not mention a ship of that size washing up."

"Oh, no," he chuckled. "I left her further south, moored in a private harbor with a skeleton crew. I brought only a lesser ship and myself up north."

"And why exactly are you here?"

"I said I wanted to speak with… Ferrin," he smiled wickedly as he said her true name.

She knew what he was doing. Trying to throw her off. Confuse her. Frighten her.

It was working.

"And she's here. Say your piece." Helene crossed her arms, looking nearly out of patience.

"Love," he shifted his attention back to Ferrin. "Won't you even say hello?"

"What," she asked through clenched teeth, "are you doing here?"

"It's nice to see you, too."

She might as well have had a rock stuck in her throat for how hard it was becoming to breathe evenly. Why was he acting so cavalier?

"What do you want?" she repeated, her voice almost unrecognizable to her own ears. Quiet. Reserved.

"Come now, didn't you miss me?"

"Can you confirm his identity?" Helene asked.

Ferrin nodded reluctantly.

"Can you also confirm he is not a Bourjon spy?"

Ferrin snapped her head around to Helene.

"For legal reasons," Helene explained, "we cannot keep him locked up much longer without cause."

"He's… you can't trust him."

"What if I told you that everything I did this past spring," Zare began, "was in service to a larger goal, one you stand to benefit from?"

"No. No. I'm not listening to this." She backed away. "You can't trust him. Not a word out of his mouth," she repeated to Helene, without taking her eyes off Zare.

"Well, I have to do something with him," Helene gestured.

Ferrin shook her head again and swallowed down the bile making its way up her throat. She turned and stalked out of the room, waiting until she made it outside to break into a run.

CHAPTER TWENTY-ONE

Duke Hadringston—Cal, as Soviel had learned his first name was—kept to a fairly regular and rigid schedule.

He awoke early, with the sun most days. He drilled on the lawn with swords after running a wide loop around the manor and the town. He kept himself in remarkable physical shape. He then retreated into his study for breakfast, where he took his coffee black, his eggs over-hard and his toast medium-brown. He worked in his study until mid-afternoon on gods-knew-what, and then took meetings in the conservatory with ambassadors, officers, commissary officials and merchants.

Then he went for a ride to the east. Where, Soviel wasn't sure, but she made a note of it anyway. He came home for dinner, which he ate without complaint and said little to his wife, her entourage, or even the servants, beyond a few passing words. Then, he retreated to somewhere in the house that she had not been able to ascertain, as he always left mid-dinner, before she had any hope of being excused.

He and the duchess kept separate quarters, which wasn't uncommon, but it seemed they rarely, if ever, ventured into each other's rooms.

In the early hours of the morning, Soviel had detailed all of this in her report before rolling it up and shoving it down the front of her stays. She finished dressing herself and went out to the edge of the woods to leave her report in the drop-spot she had designated in her initial letter. She was nearly halfway across the green when she caught sight of Hadringston jogging toward her.

He was in his shirtsleeves and a light waistcoat, unbuttoned at the top. Absent the powdered wig, he looked even younger, the chiseled planes of his face brought out by his short dark hair.

"A little early to be up and about?" he queried, his tone flat.

"I've always been an early riser," she said.

"Are you lost?"

"No," she blanched as he stepped closer to her. "Just on a stroll for some fresh air."

"Be careful." He glanced towards the woods. "Lots of hungry animals prowling about at this hour."

"I will be," she nodded.

"I didn't know Njorski socialites liked to exercise early in the morning," he said, and she realized he was trying to make polite conversation. His ever-present stony expression and sharp, flat voice made it hard to tell.

"I grew up hunting with my father," she shared. "We'd leave the estate by sun-up to make the most of the day."

"I see," he narrowed his eyes and nodded. "Well, enjoy your walk."

And then he was gone, launching back into his quick-paced jog around the grounds.

She didn't quite know what to make of the interaction, and continued her walk down to the woods to leave her correspondence in the hollowed-out tree feeling a little unsettled.

Rhi awoke early the next morning and headed down to the barracks. Despite any heaviness left hanging in the air between them, he and Lachlan had made up and he was glad of it. He was relieved to have settled into some sort of routine, drinking strong coffee with Lachlan, and working through whatever the newest issue at hand was each morning. He stopped by the kitchens and grabbed two tin cups, wrapping a dishtowel around each of them before proceeding to the row of soldier's tents. Lachlan, it seemed, was a bit of a walking disaster when he first awoke. He was prone to burning his hand on hot mugs and then spilling black coffee all over the floor of his tent when he inevitably dropped them. Rhi was surprised there wasn't a permanent mud puddle on the ground.

Rhi breezed through the tent flaps and found Lachlan still asleep. The light slanting through the flaps illuminated his face and hair in a gleaming halo, a sprite of eternal summer. His features were softened, more gentle in sleep. Rhi didn't want to wake him when he looked so peaceful. He wanted to sweep the red strands out of his face and let him rest.

He quickly batted the thought away, as there was no time to entertain such fantasy. Not with so much to do.

"Wake up," he said softly, jostling Lachlan's shoulder and quickly stepping back, waiting for his typical swing-into-consciousness fists first.

As expected, Lachlan sat bolt upright, grappling at whatever or whoever he expected to be there. His eyes landed on Rhi and he relaxed, looking a little embarrassed by his reaction.

Rhi had not previously noted his state of undress, but as Lachlan climbed out from his cot, he saw that he had no shirt on, only the breeches he'd dozed off in, hanging low on his hips.

Lachlan turned to stretch his muscles, oblivious to Rhi's state of stupefaction. His back rippled and flexed, and Rhi turned away to find a surface to set their coffees on.

"So, I'm told Soviel's latest intel was delivered last night," he said, his voice coming out an octave too high.

"Yeah," Lachlan confirmed, holding up a rolled-up copy of the report. He tossed it to Rhi then pulled a fresh shirt off the end of his cot.

"Did you read it already?"

Lachlan shook his head. "It was only delivered just after midnight. Apparently it's been a hectic night for everyone."

Rhi had almost forgotten his own words the previous evening. His admission of what the ghosts of his own mind had nearly pushed him to do under the influence of the tainted drug.

"Sit," Lachlan dropped back onto the cot, patting the space beside him. "We can go over it together."

They both pored over the copied page-and-a-half report. According to Soviel, the Hadringstons and their entourage were to travel to Everness, the old capital, for the duke's work. They'd be staying a week, and Soviel hoped to get eyes on the second workshop of *popava* production and experimentation that she suspected might now be operational beneath the old castle. Rhi's old home. On the way, she'd be stopping through a grain supplier for the allied Bourjon-Lindbarrian commissary. She also mentioned that both the Bourjon Navy and Hadringston himself were sending ships into the Meddemara to hunt down some mythic-sounding gem.

"Gods," Rhi breathed, letting the paper fall between them.

"Another lab." Lachlan's sleepy tone had turned glum. "Let's hope she finds something useful."

"Let's just hope she makes it back in one piece," Rhi responded. "I miss her."

Lachlan shot him a look bordering on derisive.

"Alright, let's hear it. What issue do you have with Soviel?"

Lachlan frowned.

"You were rude to her when she was helping with the initial patients. She wasn't even a part of the prison break this spring," Rhi said. This last part wasn't explicitly true, but he wasn't going to elaborate on that now. He stood to pluck up one of the coffees and leaned back against the table, mug in hand.

"I don't trust people like that. People who just," he waved his hand dismissively, his voice gruff, "switch their personalities on and off."

"That's a bit harsh." Rhi frowned. "She's a spy. She's doing what she has to."

"Oh, and is there a real version of her that you know intimately?"

Rhi choked on a laugh. "If I didn't know better, I'd think you were jealous."

"Good thing you know better, then," Lachlan quipped.

"She is kindhearted. She's one of my closest friends. Maybe you could stand to take a cue from her once in a while."

"I don't see the point in doctoring your persona to fit every given scenario," Lachlan crossed his arms and fixed Rhi with his gaze.

Unwilling to repeat their fight in the borderlands, Rhi shrugged. "I admire your authenticity, but I think you're being unfair to her. Everyone's survival comes with a different price tag."

"Don't use your diplomat voice on me," Lachlan said.

Rhi's next words died in his throat. For a second, Lachlan had looked genuinely hurt. But it was gone almost as quickly as it had come.

"I'm sorry. It's second-nature," he said with a deflated laugh. "I really don't know how to stop sometimes."

Lachlan stood and closed the distance between them in one long step. He braced one hand on the table next to Rhi, and leaned in close. His voice was low, rough, almost vicious when he said, "I don't want you to ever polish your words for me. I don't want you to show me what you *think* I want to see. I don't want you to tell me pretty half-truths that you think will smooth my edges. If you can't live with that, then we're done here."

"Understood," Rhi said quietly, without balking. Their faces were only inches apart.

"I don't care for easy. I don't care to be well-liked. I've certainly never looked for perfection and I won't start now. If you try to smooth-talk me again, I'll throw you out of this tent on your ass."

"Will you?" Rhi asked, leaning in a fraction of an inch, baring his teeth. "There may come a day when my 'smooth-talking' is the only thing that keeps you from being kicked out of the army. Or worse, considering that temper of yours."

Something in Lachlan's eyes flared with delight at Rhi's words, at the fearlessness unmasked behind them.

Rhi continued, "I'll say it again in your particular dialect, then. Soviel is risking everything for this cause. She is going out of her way to get us information for our particular project. You have no idea the kind of mental distress it can put a person under, doing what she does, but *I* do. The fact that she has even a shred of a sense of self left is a fucking miracle. She has saved my life on more than one occasion. The next time you speak ill of her, we'll see who's getting thrown out of this tent on their ass."

Satisfaction at having riled Rhi, and something else - something almost defeated, warred in Lachlan's unflinching gaze. He pulled back, and took his coffee with him. That's when it struck Rhi.

He *was* jealous.

"And no, if you're wondering, I'm not fucking her. She's only ever been a friend."

"I wasn't wondering that," Lachlan snapped.

"I thought you didn't like people doctoring their personas."

"I'm not."

Rhi couldn't help a faint smile from behind his mug as he took a sip. The coffee burned, hot and bitter all the way down.

CHAPTER TWENTY-TWO

O i." Something jabbed Lukas in the shoulder, rousing him from his fitful sleep. Ignoring the intrusion, he pulled the blanket tighter over his shoulder and rolled away from the annoyance.

"Lukas!" Ash's voice was piercing, as only little sisters' voices could be.

He grumbled something unintelligible back at her, pulling the blanket over his head. No force was moving him from this cocoon for at least—

A rush of cold bombarded him as the blanket was wrenched away.

"What is wrong with you!" he barked, sitting up. The harsh reality of the morning finally slapped him awake.

"The boat is leaving in an hour, get dressed! Unless you no longer plan to accompany me to Avaree?"

He groaned. "Right, I forgot. Give me a few minutes."

"I'm not delaying for you," she said, and crossed her arms pointedly.

"Then get out and let me get dressed."

"Where's Rhi?" She jerked her chin at the empty half of the bed.

"I suspect he's got an early start on whatever he and that Lachlan fellow are working on. They were going on about how the druggings are related to the work in the prison's lab."

Ash nodded, slow and thoughtful. "Interesting."

"You ought to go see them later, tell them about your experience in Danvery."

"Already told them everything," Ash said. "Get dressed." She left and shut the door, leaving Lukas to ready for whatever the day would bring.

He'd been planning to head to Avaree to see what he could turn up on Ryder's whereabouts, while also rooting out a few old contacts from Everness. He was low on funds, and had too much time on his hands without all his old smuggling jobs.

He dressed quickly and splashed cold water on his face to scrub the sleepiness out of his eyes and made his way out the door, where Ash waited, leaning against the wall.

"Ready?" she asked, her coat slung over her elbow.

"Lead the way," he said.

The docks were less busy that morning; presumably a lot of fishermen and patrol workers were getting a late start after the previous night's festivities. Ash strode down the pier with a new, solid confidence that Lukas hadn't seen before. She'd never been a shy girl, but this new job had given her an air of self-assuredness that made her seem older, wiser. It was strange to see, especially when he had missed so much of her growing up. She was no longer the child climbing onto the roof to flee the threat of bath time.

"Here we are," she said after they turned onto a dock beside a small berth.

A small ship, perhaps twenty feet long, sleek and narrow, sat bobbing in the waves. It was single-masted, and two men already sat chatting and loading messenger capsules into the tiny cargo hold.

"Toscan, Rorin, this is my brother Lukas," she said, gesturing at each sailor. "Lukas, my capable crew."

"Hello," the broader of the two men, Rorin, said, lifting a hand to wave. He had dark brown hair and lightly tanned skin.

"Welcome," said Toscan. He pushed his gold wire-rimmed glasses up his nose. He seemed rather slight for a sailor.

"Only three of you?"

"And you make four," Ash said, pressing a folded up scope into his hands. "I trust you can manage the front gun should the need arise?"

Lukas eyed the ship again. If a normal-sized vessel fired upon it, they'd be splinters in one shot.

"Sure," he agreed, not entirely confident.

Ash went on to explain a bit about the vessel and its workings. "Toscan's just finished up repairing it after the big storm-thing last week. She's fast, and a bit temperamental."

This earned a frown from Toscan.

"So, when the sail is on the port side, you may need to shift weight to the starboard side, and vice versa. Understand?"

"I've sailed a small vessel before, Ash."

"Yes, but this one is a lot more sensitive to weight change than your average skiff. And *fast*. You'll see."

"I understand," he said, trying not to sound snappish. They were too old for childish sibling bickery.

"Alright then, in you go," she said, pointing to the bench just ahead of the centerboard casing. "Carefully!"

As he set foot on the deck, it did indeed bob and sway. He shot out a hand to grip the mast and steady himself.

"Easy there, lad," Rorin jested.

"Yeah, I've got it." He planted himself on the centerboard seat.

"Rorin, deal with the main please," Ash said with a grunt as she squatted down to untie the cleat at the stern. She held the end of the rope in her hand, and planted one foot in the boat. With a quick kick, she pushed them away from the dock and hopped over the rail, seating herself at the tiller as they drifted out of the berth.

There was a loud *whoosh* as Rorin yanked the rope in his hand and raised the main sail. He tied off the halyard on a small cleat at the mast, and the ship took on speed. It immediately leaned a few degrees, and Ash scooted closer to the rail on the opposite side of the sail. Toscan, who was on the same side as Ash, leaned his weight over the side of the rail until the ship flattened itself out.

Then they were speeding towards the mouth of the harbor, waves slapping the hull beneath them.

The sail to Avaree was short, thankfully. Ash was in her element aboard *The Brisk*. Lukas was not. He had queasy memories of the dive rafts, and of sailing back and forth on the strait to smuggle shipments of food and pipeweed into Everness. The journey was rough, and every bump seemed to rock the ship with a force. His stomach was churning by the time they turned into Avaree's harbor.

It was shaped differently than the harbor at Galan, much longer and narrower, and without the rocky prominence to guard it. In lieu of towering rocks and cliffs, there were soldiers in high watch towers along the entrance, and a harbor patrol ship that swept up beside them.

"Hello, Tosc! Captain Ash, Rorin," a brunet man with broad shoulders and a dark green coat called over the side of the much-larger harbor patrol ship. "Be right down."

A second later, there was a thump that sent the ship jolting.

"Fine morning for a sail, aye?" he asked, straightening.

"This is Colren, he's Toscan's brother, and harbor patrol for the city of Avaree."

"And your strapping new passenger is…?"

"My brother, Lukas. He's tagged along to look for a friend he believes may be here," she explained.

"Right," Col nodded. "And the rest of your business in the city today?"

"The usual," Ash sighed. "Running correspondence to the manor so Kenrose can purposely ignore the dire requests for aid and make me read to him the progress of his own trade ventures," she added cheerily.

Colren smirked.

"Honestly, man, I don't know how you put up with it working around here. Is it true you lot were without fruit rations for three weeks?" Rorin asked.

Colren shot him a look. "Something like that. Fortunately for *me*, my transfer request was approved yesterday morning. Looks like I'll be in Galan by month's end, should things go my way."

Toscan crossed his arms petulantly. "Well, I don't have space for you in my abode."

Colren's brown eyes rolled back so far, he could have seen the inside of his skull. "Thank you for your warm welcome, Tosc, but I don't much fancy dozing on top of a pile of mathematical papers, or having a metal contraption fall on me in my sleep."

Toscan scoffed.

"…Besides, I'll be put up in the barracks. It'll be nice to see you more often."

Toscan smiled just a little bit.

"Alright! Well, I'm going to let you get on your way. If you leave after mid-afternoon, you'll need to check in with whoever is on duty on the main docks."

"Thanks, Col."

"Good luck."

They docked at a long, narrow pier before a huge building, fresh and crisp with mint and white paint. A long, emerald lawn stretched before it, and a large colonnade propped up its awning.

"Whoa," Lukas said. "Now *that's* a manor."

Ash made a derisive snort as she leaned over the cargo hold and began shuffling the watertight capsules into the satchel she wore over her shoulder.

"Is it true? What you said about Kenrose?"

"Yeeuup—pretty sure his inattentiveness is responsible for the lack of civilian communication between the two cities."

"So why is he still in charge?"

Ash shook her head and shrugged.

"He's rich and has loads of connections. He and Ashwife were cronies in the military academy before they defected to the cause," Rorin explained as he spat over the side of the dock.

Lukas frowned thoughtfully. "I see."

"Alright, lads." Ash patted her messenger bag as she eyed the manor. "Meet back here in a few hours? Unless you two want to wait in the manor again…"

"No!" Toscan and Rorin said in unison.

"We're going into town," Rorin said.

"I do *not* want to talk to that woman again," Toscan cringed. "She pinched my cheek like I was an infant."

"Madame Kenrose is a sweet and affectionate lady."

Ash rolled her eyes. "Fine then, go on, have fun while I deal with the hot-air bag."

With that, she turned on her heal and stalked across the lawn.

"So, Lukas, who is it you're looking for?" Rorin asked. He seemed the more social of the two.

"Ah. A friend of mine from Everness. I lost track of him just before the invasion, and haven't heard from him since. Hoping he wound up here with the refugees."

"Good luck with that, it's a *mess* down there," Toscan warned.

"Thanks," he said drily.

"You know anyone else here? Someone who might be able to help you find him?" Rorin asked.

"I'm not sure," Lukas admitted. "I had a few contacts for…" he trailed off, not sure where these two sailors stood on the issue of smuggling. "For trade."

"You were a merchant?" Toscan asked doubtfully.

Lukas smirked. "Not exactly."

"Wow, criminal twins," Rorin laughed.

"Ash and I aren't twins," Lukas said with a frown and a laugh. So Ash must have told them about her own past.

"Oh, right. Well, criminal siblings." Rorin pantomimed two pistols with his thumb and forefingers.

"That's a bit extreme."

"Not my jurisdiction. Anyway, do you have a 'trade contact' for Corsovenan Arimopo? The kind you chew?" Rorin asked.

"*Ew.*" Toscan winced.

"It keeps me awake! Better than that bitter coffee *you* like."

Lukas stifled a chuckle. "Yeah, I can see about that. It's a lot more difficult to get things onto the isle now, though. I'll warn you, it'll be more expensive."

"Eh, get me a price and maybe I'll put in an order?"

"Yeah, I'll see what I can do," Lukas agreed.

"So how much older than Ash are you?" Toscan asked.

"Four years," Lukas said.

"You're twenty-two?"

"Twenty-three. Two months ago," he amended.

They were nearing the center of Avaree now. A tall bank stood at the junction of two main roads. Beside it was a tavern, a laundress-shop, a milliner, and so-on.

"Well, I think we're due a drink," Rorin said, slapping a hand on Toscan's narrow shoulder. "Come join us if you don't have luck finding your friend."

"Thanks," Lukas nodded once, "I will."

The refugee center was, indeed, a colossal mess. One huge tent stretched half the size of a city block, with rows upon rows of cots, until they'd apparently run out, and the rows turned into piles of blankets and sheets along the floor. People looked *miserable*. A few soldiers milled about the edge of the tent. Lukas approached the pair nearest to the road, hoping to find a familiar face. He didn't.

"Morning," he said in greeting. "I'm trying to track down a friend of mine. He'd be a refugee from the capital, any idea where I might start?"

One of the soldiers jerked his chin at the interior of the tent where, through the crowd, a desk with a lone soldier was visible. "You'll want to talk to Sergeant Mallon. They're in charge of refugee comings and goings here."

"Thanks," Lukas said with an appreciative dip of his chin. As he made his way into the tent, he took stock of everything. There was one information desk, and one cauldron of soup being cooked at the opposite end of the tent. There must have been two hundred people under the covering, all in all.

"Hi," Lukas said as he approached the information desk. "I'm looking for a friend."

"Name?" the administrator asked, flipping their chin-length chestnut hair out of their face. A badge on the front of their faded green tunic read *Sergeant Mallon*.

"Ryder Berry," Lukas said.

Mallon flipped through the dense notebook on the desk to the *B* section, where they scanned down the page with a gold-ringed finger. "I have a Ryder *Baron*, could that be him?"

Lukas felt his mood darken. "No, that's not him. Can you check again? Or maybe for his wife, Tolline Berry?"

Mallon fixed Lukas with a pitying expression for a half-second before turning back to the book. They scanned the page and raised their gaze. Something in the set of their shoulders told Lukas he wasn't the only person searching in futility that day.

"Nothing, I'm sorry. It doesn't mean he isn't here," they said with a sigh. "Frankly, I think there're more people in this city *not* listed in this book than are."

"Well," Lukas shrugged. "Thank you for your help. Mind if I look around?"

"By all means," Mallon said, gesturing to the floor.

Lukas took his leave and paced down the aisle, the feeling of so many eyes on him a heavy weight. He made it halfway down the tent when he heard someone step into the path behind him.

"Lukas?" The deep voice was familiar and rich.

He turned and saw a tall figure clad in a uniform, his dark hair cropped close to his scalp.

"Akachi?" Lukas said, taken aback.

The soldier approached him with a grin. "How have you been?"

Lukas returned the man's smile. "I'm alright, I suppose. What are you doing here? I thought you'd gone to Karlgiard."

"I did, just got back on the most recent boat," he laughed. "A little gray there for my tastes," he added with a grimace.

"It's good to see you."

"It's good to see *you*," said Akachi. "We weren't sure the three of you made it out of Danvery."

Lukas tilted his head and took a breath. "We nearly didn't."

"I heard about the findings of the army's rescue mission there: gruesome."

"Say," Lukas said, falling into step beside Akachi. "You haven't seen Ryder since then, have you?"

"He was here when we arrived with the prisoners, then he said he was heading to the capital to fetch his wife and his dog."

"And since then? Any word?"

"No. He did say something about heading north to hide out."

Lukas twisted his mouth as he thought. *Of course* Ryder didn't want to be found. Not with all the trouble he'd had with the law in the past. He and Tolline were probably living under fake names in some village south of here. Or they'd been caught in the forest on their way north…

"Alright, well… if he's hiding out, there won't be much I can do to find him," Lukas admitted.

"Leave him a message at the desk," Akachi suggested.

"Right, probably the best idea," he agreed, and turned back to the desk.

After leaving a message with Mallon for Ryder, Lukas jogged out of the cramped tent, anxious to be free of its stale air, and met Akachi on the grass. Though his chest was still heavy with worry and guilt, he had a renewed spring in his step, knowing that *someone* had seen Ryder since the prison break, and that Ryder had had a plan.

"So you've been here how long?" Lukas asked, as they strode toward town.

"About a week," Akachi said, running his hand over his scalp. "Place has been turned upside down since the coup."

"So I've heard," Lukas nodded. "What've they got you doing here?"

Akachi's expression was somewhere between a smirk and a grimace. "Well, since the coup has outed the army, it no longer mattered that my cover was compromised—I'm back in intelligence, but mostly in a scouting capacity."

Lukas whistled. "Where have they sent you?"

"Nowhere yet, but I'm going south later this week. Can't say where, specifically, I'm afraid."

"Wait—Ferrin was reprimanded for the prison break, what about you? Hatra and Petir?"

"Keep your voice down," Akachi said pleasantly through his teeth. "My involvement is not confirmed, therefore no consequences have befallen me. I'd *prefer* to keep it that way, if you please." It wasn't a request.

Lukas nodded. "Understood."

"And you? What busies you in Galan?"

Lukas blew out a long breath. "It depends on the day. Sometimes, fishing artifacts out of sea caves, sometimes writing three-dozen letters to track down old contacts. I try to keep busy; idle time doesn't sit well with me."

Akachi laughed in understanding. "I can relate. You need to find something consistent."

"Believe me, I know," Lukas chuckled. "Think you'll come to Galan at any point?"

"I'd like to transfer there, given the leadership here," he grimaced. "But I suspect I will be shipping south to the front in the next month or so."

"To the front? In Efel?" Lukas asked with shock.

Akachi nodded. "The tension on the continent thickens. Since they've taken the bulk of the isle, they will shift their focus to the border between Efel and Bourjony."

"That border is a mountain range—it must be near impassible."

"It was," Akachi explained. "But they've made modifications to the cliffs and mountains. Metal rungs and bridges made of narrow rods. They're calling it the iron road."

"How?"

"The Bourjons did it first, so I hear. They drilled into the rocks deep in the night during a thunderstorm, so the Efelian soldiers would not hear the pounding and cracking. Then they descended from the rocks in droves, took out an outpost just before daybreak."

"So the Efelians did the same?" He turned to face Akachi. They were just outside the tavern Rorin and Toscan had gone into.

Akachi nodded again. "They built their own paths, high in the Andal mountains, where the air grows thin and the winds cold. They traverse the peaks with speed and silence. Stone demons, they're called."

Lukas could only imagine the fright of an enemy soldier descending silently from the crags to take vengeance in the pitch black of the night. "It's certainly inventive," he admitted.

"And deadly."

There was a lengthy pause while they both considered the impact of these iron roads. "Well… care for a drink? Some of the sailors I hitched a ride with are in here," he said, gesturing behind him at the tavern called *The Cat and the Egg*. He puzzled at the title, wondering what it could possibly be named for.

Akachi looked like he was going to say no as he looked from the tavern sign to the window to Lukas's face. "Alright, one ale," he conceded.

Lukas clapped him on the shoulder. "Wonderful. It may not be a rainy countryside tavern with Petir's lover as the barkeep, but… I'm sure it's fine."

"You know, Petir and Andran are living together now," Akachi laughed. "After *years* of dancing around."

"Really?" Lukas pushed the front door open. A bell above his head rang.

Rorin and Toscan turned from their places at the bar. The former threw up an arm in greeting. Patches of rose had bloomed on Rorin's cheeks, and Toscan looked significantly less uptight than he had that morning. Somehow, they must have managed to drink a fair bit of ale since he'd left them, despite it being so early in the day.

"Yes, about time," Akachi went on. "They seem happy. Petir is so much less restless."

A warm feeling went through Lukas as Ferrin crossed his mind, with her own bold streak of restlessness. He thought of her dangerous curiosity, and how it so often teased out his own. He soured, recalling his argument with her the night before. He didn't know what was wrong with him, why he kept picking fights with her, with everyone.

"There's my… boat-mates," Lukas said as he gestured to Toscan and Rorin. He and Akachi made their way through the crowded tavern towards them.

"Lukas!" Rorin slapped him on the shoulder. "Is this Ryder?"

"Hm? Oh, no, this is Akachi. He's a friend."

"We're just killing the afternoon here waiting for Ash to be done at Kenrose's. It takes *hours* sometimes." Toscan leaned forward, sloshing a bit of foam from his ale flagon.

"This is Toscan and Rorin." He pointed at each of them, fairly sure he hadn't mixed up their names. "Who do I have to threaten to get an ale around here?" He asked with good cheer.

"Barmaid!" Rorin hollered over the din.

"How are there this many people here so early?" Akachi asked quietly as he examined the room.

"Lots of people with nowhere else to go," Rorin said, his voice slurring slightly.

"And the ale is so good. *And* the barmaid is pretty," Toscan added with a bashful dart of his eyes to the blonde woman serving up ales by the six. Her hair was curling in the heat, the loose strands that had escaped her bun puffing around her face as she moved.

"Aye, she is," Rorin said in a loud, conspiratorial whisper as he yanked Toscan toward him. "And what are you going to do about it?"

"Uh—"

"Go on! Talk to her!"

"Two ales for you," she said as she swept by, slamming down Lukas' and Akachi's drinks. "It'll be six."

Lukas fished into his pocket for his coin purse while Rorin talked up Toscan to introduce himself to the barmaid.

"Come on, even if nothing comes of it, you never have to see her again."

"Really?"

"Oh, are you frequenting… what is this place called? *The Egg Cat* terribly often?"

Lukas choked on his first sip of ale.

"B-but—"

"Oh, come *on* Tosc. You're a top engineer in the Caelish Army! Lasses *love* smart men."

Toscan's brow crinkled. "Are you *sure*?"

"Yes!" Rorin cried.

"He's right, you know. What is there to lose? You need not come back here if it should go sour," Akachi offered, sipping from his flagon with a mischievous smile.

"Well. Alright," Toscan agreed, squaring his shoulders.

A little over an hour later, Ash entered the tavern with an uncharacteristically stony expression on her face. Her messenger bag was slung across her chest, and her shoulders were tense. She spotted their group, and her face immediately softened, though her posture did not.

"Have you lot been wasting the day away in this *dump* while I had to *read, out loud as if to a child,* Kenrose's letters? He's lucky I *can* read. I swear, that man has not a lick of sense or propriety. He wrote off responses while I waited, but *only* for his personal business enquiries. *And* he continues to call me 'dear'."

Toscan was red-faced and smiling, Rorin had a wide grin on his face. He'd just chatted with the barmaid, a miss Denile, or Donalia, or something, and he was practically glowing.

Lukas sipped his second ale as Ash slid onto the stool beside him.

"Doing alright?" he asked.

She gave him a long look, and turned back to the bar. "Fine," she sighed. "Just a long day."

Lukas raised one teasing eyebrow. "And yet, you still must sail us all back to Galan tonight."

CHAPTER TWENTY-THREE

Ferrin was on the roof when Rhi found her at last. He'd stopped by to share Soviel's news and had found her nowhere in the manor. After some careful thinking and climbing, he slipped from the window and up onto the slats. She was staring out at the horizon, her chin propped up on one knee and a mug of tea or coffee steaming idly in one hand.

"Hey," he said, easing out next to her. He was cautious in his footing, not as prepared for a stumble as she was with their mother's magic ring. In the early weeks in Galan, Ash had asked Ferrin what would happen if she tried it. Ferrin had explained that she'd had to jump off a roof to get the thing to work. Ash and Rhi had stared at her, perturbed, while she offered a casual expression.

He had only used the blasted thing once since the escape, and he found that the sensation of flying unsettled him more than he liked. Had he not been exhausted, terrified and dehydrated, and had his life not depended on it that day in the tower, he never would have let himself jump out a window trusting in such a thing. "Haven't talked much lately."

She drew herself up straighter with a deep breath. "I know, I'm sorry."

"Don't be," he said. "We've both had a lot of new responsibility lately."

"Sort of," she said, fidgeting. "Did you have a nice time at the fire?"

"Sort of," he snorted. "Did you?"

"Briefly," she said, setting down her mug. "After Ash left, I got into it with Lukas, and then…" she trailed off, shaking her head half-heartedly.

"He's been on edge lately," Rhi said in solidarity. "Is everything," he frowned, searching for the right words, "alright between the two of you?"

She gave a noncommittal grunt and shifted to face him. "There's something I've been putting off telling you. First, you were gone, and then so much was going on with Soviel leaving and all and…" she flitted a hand at the horizon. "Anyway. You need to hear this from me." She closed her eyes briefly. "I saw Mother."

"You *what*?" Rhi started, nearly losing his balance and skidding off the roof. "Where is she? How?"

"I take it Lukas told you about our foray to the strange spot on the map?"

"He did," Rhi confirmed.

"Well, the ah… portal-guardian-creature told to me to 'keep the way open' when I fell asleep and that Mother would communicate with me in my dreams. And she did. She had a lot to say."

Rhi was confused about exactly what a '*portal-guardian-creature*' was, but decided to hold his questions for after. "Like what?"

"It wasn't exactly a happy reunion," she said, staring down at her hands, picking the skin of her nails.

"Oh, I see," Rhi sighed wearily. "Your perfect, glowing image of her has finally been shattered, hasn't it?"

"What? I did *not* have any certain image of her!"

"Relax, Ferrin. I'm not accusing you of anything." He leaned back on his palms on the slanted roof. "I only mean our perspectives on our parents were a little different. For you, Mum could do no wrong, and Father was the instigator of all things bad. I never saw it like that, I suppose. At the end,

Father did some despicable things, but even before that point… well, they were both incredibly flawed human beings."

Ferrin groaned. "That's sort of what this is about. Our father."

"Henrik?" Rhi asked.

"No, Rhi. Not Henrik."

He'd heard no shortage of rumors growing up that his mother had been disloyal to his father. The idea wasn't new to him, but since those whispers had died down, he'd never given them much stock. It always seemed to come from pissy Lundi nobles who were bitter that their own relations weren't chosen for the throne all those years ago.

"Who?"

"Alick. Alick MacVale. They were close friends growing up, and I guess she-she found out she needed to fulfill another generation of Caelish resistance on the throne. Among other things."

Rhi winced. "What? Did he know?"

"I don't know. I was too mad to ask."

Rhi was quiet for a few moments before he asked, "What's he like, anyway? You were always hanging around the barn with him. Is he a decent fellow?"

"Yeah," she scrubbed a hand across her eyes. "That isn't the issue at all."

"I know," Rhi said quietly.

"She *made* us. For a purpose. As if… I don't know, as if we were weapons forged to be wielded at the right time."

"What do you mean?"

"There is some fanciful island I am supposed to visit to find some special power or knowledge or… I don't know. She tried to go herself and said the timing wasn't right. That she was a generation too early."

"And it has to be you?" Rhi asked. Once again, Arabella was casting him aside.

"Yes. No. I'm not sure. One of us has to be around to take the throne. Whoever takes the quest can't—won't—be able to be a ruler. She wasn't very forthcoming as to why."

His heart constricted at the weariness in her voice. "Ferrin," Rhi began, exasperated. "This is so fucking typical of her. Leaving her messes around for everyone else to deal with while she vanishes into the breeze."

She flinched. He hadn't meant it like that, but he could tell she had taken his words as a personal jab about her own disappearance.

"Hey, hey—not what I was saying," he reassured her, grabbing her hand. "You're not her."

Ferrin turned to the horizon, eyes misting.

"Shit," Rhi sighed. "Everything is falling apart."

"It has been for a while," she gestured at the half-ruined barracks below, the crumbling promontory, the manor around them. "We fled our home pursued by an army, Rhi. Things have been a mess for a long time." She sniffed and wiped away a single tear. "Everyone is struggling."

"Go easy on Lukas," he said, catching her meaning. "I think… I think Ryder's disappearance is reminding him of something from his past he might not be ready to talk about."

She clasped her hands behind her neck and raised her head with a heavy sigh.

"What else is bothering you?"

Her next words came out so flat he almost thought he'd misheard her when she said, "Zare is here."

"In Port Galan?" Rhi balked.

Ferrin nodded.

"How? Why?"

She shook her head. She looked exhausted. "He's being let out of holding today because they can't find proof of him being here for malicious intent."

"What? That's madness! Is he here for you?"

She shrugged.

"*Strata* above."

"I have to go find Ash," she said vacantly. "Later… we should talk about all this more."

Just as he finished nodding in agreement, she launched herself off the roof.

The sun was setting, and Ferrin was heading down to the docks, cutting through the barracks and trying to keep her grip on the present moment. The last thing she needed was to nosedive down some long-lost memory and slip up because of it.

She needed to find Ash, needed to warn her before she, too, was blindsided by Zare's reappearance. She wouldn't let him get near her again, not when he'd nearly killed Ash for questioning him. She'd meant to tell her yesterday, but she and Lukas hadn't yet returned from Avaree when she finally fell into bed exhausted.

She'd flown so far earlier in the day, aimless and with no direction, until she had to make herself turn around and head back to Galan, exhausted. She'd made it more than halfway to Everness. staying high above the trees so no passing scouts would catch a glimpse of her. She'd brought a scope and dressed warmly, hoping to find out something useful, but had come up short.

She wondered what would happen if she just kept flying south, how far she could go.

Her resolve had been badly shaken by the events of the last month. She hadn't slept more than a few hours in a row for weeks now. There was too much coming at her from every direction. Perhaps she should make that leap, head to the Door, go to the island, if only to escape the tangled mess her life in Galan had become.

She was only halfway through the encampment when Zare appeared walking beside her.

"Quite the set-up you have here," he said as he fell into stride.

"Leave me alone," she said with strained civility, staring straight ahead.

"Won't you at least hear me out? For old time's sake."

"So you can spoon-feed me some elegant lie you've no doubt spent the last few weeks cultivating once you realized you wanted something from me?"

"No," he said. "I just heard tell of your plight here in the north, Everness being raided and all. I happen to be in possession of something—a few things—that you might find very intriguing and useful."

"Go on and tell me what, then."

There was a beat of silence just a fraction too long, and she realized that he'd expected her to jump on his bait at the first whiff. How pathetic she must have been.

"Well, it's much more complicated than that."

"Of course it is," she groaned just as Lukas rounded a corner two buildings ahead and locked eyes on her.

"*Fuck,*" she swore under her breath before she could stop herself.

Zare's eyes landed on Lukas and then returned to her. She could practically feel the smugness rolling off him in waves as he realized what was happening.

"Ferrin," Lukas said, halting in front of her.

"Lukas," she said, shifting nervously on her feet. Things between them were precarious as it was, the last thing she needed was for Zare to swoop in and stir the pot. Or, more likely, tip the pot over and set it on fire.

"I was hoping I could talk to you about—" he stopped, eyeing Zare. "Who's this?"

"No one important," she said quickly at the same time Zare began laughing softly. "Can you please find Ash? I *really* need to speak with her."

"I need to talk to you about something," he said again, eyes flicking back to Zare, who was maintaining a neutral expression.

"Lukas, *please*." She flared her eyes in silent warning. "Find Ash."

He narrowed his eyes at Zare and looked him up and down. "Do I know you?"

"Doubtful, I'm new around these parts," Zare drawled. "Shellfish trade."

"Will you *please* stop talking?" She glared at him before turning back to Lukas. "I will explain later but I *really* need you to go get Ash."

Lukas stared at her and eyed Zare with deep suspicion before nodding slowly and saying, "Sure, I'll have her come find you."

"Thank you," she breathed, her heart hammering in her throat.

When Lukas was out of earshot, Zare spun to face her, a look of pure incredulity on his face. "I'm sorry, you mean to tell me *Ash* has ended up here somehow?"

"You mean after you tried to have her killed?" Ferrin shot back.

He winced. "I had hoped you wouldn't find out about that."

"Perhaps you should have chosen a different island to dump her on."

"Well, someone needed to take the fall for those stolen customs papers. It was an unavoidable cost, I'm afraid."

"You can't truly mean to win me over with another scheme like this, can you?"

"As I was saying. I have in my possession something that is worth a great deal. Something that will be invaluable in

268

changing the tide of this war that is beginning to spread across our seas."

"And this has *what* to do with me, or for that matter, with your supposedly noble motivations for poisoning and selling my unconscious body to the navy?"

He winced again. If she didn't know better, she'd think his expression of regret was genuine.

"I should have told Helene you were a Bourjon spy intent on infiltrating this city," she gave a clipped, humorless laugh. "Should have put a bullet in your head and damned the consequences."

"But then you'd never get your hands on the cetamaris."

"The what?" It sounded familiar but she couldn't place it.

"You heard me right. I found it. Well, one half of it, but the crew is hard at work back on Tunis trying to locate the second half."

"You're lying," she said as she correlated the strange word with something she'd pulled out of *Legends and Truths* only a few months ago.

"Would I have come all this way, on a mere skiff, all by myself if I didn't have something worth your while?"

"Fine, let me see it," she sniped.

"Oh, sweet Gillian. Have you forgotten? I never put all my eggs in one basket. That gem is hidden in a place only I can find it, and will remain so until I have the assurances I need."

She let out an exasperated sigh and stomped her foot. "What is it you *want* here, Zare?"

"A few things, starting with some answers. Who is Lukas?"

"Absolutely not. I am not playing this game with you. You lost any privilege to information about my personal life the day you decided—"

She didn't get to finish because a fast-moving blur plowed into Zare out of nowhere, and decked him in the face.

Ash.

Zare went down with an *oof*.

"Are you," —she kicked him in the ribs— "serious?!"

"Ash," he coughed.

"I don't want to hear another *breath* out of you!" she spat before rounding on Ferrin. "Why isn't he in shackles? Better yet, six feet deep in the ground?"

"He was in lock-up. But Helene said they had nothing to hold him on."

"Oh, that's rich. Give me one good reason I shouldn't slit your throat right here?" Ash seethed, drawing the knife from her belt.

"He's claiming to have important information and some rare gem in his possession." Ferrin rubbed the bridge of her nose, unsure why she was bothering to defend him.

"And you believe him? No. No way. We can't believe a *thing* this piece of shit says. I don't care *how* sweet the offer— HEY." She planted her boot on his upper arm, stopping him from getting up. "Stay down. I'm not through with you yet."

Upon seeing the commotion, a few soldiers dragged Ash off of Zare before she could inflict any real damage, but her golden brown eyes were molten with rage nonetheless as Zare was escorted out of camp. Ferrin stepped closer.

"Are you alright?"

"No, Ferrin, I'm not alright! I don't understand how you're being so cavalier about this." She flung a hand up in the direction Zare had been marched off.

"I'm not," Ferrin said, turning away from Ash and bracing her hands behind her head as she paced.

"Well you seemed to have no issue taking an evening stroll with him."

"I came down here looking for *you* so I could warn you. He blindsided me and I didn't want to make a scene. This camp resents me enough as it is."

"Do not let him use you again, Gill—Ferrin. *Fuck!* I cannot believe this. He's already messing with our heads again," Ash carded her fingers through her short hair and shifted anxiously on her feet.

"I won't. It isn't like that anymore."

"Maybe not yet," Ash shook her head frantically. "But piece by piece he'll try to wear away at you again, just like last time. Don't give him a damn inch. You hear me? Not an inch."

"I won't, Ash. I have no illusions regarding what he is capable of."

"I hope not," Ash said intently, clasping Ferrin by the shoulders. "I really, really, hope not."

When Ferrin returned to the rooms, she found Lukas leaning against her bed. His hands were in his pockets and he was staring wistfully at the ground.

"Are you alright?" he asked quietly when his gaze settled on her face.

She released a breath she felt like she'd been holding since walking into Helene's office and finding Zare there, or since she'd stormed away from Lukas at the bonfire, or since she'd flown into that tower in Everness. It came out choked, and she brought a hand to cover her mouth as if she could hold in the sob waiting to break free.

"Was that…" he began, brow furrowed in concern. "Was that who I think it was?"

She nodded, blinking back the burning in her eyes.

"Oh, hey." He pushed off the bed, starting toward her. "Are you alright? Did he hurt you?"

She shook her head and squeezed her eyes shut as he put two steadying hands on her upper arms and pulled her to him. His hand cupped the back of her head.

"If you want, we can go back down there now and I'll hold his arms back while you take a few swings at him," he said, half-joking.

"Ash already kicked the shit out of him," she choked out.

"Well, that's good, at least." He rubbed slow circles over her shoulder, sending shivers down her spine.

She managed a half-hearted laugh, composing herself with a final sniff. "You wanted to talk?"

He straightened. "I… I wanted to apologize for snapping at you."

"Oh." She collected herself and looked up at him. "Lukas, I didn't mean to act like I knew better. I just," she broke off. "Doing nothing, sitting still, it makes me… itchy. Even worse, when someone I care for has a problem, I *have* to do something. Even though sometimes there's nothing I *can* do," she added the last part in a quiet voice.

"I know," he said, resting his forehead against hers. He hadn't let go of her yet, and sighed deeply before continuing, "Ryder was—is—my friend. And I dragged him into this mess, and now he's missing. Whatever's happened to him is on me."

"Luk," she whispered soothingly, reaching up to cup the side of his face. "It is *not* all on you. Ryder is strong, and capable, and he made his own choices."

He looked for a moment as if he was going to say something else on the matter, but changed his mind and the subject. "So," he said, "any idea what you're going to do about Zare?"

She drew back and took a shaky breath. "I have a lot to decide soon. Zare claims to have one half of some special sea-gem, the cetamaris."

"That's real?" Lukas asked, perplexed.

"You've heard of it? I only barely remembered reading the word in *Legends and Truths*. I'd assumed it was an elaboration.

Too bad that book is probably pulp in Everness now." She let her hands settle on his back, holding him close.

"Ah, this really is funny."

"How so?"

"A few nights ago, I couldn't sleep. So I went down to the docks and ended up helping some old fisherman repair his nets in exchange for a story." He laughed. "He told me the tale of the Witch of Galan."

"The Weeping Woman? What does that have to do with the cetamaris?"

"According to Old Salty, she created it."

"'Old Salty'?"

He laughed, but did not elaborate. "She took the gemstone from her wedding ring, when her would-be husband died in a storm of her own making before they wed. She cursed the gem, or something, and used it to control the sea."

"I have never heard that version of the story." She narrowed her eyes skeptically.

"To be fair, he did contradict himself a few times while telling it."

"That's mighty interesting."

"I can see the gears turning." He angled his head, looking down at her. "What are you thinking?"

"I'm thinking I might want to meet this fisherman."

"I'm starting to think *he* was the ghost." He smirked, lifting her chin with two fingers. "But, I'll see if I can track him down."

"If anyone can find some ghostly old fisherman," she sniffed, "it's you."

"I knew you'd come to appreciate my talents," he joked, placing an *almost* chaste kiss on her temple.

She laughed huskily, becoming increasingly aware of their nearness. "I missed you while you were in Avaree," she said coyly, letting her gaze fall to his lips, before bringing it back up to his eyes.

His stared at her a moment longer, then leaned forward with a hint of caution, and claimed her mouth with his own, pulling her into his chest. Everything about his movements was gentle and cautious, tender and soft, until she wrapped her arms around his waist and crushed him even closer.

The severity of their embrace, the sudden heaviness of it, sent a shock down her spine. Something fluttered in her belly and she instinctively leaned into him, pressing her chest against his as he kissed her hard enough to bend her backwards. A soft moan of surprise escaped her throat.

She reached up and snaked her arm around the back of his neck as she curved into him, winding her fingers through his curling hair before cupping the back of his head. The skin of his lower lip was soft and pert when she pulled it into her teeth with a gentle, insistent pressure. She felt him inhale sharply in response.

Her skin went taut as his hands moved down her back, over the fabric of her jumps and shirt, down to cup her backside. For a second, he dropped low, but only to scoop her up by the backs of her thighs. She gasped in surprise, and wrapped her legs around his waist as he walked her backward three steps to the dresser. He set her down without a hint of gentleness, and pulled away to yank his shirt over his head.

Ferrin watched the muscles rippling under his bronze skin. He was stunning, every inch of his body was powerful and strong in more ways than one. His sea-green eyes bore into her when he caught her staring, and she reached out and ran her hand over a long-faded scar on the left side of his chest. She wondered what had put it there. The heat of his skin was enough for her to forget all her questions and pull him back into her reach.

She started unlacing the front of her stiffened gray jumps, the air cool on the tender skin of her breasts as the fabric of her shirt loosened.

He surged forward, kissing her again. She parted her lips for him and angled her head back to give him access. His tongue met hers, moving in slow circles as he reached through the unlaced front of her jumps, caressing the underside of her breast. With a low, sweet moan, she encouraged him on.

He palmed her breast, and rubbed a thumb over her nipple, which had gone taut with desire and anticipation. The place between her thighs was aching and throbbing with need, and she wriggled closer, sliding her hips to the edge of the dresser as she tried to pull him closer with her legs.

He ground against her and swore. She could feel his hardness through both their breeches, and decided, *to hell with it*. She undid the rest of her shirt and shrugged out of it, letting out a little yelp of pleasure as he rolled her nipple between his thumb and first finger.

"*Lukas*," she moaned, eliciting a deep inhale from him as she rolled her hips against him again.

He relinquished her breast, but only to attend to the ties of her breeches. A second later and he was leaning further over her, his hand inching closer and closer to where she wanted it.

"Don't you dare tease me like—" her eyes bulged wide, choking off her sentence with a gasp as he did *something* with his middle finger on the most sensitive part of her.

He did it again, rolling over the peaked bud of flesh, coaxing another moan from her lips. The sensation was sharp and sweet and all consuming. Her blood was pumping. He did it again, and this time slid one of his fingers inside her. She was already slick with desire, desperate to claim him with her body.

She let out another moan as he worked her with his hand, again, again, again, *again*. Until she was panting and her pulse was slamming in her chest and she was seeing stars and something inside her went incredibly rigid, right before snapping, shattering into a million bright pieces.

Still gripping the waistband of his breeches, she let her head fall back against the wall as her breathing evened out. Lukas was still stroking into her, slower now as he brought her through the aftershocks.

As she came back into herself, she let her eyes float open and found him watching her with satisfaction and awe. She smirked wickedly, and yanked him forward by his waistband. "My turn."

Surprise flashed in his eyes, and she palmed him through the fabric as she leaned in for another kiss. Her own trousers were still half-way off.

She had just managed to undo the front of his breeches, and based on what she'd felt straining against the fabric, was anticipating the next few steps with a wild hunger, when a loud rapping came on the door.

"Hey!" Ash's voice cut through the room like an axe, causing any and all tension to go slack as she cracked the door open one inch. "Get up."

Lukas jerked back, his lips as reddened and swollen as Ferrin's felt. He held her gaze for two breaths before straightening, his hands flying to the front of his breeches.

"One moment!" Ferrin called to Ash. "Don't come in!"

As she shimmied back into the rest of her clothes, she heard Ash mutter something about needing to find better quarters.

Lukas scooped her shirt off the floor and tossed it to her. She shrugged into it as he cracked open the door.

"Yes, Ash?" The impatience in his voice was not easy to miss.

"This is *my* room. Move," she ordered, shoving past him. "Word from Soviel."

"At this hour?"

"The decoded message has only just been released to me."

"What did she say?" Ferrin tumbled off the dresser, still rumpled and blushing, earning a sidelong glance from Ash.

"They only gave me the relevant notes, but what I've been told is that whatever is going on down in Everness, she's headed there with her charge. She suspects they have an operation there similar to that of Danvery Prison."

Ferrin scooted into the seat at the desk beside Ash and pulled her hair up into a messy top-knot.

"What does this mean? She's going into the castle?" Lukas asked, buttoning his shirt back up and pacing to the other side of the desk.

"It means whatever was going on at Everness, the *popava*, the tunnels, the pit-creature, it didn't stop when we left," Ferrin said. "Hadringston *was* at the prison when we broke in."

"What else did she say?"

"You won't like it," Ash said with a grimace.

"What?"

"She mentions the same jewel Zare claims to have hidden. The cetamaris."

"What about it?"

"Bourjony is searching for it, too. They've deployed mercenaries to the Meddemara to find it."

It was past midnight when Ferrin and Ash filed into Helene's office. It seemed Zare's appearance had been enough to make Helene drag Ferrin back into the fray. Whether or not that was a good thing, she wasn't sure. Despite the hour, Helene was up and pacing about in her office.

"I need the two of you to extract the information from your *friend* by any means necessary," she said, red braid swishing down her back. "Find the location of that gem. I don't care what you have to bargain."

Ash bristled. "You realize he tried to kill me, right? And he poisoned Ferrin."

Helene squeezed her eyes shut and pinched the bridge of her nose. "I am well aware of the situation's complexities—"

"No, you have no idea!" Ash burst out of her seat. "He's an expert manipulator. If he's asking for something, it's going to come with ten other things that we won't even realize until we're sitting there robbed blind."

"You're a smart girl, don't *let* him take advantage. Either of you," Helene said icily, gesturing between Ferrin and Ash.

Ash was fuming. Ferrin had gone stony-faced and silent since hearing the news corroborating Zare's information on the cetamaris. Tension was rippling off of her in contagious waves.

"Do we even know where he went after you *let him out of jail*?" Ash asked through gritted teeth.

"I have it on good authority that he's been staying at the Whitecliff."

Ferrin uncrossed her arms and pushed her chair out. She stood and stalked out of the room without another word.

Ash threw up her hands and groaned. "We'll try, but hear me now: the cost will be steep and we will all regret it."

"We have resources," Helene countered.

Ash gave a joyless, hollow laugh. "That's not what I meant." She turned and walked out of the room.

Ferrin stood outside the front door at the Whitecliff Inn, staring up at the three story building with barely-bridled disdain. It was the dead of night, and the street lamps barely burned high enough to illuminate her features, but Ash could see it in the set of her shoulders, the tension in her jaw. Zare was in there somewhere, still asleep, or up plotting his next devious move. Either way, Ash wanted nothing to do with him.

"Are you going to be alright?" Ash asked as she stepped up next to Ferrin to join her in surveying the inn.

"Yes," Ferrin said in a low voice, swallowing thickly. "I'm willing to do what needs to be done." A beat of silence followed. "Are you? Going to be alright?"

Ash gave a small, tight nod.

"Then let's find out what the hell he wants."

They breezed up to the tavern on the first floor where the dark-haired bartender was cleaning up for the night.

"We need to speak with one of your patrons," Ash said curtly.

"And?"

"We need to know what room he's in. Early twenties, brown hair, gray eyes, loves the sound of his own voice?"

The bartender slung his towel back over his shoulder. "Sounds familiar. You got anything to help me remember?"

Ferrin rolled her eyes, and Ash slapped two silver coins on the bar top. "Ringing any bells?"

The barkeep pulled the coins back over the edge of the bar top and pocketed them. "Yeah, fellow like that is on the third floor. Room six."

Ferrin turned without another word toward the stairwell.

"The resistance appreciates your service," Ash said with a mock bow before turning and darting up the stairs after Ferrin.

When they reached room six, Ferrin banged her fist on it four times, hard enough to bruise.

"Zare! Get up!" Ash shouted through the door.

A moment later, Zare opened the door. He was fully dressed for the day, not a button out of place and not a hair out of line, as if he had been waiting for them.

"Good morning," he greeted them with a knowing smile.

Ash shoved her way into the room, forcing him back a step. Ferrin followed, looking around the room before yanking the door shut behind her.

"Where is it?" she asked.

"Well, you're in a mood," he mused. "No, 'how'd you sleep, darling?'"

"I wouldn't taunt her, she's been murderous since I dragged her out of bed," Ash bit back.

"Ladies, I've already told you. For my *own* safety," he glanced sidelong at Ferrin, "I've hidden the gem somewhere I, and I alone, know. I will disclose the location once my terms are met, and once I know I am not going to be murdered on the spot."

"We're not working with you, we're not negotiating with you. Recall the time you tried to *kill* me?" Ash pointed out.

"An unfortunate turn of events. My apologies," he said primly, as if he'd merely spilled a spot of tea on her tablecloth.

"We're not *giving* you anything, short of dropping your ass on the nearest spit—"

"What do you want?" Ferrin's question was hard, flat, level.

A beautifully malicious smile spread slowly across Zare's face. He looked like a snake.

Ash nearly recoiled. How Ferrin had ever found him attractive was a complete mystery to her. "I knew you'd be willing to compromise, Gillian."

"Ferrin, *what* are you doing?" Ash hissed.

"What. Do. You. Want?"

"One," he said, "I wish to be licensed to hunt on behalf of this 'Caelish Resistance'."

"You want letters of marque?" Ash squinted.

"*Two*, I want a trade deal."

"And, pray tell, what else?" Ash laughed in disbelief.

"Gillian—*Ferrin*—will have dinner with me. Tomorrow evening."

Ash threw up her hands in exasperation. "Are you serious —"

"Fine."

She whipped around to look at Ferrin in shock.

"So, we have a deal, then?" Zare raised one eyebrow, cool and calm. He knew he'd won.

"No, we most certainly do not," Ash answered.

"We do," Ferrin said, leveling her gaze at him. "I'll see you tomorrow."

Ferrin turned on her heel and left, fists clenched at her sides.

Ash turned back to Zare and took one menacing step toward him.

"I know what you're doing," she said in a quiet voice. "If you think you can spin us the way you did before— no—if I get even a *whiff* of something off about all of this," she took in a deep breath and let it out slowly as she met his eye. "I'll carve you a new smile that will be so incapable of charming anyone, they'll turn you away at the gates of the dead. And that's a promise."

CHAPTER TWENTY-FOUR

W ell," Helene said the following morning. "The letters of marque, I can do easily." As always, she looked exhausted. Her hair was absent its usual neat braid, and was instead twisted into a haphazard knot at the back of her head. Her shirt was wrinkled, as if she'd slept slumped over her desk rather than retiring for the evening. Based on the pile of tomes and papers on her desk, she likely had.

"And the… trade deal?" Ferrin asked, extremely aware of Ash's glare burning into her.

"I will need more information. It'll be difficult convincing commissary, but it isn't impossible. Trading what, exactly? And to whom? What is he affiliated with?"

"Ferrin can ask when she goes to the dinner she agreed to have with him," Ash grumbled, doing nothing to keep the edge from her voice.

"Ash."

"Remember last time you had dinner with him, and he poisoned you?"

"That was lunch."

"You *know* he's up to something," Ash said. "You can't joke your way around this."

"I know." Ferrin admitted, fighting to keep her features neutral as her unease grew.

"Then why—"

"Ash, *please.*"

She wanted him gone. She wanted this over with, as soon as possible.

Helene cleared her throat. "I'll have the letters of marque by day's end. The trade agreement, I'll look into." She swept the loose strands of hair off her forehead. "Ferrin, be careful."

"I know."

"You are both dismissed. Keep me updated, please."

Once they were out of the office, Ash whirled on Ferrin.

"What are you doing?" she hissed.

"I'm doing what's *necessary*," Ferrin bit back.

"After everything he's done to us? You, me, Pierre, who knows who else? You're just going to give him exactly what he's asked for?"

"We need that gem, Ash."

"I know he's got charm, but we know better. *You* know better. He is never going to give us what we need. He's going to find a way to slip out of our grasp again, taking everything from us and giving nothing back."

"I have to try, Ash," Ferrin coaxed, something in her chest going taut. "The sooner this is done, the sooner he's gone."

Ash exhaled derisively. "You're making a huge mistake," she muttered before storming off.

As Ferrin was dressing for her dreaded dinner with Zare, a knock sounded from the adjoining door.

"Come in," she said.

The door opened and Lukas met her eye in the mirror. She halted her combing mid-stroke; she hadn't seen him since Ash had interrupted their tryst the previous evening.

"How did it go?" he asked a little awkwardly, moving to lean against the dresser on the back wall.

"He had his demands, obviously."

"What were they?"

"Privateer license, trade deal, and… he wants me to have dinner with him."

He looked briefly taken aback. "And what did you say?"

"I thought Ash would have already told you. She made her opinion on the matter very clear."

"You're *going*?"

She set down her comb and turned in her chair to face him. "It's only a dinner."

"I was under the impression that you wanted nothing to do with him."

Something about his icy tone really pissed her off. "Are you *jealous*?" she scoffed.

Lukas bristled. "No."

"Why is everyone so bothered by my negotiating with him?" She stood and fetched her boots from the armoire. "He is a potential—even if not ideal—ally, with important information that we should be trying to get at any cost. Regardless of my personal history with him."

He squinted at her. "You told me he'd find a way to use everything you tell him against you—"

"You forget that I am the one who knows him best," she stomped back to the vanity chair with her boots, sitting to put them on. "I am the one he betrayed. Not you."

"I am not arguing that. You want to go ahead and throw yourself into his waiting teeth, be my guest. But you seem to forget he also hurt Ash. My sister. So perhaps consider her when you're going about this with your newfound pragmatism."

A sharp pang lanced through her gut and she recoiled.

"It's not as if I'm crawling into bed with him!" she exclaimed. "You can't ignore the importance of what he has. Access to the cetamaris, and whatever other information he has… it could save our lives. All of our lives. Whatever the cost, we need it. Despite any blows to my pride."

"That's all you think this is?"

"Lukas, don't. I know. I know what he is. I have to do this."

He came closer and braced a hand on the back of her chair. She turned from the mirror, twisting in the chair to face him. With one finger, he lifted her chin, forcing her to meet his eye. "I know. But there has to be another way that doesn't involve you and Ash selling yourselves out to work with him. Kill him and be done with it," he urged, dropping his hand to his side. "Or, if you can't stomach it, I know Ash would do it with a smile and a song."

"You underestimate him." She stood. "If Zare says he's hidden the gem somewhere untraceable, even you couldn't find it. Even if you tore apart the world."

He watched as she walked to the bed where she'd flung her coat.

"Besides, there is something else I wish to find out about from him."

"About the gem?"

She nodded, pursing her lips.

"Whatever it is you're planning, Ferrin," he said in a clipped voice, "I hope it's worth it."

Without another word, he turned and walked out, letting the door shut behind him with a discordant note of finality.

The tavern was well-lit and surprisingly close to empty, given that it was well into dinner time, and given that this place boasted to have the 'best lamb stew in town'.

Ferrin slid into the seat across from Zare, the letters of marque secure in her coat pocket.

"The cool air suits you," he complimented. "Perhaps you were always meant to rule in the north."

"I'm not meant to rule the north," she said. "Rhi is."

"Ah yes, *Rhi*," Zare chuckled. "You used to say his name in your sleep, you know. At first I worried you were seeing another man behind my back, but it became clearer and clearer that you had a family you'd left behind when you washed up on Tunis."

The memories dragged her back, unbidden. The day she'd hopped off the cargo ship onto the white sands of Tunis, waved goodbye to the merchant she'd bribed to let her aboard, and walked into town disguised as a young boy. She'd met Zare and Captain McGidrew as they recruited new sailors after a few of their number had been killed in a raid gone wrong. She wondered now if Zare had had anything to do with that.

"Once I connected the fact that *Rhi* was the name of the first in line for the Barrian throne, I began to suspect there was even more to you than met the eye."

"Are you going to gloat in your own cleverness all evening?" she snapped.

"Apologies, lost my thread," he winked.

"Get on with it, then."

"I wanted to ask you to join me. Once everything is ready, come south with me. Back to the crew. Let's rule the seas together," he leaned forward, a conspiratorial grin on his face.

She choked on her drink. Despite herself, a tiny part of her wanted very badly to lean in, too. To believe him. To agree with him. "You must be delusional."

"Any food for you this evening?" the barmaid said, stepping up to refill their drinks.

"I think we'll both have the dinner special," Zare said without missing a beat.

The waitress blushed at the charming smile he flashed her and retreated with her pitcher.

"Now why would you say that?" Zare returned his attention to her, not acknowledging the poisonous glare she was giving him for picking her dinner without her say.

He'd already taken control of the conversation. Ordered her food for her before she could make her own choice. She set down her drink and stood up. "I am not entertaining this. Say what you really came to say, or let me be."

"How I've missed your sharp tongue," he chuckled. "Sit back down, I have what you asked for."

"You have the gem?"

He shook his head. "I'm not a fool. I know Ash will kill me the second you give her the nod. Still at your beck and call, is she?"

"Ash has *never* been at my beck and call," she seethed, sliding reluctantly back into her chair. "Don't you dare try to drive a wedge between us. You will not succeed."

"Apologies," he said, raising his palms in submission. "Old habits. I don't have the gem on my person. However, as a show of good will, I will tell you what I know about it."

She gestured for him to go on.

"The cetamaris," he began, pausing when the waitress returned with a basket of bread.

Ferrin had no appetite.

"Is split into two parts," he continued, tearing a roll in half. "It was created hundreds of years ago by an incredibly powerful witch, as a means of controlling an ancient power that lurked beneath the waves. When she realized its power, she split it in two for safe keeping, and hid both pieces. One was in a necklace that she wore until she died here in the north. I found it off the coast of Njorske. Believe me when I say it cost me *greatly*."

"Continue," she said, breaking his dramatic pause.

"The second half, I suspect, is in the south. But you already knew that, didn't you?"

She grunted noncommittally.

"You remember Tabka's special charts, yes? The ones he swiped from that warlord off the coast of Marak?"

She nodded again. The enchanted set of charts were the most magical thing she'd seen at the time—old and weathered, yet still in perfectly legible condition. They seemed to show exactly what one needed to see in order to find what they sought. They could be folded into different patterns to show current winds, lurking threats and even lost treasures. Every time they were opened, they showed something new.

"Well, it's troubling, you see. The gem itself must be of a similar magic, because it is nearly impossible to track on the charts. It is almost as if it has a consciousness, as if it is moving across the sea."

"Maybe it's already aboard a ship, and someone is merely moving it without knowing," she said matter-of-factly.

"Perhaps," he agreed. "My letters?" He laid his hand out, expectant.

She fished the sealed envelope out of her coat and dropped it in his palm without ceremony. "You'll get the rest when I have the gem in my hand."

"Certainly." He cleared his throat. "There's more, though."

"What now?" she demanded.

"I have relevant information on Bourjony. That is who you're enmeshed in this little skirmish with, is it not?"

"And I suppose you want something more in exchange for this information?" she sighed.

"You can't have something for nothing, sweet Gillian."

She flinched. "Don't call me that."

He watched her in silence as the waitress brought forth two plates of roasted chicken. He was noting her reaction, tucking it away to use against her later. She cursed herself for allowing her flinch to show. She *needed* to keep her discomfort less visible.

"Well, what is it?" she asked when the waitress was gone.

"All in good time. Now, let's discuss what's going on here. You're gone for a few months and already you've replaced me.

Albeit with a more… rugged version." He took a too-casual sip of ale as he eyed her over his cup.

"Leave him out of this," she snarled in a hushed tone and picked up her mug again, if only to have something to do with her hands.

"Lukas, is it?"

"I already told you. We are not doing this."

"Doing what?" he asked lightly.

"This thing where you act like we had a mere spat before parting ways."

He gave a low, slow laugh. "*You lied to me for years*," he said, sitting forward and dropping his voice low. There might even have been genuine hurt crossing his features. It was gone in a blink.

"And you manipulated me and everyone else around you for years," she countered, her voice gravelly and quiet.

"Oh, please. You knew what I was," he reminded her. "You just chose to pretend it would never come around to your end. But me? I was in the dark for *years*. Who knew what a sweet little liar freckle-faced Gill could be."

"Are we done here?" she set her mug down with a satisfying thud.

"We have yet to discuss Bourjony," Zare said coolly.

"Go on then, tell me this tide-turning information."

"Not without something in return." He leveled a cool stare at her.

She scoffed. "No. I'm not wasting any more of my time playing games with you." She stood.

"Right, of course. You should get back to…" he let the question hang in the air before he gave it voice. "What is it exactly you're needed for here?"

She halted, her back still to him, fists clenched.

"I know where they're hiding their southern fleet."

She took one deep breath, steeling herself to ignore his words.

"I know what lurks in the harbor on Calixta, what they're breeding in that lab of theirs."

She turned around slowly, forcing her features into a mask of neutrality. "Another lab?"

A serpentine smile crossed his face. She knew that look. A predator who knew when his prey was cornered, all he needed was to wait for her to fall into his waiting teeth.

"And how did you come by this information?"

"You know me, I always have one eye open."

She closed her eyes slowly, preparing herself to shave down her dignity even further and begin negotiating with him.

"What is it you want?"

"To be blunt, I need money."

She couldn't stop the laugh that burst out of her. "Did my father not pay you a small fortune for stabbing me in the back?"

"And a new ship to return south on," he continued, ignoring her question.

"What makes you think I have any coin to give you?"

That cool smile returned. "I know you have funds. Perhaps your crown is gone, but the credit lines of the Lindbarrian Royal Family run deep, I'm sure."

She glared at him with fire in her eyes.

"Hunting down the cetamaris was not cheap," he said, his expression transforming into a stony, joyless one. "I lost a lot. Sailors, money, supplies. The accounts were all but drained."

She tilted her head curiously. He'd taken a huge risk to get that gem and get here, so he had to be sure this was going to pan out in his favor. Zare did not take risks without careful calculation. Either he was lying, or there were yet more cards up his sleeve.

"Get me enough money to outfit a new ship and fill its coffers, and I'll tell you everything I know about the southern fleet, and Bourjony's newest ally."

There it was. The final play. He knew he'd snared her, and she was going to get him what he wanted. Maybe not right away, but he'd won this round.

"And how do I know you're not making any of this up? What confirmation could you possibly offer me?"

"I'm not saying more until you agree to get me what I need," he said smugly, crossing his arms.

"Whatever. I'm not desperate enough for that," she lied. "Meet me out on the docks at dawn in two days to do the final trade for the gem. I'll have your papers in order by then."

CHAPTER TWENTY-FIVE

The following days in Bramblehall passed with little importance. Soviel's days were filled with teas, luncheons and strolls, her evenings with feasts, wine tastings and balls.

The morning of their departure, Soviel awoke early and quickly stashed her most recent set of notes in the tree before scurrying back to the estate to attend Samia with packing for the day ahead.

The idea of returning to Everness was daunting, and she wasn't sure it was a smart idea. There were informants who might still be employed there who could identify her. However, there was much left to be investigated. And, if she was being honest, she was curious to see how badly she and Lukas had damaged the old wing of the castle when they'd blown up the beast.

They were to leave around lunchtime, in a caravan of four carriages stocked with servants, gifts and goods. Samia was flitting about in her usual state, chirping out her stream of unfiltered consciousness. If only she were the one with important information; she seemed to have no refining process whatsoever for her words. She'd just plucked up three sets of silk slippers from the floor and was flinging them onto the bed to be packed when she started sniping at Erina for her un-polished hairstyle choice for the day.

With a barely-suppressed sigh of annoyance, Erina excused herself to go freshen up.

"How long until we leave?" Soviel asked, picking up and folding a petticoat that had been flung over the bed's footboard.

"An hour," Samia wrung her hands. "There is too much to do."

"What exactly will we be doing while in Everness?" Soviel asked. "Aside from the ball, I mean."

"Well, my husband will have various meetings and duties to attend to," Samia huffed. "And I suppose we'll have time enough to do as we please: teas, luncheons, perhaps there will be musicians to listen to."

"Samia, are you certain you need this many sets of stays?" Jorde asked. "We're only there four nights."

"They each go best with a specific dress," Samia pouted.

"Maybe so, but look here," Jorde held up a set of dove-gray stays. "This one matches all of them."

Soviel was trying not to roll her eyes at Samia's trivial crisis.

"Very well, Jorde. I suppose you're right."

Finally, they finished packing and rang the footman to collect the various trunks to be brought down to the carriages.

The duke was waiting outside, his valet and one of his usual associates, the second son of a lord of a neighboring territory, stood with him chatting idly while he checked his pocket watch.

His appearance was polished as ever, and he wore a tight scowl, and a tense set to his shoulders. He was in a mood, it seemed. Once everything was settled into its place in the caravan, he climbed into his own carriage, separate from Samia, and slammed the door.

Samia took Soviel and Jorde into the second carriage, and relegated the other girls to the third.

Everness was mostly unchanged. Though the people were new, and the flags flying from its spires and turrets were different, the bare rock and hewn marble of the palace had remained the same. Some things were unchangeable, she supposed. When a place had stood over a thousand years, lasted through dozens of sieges, generations of changing power, and endless amounts of spilled blood, it wasn't as if one more occupation would alter it. Dynasties rose and fell, but stone persisted.

The new regime had left its marks, though: a gallows had been erected in the courtyard, mere feet from the flower garden from which Soviel had once collected herbs. Soldiers drilled on the lawn with a fearsome tenacity. Diplomats milled about the halls, busy as ever.

Soviel marked a few faces she vaguely recognized from her time in the capital. A few nobles who must have weathered the change of power through money, luck, or complicity.

"How positively barbarian," Samia said in regard to the rough stone architecture in the oldest part of the castle.

"Oh, you can't even imagine how cold these stone floors get in the winter," Soviel said. "Getting out of bed in the morning was a feat of bravery in itself. But it did keep us cooler in the warm months. A small blessing."

"Och," Samia grimaced. "We have a floor heating system built in at Bramblehall. Some ancient Efelian invention once used in their public baths."

"How does it work?"

"Some hollow beneath the floors that connects to an interior chimney tended by the servants," she waved a dismissive hand.

A hollow beneath the floor. Soviel wondered if it was big enough to crawl through, or if it, too, would prove useless to her own purposes. She tucked this bit of information away for later, as she had more pressing things to deal with here. More important floor-hollows.

Once she and the other ladies had helped prepare Samia for bed, Soviel excused herself to the guest room she'd be occupying, before setting out to examine the halls she'd walked countless times before.

She supposed it was unsurprising that under the new regime, the halls were more heavily guarded than before. Certain areas were marked completely off-limits without proper credentials, and it seemed that the lower half of the old wing was completely unsafe to set foot in. Apparently, when she and Lukas had blown up the pit-creature, it had damaged several floors above the underground tunnels.

After an hour of casual exploring, she turned back the way she had come, aiming to pass by the wine cellar where she and Rhi had found those barrels of *popava* stashed. If the strange system of tracks and tunnels she'd seen were now operational, she needed to find out why.

She passed a few servants bringing tea and warm milk up to their mistresses and masters; none of them seemed to pay her much mind as she headed downstairs. When she reached the entrance to the wine cellar, she found two guards outside, standing sentry. She pulled up short before rounding the corner, before they could spot her. *That* was a new development.

She listened for a minute, as they chatted idly about what they wanted to do when their shift was up, but despite the chatter, they were attentive and alert. There was no way for her to slip past them, and no charming her way in, either. Too risky.

She had four free days here. Surely that was enough time to find a way to temporarily incapacitate the guards.

All she needed was to learn their schedule. She knew exactly where she needed to go.

The following night, Soviel dragged Erina with her to breeze by the guardhouse under the guise of making acquaintances before dinner. Erina looked mildly disinterested in every soldier who looked her way, but perked up when a tall, uniformed brunette leaned over the back of her chair to introduced herself with a cool, confident, extended hand.

The two began chatting, Erina leaning in, far more engaged than she'd been when speaking with any of the gentlemen. Soviel made a mental note not to bother Erina with any more noblemen in the future. She was surprised she hadn't picked up on Erina's interests sooner, but she supposed so many new faces at once had kept her from piecing together details about each of their lives. Especially, when she'd been spending so much of her time trying to schedule a way to get into the duke's office.

She returned her attention to the young guard she was speaking with. He was mild-mannered, a bit bland, with a placid expression on his symmetrical features. She nodded, slightly doe-eyed, at what he was saying, while memorizing the guard schedule that was posted on the wall just behind his shoulder. She'd once had a few passing friendships with some of the guards here, and fortunately, it seemed her cover was still entirely intact with all of them.

When she'd gathered what she needed from the schedule, she politely excused herself and gathered Erina to return to their rooms for the evening. Tomorrow was the ball, and the night after that, she would make her move on the wine cellar.

Eddanie Handrickx and Trent Mullein - Sentry duty, Wine Cellar, Midnight-Dawn.

Mullein - that name was familiar. He'd been one of Grey's targets for intelligence. A wealthy second son of a merchant or somesuch. She'd even met him once or twice.

Yes, she could find a way to make this work. If she could dose them with something just after dinner and make sure it didn't kick in until they were already on duty, it would be simple. She'd only need a day to gather the ingredients.

The evening of the ball was a clear one, and unseasonably warm. The large windows of Everness's ballroom had been thrown open for more airflow, and Soviel had broken a sweat as she rushed to Samia's rooms to ready her for the big event.

Samia had had an array of gorgeous gowns made specially for them at an expedited rate; Soviel didn't even want to think about what Theo's bill to the duchess would look like for that month. The gowns alone had to cost a fortune, and to have had his entire staff drop everything so they could finish them on such short notice would have tolled a king's ransom.

The burgundy silk of Samia's gown flashed bright crimson when it caught the light, and was layered over a contrasting petticoat of midnight and cream harlequin checks. Its sleeves billowed with excessive fabric, draping romantically to her elbows where they fastened with gold buttons. All she needed was a red and black lace mask, and she could be the Carnival Queen of the *Drama Macabre*, the famous Bourjon opera about wives murdering their husbands that had gained popularity over the last half-century.

Tavara was sorting through Samia's jewelry while Jorde held up rouge samples, trying to help Samia decide on which particular berry shade would do.

Soviel had just located the box carrying Samia's and Jorde's new shoes for the event, shoved among the near dozen trunks the duchess had packed for the week's journey.

"Found them!" she cried, holding up one of the brand new ruby red slippers.

"Perfect!" Samia clapped.

"Here's the black diamond earrings," Tavara said, approaching the vanity with the box in her hand. She clipped the earrings into Samia's earlobes one at a time.

"What exactly is it we're to be celebrating at this ball?" Erina asked boredly from where she'd sprawled on Samia's bed. "I don't want to make an ass of myself when making conversation."

"The new governor's appointment, of course," Jorde said.

"Right, but wasn't he appointed weeks ago? This seems delayed."

"Yes, but there's been so much to do. Power shifts take time," Jorde explained.

"Right," Erina drawled, picking at her nails.

"I'm just looking forward to the wine," Lucelle mused. "The new ambassador is here and there's simply no chance they'll put out anything but the best."

"Which ambassador?" Soviel turned, still twisting Samia's brushed out hair in one hand.

"Ambassador Nouie Fremange of Larais. My cousin. Distantly," Lucelle added with a wave. "He's already married."

"Just curious," Soviel said casually.

"It's not as if he's the faithful type," Tavara scoffed. "Luce practically had to swat his hand off my ass with a serving tray the last time he visited."

Lucelle shrugged. "I doubt Soviel is looking to be some nobleman's one-week fling. She wants a wealthy match and an easy life, yes?"

Soviel shrugged and smiled. "Well, don't we all?"

It couldn't be further from true, but the lie was easy. She had nothing against women who wanted such a thing— security, comfort, ease—but the idea of some strange, faceless man she hardly knew pressing up against her, kissing her, doing more, was a lot to stomach. The very few courtships she'd had had only come after she'd known the person and worked with them for a long while, building a strong bond of friendship and trust before it ever progressed into anything more.

"Well, he's taken, but I'm sure I can find a few of his pals to introduce you to," Lucelle offered good-naturedly.

"Thanks," Soviel said with a sheepish half-smile.

"Don't feel badly, Tavs is in your position as well."

"Oh?" Soviel shifted her attention to Tavara, who was adjusting her poppy-red lip-paint in the mirror.

"Yes," she grumbled, dabbing red rouge on her lips in the mirror. "Unfortunately, my family had a large stake in some business with a former mining magnate of Khalim. When that business fell through, they lost a great deal of their fortune. If I or my brothers don't marry rich—and soon—it'll be a lean year indeed."

"Sorry to hear that," Soviel said.

"It's a fixable problem." Tavara said coyly before turning back to the room. "But, don't repeat that to outsiders. I don't want to come across as desperate."

"Right, of course," Soviel nodded.

During the last few years of Henrik's reign, the ballroom at Everness castle had fallen into disuse. Apparently the man had little taste for parties and large social events. In fact, the last time Soviel had seen people in the ballroom had been the Royal Wedding between Henrik and Nerena, almost four years prior. Somehow, the Bourjonaise gent-folk had already seen to dusting off each chandelier, polishing each marble column and granite tile, and cleaning each mirrored wall panel. The ballroom had been restored to its former gilded grandeur.

"Oh, my," Soviel breathed when they entered via the balcony. She did not have to feign her awe. "It certainly looks different than it did when I was last here."

"This puts the rest of the ancient building to shame," Lucelle commented, flicking out her fan.

"Come, let's make our entrance," Samia urged.

The six of them truly made a picture: Samia's dramatic red dress, Tavara in white and gold flowing silk, Erina in a sleek, skin tight dress of dark emerald that flowed out at the thigh and trailed behind her like a rippling pool, Lucelle's deep fuchsia gown with its cream and teal accents, Jorde's saffron chiton that hugged her waist and flowed into a slit skirt, showing off one of her long legs, and Soviel's gown of two-toned silk that flashed gold in the light and ultramarine in the dark, with translucent sleeves like mothwing wisps falling just off her shoulder.

The entire crowd was coiffed, bejeweled and bedecked in their finest clothing. Soviel tried to get a lay of the land as she descended the staircase slowly behind Samia and Jorde. Erina was beside her, and Lucelle and Tavara behind them. She found it odd that Cal hadn't entered with Samia, as was typically custom for husband and wife to do, and wondered where the duke had run off to, until she spotted him speaking with a man with deep bronze skin and a pale pink silk jacket.

"Who's that speaking with His Grace?" Soviel asked Erina under her breath.

"Oh him?" Erina's gaze caught on the man. "He's one of the wealthiest land-owners south of Larais. His name's… ah… Rovelian or something. My parents are desperate to get in good with him. His main business is a shipping concern out of Khalim, but he owns stake in a dozen or so farms and plantations from the Wee Isles to Marak."

"*Popava* plantations?" Soviel surmised.

"Popava, arimopo, sugar, spice, tea, grain, you name it," Erina explained.

"Incredible," Soviel widened her eyes. "Where does he ship to?"

"All over. As far as I've been told, Hadringston has been trying to buy an interest in his company for months now. Maybe something will finally come to fruition this evening."

Soviel nodded, tucking away that bit of information for later.

They reached the bottom of the stairs and assimilated into the crowd. A moment later, Tavara linked an arm through Soviel's and whisked her away, placing a glass of champagne in her hand.

"Come, I want to speak to Lord Dresden, and his brother who never leaves his side has a proclivity for fair-haired women."

"Alright," Soviel agreed with a surprised laugh.

Tavara deposited her in front of two men who were nearly identical, other than the fact that one looked like a worn out copy of the other—their features were alike, yes, but the man on the right was pallid where his brother was sun-kissed, unassuming, while the other was magnetic.

"Hello, Lord Dresden," Tavara said with a well-practiced curtsy. "This is my dear friend, Lady Soviel of Korolsk."

"My Lord," Soviel said, mimicking Tav's curtsy.

"A pleasure to meet you." He took her hand and kissed it. "Allow me to introduce my brother Filivid."

"Just Fil," the faded one said with an incline of his head. "Nice to make your acquaintance."

"And you as well," Soviel said politely.

The four of them got to chatting. Soviel had to admit, Tavara was an expert conversationalist, if a bit openly flirtatious. When the conversation turned to the weather and Dresden began losing interest, she leaned in with practiced conspiratorial interest.

"Now, who would you say is the guest of the hour tonight? Besides our esteemed governor, of course," Tavara said in a stage whisper.

"Oh, now that *is* tricky," Dresden said, leaning in and surveying the crowd. "Ana Lela Maufin is here, somewhere. She's one of the top—if not *the* top—developers of naval weaponry north of Khalim."

"And who is Madame Maufin's competition for the title?" Tavara linked her arm through Dresden's, scanning the crowd.

"Perhaps him," Dresden said, pointing with his drink at a short man with curly red-brown hair and olive freckled skin weaving through the crowd. "Kalassan ambassador. Here on serious business, I'm told."

"Oh really?" Tavara asked. "An ambassador, that doesn't sound very exciting."

Desperate to keep the conversation from shifting, Soviel cut in, "is he not the one who was having the affair with… oh… what was her name—"

"Pannery Levin? No. That's not him. He's here on business regarding the troops to be lent."

"Pannery Levin was having an affair with a drill sergeant from Frise," Fil interjected.

"Fil, you're an insufferable gossip!" Tavara exclaimed with a laugh that was a touch too forced. She was losing her handle on the conversation, and if she kept at it, she'd drive away the sources of information Soviel was keen to keep close at hand.

"What are we selling to Kalassa?" Soviel asked.

"Nothing, I said *troops*, dear," Dresden said, his words dripping with condescension.

Soviel willed a blush to her cheeks. "My mistake."

"Worry not, such things are often confusing," he said in a benevolent tone that made Soviel want to roll her eyes. Tavara was in dire straits indeed if she was willing to throw herself at this kind of man. She'd listened in on some of Tavara's conversations with Erina and knew her to be quite learned.

"So, what is he doing here?" she asked, doing her best doe-eyed simper. Tavara shot her a look that said she knew *exactly* what she was doing and she'd better back off her mark.

Wrong kind of mark, Tavs, Soviel thought to herself.

"Well, nothing is set in stone, but a deal is in the air for our Kalassan allies to loan us troops numbering five-thousand," he said.

Her heart jumped into her throat. If the Kalassans allied with Bourjony, it would tip the scales remarkably out of favor for the resistance in the north.

"Oh," she nodded dumbly. "What are we giving in return?"

"No, dear girl, I said it's a *loan*, not a trade," he said sympathetically.

Tavara shot her another look.

"I think I've have had too much champagne." Soviel fanned herself lightly.

"Maybe you should go get some food, Sov," Tavara said pointedly.

The shortening of her name twisted her heart. She missed her friends, she missed being able to speak freely, to come out of her veil every so often and just *be* without putting on a constant performance.

"Maybe I should," she nodded. "Please excuse me. Gentlemen, it was lovely to meet you."

With that, she ducked away from the group, her lovely skirts swishing behind her as she pushed through the crowd, plucking a shrimp from one of the platters as she doubled back around to get closer to the Kalassan ambassador. She swapped her full champagne glass out for one that had been half-drunk and left on the edge of one of the food tables, then swept into the crowd.

After a moment of wandering, someone grabbed her free hand and cupped the back of her waist, sweeping her into the waltz that had begun. Her heart ratcheted up when she realized it was Hadringston.

He looked immaculate in his sharp gray coat. His hair was absent its usual powdered wig, and was pulled back neatly. His hard gray eyes matched the color of his silk clothing as they bore into her.

"You looked lost," he said.

"Your Grace," she hiccuped. "Are you enjoying the ball?"

"The new governor is a colleague of mine. I'm pleased he's finally had the time to celebrate his appointment," he said. A pleasant non-answer.

"It's lovely," she nodded. "After so much strife in this castle, it's nice to see it so cheery."

"And you? I trust you're enjoying the evening?"

She nodded, feeling awkward and pinned by his unrelenting gaze. The coldness in his eyes never ceased.

"I like to get to know the people my wife employs. I make a habit of having conversation with the people hanging about my estate. You'd agree that that's prudent, yes?"

"Of course," she nodded.

He looked her up and down. "How are you finding Bramblehall? The other ladies?"

They continued through the steps of the dance. "It's excellent, the amenities are the best I've ever lived with, the girls are a fine time, and S-Her Grace is a benev—"

"I didn't ask about my wife."

Oh, this was looking to be an uncomfortable situation.

"The other girls are fascinating," she continued, trying to keep control over the conversation. "Jorde is so smart. I swear, she knows everything there is to know. And Lucelle is so compassionate, even though she acts like she's above caring for anyone besides herself—"

"Hm," he snorted. "You try very hard to impress people, don't you." It wasn't a question.

"I'm not sure I know what you mean."

He spun her in time with the music, catching her to his chest on the beat, so her back was pressed against him, and her hand was clutched in his.

Her skin crawled. In her time as a spy, she'd chosen safety and swallowed her pride on many an occasion. She hoped Hadringston and his cold eyes would not turn into one of those times.

"*Try less,*" he instructed in her ear. She caught a strong whiff of liquor on his breath. This hair-line indiscretion must have been the most un-composed transgression he was capable of, even drunk. *What a rigid way to live.*

The song ended and he relinquished her, turning and stalking back through the crowd without another word. She swallowed, thoroughly put off by the entire encounter.

The ball wore on, and Soviel tried to put Hadringston's unsettling advance out of her mind, focusing on the task at hand. She'd set her sights on a group of refined-looking scholars, chatting at the edge of the ballroom floor, champagne glasses in hands, posture elegant. The woman pointed out earlier by Dresden was among the group, her graying brown hair piled into an elegant, conservative knot at the back of her head. Ana Lela Maufin, one of Bourjony's chief weapons developers. A brilliant mind, who'd studied in Dromata's great university, as well as a dozen others, perfecting and spearheading the field of engineering.

She'd switched out her champagne glass multiple times among the crowd, sure to keep the illusion up that she was drinking as much as the rest of them. She'd gone as far as dabbing some liquor under her chin and ears so she'd smell the part.

"Soviel!" exclaimed Samia, as she grabbed Soviel by the wrist a little less than gently. Some of her champagne sloshed to the side. "How is your evening going? Have you made any acquaintances?"

"Splendidly," Soviel gushed. "I've met Lord Dresden, his brother, and a Mr. Elbroucke? Who hails from Fairjold, do you know him?"

Samia shook her head blankly.

"Oh, well, he boasts to own half the iron mines between there and the Veiran border."

"Oh, *Jensing*," Samia said in recognition. "He's my third cousin. You've never seen someone hold their liquor like him."

Soviel laughed. "Yes, that sounds like him."

"Will you retire to the after party with me when the time comes?" Samia urged, taking ahold of Soviel's elbow in her gloved hand.

"An after party?"

"Yes, to take place in one of the smoking rooms."

"I don't see why not," Soviel giggled, maintaining her carefree, doe-eyed persona.

"Come find me when the clock strikes midnight!" Samia said with a squeal before peeling off into the crowd to find her next target.

Soviel released a breath. She took a false sip from her champagne glass and turned back to where Ana Lela Maufin's group had been.

Only, they were gone.

She deflated slightly and turned to search the crowd. She spotted Maufin just a few groups away, but her joy was quickly crushed when she saw that the lady was deep in conversation with Jorde.

Of course she was; Jorde was brilliant, a scholar through and through. That was what made Soviel nervous from the get-go. Jorde had been disapproving at best and suspicious at worst wherever Soviel was concerned.

If she swooped in now, she would kill whatever conversation they were deep into, or worse, give Jorde cause to be even more suspicious of her motivations for being there.

She huffed and set down her glass. Without moving too quickly, she made her way up the table, edging closer and closer to where Jorde and Maufin were speaking quietly.

With careful fingers, Soviel plucked miniature cakes, tiny fruit pies and little pusties off of the various buffet-style trays, absently scouring the options as she came closer to the scholars.

Finally, she was within earshot.

"…primary issue we faced in the earlier stages was the weighting, you see. This wasn't an issue for the land models, of course, but the ship-mounted versions? They'd be more a hindrance than a help," Maufin explained in her elegant, accented voice.

"And the initial models were comprised of…?"

"Iron, but our stores ran low, so we switched to bronze bases with iron components."

"And what of other nonferrous metals? Iron at such a scale *would* be far too heavy on a warship—"

"Yes, well that's the point of contention my team has been having," Maufin explained. "What lightweight metal is strong enough to sustain it? What is abundant enough?"

Jorde puzzled a moment and seemed to come up blank. "Well, aside from scaling it down, I just don't see how it could work."

"Yes, I've said as much to the investors, but they don't like that very much. So production has hit a snag for now, I'm afraid," Maufin sighed. "But I'm always happy for insight from younger minds. You've been applying to return to university, am I correct?"

"Yes," Jorde said a bit irritably. "Though I haven't seen much luck in the matter."

Maufin considered a moment. "I'll have a word with a good friend of mine on the board at the University of Khalim, see if he can find a space for you."

With the conversation no longer relevant to her purposes, Soviel cleared out before anyone noticed her lingering too long.

Midnight rolled around with an ominous chime of the fifteen-foot-tall gilded clock that stood at the head of the room, and Soviel, ever the dutiful charge, set out to find Samia.

She found her in a drunken knot of people crowded onto a bench overlooking the moonlit gardens, awash in laughter, and enjoying a plate of strawberries.

"Oh, oh!" Samia choked down her laughter as she saw Soviel approach. "Is it midnight already?"

"Yes, Your Grace," Soviel said, setting down her fifth glass of champagne.

"Splendid," she giggled, disentangling from her group of pals. "Let's go find my grouch of a husband before we go."

Soviel bristled. She was still feeling out the dynamic of Samia and Cal, and she didn't want to do anything that would further encourage his interest in her. That would be a dangerous last resort, should *everything* go wrong.

Samia dragged Hadringston from whatever conversation he had been in, apparently oblivious to the murderous scowl on his face as she pulled him down the hallway. Soviel trailed behind awkwardly until, thankfully, she was joined by Erina.

"And how has your evening been going?" Erina asked cheerily, linking her arm through Soviel's elbow. Her wide brown eyes and heavy lashes reminded Soviel wistfully of Ash's, though they were absent the flecks of honey-gold and amber that caught the light in Ash's.

Soviel burst out in a giggle, drawing on fond memories as she played up her drunkenness. "I'm drowning on bubbles, I think," she admitted in an unquiet whisper.

Erina bust out laughing. "Well, I hope you're ready to swim. Apparently these after-parties are an absolute carousal. Word is, the room's previous owner left behind a host of exotic liquors and smokes."

Soviel's heart sunk when she realized they were headed straight for Rhi's old chamber. Her chest tightened and it took everything to keep her giddy, lazy smile from disappearing.

"I suppose I could drink a little more," she said, hiccuping on command.

Erina laughed again and clapped her on the back. "Great, just don't get sick on my things. We're sharing a room, remember?"

Soviel giggled again as they passed through the threshold of the familiar room.

"The crown prince was kind enough to leave us plenty of goods when he ran off to Galan!" A man in his shirtsleeves was standing on the bed, a crystal decanter clutched in one hand, an *arimopo* cigar in the other. He'd loosened his cravat and shoved it up around his forehead like some kind of warrior-headband, to hold back his golden curls. He wasn't someone she recognized, but he seemed to be hosting this party.

"A toast!" he continued in a boisterous tone, cheeks flushed pink with drink and heat. "To our esteemed runaway prince and princess, for vacating such fine rooms!"

Another similarly boisterous man on the side was holding up a translucent silky shift that he must have dug out of Ferrin's room. With a snigger he paraded it around before tossing it at the man standing on the bed. It landed over his face but not before being singed by the end of his cigar.

Soviel laughed as she steamed inside. "Where are our other ladies?" she asked Erina as she surveyed the suite.

"Oh, this isn't their sort of thing—Lucelle is probably having some deep, pretentious philosophical conversation while neck deep in smoke with some of the university students —she has such a thing for scholars. I swear, put a person in spectacles and she falls head over heels—and Tavara is probably letting Lord Dresden catch a feel behind a potted plant. Jorde is obviously much too intelligent to attend one of these things. She wouldn't want to waste the brain-space with such useless memories."

Soviel nodded and picked up an open bottle of red wine from the desk before her, pouring herself a glass. "And you? Is this your sort of party?"

Erina looked around and smirked. "It's getting a bit too rambunctious by the looks of it, but I'll stay."

Soviel scanned the room again, and her eye caught on one of the ladies across from her. Her heart leapt into her throat. *Nimhe?*

Then she turned, it was not Nimhe.

It was just another young woman with red hair. Though, hers was a little darker, and she was a little older. She was drinking straight from one of Rhi's more expensive whiskey bottles.

She didn't know why she'd thought it was Nimhe—the similarities ended after the bright hair. This woman was tall and willowy, and cut an impressive figure in a tailored jacket and matching breeches.

She needed to relax.

"Now, everyone knows the rules!" the man standing on the bed shouted, turning in a circle and spilling precious drops of liquor all over the duvet. "You have to have a substance on hand at all times," he slurred, "I care not if you're smoking it, drinking it, dropping it on your eyeball!" He laughed again. "To the new governor!"

The room echoed his toast and the revelry ensued.

CHAPTER TWENTY-SIX

Soviel's following day had begun with a late start, unsurprisingly, after pouring Samia into bed still half-dressed around three in the morning. By the time evening rolled around and all had more or less recovered from the night of indulgences, Soviel was feeling withdrawn and too-quiet, as if she'd been wrapped in cotton that muffled everything around her, as she plotted her post-dinner plans. She'd tried and failed several times to shake herself into the present moment.

Samia seemed to be cycling through topics at the speed of a bumblebee's wing as she picked at roast pheasant. Soviel barely managed to get down half of her dinner, the vial of sleeping draught growing heavy in her pocket.

During the first course of the meal, served feast-style in the Great Hall, she spied Mullein down at one of the lower tables. He was laughing and chatting animatedly, as if half of his comrades hadn't been slaughtered and imprisoned mere weeks ago. It seemed like he was already well into his cups, quite deeply, in fact, for someone who was to be awake and on sentry duty all night. Quite convenient for Soviel.

"Does it sadden you to be back here, Soviel?" Jorde's voice sliced through her planning and drew her back to the present moment.

She sighed lightly. "Only a little, I have some unpleasant memories from the whole ordeal. People I thought were my friends turned out to be sympathizers to the Caelish, or were killed in the fighting that broke out." As always, the lie rolled smoothly off her tongue, and she let her discomfort show.

"I thought your parents were Caelish sympathizers before the Unification?" Jorde asked, her voice almost bored.

Soviel stiffened. "My parents made a series of bad investments during war time, and bet on the wrong horse. I've learned from their mistakes. Those in the north who insist on keeping this conflict burning do so to all of our detriment."

Jorde considered her words, and crinkled her nose in distaste. "How grim."

"Yes, it is," Soviel admitted, sipping her wine.

Jorde studied her for a moment too long. Of all the ladies, Jorde was the one to watch out for. Lucelle was here for status, Tavara for money, Erina for some combination of the two, perhaps. She was still figuring out what exactly the girl's lack of ambition could mean. But Jorde was sharp-eyed as a hawk, and wise, too. If anyone was going to spot a hole in Soviel's story, it was Jorde.

Not that she was willing to underestimate any of them. Even vapid Samia could have unknown motives.

"I must say, I find the amenities here quite charming, almost vintage," Lucelle observed, popping a cherry-tomato into her mouth.

"I'd like to see the grand library while we're here," Jorde added, pushing her dainty gold glasses up her nose. Soviel was beginning to wonder if Jorde truly needed her spectacles, or if it was another part of Samia's decorating the lot of them how she saw fit.

"I can show you the way there tomorrow, if you'd like," Soviel offered.

"I prefer to read alone," Jorde replied coolly.

"Understandable," Soviel said, willing a relaxed agreeableness into her tone. She ignored the sharp eyebrow-raise from Tavara at Jorde's dismissal.

Fine, then. I have better things to do with my time anyway, Soviel thought.

"I'd like to stroll in town tomorrow afternoon," Samia announced.

And that was that.

By her calculations, Soviel had positioned herself in precisely the right place to run into Mullein just after dinner. She was perched on a lounge chair in the lower salon, where nobles and commoners alike might retire to sip a brandy or a whiskey while smoking and chatting after dinner.

She'd dosed the entire jug of wine before her with the sleeping draught, one she had engineered herself last year. It took just about four hours to kick in on an average-sized man. As long as the intended target drank enough of it, it required only a quick bit of magical maneuvering from her and the draught would activate, triggering a response from the chemical that made a person drowsy. If she didn't activate it, the drug passed from their system with no noticeable side effects. This method made it safe for her to drink alongside her target, casting any suspicion away from her.

At just past nine o'clock, the soldiers who'd been at dinner strolled in, their mood loud and rowdy.

She made a show of slowly looking up from her novel, making eye contact, and holding it for a beat before dropping her eyes back to her book.

Like clockwork, her feigned disinterest pulled him right in. She could feel his attention on her as she flipped to the next page of the novel she was pretending to read, and she shifted in her chair, arching her back the slightest bit.

"Hi there, you look like you could use some company."

She set down the book and looked up slowly through her lashes. Then, she let the smallest spark of recognition show.

"Trent, right?" She tilted her head to the side, as if recalling a distant memory. "Trent Mullein?"

"Yes." He looked her up and down, not quite recognizing her, but certainly piqued by her interest in him. A slightly smug expression fell over his features.

"It's Soviel," she pressed a hand to her chest, leaning forward slightly, showing the low neckline of her gown. "We met a few times last winter at Grey Emmin's parties."

His eyes latched onto her face. *Curses*, no one *ever* remembered her face. It was usually a blessing.

She fluttered her lashes and let her lips part. *Come on, you fool, at least stay interested if you don't remember me.*

"Right! Soviel. You were one of the queen's ladies?"

"Close, I attended to the former princess," she corrected.

"Ah, yes, and what's brought you back to the castle?"

"I'm in the employ of Duchess Samia Hadringston of Bramblehall, now," she said, sipping her wine.

"Are you now?" He made a show of taking in her appearance; the lavish dress, the fashionable hairstyle, the expensive jewelry.

She merely nodded and bat her eyelashes with an impish tilt of her head.

"How are you liking things over at Bramblehall?" He stepped closer. He already reeked if liquor.

"Oh, it's much nicer than this drafty old place." She flashed him a conspirator's grin.

"Indeed," he said, nodding. His gaze dipped down the front of her dress for a fraction of a second.

"Are you going to introduce me to your friends?" she asked with a mischievous smile.

"Of course, right this way," he said, offering his hand so she could rise from her chair, then guiding her with an unnecessary hand on her lower back.

She tucked the jug of wine under her arm and left her book discarded on the lounge.

"Friends, this is Lady Soviel, of…" he looked back to her.

"Of Korolsk," she supplied.

"Lady Soviel of Korolsk," he introduced. "She attended to that shrewish princess before the city changed hands."

"Pleased to meet all of you…" she paused, waiting for their names.

"Ah yes, my manners. This is Blaise, Artur, Eddanie and Gord."

She skimmed her eyes over each of them, nodding as she noted their names.

Soviel cursed to herself. Eddanie, blonde and youthful, was a particularly large woman. Certainly over six feet tall, and broader even than some of her male counterparts at the table. It might take a fair bit of sleeping draught to knock her out.

"Well, soldiers, I can't finish all this wine by my lonesome, care to have a game?" she said, her voice taking on a wickedly flirtatious tone.

The clock struck half-past one, and Soviel, dressed in a crummy old frock, was on her way out the door, letting it close without so much as a creak behind her. She'd been careful to oil the hinges upon arrival—she was sharing quarters with Erina for the duration of their stay, and she didn't want the lady noticing her coming and going at odd hours as a result of Everness's ancient, creaking doors.

Pulling her shawl tight around her shoulders, she moved through the halls she knew better than the home she'd grown up in, and headed for the wine cellar. If her calculations were right, the sentries would have been knocked out by one hour past midnight, but given Eddanie's size, she couldn't be too careful.

She'd just rounded the corner of the staircase heading to the lower level when she heard approaching voices. Before they could spot her, she ducked into an alcove, partly concealed by a potted fern.

Once they'd moved on, she resumed her trek down to the wine cellar.

As expected, both Trent and Eddanie were soundly sleeping, their chests rising and falling evenly with an occasional little snort, propped against the wall.

She gingerly stepped over Trent's extended leg, careful not to brush him with her skirts as she crept to the door. It was locked, but thankfully, the stolen set of keys she'd long ago hidden beneath the floorboards in the servant's passages had still been there.

She opened the cellar door and stepped inside.

The room was cold, crisp, and dry as Soviel padded through the darkness. When she reached the middle of the room, by the rack of merlots, she knelt and peeled back the rug covering the trap door. The O-ring flipped back and she slowly pulled it open with minimal resistance.

As Soviel's eyes adjusted to the darkness, she could see that the barrels of *popava* she and Lukas had commandeered to aid in blowing up the pit-creature had been replaced. When she popped the top off of one, she saw that they were again filled to the brim with dried, primed *popava* leaves. She took a deep breath and swung herself into the ditch beside the barrels.

The first thing she noticed was the distant echoing of metal pinging, and creaky wheels on tracks. Strangest of all, unlike the last time she'd been down here, the air was full of reddish dust and movement. Dim torchlight extended hazily from the distance, far beyond where she could see.

She slung her plain cloak higher over her head and hunched deeper into the tunnel. As she made her way along the tracks, she found that the tunnel opened into a large, underground cavern, one that in all her years of snooping, she'd never known to be beneath the castle.

Long tables sat in rows, crammed with dozens of people standing over them, working by torchlight, backs bent as they toiled over something. *What was it?*

She crept closer and saw a man standing with his back to her, head bent as he scanned the open book in his hand. A ledger on production, or quantity reports, perhaps.

"You! Get back in line!" a deep, sharp voice rumbled to her left. "Your break ended five minutes ago!"

She lowered her head in subservience and slipped between two workers at the table, blending seamlessly into the line. Before her there were dozens of tins and tinctures, bundles of herbs, oils in jars, and rows and rows of empty glass vials stacked in stands. They looked exactly like the vials Madame Leone had used to store highly-potent liquid medicines.

The woman next to her had her hands wrapped in dirty linen bandages, but worked nonetheless. The flesh beneath looked badly burned, recent enough to still be scabbing. Her movements were nonetheless nimble as she packaged the mixtures into the strange vials. One small scoop of powder, one folded and dried *popava* leaf, two small scoops of the milky liquid, one pinch of the blue-gray powder. Then, the vial was capped off and placed in the basket on the table where it nestled amongst its glossy brethren.

Soviel tried to note everything as she took it all in.

Once the basket on the table was filled, one of the workers moved it to the cart on the tracks behind them, and replaced it with an empty one, and the whole process continued on.

She'd been standing on the assembly line trying to look busy for ten minutes when the nearest cart filled, and one of the overseers pulled a lever that sent it careening away into the tunnel on its tracks.

She narrowed her eyes in the direction it had been whisked away. Where were they sending it?

A fresh cart rolled up from behind her by the second station, and she saw her opening. In her peripheral vision, she watched it fill for a few more minutes. Then, in a show of impulsivity she'd later consider wildly unlike her, Soviel looked both ways before hopping over the side and climbing into the cart, pulling baskets and folded linens over herself until she was completely covered. A moment later, there was a mechanical hiss, and she was on the move.

The cart skidded on, carrying her along its tracks into the tunnels. Her heart thundered as she let it take her blindly deeper into the castle's underbelly. It went over bumps that jostled the cargo above her, and she managed to snatch one vial and tuck it into her pocket. If she could manage to smuggle it out, she could send it back to camp to have tested. It could be the key to Rhi and Lachlan's research.

The cart squealed to a controlled stop, and she heard voices approaching.

"Pull the track shift, will you?"

"What?"

"These are needed in the lab. There was another… incident," a pleasant male voice said from above. "They need more vials immediately, so get a move on."

"That's the second one this week," hissed a second voice, female this time. "We're going to start running out of willing subjects."

"It's part of the process. It's a risk we *all* knew was possible."

"I know. But you're not the one up there, recruiting," she said.

Soviel didn't recognize either of the voices. *Recruiting for what?*

"Never mind that, just get a move on."

The cart slid forward another few feet before jerking to a stop again. She felt someone drop their hands on the rim of the cart and heard a metallic groan. *A track switch?* she wondered.

Oh gods. What had she done? Once they unloaded this cart, surely they'd find her stowed away in here. She'd be thrown in prison, or worse.

One basket shifted and she heard footsteps retreating.

Think, think, think. How could she slip out of this without notice?

A second basket shifted above her. The hem of her dress would be exposed now.

She twisted under the weight of the baskets, fabric writhing beneath her.

Fabric.

She squinted in the dim light—was that a soldier's jacket?

She'd have to hitch her skirts up beneath the fabric, but it might let her slip away. She'd worn breeches beneath her dress just in case.

She pawed at the fabric some more, pulling back the layers of what appeared to be the laundry and met with something hard beneath. She choked on a gasp as her palm slapped against what was unmistakably dead flesh.

She squirmed as far from the body as she could, and drew a piece of linen over her head as she looked over the edge of the cart. She could see the entire room now—gray stone walls blushed red with the lantern light. Dust hung in the air, casting a haze over everything.

She peered into the space, it was small. More people, better dressed than the assemblers, were gathered around low tables. A woman turned around and Soviel saw she was wearing some kind of protective eyewear, and a set of coveralls like she herself had once donned at the infirmary.

Slowly, she let free a tendril of her power, exploring, stretching to see if what she suspected of this room was right.

She drew in a sharp breath through her nose in shock. They were like her. Healers. Or people with some trace of healing magic, at least. As her eyes adjusted to the dimness, she could see what was on the tables around them. Among the scattered vials and bottles were… people. Dozens of strapped-down people, mostly unconscious, but a few were tied down to chairs, groaning in pain as they were injected with whatever was in the vials.

"Get this one sedated!" a female voice screamed from the far end of the room. The figure before her thrashed against his bindings to the point of the metal table groaning, *bending*. He opened his mouth and let out a visceral scream as he arched off the table.

Hands shaking, she peered higher over the lip of the metal cart. Just as she laid eyes on the attendant with the sedative in hand, the man on the table roared—and the jug on the table beside him began to quiver before the water inside exploded out the top and shot toward one of the healers. The shaft of water hardened, crystallizing into an icy spear in the blink of an eye just as the attendant managed to block it with the empty pail she held.

Soviel's eyes widened; it was very similar to what she had seen in the secret infirmary tent with Rhi and Lachlan. Only instead of fire bursting from the victim, it was water, turned to ice.

They sedated the patient and went back to working on whatever it was they were doing. Glass vials were being attached to a gun-like device with a long, thin needle on the end. The very same vials that were being packaged on the assembly line! That was what they were injecting into the restrained people. Somehow, it allowed them to summon intensely potent elemental power, the likes of which hadn't been seen in years.

Then she remembered the flying woman who'd attacked them when they'd fled this place earlier in the spring. That soldier had had power like this, had been created like this.

She had to get this information out, get it back to Galan.

"Get me linens," someone ordered.

With a jerk, the cart squealed into movement again. Before she could do anything about it, someone tossed a heavy ball of dirty linen on top of her. She batted it away from her face and kicked out from under the pile, trying not to let the thought of what she was sitting on undo the rest of her nerves.

A draft blew through the tunnel, and she cautiously poked her head over the top to see that she was careening downhill on the tracks. She gasped. The thing was going a bit too fast for her liking. She ducked back down again just as more linens and waste were thrown into the cart from far above.

She bit back a gag, grimacing as she shifted the mess away from her face. The air in the cavern seemed to be warming, and she had no idea what she was going to do with this filthy dress when she found her way out of this place. Something lukewarm and oozy had leaked onto her through the dirty linen. At last the cart screeched to a halt.

Suddenly, it lurched to the side, tilting all the way over on its edge.

She inhaled a sharp breath as she slipped and scrambled to keep from toppling out. And thank the gods she did, because below her, there was about a twelve-foot drop into a pit of flames and red-hot coals. An *incinerator*!

The heat dried her eyes and warmed her cheeks as she scrambled to stay upright. The cart at last righted itself and she popped up, looking over the edge.

There were two doors ahead, and voices coming from behind. She leapt over the side and ran for the first door she saw, bursting through to find a set of cellar stairs. She ran up, blind to what might be ahead, until she came to another door.

She threw herself through it and immediately tripped and tumbled down a grassy hill. She was somewhere outside the castle walls.

Finally, she stopped rolling and managed to right herself. The moon was high overhead, and her breath was coming hard and fast as she got her bearings.

Shit.

How was she to get back in the castle, at this hour, no less, looking like a ragamuffin?

She dropped her skirt, leaving the breeches beneath visible, and pulled it around her shoulders like a shawl before moving closer to the walls. There had to be some way in that didn't involve giving all her information over to the guards. Perhaps she could clean off in the stream, and then head back in…

No, it's much too cold for that, I'll freeze, she thought.

She walked the perimeter of the castle, avoiding the main entrances and the outposts. It was hopeless. Bourjony knew of most of the clandestine tunnels, and had blocked them off upon taking the castle. She'd already checked.

She could trek down to town and barge into the laundress's shop. There was a chance they'd be open at this hour.

She looked down at herself, at what had contaminated her clothes and skin in that cart. At least it didn't appear to be human fluid of any kind.

With a groan, she squared her shoulders and stomped down the hill, her mind still spinning with all she'd just seen.

Light was starting to peak over the horizon by the time Soviel trudged back up to the castle. When she'd found nowhere to get clean in town, she'd taken a painfully cold bath in a stream, nearly losing her footing to the current in the process, and had swiped a robe from a nearby clothesline to don while her dress finished drying, which, in the misty air, it hadn't. She was chilled, damp, and completely exhausted.

Her timing was perfect. The milk cart was just winding up the main road to the castle, and she slipped on unnoticed just before it came into view of the guard station. She had—at best—half an hour before Erina awoke and found her missing. Her dress was still damp and a little dirty, so she'd have to change quickly when she got back.

The milk cart stopped, and she heard the voices of the guards as they questioned the driver with their usual spiel.

"Anything besides milk you're bringing in?" one asked, his Bourjon accent thick.

"No, sir," replied the milkman.

"Papers, please."

A rustle of paper on leather, a brief pause.

"Go on then."

"Good day to you, sir."

She released a breath when the cart again hobbled forward.

The cart stopped a few minutes later, and Soviel heard the telltale sound of boots hitting the ground as the driver prepared to come round the back. She scooted up the cart, away from the back, and crawled out the front end of the covering just before the man poked his head into the carriage to begin unloading his goods.

She ducked in a servants' entrance of the castle's main wing and ran all the way to where she and the other ladies were staying. She was breathless by the time she reached their hallway.

Not a moment too soon, she eased open her door and saw Erina still asleep in her bed. As silently as she could, Soviel crept towards the bathing chamber and stripped off the rest of her clothes, removing the stolen vial from her pocket before tossing them in a heap and kicking them into the corner to deal with later. She washed her face and hair once more before tying her hair back. Finally, she pulled on her second, clean shift and launched herself into bed.

She sat, covers half over her, brushing through her damp hair, as if she'd merely risen early to bathe before her roommate awoke.

Minutes later, Erina stirred and rose with a stretch. "You're up early." She squinted. "What time is it?"

"A little after dawn," Soviel said sleepily, rubbing her eyes. The loss of a night's sleep was going to cost her.

"And you've already bathed?" Erina asked with astonishment.

"I'm a morning person," Soviel answered cheerily.

"If I drank wine the way you did with those soldiers last night, I'd be on my ass until noon," Erina yawned.

"We Njorskis have incredibly high tolerances," she said, swinging her legs out of bed. She walked to the bathing chamber and shoved her filthy, damp dress into the basket meant for dirty linens. She'd need it laundered properly, and soon. "Do you know what Samia has planned for today?"

Erina let out a string of Kalassan that was much too quick for Soviel to catch, but judging from the tone, she knew it was not positive.

"Likely ogling soldiers while we gorge ourselves on bonbons," she said lightly.

"Do you not enjoy bon-bons?" Soviel asked, raising one eyebrow.

"Oh, the bon-bons are lovely," she scoffed.

Soviel dropped it before she said too much. "Well, at least the soldiers are good-looking. That soldier, Corioni, seemed rather intrigued with you after dinner last night."

Erina shot her a sidelong glance. "Major Ennalise Harleaux is the only soldier here I find myself remotely interested in."

Soviel gave a slow nod. "I'd be inclined to agree, she's stunning. All that red hair."

Erina smiled lightly, then asked, "Any you have your eye on?"

"I'm not picky," Soviel sighed as she rose from her bed and began to dress. "I'm looking for a smart match. It turns out I have very little to lose, coming from a family on the edge of disgrace."

"Well, I *am* picky," Erina said, buckling her shoe. "My family is rich enough that I could die an old maid in possession of three houses and still not burn through our funds."

"Fortunate for you," Soviel smirked as she pinned the front of her gown closed. "So why, then, are you in Samia's service?"

"My parents sent me here to make connections for their imports company. They're in a sort of loose business partnership with His Grace, and they wanted to earn his favor."

"Oh," Soviel nodded. "What sort of business?"

"A bit of everything. My parents are primarily in the orchard business in Kalassa and the northern parts of the Meddemara. They're looking to grow their reach through Hadringston's company. Westerbarrian Importing has a foothold in colonies across the Meddemara, as well as the mainland."

"He's quite the business man," Soviel mused aloud.

Erina rolled her eyes. "You needn't keep up the doe-eyed bullshit around me. I know what you're doing."

Soviel's stomach leapt into her throat. "What do you mean?"

Erina lifted a casual shoulder. Too casual to be accusing her of treason. "I know you're only playing a role to gain favor with Samia and gain a match above your station. Believe me, I understand why, but it's a little tedious."

"Well, if we're being frank, then," Soviel admitted. "Just… don't mention it to anyone," she said in a more relaxed tone.

"My family needs me to pull a wealthy match, or we'll be ruined."

"It's no sweat off my brow," Erina quipped, fixing her hood where it sat on her shoulders. "Like I said, I understand. If I were in your position, I'd be doing the same."

"Thank you," Soviel exhaled, her relief genuine.

"Ready to go? There's a duchess that needs her daily ego fluffing."

CHAPTER TWENTY-SEVEN

The refugee ship cleared the harbor mouth from Avaree at noon. Two dozen souls aboard, not including the sparse crew.

Lukas was down at the docks the second he became aware of the arrival. His heart was leaping in his chest with a mix of dread and hope.

"Form an orderly line, folks! These people are tired!" crowed one of the guards, placed there to maintain some semblance of order.

Lukas filed into the line, despite knowing that the guard in question, Lenson Mortgarth, had a penchant for dangerously strong Corsovenan stimulants that only, very occasionally, entered Port Galan one way. Him.

But he followed the rules, stepping into the queue.

The second soldier, a dark-haired woman in her forties who Lukas didn't recognize, began to read off names.

"Callameen Throckmorton!"

A woman with a young child rushed forward to give their information to the lady at the desk. Agneath, again on duty. He made a mental note to bring the woman a pie sometime.

"Larrin Prealneth!

"Orga MacNolin!

"Denison Fairbora!"

That name sounded familiar. Hadn't she been some socialite favored for Rhi's hand? The thought made Lukas uneasy. The entire idea of Rhi being expected to wed a woman just for the purpose of popping out heirs… it was horrible to expect that from him *and* the woman forced into a lie of a marriage. One of the better aspects of the current situation was that Rhi was now *free* of that expectation. What if she was here to cause trouble?

"Cora Phelps!

"Darrick Parkington!"

Darrick Parkington used to seek him out to purchase custom cigars packed half with *arimopo* half with *popava* with a special dusting of glisten powder, for a hefty price. He was also a sometimes-paramour of Rhi's, if Lukas remembered right. He'd worked in the printer's shop in Everness.

"Cara Lourdes Forsyth!

"Dean Atkillian!

"Gerred Leominwaith!

The names went on.

"Tolline Mordiel!"

His head snapped up.

Tolline.

That was Ryder's *wife*. And her maiden name—he knew she'd taken Ryder's after their marriage. Tolline Mordiel-Berry. He'd only met her a handful of times, but he was certain he could pick her out of a crowd. If she was here, perhaps Ryder was too, traveling under a false name out of caution after Danvery…

Lukas made his way forward to Agneath's table. "I'd like to give my contact information over for Tolline Mordiel."

"Relation?" Agneath asked, peering at him over her spectacles.

"Cousin."

"Very well. They're all going through a health evaluation before they're released. I'll send her your way after."

"Thank you. Do you know if she traveled with anyone?"

Agneath leveled an unamused stare at him.

"Right then, sorry."

He moved along and retreated down the docks.

He'd only made it a little ways into the town center when a light voice stopped him. "Sir—sir Lukas?"

He froze, not recognizing the voice.

He turned and found a woman with wide brown eyes, pinkish skin, and golden hair chopped to her shoulders hanging loose. She had a light blanket tugged round her shoulders over a plain blue frock.

"Can I help you?" he asked, a bit perplexed. He didn't recognize her.

"My name is Denison," she clarified. "Denison Fairbora. I'm hoping you can help me find someone."

"That's a task for Miss Agneath back at the refugee center." He made to turn, but she caught him by the elbow.

"Please, sir," she said, her eyes round and desperate. "I know it's pathetic to plead. But I've seen you around the capital. I've seen you with Prince Rhi and Lady Soviel. I need to find them, find *her*."

"Look, I know all about Rhiach's charms, but I promise, he isn't going to marry you. There's no crown left, anyway."

"What?" she squawked. "I've no interest in Rhiach's crown, or his hand in marriage. I'm looking for Soviel."

"Oh," he said apologetically. "May I ask why you're looking for her?"

Though she was dressed in drab, droopy fabric, her reaction resembled the preening of a fluffy young bird. "She helped me once. I seek answers and, well, I know no one else here."

He puzzled at this. "Soviel has… left Port Galan." He stopped a moment. "I don't know if or when she'll be back, but I'd be happy to bring you to meet the rest of our friends…"

Even as he said it, it sounded strange.

"She's left?" Denison said, visibly deflating. "Oh, no. Oh dear."

"Can I help?" he tried, not really sure what else to ask.

"I should have just swallowed my pride and stayed in Avaree," she cursed, shaking her head. "This won't do."

"Lady," he started awkwardly. "I would be happy to bring you to Rhi and my sister and Ferrin. You know *her,* right?"

Denison grimaced just a little bit at the mention of Ferrin's name.

"Look, Lady D—"

She waved her hand. "I truly don't see why we must keep up all that. I've lost everything as it is, why not the title as well?" she said with a slightly unhinged laugh.

"Uh—"

"Very well, bring me to Ferrin and the others. At least one of them must have some sense of what's happened."

Lukas tensed, but agreed. "Very well, Miss."

As soon as he had ushered Denison into the manor and up to the wing where the adjoining rooms were, he'd grown uncomfortable and tense. When would Tolline be out of medical? Would Ryder be with her? Would she at the very least have news of him?

"This castle is quite… quaint," Denison observed for the third time. Only the first two times, she swapped out *quaint* for *rustic* and *cozy.*

"It certainly keeps us all warm and dry, despite the state of things," Lukas countered. "So… why did you flee, exactly?"

She pursed her lips. "Don't ask me in such a condescending tone. Just because I played by society's rules does not mean I'm incapable of adapting."

He didn't respond.

She sighed with resignation. "My parents had arranged a marriage match to someone I didn't like very much," she explained.

"Sorry to hear that," Lukas nodded, stopping in front of the doors to the suite. "Well, here we are." He knocked.

"Thank you. For bringing me," she said, far too formally.

The door swung wide and Rhi answered. He squinted at Denison for a moment, taking in her shorter hair, dirty dress, wilting countenance. "You look—"

"Oh, please," she rolled her eyes, completely transforming into a confident woman. "You know who I am. Lady Denison? Our fathers threw us at each other in our youth? I rode horses against your sister?"

Recognition dawned on Rhi's face. "Right, right. Lady Den —"

"Just Denison is fine," she said, throwing up a palm. "I am by all counts no longer affiliated with my family, assuming they've survived the invasion."

Lukas met Rhi's confused gaze over Denison's head and shrugged as she flounced into the room.

"Is your sister here?" Denison fired at Rhi.

"Not at the moment," he answered hesitantly.

"Shame, a familiar face, no matter how hostile, would have been nice," she said, crossing her arms. "Well. How have you all been faring?"

Lukas blinked.

Rhi peered at Denison curiously. "I'm sorry. Did you track us down to ask how things have been?"

"No." She bristled. "I've been alone in Avaree this whole time, where, by the way, the conditions for refugees are *abysmal.* You might want to do something about that," she said, gesturing to Rhi.

"I am sorry to hear that, however, most dulcet dove, I am not in charge of that in any capacity. I can submit your complaint through the army channels, but based on their backlog, I would not hold my breath."

Denison looked like she was going to pop. "Do not," she scowled, "talk to me like I'm some flittering fool. I've fought like hell to survive to this point. I did not stroll up north in a gilded carriage on a whim. I fled. Just like the rest of you, I'm sure. And I'm telling you, whoever runs things in Avaree is shoving refugees into the tiniest, dirtiest encampments and offering no answers and no way out. Your Highness," she tacked on the end.

Rhi stared at her for a moment. "My apologies. And please, as you've said, let us do away with the formalities." He shot Lukas a look. "Are they keeping track of who comes and goes in this refugee encampment?"

"To some extent, but not very well. I spent two weeks searching for record of my lady's maid. They told me over and over she wasn't there, and finally I ran into her at the soup station. Said she'd been there *twelve* days!"

Something flared in Lukas's chest. Hope.

"How many people would you say are living there?"

"Oh, I don't know. Two hundred? Maybe more."

Rhi muttered something under his breath. "I'll see if I can find anyone willing to take some of the pressure off Avaree, find another place for some of the refugees."

"Twelve days," Lukas repeated. If people were slipping through the cracks in the system so easily, it was more than possible that Ryder was in Avaree, lost in the shuffle.

Ash strode into the room then, her eyes going wide when they caught on the unfamiliar figure.

"Who's this?" Ash looked Denison up and down and Lukas had to restrain himself from rolling his eyes. Ash had always had a weakness for a pretty face in a nice dress. Even if Denison was smudged and dirty, she was still beautiful, and she carried herself in a way that said she was well aware of that fact.

"This is Lady Denison, she fled the capital this spring as well," Rhi introduced. "She was just telling us of Avaree's poor refugee conditions."

"Oh," Ash said, nodding. "The general out there doesn't allot much for the cause, is what I've gathered."

"Who is it?" asked Rhi.

"General Kenrose," Ash answered, turning her attention to Rhi. Her hand twitched at her side, a nervous tick Lukas knew well.

"Ah, I've heard of him. Lachlan does *not* have good things to say from when he was stationed there." He paused, considering. "Denison, how ever did you end up in Avaree? Why would you not flee to one of your father's estates?"

She turned a dark look on Rhi. "I told you. I can't go back there."

His brow furrowed, and then relaxed as he recalled what she'd said months ago. "Your betrothed."

She nodded furiously.

"So your family has no idea you're alive?"

She barked a joyless laugh. "My family may well remain in Everness, kowtowing to the highest bidder as they have always done."

Lukas raised his eyebrows.

"Why have you come here, then, to Galan?" Rhi asked.

"I've told you, I was hoping to find Soviel. She was kind to me and warned me out of the capital days before it fell. I wanted to thank her, and to be frank, I didn't have any other priorities to see to."

This girl was blunt and unapologetic, a far cry from the simpering lady featured in Ferrin's childhood stories.

"She isn't here," Ash shared, her words a little strained.

"Yes, these two have told me as much. Who are you?"

"I'm Ash."

"Hi," she gave Ash a once-over. "Well, if that's all then, I suppose I'd better go find somewhere to wash up. That sea journey was disgusting; someone's infant puked all over the floor of the ship and I can still smell it," she muttered. "I'll be back to speak to Ferrin when I can."

She strode out and shut the door behind her, and the three of them were left gawking after her.

CHAPTER TWENTY-EIGHT

It was mid-morning the next day when Lukas received a summons from the refugee center. He'd slept terribly, the anticipation of the following day's potential overwhelming him. What if Tolline refused to speak with him? What if she sought him out only to tell him Ryder had been swept away by the invasion, or had never returned? He could almost see her face twisting with distraught accusation as she hurled the blame at him.

He'd deserve it. Ryder was kind, and always showed up for his friends. Lukas had dragged him into a horrible situation Ryder never would have said no to.

The day was already humid and bright when he pulled on his faded green shirt and rolled up the sleeves against the heat. When he arrived at the refugee center, there was already a queue forming for people to reunite with their friends and family. Agncath, gruff as ever, was directing them to form two separate lines.

At last, he reached the front of the line and found an unfamiliar attendant, with graying brown hair and milk-oat skin. Her dowdy glasses were pushed far up her nose as she smoothed her hand over the tired list of names in front of her.

"Hi, Lukas Mazrihn here for Tolline Mordiel," he said in a soft voice. The woman looked about as ready to startle as a field mouse.

"Alright," she said, scanning down the list. She licked one finger and flipped the crumpled page. "And you're her cousin?"

"That's right," he lied.

"Please wait over to the side, and she'll be discharged momentarily."

He did as instructed. Ten minutes passed, and the back tent vomited out a handful of weary-looking people. He instantly spotted Tolline, her reddish gold hair messy and pulled back, her face dirty and hollowed, her light blue dress practically beige with dust.

He raised a hand to get her attention, and met her with a tight-lipped, grim smile.

"Lukas Mazrihn," she acknowledged as she stopped in front of him. "What have you gotten yourself into?"

He brought her to the coffee house in the town square, and told her to order whatever she wanted. She must have been starving, because she directed the young waiter to bring her a plate of butter-biscuits, a ham-stuffed croissant and a cup of tea with honey and milk.

She devoured two of the butter-biscuits before she said a word.

"I am furious with you. But—" she said, licking her fingers. "I'm too hungry to be mad. The little one is taking what little strength I have," she muttered.

Lukas's eyes widened. "You're—"

"With child, for four moons now. I know, I don't look it," she smirked. "Nor did my sisters or my mother, not until further in."

"So..." he began.

"You want to know where my oaf of a husband is, so you can drag him into another of your little schemes, is that it? I know you didn't bring me to this pastry shop just to enjoy my company."

"Not exactly. I've been worried about Ryder. I haven't seen him since he left Danvery."

Her laugh held no joy in it. "Yes, Danvery. The prison in the northern forest where they were torturing inmates. So glad to know that while I was in the throes of morning sickness, my husband was being chased by soldiers on your word."

"It wasn't on my *word*." A pang of guilt lanced through his chest. "Look, I'm sorry. I didn't anticipate the extent of that job."

"*Job*." She fixed him with a pointed stare.

"Expedition."

She sighed, took a long drink of her sweetened tea, and set the cup down with a clink. "I'm sorry, I'm being harsh. You want to know where Ryder is? I can't tell you precisely. He's been on the move to keep from being found. Soldiers identified him in Avaree, before the coup went down. He was already wanted on smuggling charges from a year ago. Now a prison break? He's been lucky before but he and I agreed it was time to lay low. He's in Taroch, in a cabin, waiting to hear from me."

Lukas nearly jumped out of his seat. "He's in the north? Safe?"

"Well," she scoffed, "I don't know how *safe* he is, being so close to the borderlands. He's grown an impressive beard, though."

"Can you get word to him?"

She picked up her teacup and took a long sip as she watched him with coy interest. "You've really been up your own ass about this, haven't you? You must have felt *awful*."

"Tolline," he explained. "He's my friend. I know we've gotten into foolish situations, but I care what happens to him."

She chuckled and set her cup down, opting to eat another biscuit. "I can get a message to him. You remember those birds?"

"The pigeons?"

She snorted. "Flying rats, if you ask me." She crossed her arms and leaned back in her chair. "The ones he was always feeding in the capital… they sort of imprinted on him. I don't know why, I suppose because he always left them scraps. Soft-hearted fool," she sighed lovingly. "When he came to fetch me this spring, he coaxed three into a basket and brought them with us. I thought it was just silly sentimentality, until he began using them to communicate with old contacts in Everness."

Lukas shook his head in disbelief. "No. How?"

"Something about them always returning home? I'm not sure. But I have one of them with me. I had to fight the officers to let me bring the damn thing on the boat. They said they can carry disease." She rolled her eyes. "I will send him a message when I know he can get into Galan safely. Not a moment sooner."

Lukas nodded in agreement, barely able to restrain his relief. "What can I do to assure you of that?"

She assessed him for a moment. "Find a way to sneak him in. I don't trust these military types, no matter which side they claim to fight for. Find a way to get him into the city limits without anyone checking his papers, and I'll send word."

CHAPTER TWENTY-NINE

Ash was just rounding the prominence that marked the entrance to the hidden inlet a mile south of Bramblehall as the sun reached its zenith for the day. It was her third messenger-run of the week on *The Brisk*, now freshly repaired, and the winds were more than favorable. Assuming all had not gone to shit, Soviel would have arrived back from Everness the previous afternoon, hopefully with some useful information.

She tied off the boat and left Rorin and Toscan with instructions to flee and leave her should anything go wrong as she made her usual hike into the woods surrounding the estate where Soviel's letter should be waiting. It made her sad, these messenger runs where she'd be coming so close to Soviel and not even be able to see her.

Ash had nearly reached the drop-spot when a pale figure slammed into her. She went for her knife, but stilled a second later as she caught the scent of familiar perfume and an aura of peacefulness and safety that seemed to follow Soviel everywhere. Ash's breath rushed out of her as Soviel squeezed her in a tight embrace.

"*Good gods, Sov—*" Ash wheezed.

"You have no idea how happy I am to see you!" Soviel stepped back without relinquishing her hold on Ash's shoulders. "How's Galan? How is everyone?"

"We're all doing fine, more or less," she said, surprise still writ across her face. "I thought we were never supposed to overlap? That you were to drop the letter and be gone!"

"I know, I know, it's just—this was too important to leave to chance. Listen," Soviel said, backing Ash further into the thick cluster of trees. She reached into her pocket and produced a tiny glass vial. "You have to get this vial to Lachlan and Rhi. Tell Wilcoe, but it must go to Lachlan. Everness has a workshop, a lab, beneath the castle, and *this* is what they're making and using. Test it, find out what it is. Somehow it's able to trigger an intense magical response."

"What? How?" Ash's eyes flitted between Soviel and the vial. The liquid inside was milky and gray.

"There's more; it's all in my letter," she said, placing the folded square of paper into Ash's hands and pressing it to her chest. Ash stared a little dumbly at Soviel's face. "*Gods*, I've missed you. All of you. Tell the others for me," she said, her lovely earthen eyes filling with longing.

"I will," Ash promised, mirroring Soviel's touch and squeezing her arm. "You're alright? You're keeping safe?"

"I nearly got myself incinerated in Everness a few days ago," she admitted drily. "But, yes. I am keeping mostly safe."

"Good. Good," Ash nodded, swallowing. She wanted to tell Soviel everything about what had happened in Galan. Zare's reappearance, the tension in the army, all of it. But there wasn't enough time in the day. "Just… find out what you can and come back to us. Amongst the five of us, you're the only one with half a wit of sense."

"Oh, that's not true," Soviel laughed. "Lukas has the other half a wit."

Ash snorted. "He does *not*."

Soviel laughed again, the skin around her eyes crinkling with cheer. "How are the others? How's Rhi's research?"

"Good, I suppose. Though he I don't see him much. Lately he spends all his time down in the barracks working with *Lachlan*," she dropped his name suggestively.

"Is there a new development on that front? Are they involved?" Soviel asked, hungry for fresh gossip.

"Well, I'm not sure how *involved* they are, but there's certainly more than research going on between those two."

"Somehow that makes sense," Soviel narrowed her eyes in thought, as if she were parsing out how their two personalities would fit together.

"A Lady Denison has arrived with refugees from Avaree, claiming to know you. Said you'd helped her once."

Soviel stiffened. "Denison, yes. She was among the early druggings in the capital. I told her to run. She's safe?"

"Yes," Ash said slowly. "She seems to be. Very riled up, but safe."

Soviel snorted. "Has Ferrin run into her yet?"

Ash smirked playfully, and Soviel chuckled. "They always had the stupidest rivalry growing up." She paused, considering. "And Ferrin is well? Any word on the island? Her mother? Have she and Lukas—"

She cut off after seeing Ash's expression.

"What? What is it? Please, I'm dying for some interesting news that isn't about all this," she gestured a hand back at Bramblehall's distant marble columns and manicured lawns.

"They've been hot and cold for weeks," Ash admitted. "Which makes it fucking awkward for me, the person who is around them *all* the time."

"Oh, dear," Soviel sighed knowingly.

"And, well, I don't want you to worry, or be distracted by this, but… Zare has reappeared. The captain that Gill—Ferrin and I sailed under. He was her lover, before."

"Right, I remember," Soviel nodded. "What is he doing in Port Galan?"

Ash shook her head, lips pursed.

"Gods," Soviel sighed. "How are you two faring, having him there?"

"Fine," Ash grumbled, crossing her arms. "I'd sooner see him dead than speak with him, but unfortunately he seems to have useful information."

Soviel stiffened. "Such as?"

Ash gave her the briefest overview and earned a few resolute nods.

"He's not lying. You'll see it all in my letter, but it's true—the weaponry, the alliance with Kalassa." Soviel shook her head, looking grim.

"He also claims to have in his possession half of the cetamaris."

Soviel gasped. "Bourjony is looking for that."

"I know, I read your last letter."

"Dammit," Soviel cursed, turning to pace before whirling back to Ash. "Be rid of him. Soon. I have a bad feeling about his presence there, even if his information may be good."

"Believe me, I know," Ash agreed.

"Be careful, Ash," Soviel said.

"I know, Sov, we will," she repeated more quietly, remembering the day she and Pierre had confronted Zare about his plans to betray Gillian, and how he'd reacted.

He'd slit Pierre's throat without a twitch of his brow, then bashed her over the head with a whiskey bottle before stuffing her pockets with some contraband he needed to be rid of, and dumping her off the coast of Avaree for some patrol to decide her fate.

"I suppose Ferrin isn't taking his return well?"

Ash shook her head. "She's had other worries distracting her, this is just one more."

Soviel nodded. "Well, anything you can get out of him about this mysterious new weapon they're building would be beneficial. I haven't had much luck, and one of the other ladies here seems intent on blocking me from the answers."

Ash nodded. "We'll try."

"Just don't pay too much for it."

"We won't."

A shot sounded in the distance and Ash jumped.

"It's only the morning hunting party," Soviel assured her with a squeeze to her upper arm. "It'll be a while yet till they reach these woods, but you should be off nonetheless. We've lingered here too long."

Ash threw her arms around Soviel one last time. "Be safe. Come home soon."

"I will," Soviel promised. "Be careful."

Ash hurried off back to the inlet with Soviel's hard-won intel secure in her jacket, already feeling Soviel's absence more keenly than she'd thought possible.

CHAPTER THIRTY

Ferrin was glad to have been asked to sit in on Helene's small debriefing regarding Soviel's intel. Grey and Ash were there, as were Lachlan and General Alemont. She suspected her presence was a begrudging concession by Helene at Ash's request. She was thankful to have something to do; Zare's presence had set her on edge more than she liked to admit. Over the edge, really. Every noise made her jump, every time someone said her name, her breath hitched. She couldn't seem to fall asleep if she was alone.

She wasn't thrilled about Denison's arrival in Galan either, but the issue of a childhood nemesis was a trifling matter compared to everything else going on. Zare was still lurking around every corner. Soviel was traipsing around at the mercy of a despicable mastermind. Lukas was looking for a way to sneak Ryder into the city, despite the potential risk. She gnawed on her pinky nail as she replayed the argument they'd had. It had been almost a *week*, and they'd barely spoken since. She wanted to tell him to mind his own business. She wanted to pull him close and protect him from the ghosts eating away at him. She didn't know anymore.

Ash had been quiet and thoughtful in the hours following her return from Bramblehall. She had fetched Ferrin from the manor with only one three words: "News from Sov."

Lachlan Tarrish was also present, and had been handed a vial of grayish-bluish liquid. He'd pocketed it without a word.

Helene stood and strode to the door, glancing outside before closing and latching it behind her.

"It goes without saying that the information disclosed tonight does not leave this room until properly released," Helene said forcefully. She moved to her desk and sat down, laying Soviel's letter before her.

"The Kalassans have allied with Bourjony."

There were several gasps around the room, and Ferrin was surprised to see the expression of shock on Grey's face, of all people. Then she remembered that he and Soviel had briefly courted. His feelings about her current whereabouts went beyond mere professional concern.

"There's more," Helene continued. "Bourjony has a top weapons developer working on something big. Something that will be used both on land and on their ships when it is ready. Our agent doesn't have more information on that, save that they are having difficulty sourcing proper material for the ship-mounted model of whatever it is. But, it seems they've had successful test-runs of it on Galus and Corsovena."

"How can our agent know about the Kalassans?" Alemont asked.

"The ambassador was at the Governor's Ball in Everness, at which our operative was also present."

"To what degree have they shown their support? Are they trade partners? Are they lending military aid? We're going to need more details on that," said Alemont.

"This is all I have at present on the matter, General," Helene responded.

Alemont looked exasperated. "What else?"

"Everness is harboring a lab similar to the one most recently dismantled in Danvery Prison," Helene continued. Lachlan, who stood at the far side of the room, frowned.

"Our operative observed multiple test subjects being injected with a substance, multiple humans displaying very out-of-the-ordinary control over the elements—ice, water, flame. She observed what looked like a heavily reinforced training room, an assembly line for the injectable medicines, and an incinerator for the rest. It all runs on some kind of track system, spanning over a large area beneath the castle."

"I'll see that this vial is tested," Lachlan said.

"Thank you, Lieutenant Tarrish," Helene nodded.

"It seemed that there was a ratio of dead to surviving subjects, and that there was some sort of recruitment going on to find people willing to participate. That's odd," she paused, shuffling back to the first page. "This is the first mention of anyone being willing to undergo these treatments, whatever they are."

"Ah. I might have some insight on that," Lachlan interjected, pushing off the wall he'd been leaning against. He glanced impatiently at the front door and frowned when nothing happened. "Just waiting…"

There was a near-perfectly timed banging on the door.

"Could someone please let Rhi in," Lachlan asked.

Ferrin glanced to Helene, who glanced to Alemont, who shrugged. "Go on."

Ferrin went to the door, unlatching it and pulling it open.

"Hi. Apologies for my tardiness, did I miss anything?" Rhi panted, practically breezing in.

"Was just about to bring up what we'd been researching," Lachlan said.

"Great," Rhi nodded, shoving the envelope he was holding deep into his coat pocket.

"Pending the testing of this vial," Lachlan began, "we, that is, Administrative Ambassador Valcara and I, have an idea of what may be being done to the people in the labs. With the end-goal being highly-powered soldiers with access to magic more potent than anyone has seen in centuries."

Ferrin smirked at the title she was fairly certain Rhi had fabricated.

Helene was aghast. "Artificial magic?"

Alemont nodded for him to continue.

"It started with us looking into Gerreway's theories," Rhi took the floor from Lachlan. "The idea that magic is brought about through necessity—whether or not that comes from the environment or some kind of artificial inducement. The working theory is that the hallucinatory *popava* strain that was running rampant through the capital this spring, just before the big prison round-up, if survived, acts as a key. It unlocks any trace of magic that might have been slumbering inside the affected person."

"And how did you come to this conclusion?" Alemont narrowed her eyes, interest piqued.

"Well, the timing of the dosings coincided too perfectly to not be related, so we looked into the theories further. But it still didn't explain a soldier who was present at the invasion of Everness—what was her name?"

"Monroe," Ferrin offered helpfully.

"Right, Monroe was able to fly, was incredibly strong," Rhi explained. "But she clearly wasn't some poor soul who was pressed into duty. She was a volunteer."

"So why were there so many bodies at the prison? Why were so many from the lab dead? Lieutenant Tarrish, you described the scene as a bloodbath; dozens of corpses, all clearly having been experimented on to the point of death. If what you're suggesting is correct, the success rate must be negligible. Who would volunteer for that?" asked Alemont.

"That's what we were trying to figure out," Rhi replied, coming around to stand beside Lachlan, who looked like he was already starting to lose patience. "There are two outcomes, two kinds of subjects entering the lab.

"At first, we assumed the prisoners were mere test subjects, so they could see what worked and what didn't before applying it to their hand-picked super-soldiers."

"But it's far, far worse than that," Lachlan finally spoke, his voice edged with rage, abrasive as gravel.

"There are *two* kinds of subjects in these experiments," Rhi explained. "The unwilling are used as…" he grimaced, "fuel, sort of. Once the subjects magic is unlocked, it's still not enough to make them into unbeatable war-machines like Monroe. So that's when the healers come in, er, not healers but —"

"People with life-magic," Lachlan said. "They move the power."

"They move it," Alemont repeated skeptically.

Ash cocked her head to the side. "This may be a dumb question. Is it the same as when a healer draws on energy from something else, like a specific plant?"

"Yes." Rhi nodded grimly.

Ferrin's stomach turned, thinking of the leaves withering in Soviel's hands, and she didn't need to hear Lachlan's next somber words to understand just how perverse the process of making these weapons was.

"The unwilling subjects, like, say the healthy prisoners back in Danvery, have their life-force pulled out of them by a team of healers, and channeled into the soldier."

"How many?"

Rhi shook his head. "We don't know, but at least a few dead for every one soldier. Likely upwards of a dozen. We're thinking, if we were to target their *popava* sources, it would prevent them from further creating these soldiers."

Ferrin realized with horror that Rhi and Lukas had both been dosed by the strain of *popava*. This very fate could have befallen either of them. Drained and used for whatever power might have lain dormant in their blood.

"And this research, could you recreate it here?" Alemont asked.

All eyes snapped to the general.

"Did you not hear me? It could be a dozen dead *per person*!" Lachlan snapped.

"I'm not suggesting we do it en masse," Alemont said. "But why not return the favor? Take their prisoners of war, copy the results, hit them back with our own soldiers."

"No," Lachlan said, his voice low and rough. He'd gone taut as a bow string, ready to launch forward, only to halt mid-stride with Rhi's hand firm on his arm.

"As I was saying," Rhi went on, shooting Lachlan a look that said *calm down before she throws you out.* "This is only theory—but once we can test that concoction and find out what's in it, we'll know more. This new information from Bramblehall supports our theory."

Helene rubbed her forehead.

"I don't care what moral qualms you have here," Alemont stared down Rhi and Lachlan. "You've gone this far into researching it, and that makes you the two for the job. Find a way to replicate this, or find me something better. Right now, we cannot withstand a hit from an army of high-powered soldiers with magical abilities. This resistance will be done by winter if we can't find a way to stand against that level of power. We have plenty of prisoners, and limited resources to keep feeding them. Get it done. That's an order."

Lachlan stared back at her, and Ferrin could feel the tension in the room, thick as cold butter.

"We'll look into it, General," Rhi said, his fingers tightening visibly on Lachlan's forearm.

"Good. You are dismissed."

Ferrin watched Rhi's hand float toward his pocket, and then relax to his side. His gaze flickered to Lachlan. "Come on, we've got work to do."

They left quietly, and Helene pursed her lips. She looked tense, exhausted.

"This all seems like it could have been a lot cleaner, had our operation to infiltrate Danvery not been thwarted at the last minute," Alemont said angrily.

A pang of nervousness clenched in Ferrin's gut.

Ash cleared her throat. "Is there anything else you need from us?" She looked back and forth between Helene and General Alemont.

"Not at present. General?"

"No. You are dismissed," said Alemont.

Lachlan managed to pace furiously for all of five seconds before he threw a punch and put his fist through one of the stable walls.

"Hey. HEY." Rhi stepped in close, locking eyes with him. "You need to stop. Breathe."

He didn't bother asking if Lachlan was alright, it was obvious he wasn't. He was fuming. Eyes wide and wild, knuckles split and bleeding, chest heaving with the effort of bridling that fiery rage that slumbered hot and coiled as a dragon within him.

"Look at me." Rhi caught his jaw in one hand, stepping even closer until Lachlan was flush in between his chest and stable wall. "Look at me," he repeated, forcing his face forward.

Lachlan's breathing slowed, but his eyes were still ablaze, as if he might explode.

"If she thinks we're going to hand over one *speck* of information about how to do that, then I'm—"

"Stop. I know. We aren't giving it to her," Rhi shook his head. "But you need to slow down." He paused, catching Lachlan's bleeding hand in his own. "We have time to learn more. Come up with a better solution."

Lachlan took a deep, shuddering breath and blinked his eyes shut once, twice.

"You hurt yourself," Rhi said, lifting Lachlan's bloodied hand to examine the split knuckles. "Come on. Let's get this cleaned up."

Rhi led Lachlan, unspeaking and rigid, to his tent, where he deposited him on the cot and slammed a glass of water down next to him. He turned back to Lachlan's small wooden chest of things and dropped to his knees to rifle through it. After a moment or two of digging, he found a half-empty bottle of Deathwater and a few linen strips that looked clean enough to bandage Lachlan's hand.

When Rhi shifted and came around to Lachlan, he found him staring oddly at him.

"Tell me what you're thinking," Rhi said quietly, kneeling and taking up his injured hand.

He let out a near-silent hiss as Rhi dabbed him with the rag.

"Talk to me, Lach."

"I'm thinking," he drew in a deep breath, still shaking. "That I appreciate you using your diplomat voice back there."

Rhi shot him a half-smile as he wound the cloth over Lachlan's knuckles, firm, but not restrictive.

"I'm thinking that Soviel is really fighting her hardest to get us what we need," he admitted. "And we could never solve this without her help."

"Glad to see you're coming around on your opinion of her," Rhi said wryly, something in his chest easing, and tightening again as soon as he caught sight of the way Lachlan was studying him. Open, yet cautious.

"And I'm thinking there is no one else I would trust to move forward on this mission, to walk the fine line of progress, and keep others from using our findings to do more harm than good."

Rhi looked up from the bandaging and met Lachlan's somber gaze. He drew a long, deep breath, his stomach doing nervous cartwheels.

"Well?" Lachlan frowned after the silence wore on a moment too long. "What are you thinking? And no using fancy words to trick your way out of saying what you're really thinking."

Rhi sighed as he tied off the bandage, and stood. He kept ahold of Lachlan's hand as he did, meeting Lachlan's gaze.

I'm thinking...

"I'm thinking," he started slowly, "that when you go south with the army, I don't want us to be separated."

There. Not the truth in its entirety, but it was all he could manage for now.

Lachlan stared back, surprised. "You... don't want to separate?"

"No," Rhi continued. "We have so much more to do on this project, so much to unravel. And I..." he swallowed. "Well. I'm afraid I would miss you terribly."

He let it hang there in the air between them for a second that might as well have been a year. Rhi braced himself for some form of rejection. Awkwardness. Blowback. Leaving.

Lachlan inhaled deeply, remaining still. Rhi winced at the reaction and started to pull away, only for Lachlan's bandaged fingers to tighten on his own, halting him.

"You'd miss me?" Lachlan said, standing from the cot.

His cheeks went hot as he blushed furiously. "Well, yes."

A grin cracked over Lachlan's face. "I would miss you, too."

Rhi was still and searching for another heartbeat, waiting for something to blindside him as they shared breath, faces only inches apart.

A harsh, repetitive thump at the front of the tent had the moment snapping apart like opposing magnets.

"Courier!" a youthful voice called from just beyond the tent flap.

"Leave it at the door!" Lachlan called, breathless.

Rhi dropped onto the cot and watched the flush on Lachlan's skin as he paced to the entryway. He ducked his head out, grabbed the letter, and popped back in.

"So, you were saying?" Rhi drawled, absently running his fingers over the blanket.

"Maybe," Lachlan said breathlessly, "we should continue this conversation another time, and not in the middle of a war camp."

"Right. Yes. I was also thinking that," Rhi agreed. He'd decidedly *not* been thinking that, but he wasn't about to say so.

"Stop that," Lachlan said.

"Stop what?"

Lachlan shook his head with a chuckle. "You know what I'm talking about."

Rhi swallowed thickly and schooled his features into neutrality. "No I don't."

Lachlan laughed again.

Without thinking, Rhi picked up Lachlan's pillow and whipped it at him.

"Oh!"

"What does the letter say?" Rhi asked.

"It's just Alemont's request for our research. She wants us to compile it for her by week's end," Lachlan said, all heat draining from his face. At his side, he clenched his hand into a fist.

"Well, that's one bridge to jump off when we come to it."

Lachlan groaned. "Even if we *wanted* to recreate their soldiers, it's unlikely it would be successful. They had teams of scientists and healers to work on this, and an entire assembly line to make the solutions. This is impossible."

"Isn't that a good thing? We don't want to do this."

"Yes," Lachlan said. "Maybe. I don't know, it isn't my area of expertise. I only studied a little of life-sciences, or magical theory."

"What *did* you study?" Rhi asked, leaning back on his hands as he studied Lachlan's face.

"I had a bit of trouble pinning down one area of study. I tried philosophy—"

"Oh, wait until Ash hears that."

"Painting, politics, literature, poetry, earth sciences, animal husbandry…"

"Poetry? You?"

Lachlan glowered at him.

"You must let me read some of your work," Rhi teased.

"I will absolutely not."

Rhi laughed, and dodged the pillow Lachlan tossed back at him.

"In any event, it clearly didn't stick, because I left."

"Weren't you kicked out?" Rhi reminded him.

"Never mind that. Are you going to put in for transfer with my unit, or should I go to Ashwife?"

"I'll take care of it," Rhi said, letting the easy, flirtatious smile play on his lips.

Lachlan studied him from where he stood across the tent, considering. He pulled the pocket watch from his waistcoat, checked it and his eyes bulged. "Good. Do that," he said abruptly as he shoved his arms into his coat. "I am very late for sentry duty. I'll see you in the morning?"

"Yeah," Rhi said, sitting up quickly.

"Good, alright." With that, Lachlan strode out of the tent, leaving Rhi with his thoughts.

CHAPTER THIRTY-ONE

Lukas was perched at the edge of the pier, drink in his hand, pouch of fine *arimopo* tucked in his pocket, waiting for his client to show. Darrick Parkington hadn't waited long after arriving in the city before seeking Lukas out for some goods. Goods that were going to cost him about five times the usual, given the circumstances.

Since fleeing to Port Galan, Lukas's client list had shrunk significantly, which was fitting, given his inability to make runs between the isle and mainland. It was nowhere near the cashflow he'd had in the capital, but it was something. There was always dirty work that needed doing, no matter the city. Fortunately, the means of procuring said goods *had* given him an idea for getting Ryder into the city. There were still several kinks to work out, though.

Another restless night of poor sleep was biting at his heels, Damijan's death playing on a loop in his mind. It was like the guilt of Ryder's disappearance had wrenched open a hole inside of him, reminding him how he had been solely responsible for the death of his dearest friend, his brother in all the ways that mattered. He knew Ryder was safe—relatively— knew he was accounted for and hadn't died on the mission Lukas had pulled him into. So why did he still feel this way? The blanket of heavy, wet dread was impossible to shake, the memories of *that* day slouching back uninvited.

It had been worsening. Dragging him further and further down this spiraling pit that he couldn't seem to stop, couldn't seem to call out for help. As if he *deserved* help. He'd been the one to lead them down into that gulley.

Memories he thought he'd grieved three years ago, thought he'd locked away, were seeping out of his carefully constructed dams faster than he could stop up the holes. Ever since he'd seen Damijan's face the night of the druggings in Everness's slums, he'd been off-balance. Seeing him places he wasn't, recalling the heat of the desert and the snap of his bones.

He tipped back the ceramic growler of wine and let the spiced drink pour past his lips numbly as he watched the sun sink lower toward the horizon. He squeezed his eyes shut, as if he could ward off the memories of that day. Damijan's blood coating his hands. The mind-numbing throb of his broken arm. The dust stifling his lungs as he waited for death, only for night and the cover of darkness to come sooner. Sand and blood and death, everywhere.

"Hey," Ash prodded him. "Are you drunk?"

"Did you say something?" He turned slowly, looking up at her. The dying sun painted her red.

"Yeah, your name, about six times."

He'd barely heard her approach, and only fully registered her presence when she groaned and sat down beside him. He lowered his jug and eyed her. She was salt-crusted, tired, even tanner than the day before. Shadows rimmed her eyes; she looked as exhausted as he felt.

"Sorry," he mumbled.

"What is it?"

"Fine," he said. "I'm fine."

Ash stared at him. "Don't pull that shit. You're a mess. I thought you'd solved the Ryder problem, why do you look like you haven't slept in weeks?"

He grimaced, trying to come up with the words to explain the hole that had been reopened in his chest.

The scene that had played over and over in his mind had narrowed down to one moment. Silence, only not. The whistling, shrieking sound of an arrow going overhead just after the first gunshot was fired. Or maybe it had only been his ears ringing.

"Luk, you're scaring me."

He considered coming up with an excuse, but he was much too worn out for that. "Damijan."

The word was a long, pained sigh on his lips.

"Dam—oh. Is he…" she paused. "He's dead, isn't he?" Her voice was soft.

Lukas slowly nodded as he stared out at the horizon.

"How did it happen?"

He took another pull of the wine. "During the occupation. A few weeks before I came up here. I made a mistake. He took a bullet for me. Then died choking on dust in the desert just outside the city."

"Oh, Lukas," Ash said, her face crumpling. "I'm so sorry."

He swallowed his *no one's fault but mine*.

"Hey." She leaned forward and grabbed his elbow, picking up the wine jug and setting it down on her other side. "Do you know how pissed he'd be if he saw you moping around like this?"

He tried and failed to summon a smile for her efforts, the ringing still clogging his ears. "I know."

"Well… I can't tell you what to do," she said, "but if you want to talk about it, you know I'm here to listen."

He nodded again.

"In whatever capacity," she added.

A beat of silence followed.

"I just saw Soviel," she said. "If you want to hear some truly insane news about Everness…"

He turned to her and nodded. She launched into the tale.

He watched her speak and attempted to listen, but try as he might, he couldn't seem to stay in the present.

It was late by the time Ferrin wandered back to the manor, hungry and weary. She'd walked along the cliffs and watched the sun sink, an inexplicable feeling of foreboding taking root in her chest. Then she'd stayed out there until long after the light was gone. She didn't want to see anyone. Didn't want to pretend like everything was normal or alright. *Nothing* was normal. She didn't know what normal even looked like for her anymore.

She'd sat with her knees curled to her chest, overlooking the crashing waves below, dark in the dim afterglow of the sunset. What was she doing here? What was she contributing?

What was the point of staying?

Though she dreaded the particular piece of the unknown that was the Door, she knew the time for it was coming. She knew she needed some direction, something to run *toward*. Even if there were things she wanted to run away from here.

When her teeth began to chatter from the chill of the night, she pushed herself off the ground and wished she'd brought a coat with her so she might go on avoiding everything for just a little longer.

She walked on stiff legs down the path back to the manor. The old stone building nested atop the promontory like an eagle guarding its clutch, ready to swallow any sign of weakness.

Hoping to hunt down something to eat, she detoured to the kitchens in the lower level. She hadn't had a scrap of food since midday, with rations tightening. The pit in her stomach might have been dread *or* hunger.

Before she reached the hallway leading to the kitchens, she saw Lukas. His eyes were red-rimmed.

"Hi," she said a little awkwardly. They hadn't spoken more than a few sentences to each other since the argument they'd had over her dealing with Zare.

"Evening," he said by way of greeting. "You miss dinner too?"

She nodded grimly. "Lost track of time after the meeting."

"Ah," he said. "Ash told me. About Everness and Danvery and all of it. Soviel and I saw the tracks and things when we were blowing up the *ras*."

"Ras?"

"Sure, why not? *Rasernemaud*'s a mouthful, don't you think?"

She let the ghost of a laugh slip through her nose, and continued walking as he fell into step beside her. "True enough."

"So, I take it you've worked out some sort of deal with the captain?" he asked when the silence had gone on too long.

The air between them went taut, and she felt her instinct to fight or flee snap into place.

"Yes. Ash and I will meet him tomorrow morning for the exchange. We've told him that *I'm* taking the gem south. But really, Ash will take the gem and go south soon, and I will seek out Norhi to bring me to the Door. Anything we can do to keep him in the dark will be in our favor," she said.

"Hang on, Ash plans to take the gem south?" He stopped in his tracks. "I thought the two of you were going to go together, once things were squared away up here?"

She shook her head. "I can't go. I have the other thing to see through."

"What? You're *going*? After everything that creature said? You really think it won't be a trap? Some ploy?"

"My mother told me. She confirmed it's real, it's important. I *have* to go, Lukas. No matter how strange it seems."

"You have to see how suspicious this is. You don't know *where* this 'Door' will lead you. You don't know who's on the other side. You can't abandon Ash to the pirates to go through with this. It's suicide."

"It is *not*." She crossed her arms. "It's strange, yes, but I saw my mother in the dreams. She ventured through the Door, to the island. Many years ago, before I was born. She said she was too early and that the timing wasn't right until now."

He took a deep, anxious breath. "This is rash of you."

"I beg your pardon?"

He shook his head, a pained expression crossing his face.

"I can't stand by while you and Ash recklessly throw yourselves into danger. I can't do this again."

"Oh? I don't see you charging down to chastise Rhi for his involvement; you heard his story about the river. You know he was chased through the forest by a Bourjon patrol party. He's more involved with the army than—"

"This is not the same!" His voice rose sharply.

"Why not?" She matched his tone, close to shouting.

"Because Rhi never kissed me only to shackle me to a table!" His mouth and his eyes snapped shut, as if he couldn't quite believe he'd said that. "And Rhi isn't going off to hell knows where alone."

She dropped her hands to her sides and took one step back. "Don't ask this of me, Lukas. Not now, not with *him* here. Don't ask me to give you control of my life like this."

"*What?*"

She held his gaze, and then looked away, shaking her head slowly. "I can't do this. You need to find a way to make your peace with this, because it's what's happening."

"I'm not *asking* to be in charge of your life. I'm asking you to consider the risks before you go flinging yourself into some task on a strange island on the word of a cryptic sea monster!" He broke off with a frustrated grunt. "You never want to think these things through, Ferrin. You can't just march right in to every situation with a half-baked plan, and expect the people who care about you to come fetch you when you land in trouble."

She scoffed and stumbled back one step. "Is that what you think?"

He didn't say anything. He had the decency to look away, a touch of remorse taking up residence in the skin between his eyebrows.

"I don't have to sit here while you berate me," she said, raising her hands in surrender. "I have enough to deal with before I go. Worry about your own problems, and leave me out of it."

The vitriol in her own voice surprised her. She shook her head and left him standing there in the hallway. She could feel his unspoken words as she retreated. *Run away, just as you always do.*

Or maybe they were her own words.

How had it come to this?

CHAPTER THIRTY-TWO

When Ferrin finally did fall asleep, it was into a fitful and tumultuous dreamscape. She tossed and turned all night as she saw fragments of some ancient past playing out. These dreams were completely unlike the meeting with her mother weeks before, but the strange visions were too specific to be mere whimsy.

The wind blew crisp and sharp through bare branches around the hill on which she stood. A whisper of dawn glimmered to the east, pale light traveling across the world to illuminate the circle of tall, ancient stones surrounding her. She didn't recognize this place, the way the trees shied away from the tall stones, the unkempt grasses swaying around her shins, the landscape wholly unfamiliar. And yet she could tell from the trees and the mountains around her, that she was in Lindbarrow. Lindbarrow in another time.

She looked down at herself, even her clothing was unrecognizable. Furs and leathers and ties and straps. She reached out to touch the strange material and balked.

This was not her hand.

Skin three shades darker than her own, devoid of freckles, and flecked with scars she didn't recognize. A crudely carved silver ring hugged her thumb, and there—one piece of familiar adornment— was her ring. The red cabochons were dim in the pre-dawn light, the silver dirty, unpolished.

Where *was* she?

The sun was just starting to stretch itself out from behind the trees on the eastern horizon as she found herself approaching the circle of megaliths at the top of the bald hill.

Peering around the nearest of the giants, she found the ground before her patterned with flat stones, swirling to the center of the circle. Some were plain and others were carved with markings and runes she didn't recognize. At the epicenter was a round pool of water, still as glass despite the wind whipping over the trees, the reflection of the sky a clear and perfect tunnel as if into another realm.

Without considering why, she approached the pool and knelt down, the water glassy as she took in the reflection before her.

Her hair was a light, mousy brown, pulled up into a complicated series of knots and war-braids, woven through with a few strings of hide. A strand of beads that might have been carved from bone hung around her neck over a rough-spun maroon tunic. A fur shawl, clasped across her chest with a silver broach, warded off the relentless cold, and the grip of a sword peaked over her shoulder, strapped to her back on a heavy leather bandolier. Harsh gray eyes stared back from an oval-shaped face patterned with a few lines of blue pigment. She was perhaps thirty, thirty-five.

She reached out a hand to the reflection, and the likeness mimicked her movements.

"So, you've made up your mind, then?" a familiar voice, yet not familiar to *her,* asked from behind.

She turned, fingertips a breath away from grazing the surface of the water before she dropped her hand back to her side.

"I'm not so sure," she said, retracting her arm and leaning back.

The owner of the voice was a woman dressed in a similar combination of furs and leather, her face tattooed with delicate runes in a line down her left cheek, depicting two opposing crescent moons, two stars and a sun. She had bright red hair, pulled back from her face in a woven knot. A flood of comfort and fondness opened in Ferrin's chest at the sight of her.

"Well, there it is, the answer to the big question," the woman jerked her chin at the pool. "It's so much smaller than I imagined."

Ferrin had the distinct impression that they were speaking another language, yet somehow, she understood every word as if it was in her own tongue.

She felt herself nod. "It is small, but I can feel its power. Like it's wriggling deep beneath the surface. A nest of serpents."

The sensation of the words coming out of her was jarring. It was like watching from the crow's nest as someone else steered the ship, only she *was* the ship. She couldn't help thinking this was some kind of memory from long, long ago.

"Your word on the matter is final. Don't let the elders strong-arm you into taking it, Gwel," said the woman, crossing her arms as she stepped closer.

Gwel. *Gwelie,* Ferrin realized with a jolt. Her ancestor, the queen who, according to Alick, had received the flight ring from the storm goddess.

"I know," Gwelie said with a sigh, shrugging her broad shoulders, strong from decades of wielding her broadsword. "Something needs to be done, though. Our people are being picked off each day. We are powerless against the hoards coming down from the far north. They're slaughtering us." She sounded tired, resigned.

"I know," echoed the woman a little sadly, coming to kneel beside her in the grass. "But once you take it, it's yours. No going back. That's what the *Dionas* said. And there still could be another way, one where I don't have to lose you." Her brown eyes were wide and wistful as she looked her over.

"Sig," Gwelie closed her eyes with a deep breath, resting her forehead against Sig's. The comfort she found there made her want to sink into the moment, wrap it around her like a warm, down blanket, and never emerge. But Gwelie shook herself of the notion. "I can't be selfish about this."

Sig lifted a hand to cup her cheek, silver lining her gaze when their eyes met. "No, but I made no such promises."

She opened her mouth to say something else, but Ferrin never got to hear it, because she was wrenched awake.

"Gill, it's nearly dawn," Ash's voice and the present day came flooding back into her senses. "We have to get down to the docks."

"Shit," Ferrin rubbed her eyes with the heels of her palms, still dazed from the memory she'd fallen into. She didn't know what to make of it, only that it had filled her with an overwhelming sadness, and a heavy sense of dread.

Ferrin and Ash made their way down to the docks in a heavy silence, each step on the winding staircase a reminder that neither of them wanted to be doing this. Guilt clung to Ferrin's insides over trading with Zare—guilt at what it meant to Ash, and what it meant to her. She'd been stuffing down her own qualms about cooperating with him since he'd arrived, but it felt dirty expecting Ash to do the same. Still, there was too much at stake to be anything other than objective. When they had what they needed, when they'd seen this thing through, then they could go after him and take the revenge they both deserved for what he'd done.

They'd agreed a few days before not to let him know what their next steps would be, and had agreed on a lie should he ask.

They'd tell him Ferrin was to ship south with a hand-picked crew of Caelish soldiers and privateers, that Ferrin would begin hunting down old contacts and enemies alike to get her hands on the second part of the gem.

They wouldn't tell him that it was *Ash* who'd be going. Ash who'd be picking up a few familiar faces when she reached Tunis. Ash who would get clearance from the higher-ups to establish a foothold for the Caelish in the Meddemara's web of trade. As soon as they had the first half in hand, and Zare was out of the way, and once Ferrin left for the island, Ash would begin preparations to take a ship and crew south to hunt down the gem, and take out as many Bourjon war-ships as she could while she was at it.

Zare would not, *could* not, know this.

They needed him on uneven footing so they could find out the real reason he was so willing to give up such a powerful bargaining chip, and this was the only plausible upper hand for them to have on him. Let him think that he had goaded them into this, into *his* idea. Let him think Ferrin would be traversing oceans on his word alone, and perhaps, he'd get so caught up in his own satisfaction, he'd slip up.

They could only hope.

It was Soviel's information that they'd really be following, anyway, not Zare's. Soviel had sent word about the cetamaris and Bourjony's hunt for it. Soviel had sent word about the alliance with Kalassa. Soviel had sent word about the acquisitions for materials throughout the Meddemara, and what it might mean.

Zare was an afterthought, Ferrin reminded herself.

"Don't give him an inch," Ash whispered beside her.

"I won't," Ferrin said as they turned down the thoroughfare to the docks. A sinking feeling was beginning to come over her.

They walked down the end of the docks, coming to where they'd specified to meet. When they arrived at the offshoot, where the smaller docks split off the main pier, it became clear that something was wrong.

The docks were all but deserted, save for the pair of night-watchmen they'd passed hovering at the entrance. There should have been another pair standing sentry further up the pier, but there wasn't.

Ferrin's stomach churned with anxiety as they made their way down the pier. Something was definitely wrong.

They neared the end, where they'd agreed to meet, and she saw it in her periphery.

Red in the water. An empty berth. A body floating face-down in the harbor.

Ferrin's heartbeat pounded in her ear like a galloping horse as she rushed down the gangway. She reached the water and pulled the floating guard closer, and rolled him over. Dead. His throat cut. Ash swore behind her. There was a watery trail of blood leading a few yards away. The second watchman. Dead.

"What the hell?" Ash hissed.

"No. No." Ferrin shook her head, standing and backing away from the body. "Not again." Her voice pitched and she felt the ground tilt beneath her feet. He'd played her. Again. She'd lost the game. Again.

Zare came, riled her, got what he wanted, and left. Again. Leaving a trail of casualties in his wake.

"No," she repeated, unable to stop shaking her head, unable to stop staring at the body of the guard who was surely dead because of her desperation. "No."

"I know him—" Ash said hollowly, peering closer. "It's Toscan's brother."

"But he's in Avaree," Ferrin said weakly, a dark, deep pit opening beneath her feet.

"He transferred here two weeks ago." Ash knelt. "Help me pull him out of the water."

Ferrin stared for a second longer.

"*Gillian!*" Ash barked. "Snap out of it."

Ferrin obliged and dropped to her knees to help Ash pull Colren out of the water. She didn't register the feel of the dock under her knees or the cold, bloody water on her hands, only the soft thud his body made when they pulled him onto the dock.

"How did he get past the other guards?" Ash swore again. "We should have killed him. Should have killed him the second Helene let him out of jail." She began pacing. Ferrin stared dumbly down at Colren. His face was white as a sheet and the smile-shaped gash across his neck was red red red.

"What the hell?" Ash muttered. "Ferr. Come here."

Ferrin stood slowly on legs that felt like they weren't her own.

"He left a note. And… this." Ash was holding a crisp envelope and a brown-paper-wrapped parcel, carefully tied snug with a scrap of twine.

"Be careful," Ferrin said, her first words in what felt like a year.

Ash spared her a glance and turned her attention back to the parcel, carefully unwrapping the twine and tearing the paper from the box. It was a simple thing, plain, unstained wood. A pendant rested inside. It was a dull-gold sort of metal, with a glimmering cabochon stone the size of a cherry set in its center. It almost glowed, like the ocean floor on a sunny, clear day. Ash poured it into her hand, letting the dull chain trail through her fingers as she held the pendant in her hand. The whole thing was half the size of a chicken egg.

"Why…"

Ferrin took the note from her and tore it open, skimming the words as if they could lend sense to what was happening, as if there was any sense left in the world.

Darling,

I know we were supposed to meet and make the trade this morning, but unfortunately, something's come up that has narrowed my timeframe considerably. I won't be needing those trade papers after all, since I've taken this lovely ship instead. I can only hope it will live up to its name, as I will certainly need to be 'Brisk' on the waves to outrun the angry patrol that is sure to follow me upon discovery of the missing vessel.

Best of luck with the gem, I'll see you on the Meddemara.
Z

She read it over again, and then again.

"Let me see it," Ash said, taking the note from her. Ferrin let her take it and dropped her hands to her sides as she turned and stared out the harbor mouth.

Ash groaned when she read the letter.

"Why did he leave this?" she asked, gesturing at the gem.

"You think it's real?" Ferrin asked in a hollow voice.

"I think so," Ash said with a frown. "It feels… important. Heavy."

Ferrin looked up, confused.

"It reminds me a bit of this," Ash said, reaching into her shirt and pulling out the leather cord that held one of Soviel's enchanted hagstones, "but different. They both feel a bit… magnetic? I'm not sure. What do you think?"

Ferrin carefully took the pendant when Ash handed it to her, enclosing it in her hand. "I can't feel much from it," she admitted somberly.

Ash bristled and quickly tucked the hagstone back into her shirt. "Couldn't it just be some piece of colorful glass he hired someone like Soviel to put a scrap of their power into?" she asked bitterly.

Ferrin shook her head. "I think he wanted to be rid of it, for now at least."

Ash looked at her and waited for her to go on.

"He would never have come here offering it if he didn't have some other motive for wanting it gone. What if it… attracts things? If you can feel it, what if others can, too?"

"What does that mean?"

"Well," Ferrin swallowed. "I can feel this ring." She held up her hand for emphasis. "I put it on and it's like a gust of wind rushes through me. Soviel can feel the *rasernemaud* when it's active. What if this is the same?"

"But I don't have any magical affinities."

"What if you do?" Ferrin asked, staring at Ash. "What if Zare wanted to be rid of this because it's causing him trouble?"

Ash dismissed the first idea with a clipped *hmm*. "Let's say it is. Why wouldn't he just stash it somewhere until later? Why give it to us?"

"Do you suppose the pendant part was a later addition? Or do you think the witch had it made?"

"I don't know, but it reminds me of something," Ash said distantly, looking it over again. "Think the metal is worth much?"

Ferrin shook her head.

"Come, we need to go see how the hell he was able to get away with this. Those two guards up at the entrance are in for a world of trouble."

As it turned out, Zare had studied Helene's writing and forged a note of permission to be on the docks first thing in the morning, and had stolen a signal code book off of one of the murdered guards.

Toscan had crumpled with the news and retreated into his workshop alone. Ash felt like she'd been gutted, too. Ferrin barely said a word the rest of the day, her eyes lost and distant each time Ash even managed to get her attention.

Everything was falling apart.

Helene listened to their report with stony stillness.

"Well, Ash, until the updated speed-ship is finished, you're unfortunately dry-docked, unless Neb has something for you," Major Wilcoe said.

"Yes, Major."

"We are now cut off from our agent in Bramblehall, for the time being. Should she need rescuing, we won't know until it is far too late."

Ferrin stiffened beside Ash.

Wilcoe turned her attention to Ferrin. "I do not want to see you in this encampment again. You've brought us nothing but trouble, and I never should have had Soviel waste her time recruiting you," she said in a low, even tone. "Get out."

Ferrin had simply nodded slowly, stood up, and walked out of the war tent without a word. Ash had moved to follow her, but Helene's guards sat her back down with rough hands. With an expectant glare, Helene made her tell the whole story again, this time slower, and with more detail.

She didn't tell them about the pendant that was now hanging like dead weight around her neck, how she could feel it thrumming like a slow, ancient heartbeat.

After she was finally done, she got up and walked out, off to find Ferrin, and after that, she wasn't sure.

CHAPTER THIRTY-THREE

Rhi awoke alone the next morning in the shared room. He wondered if Lukas had simply risen early, or if he hadn't come home at all. He'd been growing more and more despondent each day, despite the confirmation that Ryder had reached Avaree alive. Something else, something about the friend he'd lost back home, was eating him alive.

He sat up and rubbed his eyes, resolving to track Lukas down later and find out what was *really* bothering him.

First, he had to share Hassan's notes with Lachlan. They had arrived the previous afternoon, and were far too important to put off any longer than he already had. His stomach did a turn as he thought of the previous night. Despite their mutual attraction coming to a near-snapping point, he felt more off-balance than before. He had no idea where they stood, and after they were interrupted, Lachlan had rushed out of there so fast, he didn't know what to think.

His mood took a turn. What if he'd misread the situation? What if all there was between them was a passing attraction? Perhaps Rhi had been concocting fanciful ideas in his head when they truly had nothing between them.

He shook his head. He didn't need to borrow trouble and agonize over nothing before he talked to Lachlan.

Dressing quickly, he shoved down his concerns about his personal life and tried to focus on what Hassan's research might mean. He'd read over some of it before going to bed, but hadn't been able to find his focus. Most of the higher-level sciences went right over his head. He'd been educated on politics, bloodlines, and wartime strategy, not geology. He tucked the folio under his arm and headed out.

As he made his way through camp, he caught wind of the strange tension that had befallen the barracks. Something had happened early that morning. There were groups congregating with whispers and looks askance. The eery quiet made him self-conscious. Outside a row of tents, voices began to rise, conversation escalating.

"You were supposed to be on sentry at the docks! Not him!" The voice was fraught and brittle with bereavement. Rhi didn't recognize the soldier.

"He swapped with me! He wanted the afternoon off," the second soldier responded in a desperate tone.

"It should have been *you*. You gods-damned southern *bitch*!"

"I had nothing to do with this!" she roared back.

"Your lot had nothing to lose from this. Now my best friend is dead!" the accuser's voice broke.

The first soldier, a man with golden hair, launched at the second soldier. She threw her hands up to block him, stumbling back.

"Hey!" Rhi lunged into their circle. "Calm down, do you want to get written up? What's happened?"

"Ask *her*," the first soldier spat, his friend holding him back.

Rhi turned his attention to the other soldier. She was tall, with brown hair braided back from her tan face.

"I had nothing to do with it. Someone killed two sentries on guard at the docks before dawn, and stole a boat. I swapped times with one of them." Her voice was ragged.

"*What*? Who?" Rhi asked, his heart leaping into his throat. Lachlan was on sentry duty last night. Had he been at the docks?

"Colren Trotter and Seamus Octreal. Throats slit."

"Where did you learn this?"

"It's all over camp. They're saying that prisoner they brought in a few weeks back did it."

"Who?"

The brunette soldier shook her head. "That's just what I've heard."

"Right." Rhi nodded. "Resolve this calmly, or disperse. I have to go."

He turned without waiting for a reply, and jogged the rest of the way to Lachlan's tent.

He burst in a bit more dramatically than he'd intended, still needing to confirm with his own eyes that Lachlan had not been at the docks.

"Hi," Lachlan said, looking startled by Rhi's shocked expression. He'd been shaving, and still had a white lather of soap on one cheek.

"Did you hear?" Rhi asked as he recovered his breath and his poise.

"The two dead down by the pier?" asked Lachlan somberly as he swished his straight razor in the cup. "Yeah."

"Who did it?"

"I don't know, but I saw your sister leaving Wilcoe's office with this… *look*… about five minutes after she and Mazrihn went in there."

"*Look*?" Rhi asked. "What do you mean?"

"She looked upset."

"Oh, no," Rhi sat down on the trunk and dropped his head into his hands. "She and Ash went into Major Wilcoe's tent?"

Lachlan nodded, a question in his eyes.

"Shit," Rhi swore, rubbing his hand over his mouth and jaw, then stood. "Did you see which way my sister went?"

"She took off."

"Which direction?"

"Up." Lachlan pointed. He looked slightly amused, despite the gravity of the situation. "By the way, it would have been helpful to mention that you have a flying sister."

Rhi barked a frustrated laugh. "I have to go find her. I think I know what happened."

"I'd give it a minute," Lachlan advised. "She lit off like a hawk. Went straight out over the ocean."

"Shit."

"Was she involved with one of them? The dead soldiers?"

"No," Rhi said. "But I think the killer, if it's who I think it is—" he broke off without finishing. "In the mean time, I have something to show you."

"Alright…" Lachlan said hesitantly as he toweled off his face.

"These came in yesterday," Rhi said as he dropped back onto the trunk. "They're from Hassan."

"*What*?" Lachlan spun around on his heel.

Rhi winced. "Just look at them. It's his entire book of research on Aesterium."

"All of it?" Lachlan asked, his hands falling to his side. "How did he manage to get it out of there?" he asked, more to himself.

"I'm not sure, but I was going over it last night. It's dense stuff, but there's information in here that's mighty interesting. The theorized origins of the metal, its properties, experimental uses… Go on, look for yourself," he said, handing the folio to Lachlan, who took it and sat down on the cot across from him.

Lachlan opened the book and began flipping through its pages. "Strange," he noted. "I can't believe he sent this."

"He may have made a copy," Rhi offered softly.

"Still," Lachlan said.

"He took a huge risk," Rhi agreed. "We need to make the most of this."

"I'm not handing it over to Alemont," Lachlan said, clutching the book.

"I would never suggest doing that, Lach," said Rhi, affronted.

"Good." Lachlan nodded, a bitter smile twisted his lips. "We've got work to do."

CHAPTER THIRTY-FOUR

I t was evening by the time Rhi made his way back up to the manor. The climb was long and tiring and he got the sense that he was walking into an atmosphere far heavier than he was prepared for. There were hushed, serious voices when he passed General Ashwife's office. He recognized the harbormaster, Neb, looking enraged as she was chastised by a furious Ashwife, whose face had grown redder than usual.

He continued on, not one to lurk, and climbed the stairs up to the top floor to the adjoining rooms that were split between the five of them. Even the hallway was still and cold, despite the summer heat and the sound of gulls laughing in the distance.

He barged through the door of the room he and Lukas shared and found it empty, so he crossed to the adjoining door and knocked.

"Who is it?" Ash called out.

"It's Rhi!"

"Oh, come in," she said.

He opened the door to find her at the small dresser, folding a few pieces of laundry, a book open beside her.

"You know there's really only two options for who it is when someone knocks at that door."

"You never know," Ash said flatly.

"Have you seen Ferrin?"

Ash hesitated and set down the shirt she'd just finished folding. "Yeah."

"Do you know where she is?" Rhi asked, frowning.

"No."

"I'm confused."

Ash looked at him a moment before explaining. "Something's happened, and I think she needs time to process it before she sees… certain people."

Rhi nodded slowly. "I take it you mean Lukas? I heard about the dead guards."

She looked at him pointedly.

"Is it something to do with Zare?"

"Yeah."

"Shit," Rhi muttered. "If he tried to hurt her again, I swear I'll wring his neck—"

"He's gone," Ash interrupted. "He stole my fucking boat and left."

"He *stole your boat*?" Rhi started.

Ash pursed her lips and nodded grimly. "*The Brisk* is gone. He killed two of the watchmen at the docks and took off."

"Please tell me you at least got what you needed," Rhi said.

Ash reached into her shirt and plucked forth a brassy pendant with a blue-green stone at its center.

"Oh. That's something, at least."

"Unless it's not," Ash quipped. "There's no way he'd just leave it when he didn't have to for no reason. Either it's fake, or there's going to be a horrible catch."

"Fuck," Rhi muttered, shifting from foot to foot. "What's there to be done?"

"Nothing." Ash dropped into one of the chairs at the tiny table. "The plan will have to go on as is—I'll go south to search for the other half, and interrupt as many Bourjon operations as I can."

"And the other thing?" He referred to the quest that Arabella had burdened Ferrin with. He didn't need to clarify.

Ash shrugged. "She hasn't said much about it."

Rhi nodded again. He was so furious with their mother, he could scream. She'd always been like this, manipulative, pushy, always serving some end and putting him and Ferrin in the middle of whatever issue she had with their father—with Henrik—before they were old enough to even understand it.

It didn't surprise him that they were both *actual* pawns in her larger scheme.

"Well… I guess I'll wait for her to come back, then."

It was nearly dinnertime when Ferrin returned to the manor, easing in the unlocked window, unwilling to stomach facing anyone milling about the lower levels. She wasn't sure what she expected to find, but Rhi and Ash sitting and laughing over mugs of steaming tea was not it.

"Oh, good, you're back!" Ash said with relief as she turned in her chair. "We were starting to worry."

"Hi," she replied, trying not to sound too stricken.

"What happened to your face?" Rhi asked as he set down his mug.

"Tree branch," she grunted, climbing the rest of the way off the sill. "The wind picked up unexpectedly."

"About this morning," Ash started carefully. "Wilcoe will come around, she's just stressed about Sov—"

"No. She won't."

"Yes, she will, she has to."

"She shouldn't," Ferrin said. Helene's calm, cold dismissal of her had been playing over and over in her mind. She wished Helene had screamed, thrown the ink well on her desk across the room at her. "She's right. You were right. We should have put him in the ground the second he showed up here, and taken our chances with the rest of it. Then, all of this would have been avoided."

"Maybe. But maybe not, Ferr. You can't know that."

Ferrin pulled out a folded sweater from the top drawer of the dresser and put it on as she considered Ash's words. It didn't matter. She couldn't stop seeing Colren with his throat slit, floating face down in the water, or the chilling note scrawled in dark ink, or the empty berth and calm water where *The Brisk*, Soviel's lifeline to home, was supposed to be.

"Do you still have the gem? No one confiscated it?" she asked.

Ash nodded. "Wilcoe is still on board with what she knows of our plan."

"Well, that's good. It would be difficult to get around this without her approval."

"When?" Rhi asked, looking between the two women.

"Soon," Ferrin answered. "We have to get that second piece before Bourjony or Hadringston does. Or Zare, since now he's probably headed that way too."

Ash mumbled her agreement.

"How is that going to work?" Rhi asked.

"Ash will sail south with a skeleton crew of trusted sailors, pick up a few of our old contacts in Old Orini, and begin searching," Ferrin explained.

"All under the guise of privateering for the cause. I'll be interrupting Bourjon trade ships and harassing their navy at all opportunities."

"Wait. Wait." Rhi held up a hand for them to stop. "Just Ash? You're not both going? I thought you'd… I don't know, co-captain."

"No, I'm not going. I don't think Helene would even allow me on the mission if I asked."

"Oh," Rhi said. "Then I suppose I should extend a different invitation." He cleared his throat. "When the reinforcements go south to the Andal Mountains, I'm going with them."

Ferrin's head snapped up.

"If you want to come, too, I'm sure there'll be use for you. I can ask Lachlan to put in a transfer request through Ashwife for you, you know, to circumnavigate Wilcoe."

"Oh," she said, surprised. "You're leaving?"

"Lach asked me to go, and there's so much more to be done on what we're researching…" he trailed off. There was a warmth in his voice when he spoke about Lachlan that reassured Ferrin. She was happy that Rhi would not be alone when she left.

"I can't," she shook her head. "Every day, I can feel the pull of that place, stronger and stronger. I can't put it off much longer." She tried to keep her voice light, but the waver in it gave her away, and when she looked at Ash and her brother, her stomach twisted at their expressions of concern.

"When will you leave?" Ash asked carefully.

"As soon as possible, I think," she said. "There's not much more for me to do here. If you'll sail me out to the spot we found last time…"

"Of course," Ash said softly. "Whatever you need, Ferr."

"Thanks," she smiled sadly.

"You want to come down to the kitchens with us for dinner?" Rhi asked.

She offered him a weak smile and shook her head. "Nah, thanks but I think I'll go to bed early, actually."

CHAPTER THIRTY-FIVE

Again, Ferrin fell deep into that dream space. There was the cold, windblown hill, the heavy furs draped over her shoulders, the even heavier sword at her back.

Being in Gwelie's skin was an unsettling comfort, as she was realizing more and more how similar their paths might be. Gwelie was the one who had first been gifted with the flight ring, in addition to her abilities to ride the storms. There was more to the story, though.

In her recent dreaming, Ferrin had wound up in Gwelie's story every night. Not once had she taken flight, though the ring sparkled on her hand. Through Gwelie's eyes she saw Sig, who was fighting tooth and nail to save her from some terrible fate she had not yet discerned. She saw a little red-headed child, no older than seven, who was the light of Gwelie's life, full of energy and lover of creatures big and small. She saw the priest, old and bent but wise and quick as an asp. She saw Gwelie's people, a fearsome tribe of warriors and their families, making their home at the foot of the Icharian Mountains, at war with the raiding parties coming from across the sea, and at war with an unnamed creature that came down from the mountains under cover of dark and devoured villages whole.

The desperation Gwelie felt was not unfamiliar to Ferrin as everything fell apart around her.

This dream came on with a muted intensity, but Ferrin wasn't in Gwelie's skin this time. Rather, she was hovering over her, a formless, bodiless entity, observing from the ether above.

Gwelie was hunched over something, her shoulders shaking with emotion. The stones in the distance were splattered with blood. Far, far below, a house in the village caught fire.

What came next, Ferrin saw in flashes. Gwelie rising from the broken body she was mourning, her movements marionette-like. She unbuckled and cast aside her fur cloak and stalked into the circle. That strange pool Ferrin had seen previously was barely more than a puddle now, and blood seeped into the earth around Gwelie from bodies that littered the ground. Whatever beast had killed her child, it had come to wreak havoc on the temple and the village.

She sank to her knees before the pool, and drank.

Blink—a hurricane whirled towards the coast, powerful and furious. Blink—a pillar of lightning came down on the head of the great wolf-bear-beast that had worlds in its eyes. Blink—Sig staggered to the edge of a cliff, leaning into the wind as she stared up at the storm in bewilderment, lost in the torrent of rain and wind and static. She dropped to her knees in despair. Blink—a tidal wave crushed a wooden ship, spilling fighters and fury into the sea.

Blink, and the sun shone over the isle. Grass grew green over the land, nourished by the rain. Blink, the villages began rebuilding. Livestock was rescued from cliffs, crops grew, children played.

Blink, and Sig was strangling the priest, a well of grief and rage opened so deep in her eyes, there was no climbing out of it.

Blink. Gwelie was gone; Sig wore her ring on a cord around her neck, rubbing her thumb over the red stones as she stared blankly out at the sea, waiting.

Ferrin slung her pack higher up on her shoulder and looked around the small room in the manor's attic one last time. She'd said her goodbyes to Rhi earlier that morning when he'd left for his day's work in the barracks. The knowledge that he was going south with Lachlan was equal parts comforting and worrying. She didn't want him to be alone, but the fighting at the border was constant.

On her finger, Gwelie's ring glistened its dull silver and crimson in the morning light. She'd packed enough bread, cheese and carrots to last her three days, along with a leather pouch of water, an extra knife, a few spare bullets and powder cartridges for the pistol at her side, and a spare cloak. The paraffin coating on the outside of the canvas bag would help keep it all dry on her journey to the Door, and after that, she wasn't sure what sort of environment she'd encounter. She'd dressed in layers just in case.

With a long, resigned sigh, she turned and strode out the door.

"You're leaving?" Lukas asked, leaning against the wall in the hallway.

"It's time," she said, meeting his gaze.

"I'll walk you down."

They made their way out of the manor with minimal conversation. What was there to say, after all? They'd said plenty last time they talked. Too much, in fact.

At last, they arrived on the beach where Ash waited by a skiff.

She and Ferrin greeted each other with solemn nods.

"You have the gem?" Ferrin asked.

"Safe and sound," Ash reassured her, hooking a thumb around the long chain to pull the pendant out from under her shirt.

"Ash is still taking the gem?" Lukas asked with surprise.

Ash dropped the pendant back to her chest. "I'm right here, you know."

"That was always the plan," Ferrin explained to Lukas. "You knew this."

"Yeah… before *he* slaughtered two guards and stole Ash's ship."

"It didn't change anything."

"It changes *everything*!"

"I'm going to check in with harbor patrol," Ash said awkwardly, backing away.

She pinched the bridge of her nose. "I don't know how long I'm going to be away, Lukas. Ash is qualified to do this, and we need to make use of Zare's information as soon as possible."

"And is his information *actually* useful? Or are you sending my sister blindly into the nest of this man who's tried to kill both of you? For all we know, that pendant is some bit of polished glass he picked up from a penny-vendor in Khalim!"

She looked at him wearily. "It's the real gem."

He shook his head. Something sad and fractured lingered in his eyes. "Just because you want it to be, doesn't mean it is, Ferrin."

"Look, I know you don't like this. You've made that *very* clear. I don't like it either, but the fact is, there's a lot more at stake than your feelings, or mine," she said, the words coming out with significantly more bite than she'd intended.

He balked, defensive. "My *feelings* are not what I'm concerned over. I'm concerned about you sending my sister into a trap. That man is a manipulative liar, and you're letting your past control you, and cloud your judgment. He is using you, *again*."

It was like a slap in the face.

"*My* past?" she yelled, the anger rising so sharply inside her, she wasn't sure what would happen when it bubbled over. "And what about you, Lukas? What about your past? What about how you wake up in a cold sweat every night, losing your mind over Ryder because you refuse to deal with what happened to Damijan?"

It was the wrong thing to say, acidic and burning on her tongue as it left her mouth, but she couldn't seem to stop herself.

"I know he was your best friend, that you blame yourself for his death. You think you can shove it down where no one else will see it, see the truth that no amount of sarcasm or false cheerfulness can mask."

"Oh, and what truth is that, exactly?" he demanded.

"That you're just a coward, constantly running from your own guilt. If you're going to let it warp you into *this* person, then what the hell was the point of surviving?"

She watched the words land like a cannonball, out of her mouth and inflicting damage before she could even consider what she'd said. He flinched, only for a split second, before the facade of carelessness slid over his features again.

She started forward, teetering on an invisible threshold, her lips parted to say… what? Do what? Reach for him? Take it back? She hadn't realized how hard she was breathing as he locked down, his features going stony and unfeeling.

"Whatever you find at this island, and whatever you're blindly sending Ash to hunt for, I hope it's worth selling yourself to that bastard for," he spat

Her chest tightened, her heart felt as if it was calcifying and turning brittle. They stared at each other a moment longer, both carrying their own wounds, locked in a battle to see who could hit lower. Neither able to take back their words, neither willing to admit the bitter anguish and regret that now seeped through their veins.

Ash returned, a coil of rope slung over one shoulder and a wary expression on her face as she looked between them.

"Are you… ready to go?" she asked tentatively. "We're losing the tide."

No. She wanted to take it back, take his hand, tell him she was cracking from the pressure of it all. But there wasn't any time, and there weren't enough words in the world that *she* could string together to fix that broken look in his eye. She couldn't fix this.

"Yeah," Ferrin nodded once, wrenching her eyes away from Lukas's gaze as she said, "I'm done."

Ash and Ferrin spent the first twenty minutes of the journey in total silence as Ferrin turned the conversation with Lukas in her head over and over and over like it was a cursed trinket.

They were rapidly cutting through the waves, sailing upwind towards the place where the Portal Guardian had intercepted them the first time. Ferrin spun the ring around her finger as anxiety gnawed at her.

She had the barest details of what was to come, and beyond the information that she had been bred, created for this purpose, she had very little confidence in its outcome. What would come to pass if, despite her mother's machinations, she failed at this?

"Are you alright?" Ash asked, finally breaking the silence.

Ferrin hesitated, staring out at the waves. "I don't think I have the privilege of *not* being alright anymore."

Ash took a beat, then offered, "Whatever he said, I know he didn't mean it."

Ferrin closed her eyes, feeling the cold spray of the sea. She didn't bother to say that it was *she* who'd said the unforgivable thing. She shook her head, trying and failing to focus on the task at hand.

"So," Ash said, "do you know how long you'll be in this place?"

Ferrin gathered her thoughts and turned to Ash. "No, I don't. Frankly, I don't even know where this place is. The Door may be up here, but the island it's supposed to spit me out on could be anywhere, it could be amongst ice in the far northern sea, it could be so far west the map's never touched it, it could be… anywhere."

What if Norhi didn't come to collect her? What if everything that had happened in the last weeks had marked her unworthy of this task?

"That's unsettling," Ash commented.

Ferrin mustered a half-smile. "Just a little bit."

"You have weapons? Food?"

Ferrin patted her pack. "All in here."

"Good," Ash nodded, gnawing the nails of one hand while the other held the tiller. "I can't believe you're leaving me alone with the boys," she said with an affected groan.

"Hopefully it'll only be for a few days," Ferrin said, trying for cheerful, "then you're heading back south to our old stomping ground. You want to trade missions?"

Ash grimaced. "No."

"Exactly. Try to at least bring back some good Meroyan rum for me while you're harassing Bourjon ships and hunting down ancient gems. Any idea where you're going to start looking for it?"

Ash looked pensive. "I thought I'd start by getting my hands on Tabka's special charts."

Ferrin nodded. "What do you think you'll find when you look for the old crew?"

"Well," Ash began, "Dansk and Mitch will have to be dealt with, since they were Zare's main co-conspirators. The rest… I suppose it'll depend on what state I find them in. I'm sailing down there with a skeleton crew, but I'll take on seasoned pirates looking for a change in career once I get to Tunis."

"And, Pierre? He's definitely dead?" asked Ferrin.

Ash nodded sadly at the loss of their friend. "Zare slit his throat immediately when he resisted the plan against you."

"Fuck," Ferrin breathed, sinking her teeth into her fist.

"Yeah," Ash agreed, the word strained and tense.

"You have to kill him. If you run into him, you gut him, promise."

"I plan to," Ash said with conviction. "For both of us."

"Good."

At last, they reached the strange ridge in the water, where the waves seemed to falter and ripple around an invisible border.

A silvery, scaled, equine head surfaced seconds later.

Norhi shook a spray of seawater out of his mane as he glided up to the side of the small ship. With one clawed foot hooked gently over the side, he fixed his liquid fire eyes on Ferrin.

"It is time," he said in his ancient voice.

She nodded, still half-shocked he'd showed up, and so quickly.

She turned to Ash and wrapped her arms around her, squeezing tight. "Thank you, Ash. For everything."

"Be careful," Ash said, squeezing back.

"I will. Watch out for the others," Ferrin choked out before releasing her. She pulled back, her eyes wet. She turned to the Portal Guardian. "I'm ready."

Norhi turned, bearing his back for her. She climbed on and let him whisk her across the sea to the Door within the waves.

The waves crashed against the rocky shoal surrounding the great cavernous prominence, and sprayed onto Ferrin's face as Norhi approached the little lump that formed the Door's island.

"Are you ready?" Norhi asked, craning his neck to survey her.

She offered him a numb, silent nod and stepped off when he plodded up onto the rocky shore.

"You should know—that ring will not work where you are going. Keep it close and keep it safe, but don't bother trying to use it while you are on the island."

"Why not?"

"Some ancient laws of nature are too deep to be bent."

"Oh," she replied, only half-understanding his cryptic words, as usual.

She nodded to him before turning to face the Door. She waited until she heard Norhi slip back into the sea in a shimmer of scales and brine before she staggered forward and dropped to the ground. Sand bit into her knees as she bowed over them. The pit in her stomach threatening to swallow her whole if she let it out. A sob wracked her as she relived her fight with Lukas. Her entire body ached as she thought of Helene's dismissal, of Colren's death at Zare's hands. Of Soviel… alone in the home of the enemy. Of Rhi on his way to the front. Of Ash heading south into dangerous waters with limited information. Of her mother's revelations. Of Gwelie's choice.

Sand grated her palms as she clenched them into fists on the ground.

When she was done, spent, finished, she stood and dusted off her breeches, rinsed her hands in the sea, and faced the Door. She was ready now, she had to be.

After all, this was all there was for her to do.

With her shoulders squared, Ferrin took a step

across

the
world.

PART

THREE

Blazing, blinding light met Ferrin when she awoke on the shore and cracked open one eye. She was dry, but salty, as if she'd washed up on this beach hours ago and baked in the sun all day long. Her hair was stiff and crusted from the sea.

She tried to get her bearings. Tall cliffs of white stone shot through with deep black striations, deep cerulean ocean, not a building or a person in sight. The beach's sand was black and smooth.

Wasn't there supposed to be some sort of temple in this place?

"What the hell," she mumbled to herself. The sun was close to setting, though it had been midday only minutes ago.

She turned away from the horizon and examined the tall cliffs, where the stone was glowing with the gold light of the sunset.

In the distance, she spotted a thin set of stairs that appeared to spiral around the cliff.

Tempering her resolve, she readied for the ascent.

The climb up the cliff took nearly an hour, and she cursed whatever stupid ancient laws prevented her from flying. What Norhi had said was true. She'd checked. If she'd been able to fly, it would have taken her a minute to reach the plateau, which revealed *more* cliffs, set like layers of a cake atop one another. The grass was green as emeralds, and despite the chilly temperature, vibrant wildflowers grew from the soft ground beside the path. She groaned as she circled the prominence. *More stairs.*

She'd had to go slow on her way up, reminding herself to fear the fall, since great heights were something commonplace for her now.

At last, she came around the bend and laid eyes on a hut. It had windows, the panes too small and dirty to see much through aside from the faint glow of a fire within. The roof was thatched, and smoke rose from its chimney. Night had fallen, and Ferrin was worn and brittle from her journey through the fold in the world. She'd already eaten half her bread on the trek up the cliffs.

When she was ten paces from the hut, the door swung open and a figure stood in its light. She was middle-aged, built sturdily, with her black hair tied back in a braid that circled her head in a crown. She wore a simple gray tunic with hip-high slits for ease of movement over a pair of dark burgundy leggings. Her face was full of dramatic angles, and her skin was a muted pink tone.

Ferrin froze when she locked eyes with the stranger.

"We've been waiting for you," the woman said, crossing her arms. She had a light accent. "Come," she directed.

Ferrin hesitated, searching for the threat.

"If we wanted you dead, we'd have slit your throat while you were unconscious on your back on the beach all afternoon."

Ferrin bristled.

"The Door can transport you places very far, very fast, but it has a bit of a whiplash effect."

"I noticed that," she said, testing her voice. Her throat was raw and the words came out garbled.

The woman stepped aside, inviting her in.

Inside, the hut was perfectly ordinary. A stone floor covered partially by a rustic woven rug, a little round wooden table, fire crackling in a stone hearth and a pot of stew boiling away. The walls were wood-panels, hung with blankets for insulation. In the far corner sat a cot with a pile of blankets and furs resting on its edge.

"Sit," the woman said.

Ferrin hesitated, still taking in her surroundings. After determining nothing sinister waited to leap from the corners, she slid cautiously into one of the chairs at the table.

"For the duration of your stay, this is where you will sleep. The well is on the other side of this level, just around the bend. If you take the path around the south side of the island, you'll find it."

Ferrin nodded, unsure of what she was supposed to do from here. "What is this place?"

"Your soup should be ready to eat in ten minutes." The woman strode for the door, ignoring her question.

Ferrin stood, noisily scraping the chair along the floor. "Wait, hold on, please—you haven't told me *anything* about this place—"

"Did you think you'd just be handed the answers to the secrets of the universe as soon as you arrived here?" The woman paused in the doorway. "Be up by dawn. Then, we will begin."

Exhausted from being ripped across the world, and from the climb, and from everything else swirling through her head, Ferrin fell into a dreamless sleep.

CHAPTER THIRTY-SIX

The sail back to Port Galan was somber, and Ash had to stop herself from nervously biting her nails at least a hundred times.

She couldn't shake the feeling that everything around her was crumbling. Soviel was far off, entrenched in an enemy court, Ferrin had vanished off to some mystical island found on no map, leaving Ash in Galan with her new task, along with Lukas who seemed to be holding on by a thread, and Rhi who was set to ship south with the army in two weeks time.

At least she, too would be heading south to familiar waters again. Really, how could the breeze be so chilly here when they were well into summer?

She pulled into the harbor with minimal trouble, dropping sail and landing on the beach before hauling the skiff up the beach to de-rig it. She missed *The Brisk*.

Toscan had locked himself in his workshop ever since Zare had stolen *The Brisk* and killed Colren. Ash wasn't sure if he was working on the new design, or if he was just in there alone, spiraling.

That damn gem was heavy around her neck, pulsing with its own heartbeat as if against the pressure of the deep. Regardless of the fact that it had been resting against her bare skin for two hours now, it still felt cold to the touch.

The second half—that was what she needed to focus on. They all had their parts to play, and that was hers. While Soviel gathered intel from the enemy and Ferrin sought her destiny off the edge of the map, she would find the key to wrangling the power of the deep. Bourjony's huge, growing forces were sure to have tricks up their sleeves. The resistance needed a few tricks of their own.

When she arrived back at the barracks, things were restless. The air was so tense, she could whip out one of her hidden daggers and shave off a slice like hard cheese.

"What's going on?" she asked as she came up beside Rhi and Lachlan idling outside a war tent, the latter of whom was peeling a fat, juicy orange.

"Units readying to move out," Lachlan said, lifting a shoulder. "New assignments coming in. Strange sort of silence from across the strait."

"How do you mean?"

"I mean scouts returned from the south last night and said there's just *nothing*. No transports, no communication, no supply ships. Nothing."

"Strange," she said with a frown.

"But there is good news," Lachlan went on. "Scouts from the interior have discovered ammunition and food stores not far from here. Units are heading out to take advantage of the information at dusk."

"Good," Ash nodded. "Any update on the vial?"

Rhi shook his head. "Only what you heard in the meeting."

"They aren't still trying to… replicate it?"

Lachlan glowered.

"We're working on dissuading them from that," was all Rhi said.

"Well, I'm glad the two of you are on the job." She shivered at the idea of those horrible experiments being conducted by the people in this camp.

"When are you leaving for the Meddemara?" Rhi asked.

"Twelve days," she said. "Just getting everything figured before then."

"Well, careful," Lachlan warned. "Something is coming. I don't like this silence coming from down south. The soldiers are restless and the horses have been in a fit all week."

"Maybe it's the full moon," Ash joked.

"Maybe," Lachlan split the orange in two and passed half to Rhi. "Let's hope so."

Soviel had just deposited her newest correspondence in the oak, and was headed back to the manor to ready Samia for breakfast. She'd broken a sweat in the dewy summer heat, and in her haste. Her cheeks bore a rosy flush when she rounded the corner of the field house and nearly collided with the duke.

"Your Grace! Forgive me, I wasn't looking where I was going!"

"Lady Soviel," his voice was gruff as he put out a hand to steady her. "I confess, I wasn't either." He held up a stack of papers he'd been examining.

"My apologies," she repeated, pausing to take in his appearance. "Is there anything amiss? You seem distressed."

He grimaced. "Paperwork to deal with. There's a new customs master at Everness, and coordinating things with the blockade is… well, it's nothing I would want to bore you with," he said politely with a tight smile.

Soviel let her eyes stay wide and doe-like as she nodded along. "I know little of such things, I'm afraid," she cringed. "Where are you importing from?"

"Veira," he said.

"Oh," she nodded sympathetically. "My mother is half-Veiran. Have you tried bringing it over land?" she asked, knowing full well that it would be impossibly expensive and time-consuming to do so, unless the quantity was tiny.

"Unfortunately, that isn't possible," Cal said. To his credit, he kept the condescension in his voice to a minimum. "It's just not lucrative."

"Oh." She laughed nervously.

"I'll leave you to it," he said with a nod. "Good day."

He continued on his way and she mulled over their conversation in silence, combing it for any information that might be of actual use.

Veira had two main exports: finely dyed silk and *popava.*

If she had to guess which of those goods was on those ships, she knew what she'd bet on.

Samia was in rare form that morning, near mad with something resembling self-awareness as she readied for her day.

Soviel wondered if having more responsibility would actually be a *good* thing for the duchess. All this sitting around and these mindless activities couldn't be healthy for one's constitution.

"Oh, no, no, no, this won't do," Samia said, cringing as she beheld the dress Tavara had lain out for her. "There are new soldiers arriving today, and new maid staff, oh dear."

Soviel swept her hand over the two dresses that were being scrutinized. One was of palest blue silk with creamy lace gussets at the swooping, frothy sleeves. The second was a deep, emerald green with handsome gold detailing.

"You know, I saw His Grace on my way here from my rooms. He was wearing red and gray—maybe your striped day-frock? Think of how well it would match him, how splendid the pair of you will look to the new arrivals," Soviel suggested and threw open the enormous armoire.

Samia seemed to calm at that, her nervous energy stilling as she tilted her head, taking in the dress as Soviel held it up for her to assess.

"Oh. Oh, yes. That could work nicely, with the pearl earrings…" she trailed off, climbing out of bed to examine the garment more closely.

"Shall I fetch your matching stockings and mules, Samia?" Lucelle chimed in.

"Yes. Yes, I think this will do," Samia said, calmer.

Crisis averted, Soviel thought wryly to herself. "Perfect," she said with a small smile. "Are we to greet the new soldiers and maid staff on the lawn for their arrival? I can find your parasol."

"No, there is too much important business or whatnot." She waved a dismissive hand through the air. "We will not see the officers until dinner, and the new servants likely won't receive a formal welcome." She clucked her tongue. "Such is the way things are, now," she sighed deeply, as if the neglect of a few ceremonies was the worst consequence of the international conflict.

Soviel held her tongue and nodded as she helped Samia dress in her underpinnings and petticoat.

"Well, nonetheless, it will still be an exciting day. Where have these new soldiers come from? And how long will they be staying?" Jorde had finally asked the question Soviel was itching to ask herself.

"Only a week, then they're headed north."

Soviel's stomach leapt into her throat, but she managed to keep her features from betraying her panic.

"That's a short stay, why not just camp out further north? Is it not out of their way to come so far west?" Soviel asked casually.

"Uch. Who knows," Samia said, clearly bored with the discussion. "My husband has been in a state about it since we returned from that wretched stone palace."

"Seems a bother," Soviel shrugged.

"It is," Samia huffed. "You'd think he would be more interested in *me,* considering we have no children yet."

Not what I was talking about, Soviel thought, *but…* "Does he not visit your bed chamber often?" she asked carefully.

"No," Samia pouted.

Well, that explains a bit. The man has a stick so far up his own ass, it's a miracle he can sit at his desk as long as he does.

"Why not go to his?" Soviel suggested delicately.

Tavara made a small gasping sound, and Erina smirked. Jorde and Lucelle shared a look.

"No," Samia frowned. "It isn't considered proper for…"

"For a married couple to enjoy bedding each other?" Soviel finished. "His Grace seems like a very hard-working man. Perhaps he needs to relax. You should go to him, soothe him. It just might work in your favor."

There was a beat of silence. Perhaps she'd spoken too brazenly, perhaps she'd acted out of character, perhaps—

"I think she's right," Jorde drawled, sliding her gold glasses up her nose. "Not every man is as bold as they'd have us believe. Show him you want him."

Samia paused, considering. "I suppose I could give it a try. It would give me a chance to wear my lace-applique stays…"

Soviel gave her a smile of encouragement. "Good," she said devilishly. "I'll bet he goes wild when he sees you wearing those."

Samia beamed. "I hope so," she chirped, her attitude entirely changed. "Now, let's go have our breakfast on the lawn."

Later that night, Samia had dressed in her boudoir underpinnings and left her ladies at the door when they escorted her to her husband's chambers, which left Soviel with *at least* an hour to snoop around Hadringston's office.

After retreating to her own room and waiting for the other ladies to do the same, she stole away and doubled back towards the duke's administrative suite.

The door was locked, but she'd swiped a key from one of his assistants earlier in the day, and made quick work of letting herself in and pulling the door shut silently behind her.

She didn't dare light a lantern in case it alerted anyone to her presence. His office was a series of rooms, including side-offices and a small lab full of glass beakers and tubes. The main office was fine, if minimally decorated. Everything was neat, perfectly in line, organized.

She took a deep breath and got to work.

The drawers were, predictably, locked, but the top of his desk and the sliding platform just under the tabletop were accessible to her, and she was able to find a few papers.

Nothing important that she didn't already know, just *popava* shipments from Veira, and imports from all across the Meddemara at prices so low there was simply no way Hadringston wasn't exploiting his farmers and workers.

His trading company, *Westerbarrian Importing* was quite lucrative indeed, and not shy about making the system work for it. She scoffed in disgust. He'd even had a stake in the Veiran occupation of Akhata a few years back and had profited greatly from the salvaging efforts. It was wretched.

She scowled as she rifled through the rest of the papers on the desk, looking for *anything* she could find on the army's movement.

If they were pushing north, she had to warn the others, and quickly.

She scoured the side cabinets, and to her glee found a few drawers unlocked. Unfortunately, they only contained old wage-sheets of former employees. She bit down on her sigh of exasperation and put everything back before moving to the lab, where she prayed she might discover something useful.

As with the offices, the lab was immaculate in its cleanliness and organization. Even the graphite sticks and quills left on the tables were in perfect, parallel rows.

He really does *have a stick up his ass*.

She swept her gaze over the tabletop, then the wee cubbies beneath. At the wall was a cabinet with glass doors (locked), filled with glass vials, corked bottles, and little tins. She reached out with her power, feeling for anything familiar behind the doors, anything that might help her understand what the purpose of this lab was.

She recognized a few medicinal herbs right away; the telltale zesty energy of ginger; the sharp and sweet feel of peppermint extract; the deep, earthy vibrations of *arimopo*; and a few tins of *popava*, the same strain she'd found beneath Everness in the spring.

Nothing she hadn't already known he was involved in.

She sighed, moving on.

She was about to give up hope when her eyes landed on a sheet of paper on the countertop just behind the door. With the door all the way open, it was almost hidden from view.

It was a letter, torn hastily from its envelope. The message was dated three days earlier and was from Larais, which meant it had to have traveled by messenger hawk from the mainland. It almost seemed too easy, this information right at her fingertips.

She scanned the page and froze.

Troops were moving north from two angles, set to converge on Port Galan in four days.

Her heart hammered in her chest. There was no way she could send word by then, not without exposing herself. The messenger hawks were carefully monitored, Ash had missed her last two collection dates, and Eiran's method was unreliable at best.

That left her with only one option.

She had to go in person to warn them.

CHAPTER THIRTY-SEVEN

Soviel clutched the forged letter to her chest, the crumples caused by her own trembling hands.

"It's my sister—I've received word from the post in town, she's to give birth soon. We don't always get along but I love her and—she has a weak constitution, I worry she may have a difficult birth. I—"

The forged letter was dated from a week ago, indicating that Soviel's sister was due within days.

"I'd like to go to her, please. I'll be back in a week, maybe two, it isn't too long a journey. I'll take a horse to the coast and be on the first ship out of Everness to Karlgiard, and—"

"Of course you must go!" said Bessa, the head maid, her eyes wide. "We'll miss having you here for this weekend's festival, but we all must bear our burdens in these times."

"Thank you," Soviel said, letting a tear of relief crawl down her cheek. "Thank you. And you'll extend my deepest apologies to the duchess and let her know I'll return as soon as I'm able?"

"Of course I will. You mustn't worry about that. You can take a carriage in the morning."

"No, I'll leave tonight. I'll just take one horse so I can make it onto the first ship at dawn."

"Are you certain?"

"Yes." Soviel nodded forcefully. The last thing she needed was a watchful footman slowing her down. "I'll just gather what I need and leave."

Soviel embellished the story that Bessa was to share with Samia, adding that her sister had had a frightful accident recently and that the midwife had put her on bedrest until the birth, which would likely happen within the week. She'd even sent a messenger hawk with a bland letter attached to her family's estate so her story would hold up. Just in case.

She cursed inwardly. All the hard work of ingratiating herself to these people, of burrowing into their little circle these last weeks; it might all be thrown away in one fell swoop. But there was no other alternative, she had to warn Galan.

After she'd packed what she needed, burned anything incriminating, and slung the light pack over her shoulder, she rushed to town and paid for the fastest horse they could give her. She'd have to switch for a fresh horse when she reached the next town, as there was no time to stop and rest. Already, she was cutting it close. It would take two days to make it back to Galan, and then from there a rider would have to dispatch to Avaree to warn them and ask for aid.

She rode hard, risking dangerous paths and fording rivers if she couldn't immediately find a bridge. She poured her energy into the horse, keeping him fresh and fast, until she herself was nearly spent. Around dinnertime, she arrived at Celide, where she paid handsomely for a fresh horse, and paid even more handsomely to board the one she'd come in on for a few days.

The night was clear and the moon bright as she raced over the land, fields and moors fading into forests and foothills, the Icharian Mountains puncturing the horizon to her left as she pushed north towards Port Galan.

She changed horses one more time, with half a day's ride ahead of her. At last, when she'd been riding at full speed for nearly two days, she saw the clifftop manor in the distance.

Not bothering to slow down, she cantered straight into the encampment, reigning to a halt just before Helene's intelligence tent.

She burst through the door and announced, "The Lundi-Bourjon Alliance is on its way here, and will arrive in no more than a day and a half," before stopping to catch her breath. "By land and by sea," she finished.

Helene had frozen mid-conversation, her eyes wide with disbelief as she stared at Soviel. Lachlan's and Rhi's mouths hung open in shock.

She sucked in a deep breath, the exhaustion of the journey at last washing over her.

"Sweet Lalana, Sov. Did you ride all the way here?" Rhi jumped out of his seat and pushed the chair toward her. She collapsed into it gratefully, nodding in response to his question.

"Here," Lachlan offered her the pitcher of water from the table.

"Thanks," she said breathlessly, and took a long gulp straight from the pitcher.

"How did you come by this information?" Helene asked, standing. "How precise is your timeframe?"

"Notes, in Hadringston's office. A fleet is sailing up from Everness, and the troops marching up from Bramblehall should arrive at the same time—they disembarked before me, but would be moving more slowly. Possibly, there will be reinforcements coming later on. Something about a shipment coming from Bourjony."

"Shit." Lachlan flexed his bandaged fist.

"What are we supposed to do?" Rhi asked. "We're in no shape to face them here."

"And they know it," Soviel interjected. "But at least, now they won't take us by surprise."

"I'll call a council and get a plan underway," Helene said with a stroke of her pen. "Tarrish, deliver this to Ashwife."

"Yes, ma'am," he replied, taking the letter she handed to him.

"Soviel, I'm sure the healers will need your help. You need to rest before they come."

Soviel knew she was right but shook her head. "No. Not until after the council. I need to be there for that."

"Fine," Helene agreed. She reached into her desk and tossed something to Soviel. It was a linen sack of nuts. "At least eat something. Let's go."

Soviel stood beside Helene, Rhi, and Lachlan in the war office of the manor. General Ashwife laid out before the council exactly what needed to be done to shore up the defenses surrounding the town, manor and barracks. He'd sent a runner out to the fort with this information, along with the order to stand by for orders on the naval strategy.

"We don't know the exact numbers of their troops," Helene said, relaying everything Soviel had told her. "Without the element of surprise on their side, the odds will be a bit better. But there's more," she told them. "If you fled Everness in the spring, you may remember there was a soldier among them with great capabilities. We've had a team investigating this in conjunction with the investigation of the laboratory found in Danvery Prison. We know they are engineering super-soldiers. Some may be in fighting shape, so be ready. Expect the unexpected."

A collective gasp followed by a rumbling resounded through the council.

"How will we defend from this threat while fighting the enemy from land and sea?" someone asked.

"We will need to launch a joint defense," Alemont said, her crisp voice cutting off the chatter. "That's why you've been gathered. Our numbers are fewer than theirs, and we have the added liability of a town full of civilians to defend. The fort and the manor can only do so much."

"How are we going to avoid another incident like the one at the harbor? We can't blow them up from the fort if our own ships get in the way again," said a soldier Soviel didn't recognize.

"I've got an idea," Ash's voice pierced the room as she stepped through the door, her eyes meeting Soviel's with a wolfish grin. "Sorry I'm late, no one remembered to tell me that I *didn't* need to sail down the coast today and I was halfway through rigging up when someone finally thought to fetch me."

Three scouts on swift horses were immediately dispatched to the south to determine which of the three main roads the enemy was marching from. In addition to that, a rider was sent to Avaree to request naval support and reinforcements on land post haste.

"We need to begin evacuating the town into the manor and the fort. If there truly is a land attack coming, they'll raze the town first," General Ashwife said, setting his jaw.

"You want to bring the *entire* town into the only two strongholds we have left?" General Alemont asked with disbelief. "You know well that there may be a spy in our midst. Several, even."

"I'm not willing to bet the remaining lives of our people on that suspicion, Marin." He shook his head.

General Alemont sat with her back straight as a steel rod. "Then we need to take precautions. All unauthorized civilians will be confined to the lower levels, away from the battery."

"Fine, I'll see to it myself," Ashwife grunted. "Lieutenant Fiaral," he called, "see to the evacuation of the town."

"Yes, sir," Fiaral, presumably Ashwife's aide de camp, nodded before turning to leave.

"The barracks will need to be emptied as well," Alemont noted. "Any volunteers? Good, you round up some people for that. Now, I say we take half our units, and we meet them here," she pointed to a spot on the map southeast of the inner marshes. "And defend the city as long as we can from that strategic point. There's rocky terrain, a few wooded areas…"

"And plenty of space for fighting," Ashwife continued. "We'll harass them back until they flee."

"We should ambush them," Lachlan blurted without ceremony.

Alemont blinked, turning her acid green gaze on Lachlan. Soviel held her breath; she would *not* want to be on the receiving end of Alemont's ire.

"Apologies, General," Lachlan stood and nodded in deference, as if remembering himself. "But if we are to use the edge we have, knowing they're coming, would it not be better to lay a trap for them? We send a few small units into the woods—hidden units—pick off their officers with gunners hidden in the trees, throw them off their plan, then charge them. We know this land better than they do, we can confuse them, cause chaos among their ranks. Keep them from trapping us between them and their navy."

Alemont considered, her cool gaze unreadable and assessing.

"He has a point," she said to Ashwife. "We'd be much better off pressing our advantage earlier, before they're in sight of the manor."

"Hm. I suppose we could shift our position…What about the town? It'll be empty, we could use it—"

"No, we don't need to draw all that destruction into people's homes, if we can help it. They're struggling enough as it is." Alemont shook her head. "The woods will have to do."

Soviel remembered the woods and foothills she'd raced through on her journey here.

"Now, I'd like to hear Captain Mazrihn's plan for the harbor. Asha, is it?" Alemont asked.

Ash tensed beside Soviel, her bare, muscular arms crossed over her chest. "Um, yeah, that's me. General," she said, stepping forward. "Here's what I propose."

That night, the sun sank below the horizon in a paling wash of muted metals and crushed jewels. There was no moon in the black sky—only touches of vestigial light from stars too far away to care. The wind was frantic and insistent, as if it, too, knew the perils the coming day would bring.

Hurry, hurry, it whispered as every available sailor dressed in black and silently made their way down to the docks.

The beacon was doused for one hour. One precious hour.

Hushed and reticent, one by one, the ships left the harbor.

Hours later, the sun rose blazing red and gold on an empty harbor, pushing pink and orange light onto the empty beach with the froth of the tide.

One ship remained in the bay.

CHAPTER THIRTY-EIGHT

Dawn came in bright and unforgiving, the window in Ferrin's hut apparently facing east. She awoke and ate a few spoonfuls of the stew, which had gone cold. She dipped some of her bread crusts into the broth, savoring the taste of home.

She didn't know how far away she was. She couldn't visualize where on the map she might be. The environment did little to tell her, since it resembled no place she'd ever been. The sea wasn't the striking turquoise of the Meddemara, nor the deep ultramarine of the north. The tall white cliffs she'd climbed weren't the same stone as that of Galan—they were veined and threaded with bits of charcoal black minerals and shimmering flecks of some unidentified gem. The grass resembled the short, scrubby vegetation found high on the mountains, though the climate was warmer and less temperamental.

Still in the clothes she'd left Galan in, she pulled on her boots and tied up her hair before venturing out of the cabin. The strange woman from the night before was standing on the cliff, facing the rising sun. Her hands were clasped behind her back as she gazed out over the undulating sea.

Ferrin approached her, stopping a healthy few paces from the woman.

"For hundreds of years, people desperate for a solution to their worldly catastrophes have come here, seeking answers. *Heal the land of this mystical plague, save the island from the terrible serpents crawling forth from the sea, put an end to the cursed storms raging over our land.* It never gets any easier," she said.

"I know my mother came here, long ago," Ferrin said in response. "Why was she too early?"

"Arabella," Nesseen said with a chuckle. "Yes, I remember her well. You are very like her."

Ferrin nodded, unsure of what to say.

"I met another from your bloodline, many moons ago."

This startled her. "Who?"

The woman before her couldn't be much older than forty.

"A gifted Stormrider named Rhen. We fought together in the Iron Range, under King Yistav."

"What? How? That was centuries ago."

"It was in the years before I came to this place," the woman said with a small smile.

"Are you," Ferrin paused, squinting into the bright sun, "immortal?"

She barked a surprised laugh. "Gods, no. You'll find that time works a bit differently here, on Vaiorka."

"Vaiorka?"

"This hallowed island. We sit at the overlap of the divine world and the human world. A bit like a bridge. This temple was built long ago, even by Vaiorkan standards."

"I've never heard of it."

"That's the idea." She turned at last from the rising sun and looked Ferrin over. "Since you're rested, it's time for introductions. My name is Nesseen."

"Ferrin."

Nesseen chuckled lightly. "We knew who you were long before you washed up."

"Oh."

"What do you know of our isle?"

Ferrin shook her head and returned her gaze to the sea. This all felt like one long fever dream. "Not very much. Only that I'm supposed to be here, to gain some vague sort of power that no one seems to be able to explain to me," she said, bitterness in her tone. "That this was fated for me."

Nesseen laughed again. "We'll see about that. There is much you must do to prepare first."

"I'm ready, tell me what to do," she resolved. It no longer mattered what was going on back on Lindbarrow, in Galan. She couldn't do any more there. Here was where she was needed, where her friends were counting on her to succeed.

A knowing smile crept across Nesseen's face. "You'll need to bring a dozen pails of water up for the goats."

Ferrin stiffened. "Oh."

"This place may be magical, but it doesn't keep itself running. When you're through, come find me."

Ferrin was on her tenth trip up the second cliff, and hadn't managed to tumble over the side to the crushing rocks below just yet. The goats, at least, seemed grateful for the service, which she took a small comfort in.

She was on her way back down for pail number eleven when she finally saw another human.

The child was rushing up the stairs, dressed in the same gray-and-burgundy combination as Nesseen, although her robes fit significantly looser, as if she was meant to grow into them. She nearly plowed into Ferrin in her haste.

"Oh!" She clapped a hand over her mouth as Ferrin pushed herself flat against the cliff-wall in an attempt to let the girl pass. "I'm sorry! There's usually no one else on these stairs, I'm sorry."

"It's all right," Ferrin said, righting herself. "Where are you hurrying to with those?" She gestured to the pile of books tied up with twine in the girl's hands.

"Bringing them back to the library," she said. She couldn't have been much older than thirteen.

"There's a library up there?" Ferrin asked with surprise, squinting up the cliff. All she'd seen so far was a small farm.

"It's on the third level. Oh, right, you've only just arrived!" Her brown eyes popped open wide. "My name is Lusia." She thrust out a slim brown hand in greeting.

"Ferrin," she introduced herself, shaking Lusia's hand firmly.

"Oh, wow, this is so great. We haven't had a visitor from the outside world in a long time."

"How long?"

Lusia tilted her head side to side as if weighing her answer. "It's hard to say, with time working so different here. It's actually one of the topics I'm researching. Um, it's been maybe ten years since anyone's arrived, according to outside time? No, that isn't right. Twenty?"

A flutter of nervousness washed over Ferrin. If time worked so differently, what if weeks had passed outside when she'd only been here a few days?

"Oh no, don't worry about that," the girl said, and Ferrin wondered if she'd voiced her worries out loud without noticing. "You look panicked—time moves differently for us, we who commit our lives to this place, but you won't be stuck here while the outside world passes you by. It's not like that fairytale where one day inside the magic town passes one hundred years outside. Time is not *that* cruel."

Ferrin looked mystified, but nodded slowly nonetheless.

"Don't worry, you'll catch on once you meet everyone."

She nodded again and smiled at the girl.

"Well, I have to get these back before someone notices I've snuck them out to read on the beach again. Good luck with the goats. Oh, and if you have good balance, there's a yolk and a second bucket down behind the shed that might cut your work in half," she said with a wink before turning and darting up the cliff.

Ferrin blinked. A strange place indeed.

Thanks to Lusia's tip, Ferrin finished her water-hauling chore soon after, and returned to Nesseen before the sun was halfway to noon. She was wandering around the second level of the island for about ten minutes before she finally found the strange woman again.

"All done?" Nesseen asked, her stern brows raised.

"Yes," Ferrin nodded.

"Wonderful. Come with me."

She followed Nesseen up to the third level, which *still* wasn't the top tier of the spiraling island, but was a rather small landing amongst the winding stair that wrapped its way around the cliff.

"What exactly is it I'll be doing?" she asked, climbing after Nesseen.

"On this island, we protect some of the most vital, ancient things in the world. Things even the *Dionas* have forgotten in the last centuries."

Ferrin followed quietly and listened.

"So," Nesseen continued, "it stands to reason that access to these things must be *earned*. Not just through sweat and blood, but through strength of character. You must be deemed worthy."

Ferrin felt her pulse pick up, though it wasn't as if she hadn't been expecting this.

"How so?" she asked.

"There are a series of trials."

Ferrin blanched. "What sort of trials?"

"There are a few, and always different," Nesseen explained, turning as she crested the cliff. The glittering sea spread out before them. "They will test you in more ways than one. You may not know a thing is a trial until it is done."

Ferrin was silent, waiting for her to continue.

"Today, you will be shown around the isle, introduced to its inhabitants. The temple's opinion of you is just as important as the outcomes of your trials, since the final decision as to who is allowed access to the sacred veil is up to us."

"I understand," Ferrin nodded. A distant feeling settled over her. This island, the thing that it guarded, was apparently her entire purpose for existing, as it turned out. She had no choice but to succeed. Failure was unthinkable.

"Perfect," Nesseen nodded curtly. "Your first trial will begin tomorrow. At dusk."

She swallowed the nerves that had been building in her chest since morning. She would succeed. She had to succeed. She'd put on a little muscle in Galan, and had been spending a lot of time walking about and climbing the cliffs. She was in as good a form as she'd been a year ago, if not better. Her swordplay was nothing legendary, but she could hold her own, and her skill of fists and elbows was still halfway decent. If desperation kicked in, she would make it.

She had to.

"Ready?"

"For what?" she said, drawn out of her thoughts.

"To meet the rest of us, of course," Nesseen said, turning away and walking toward the towering stone building centered on the small cliff-shelf.

The tall, cool-gray stone of the towering temple pressed in as Ferrin stepped through the entryway. The feeling was equal parts comforting and unsettling as dozens of pairs of eyes landed on her.

They all wore variations of the same gray-and-burgundy get-ups that Nesseen and Lusia wore, but the homogeny ended there.

People of all sorts stared back at her. Some looked a lot like her and Rhi, with peach-pale skin and freckles and wavy hair. There were people with dark brown skin and dark hair in intricate braids or in voluminous clouds of curls, people with nearly sheet-white complexions and thin, pale hair, people with up-tilted black eyes and soft features that made her think of Soviel, and sent a pang of longing through her. Some of the hairstyles worn were strange and old-fashioned, like something out of an old book. People from all across the world, and from times long past.

A jolt went through her at just how lonely she felt, standing in this crowded room of strangers.

She'd been gone only a day and already she missed her friends, wished she could see them, wished she could take back what she'd said to Lukas in that moment of defensive anger.

Everything had become such a mess when Zare slithered back into her life.

She shoved the thought from her mind and tried to focus on the present.

"Hi," she greeted nervously, all too aware of the attention on her.

"This is Ferrin. She is set to undertake the trials, beginning tomorrow evening."

"Hi, Ferrin," one familiar voice said from the front row.

Ferrin smiled when she saw Lusia's impish grin. "Hi again."

"This is the main temple," Nesseen explained. as the crowd dispersed. "While you're here, you will be expected to contribute to its running. Each day there will be things that need taking care of—be it washing windows, cooking breakfast, bringing up water from the well or organizing the library, there is always something to be doing."

After being shown around the grounds, Ferrin was put to work on the farming level. It wasn't so different from stable duties, and by the end of it, her back and thighs ached with the day's effort.

The tasks had been a welcome distraction from the looming trial the following evening, but once she was done and washed up for supper, the nerves crept in.

Dinner was a huge pot of fish stew that many hands had helped to make. Vegetables from the farm, white fish trapped on the beach below, butter from goat's milk. Ferrin took her serving down to the lower level, to the little hut in which she was residing. She feigned exhaustion from the day, but in reality, she was spiraling, and she didn't want anyone to see it.

She ate half her stew, but the rest sat cold and unfinished as her fears eddied. If she failed this, what was it all for?

She sat down on the floor by the hearth and wrapped her arms around her knees, pulling them to her chest. Squeezing her eyes shut, she let out a shuddering breath and fell asleep on the rug. In dreams, a great storm plucked her up and tore her into the sky, whirling as it dropped her into the sea, a thousand miles from everyone she loved.

CHAPTER THIRTY-NINE

While the privateers, fishermen, harbor patrol and everyone else initiated into the 'naval' effort took to rigging up and setting out to empty the harbor, Rhi was stalking through the barracks as it packed itself down to the barest bones of an encampment. When he found Lachlan, he was loading provisions from the commissary into a mule-towed cart to be hauled up to the manor where it would be safe from sabotage. Only torches and bonfires lit the way for them to work.

"Need a hand?" Rhi asked as he rolled up his shirtsleeves.

Lachlan thumped the crate of oranges he was carrying onto the back of the cart and turned to Rhi. "Sure," he said.

Rhi nodded, glad to have something to occupy his hands. He hadn't seen much of Lachlan since their strange shared moment nearly a week prior. Every time he'd been in Lachlan's vicinity, someone else was always there. The time elapsed had just made him more and more anxious about what had happened and what it meant, and how it was going to inevitably come back to bite him in the ass.

He scooped up a heavy sack of flower and balanced it on his shoulder before standing and carrying it to the cart. It made a cloud-like 'poof' when he thumped it down.

"Never seen a battle before," Rhi mused, keeping his tone light. "Hope this won't be both my first and *last*."

Lachlan shot him a sideways glance, brow pinched.

"Though, when I fled the capital this spring, we did fight off some pursuing soldiers as we ran through the woods. Not really the same thing, though."

"It's not a new amusing game to be witty about," Lachlan said, hauling up another crate, this one full of jars of pickled vegetables. "It's warfare. Complete chaos, blood everywhere, too much noise."

"Really," Rhi said drily.

Lachlan narrowed his eyes. "A lot of men get this funny idea that it's going to be some glorious event like in a painting—fire in the background, golden sunlight, spears pointed to the sky, vanquishing your enemies with a shining sword. But it never is, and it's always the ones with the lofty ideas like that who end up falling the hardest."

"You forgot to mention strange horses with oddly human eyes in your painting there," Rhi added.

"Rhiach," Lachlan said, setting down the next crate. "I'm being serious. It will be a disaster. A bloodbath."

"I was only trying to lighten the mood. It's what I do," he said, facing Lachlan as he leaned on the back of the cart. "I can't help it."

"An incurable ailment, really."

"I hear you have quite a reputation on the field," Rhi said, trying to steer the conversation toward something resembling flirtation. He was usually much better at this. "A mind gifted for tactics, and an iron will to see it through. That's what Ashwife said, anyhow."

"Did he now?" Lachlan pondered. "How interesting. I thought he wanted to throw me in the brig most of the time."

"Well, I'm sure those two facts can coexist," Rhi drawled.

"Was there something you wanted to discuss? You marched over here with such conviction."

Rhi tilted his head and leveled a glare at Lachlan.

"I suppose it would be wise to clear the air before tomorrow," he said breezily. "Our… discussion in your tent the other night."

Lachlan hesitated for just a second. "Right, about when the army heads south. Did you put in a request?"

Rhi swallowed, put off by Lachlan's cool response. "I—yes. I did," he replied. "Is that still what you want?"

Lachlan stared back for a moment too long, sending Rhi's stomach into his knees.

"Yes. Of course," he said, blinking. "I don't mean to seem off about it. It's just, I've found out that my father and brother have left the estate to head south to the Andals with the army." He let the end of the sentence drop into open air with no context.

"Oh," Rhi said, trying to find some hidden rejection, some tiny movement of Lachlan pulling back. "You've never mentioned them."

Lachlan nodded.

"Are you close with him?"

Perhaps there was a strategic marriage lined up for Lachlan, and he didn't want to bring the inherent conflict of Rhiach into the mix.

"Gods, *no*." Lachlan turned back to the task at hand. He seemed more intent than ever on stacking crates.

"Ah, well. I'm no stranger to tenuous relations with parental figures," Rhi said, turning to pick up another sack of flour.

Lachlan's back went tense where he stood at the back of the cart, and Rhi winced. Perhaps he shouldn't have brought his own issues up when Lachlan was trying to confide in him.

"He's a wise tactician," Lachlan began. "He'll be an asset for the army."

Rhi said nothing, hoping he'd continue.

"But he's a snake the rest of the time. And my brother is just as bad. Worse, maybe. My father enables his behavior because he's the heir."

Rhi tried not to show his surprise at Lachlan's candor. "He's to be stationed in the Andals?"

Lachlan nodded grimly. "And he will be my commanding officer. Major Tarrish, coming out of retirement," he sighed. "I haven't seen either of them since I left for school. Five years ago."

"Shit," Rhi breathed. He wondered at the extent of the elder Tarrish's malice, at the brother's '*behavior.*'

"My thoughts exactly."

Ash stared out at the looming horizon to the southeast, elbow hooked around the mast for balance as she waited to see the tiniest glimpse of the approaching navy.

The sun bore down overhead, heat and light and heat and light, drawing beads of sweat from her pores to run rivers down her skin as she waited.

Acid had clawed its way up her throat. This was *her* idea, and if any of it went awry, it was on her. She'd never been responsible for lives like this before. Even on *The Brisk*, she was captain of no more than three people and about twenty feet of wood. Now, half an army rested on *her* idea.

People kept giving her more and more responsibility, and she wanted to wave her hands at Ashwife or Wilcoe or Neb and shout: *"HEY! I'm only eighteen, I crawled out of the gutter in Khalim and spent the last three years messing about in the Meddemara! I'm only a stupid little sailor!"* But this was war and apparently her initial success and consequent handling of said new responsibilities had been enough to persuade the higher-ups to treat her like some sort of wisened naval advisor. But they'd listened to her plan, and apparently decided it was sound.

At least, it would make finagling a larger ship out of them for her coming journey south a lot easier.

Unless, of course, her plan today went horribly wrong.

She blew out a calming breath and flinched as Rorin popped up in the crow's nest beside her.

"See anything yet?" he asked, running a hand through his dark brown hair. Though Rorin was a young man, his hairline had begun to pull back at the temples. "I remember when I first saw a Bourjon Navy squadron for the first time. They're absolutely *diligent*. Pungent, even."

Ash frowned, perplexed at what he could mean. "They… smell?"

"No. But, well, you just can't ignore them. Pungent. They demand your attention," he explained with a laugh as he drew a leather flask out of his hip satchel.

"Right," Ash shot him a sideways grin. "And all that cabbage cream stew the Bourjons eat has to smell a bit, yeah?"

Rorin guffawed before taking a swig of his liquor. He thrust his arm out in offering.

"Thanks." She took the flask from him and knocked back a mouthful of some very cheap whiskey with a cringe. "*Saolath*, Rorin. Doesn't the army pay you well enough to buy decent liquor?" she coughed.

Rorin shrugged, "It tastes fine to me."

"Oh, Rorin, I may have grown up in the lowest slums of Khalim, but even *I'm* used to better liquor than that."

"Fine then." He snatched back the flask. "No more for you."

She was about to come back with another witty remark when something on the bluff by the distant fort caught her eye —a tiny, thin, white shape. The first signal flag.

Ash raised the spyglass to her eye to confirm what she was seeing when the lookout in the ship off their port side cried out.

"Get ready!"

"Oh, *shit*, it's happening!" Rorin cried. "You have spare powder?"

"Of course," Ash said, drawing her shortcoat to the side to reveal the bandolier full of ammo and powder cartridges. "Ready to pick off some gunners?"

"In my *sleep*, Ash," he grinned as he laid his rifles out on the planks before him. Four in total.

"Great. Well, until I'm needed elsewhere, I'll be on reload duty for you. Good?"

"Perfect," Rorin grinned, his front tooth, Ash noticed, still chipped from flying debris in the *rasernemaud* attack.

Night had moved on swiftly, and Rhi had stolen a few hours of sleep before he was up and preparing to set out to the woods. By now, the scouts would have returned, and he would learn what direction they were to head out in and begin the process of laying traps and hiding in trees, an experience he was beginning to feel just a touch too intimate with.

When he'd dressed and made the trek down to the war tent, which still stood, though much of the barracks had been relocated to protect resources, he found a crowd of people arguing in low voices outside.

"What's this?" Rhi asked, ambling up beside Soviel. "What have they decided?"

"Nothing," she shook her head. "None of the scouts returned."

"What? How?"

She shook her head and shrugged, eyes wide with alarm. She looked worn thin. Shadows beneath her eyes, her skin waxen and pale, her hair tied back and limp. "I don't know."

"They must have been spotted and captured."

"Maybe. Or maybe they were killed on sight."

A chill ran up Rhi's spine. "What are we to do if we don't know which road they approach on?"

"That's the question everyone seems to have their own answer to," she said, gesturing at the growing crowd.

"People, there is *no* need to panic," General Alemont said without ceremony as she emerged from the tent. She wore what must have once been the coat from her Lindbarrian Royal Officer's uniform, though there were stitched patterns on the left breast and sleeve, and the epaulets had been dyed gray instead of cream. An army in its infancy could not afford to outfit thousands in brand new uniforms. "Most of you have duties to be attended to. See to them, or face the consequences. Anyone who's still here loitering when I come back from the fort will be written up."

The rumbling of the crowd grew in pitch as they started to disperse. Rhi sucked in one long breath. "Why is she going up to the fort?" he asked, watching the general mount her white horse.

"Not sure," Soviel shook her head again. "Reinforcements since we'll have more ground to cover?"

"There isn't time for that."

"No, there really, really isn't."

He spun to survey the crowd around them. People were tired, scared. It didn't bode well. He hoped things down in the harbor were faring better.

As he and Soviel began walking towards town and the end of the barracks, the faint sound of a bugle caught his attention.

"What is that?"

"It's the woodswatch horn, I think," Soviel said with a frown. "Come, let's go see what they've seen before this crowd turns into a mob. I don't want to get anyone's hopes up."

Rhi looked around again; it didn't look like anyone had heard the horn, and if they had, they didn't seem to care. "Alright, lead the way."

The crew responsible for seeing the elderly and the children into the manor's lower levels had just finished their last round, and Lukas was headed to the armory along with the rest of the fresh recruits.

With the impending attack, every person in fighting form who wasn't the main caretaker of a child, or needed for some other task, had been inducted into a last-minute militia—Lukas included. There were folks of all ages and sizes in the armory being outfitted with standard rifles and whatever else was left over. Most of the weaponry had had the embossed "Property of the Lindbarrian Royal Army" sanded off the sides. Most of the money the rebellion had managed to accrue in its time had been put towards feeding its soldiers, the weapons had been appropriated from the cities they'd turned.

"The lot of you are to report to Captain Morgaine, she'll be down by the water pump at the fork in the road," the weaponry master announced.

As Lukas was leaving the weapons room in the bottom of the manor, a rider burst through the door, still atop his gray horse. He dismounted before the horse had stopped, and Lukas just caught a glimpse of him rushing to the weaponry master and whispering something in his ear before he was out the door.

The weight of a rifle on his shoulder was one he hadn't forgotten. The thrum of nerves before a fight, the tang of fear and anticipation in the air as everyone around him wondered what came next. The weapons they'd had in Khalim had been stolen, too. Won with an ambush of hungry divers too desperate to let fear stop them. Those weeks of fighting across the city, hiding out in abandoned estates, creeping through the alleys after dark, felt like yesterday. Three years past and he'd never forget the feeling of that first victory, how it had felt to kill the dive-warden, how he'd thrown up over the side of the ship afterward, when no one was watching.

Today would be difficult. He knew that. The last weeks had been difficult as he'd tried and failed to shake Damijan's ghost and the guilt and shame he felt at what had happened that day in the desert. If he made it through this battle, he had to do something about the claws digging into his flesh. If he didn't, they'd drag him under completely.

The woodswatch was a small tower—not much more than a raised platform with a covering, really—where a soldier would keep watch of the southern bounds of Galan, and monitor the tree line to see if anyone came through. Many of the refugees had arrived and been heralded in this way. Across the edge of the marshland, the tower loomed above the tall grasses, a raised, sandy path like the one between the barracks and manor, cut through the muck. Rhi and Soviel hurried along it, the furious bugling of the watchman beckoning them.

It was then that Rhi saw it—a hulking figure on a dark horse, hooded and lurching like a beast from a tale of old. He pulled up short of the tower, eyes wide and horrified as the creature slouched towards the edge of the wood and toward daylight.

Soviel continued past him, halting just under the tower as the figure emerged to the light. One broad arm reached up to throw off the hood, revealing a man—mid-twenties, brown hair, brown eyes, blue-black tattoos snaking up his neck.

He squinted. "Prince Rhi?"

Rhi raised his eyebrows, drawing back. "Yes?"

"Oh, good man," the rider said with a jolly laugh. He swung out of his saddle and onto the ground. "And, Lady… Soviel?" he asked, gesturing to her. "We've met once before, briefly. I'm Ryder. I know Lukas. From Everness."

Rhi blinked, trying to make sense of what was happening.

"You need to bring me to whoever is in charge—there're soldiers on their way here, hundreds. They look like they're fixin' for a fight."

Soviel nodded, though not without apprehension as she raised a hand to beckon him forward.

"Hey! You can't just bring him into the city!" the bugler called from above.

"We have him in our custody," Rhi assured him, though he wasn't sure of it himself, the man was *huge*. Tall as a bear and just as burly. He tried to recall if he'd ever spoken to him, however he'd unfortunately spent so much of the last year drunk or high that he imagined there were more than a few acquaintances he'd forgotten.

The bugler called a few protests from behind them, but he wasn't much paying attention as he watched the big man lead his horse down the narrow path. *This* was the friend Lukas had been so distressed over stranding in Avaree? Frankly, Rhi had been imagining a helpless twig of a lad barely old enough for liquor. This man could snap Lukas like a twig; it seemed strange how torn up he'd been about having dragged him into a perilous situation. Ryder didn't look like he *could* be dragged anywhere.

"Where have you been hiding out?" Soviel asked.

"The woods," Ryder admitted. "But I sent Toll in to the city without me; she's pregnant and we were worried about things being less than ideal for the baby if she stayed with me. I was waiting for her signal, but this morning when I went out to check my snares, I caught sight of the army and figured I'd better get ahead of them, and hope Galan was safe enough to return to." He shrugged.

"Safe is very relative just now, I'm afraid," Rhi said.

"Safe from being arrested on old smuggling charges?" Ryder asked nervously. "I can't wait to eat real food."

Soviel shot him a confused look. "I don't think you're going to be getting that for some time, I'm afraid. Not with that alliance army on its way."

Ryder groaned. "I've been living off of berries and squirrel for weeks."

"They'll have some nice hot stew, I'm sure," she lied cheerily.

"Lukas is going to be happy to see you," Rhi interjected. "He won't admit it but he's been rather down about you being missing."

Ryder smirked sheepishly.

Rhi and Soviel brought Ryder to Major Wilcoe, and explained the situation as best they could while trying to skirt the fact that Ryder was, in fact, wanted for several old counts of smuggling by the authorities in Avaree and Galan. Rhi suspected that Soviel's advocating for him would be an enormous boon, as Helene seemed to favor Soviel over all her young agents.

In Alemont's office, the general stared stonily at them as they deposited Ryder into a chair, still breathing heavily. Evidently, he'd been riding hard for the last few hours since spotting the troops movement. Wilcoe stood at Alemont's side with her arms crossed, looking equal parts stressed, exhausted, and focused.

Prompted by Alemont's expectant glare, Ryder launched into a tale of how he'd received word that his wife was here, and had taken the west road up from the foot of the Icharian mountains, where he'd been living in a woodcutters cabin for some time.

"They ride by the west road. There're a few hundred, maybe more. Some mounted, some on foot, and a strange woman rides with them, all cloaked in gray. Her hair is white like snow, but she is young."

Wilcoe shifted on her feet. "She wasn't in uniform?"

Ryder shook his head. "No, ma'am."

Alemont leaned back in her chair, considering. "Well, there's nothing to do but approach with caution. The ambush will continue as planned. Time to dispatch our troops. We've lost enough time as it is," she said, standing. "The two of you need to get where you're going. Larksen, bring our informant up to the fort when you go."

Rhi stood, bowed his head, and exited the tent. If he ran into Lukas, he'd have to tell him Ryder was being taken to the fort.

They had less than an hour before the Bourjon fleet was in range of the empty harbor. With the Caelish fleet evacuated and hidden just beyond the promontory, the bay was all but empty. On the fort's second signal, the fleet would run full sail into the harbor, trapping the Bourjon ships between the well-armed manor, fort, and small Caelish fleet. The *Renni Anns* was tacking back and forth waiting for the right moment to strike, and Ash was growing itchy with impatience.

Below her, the deck was silent and stiff. The air was so thick with tension, she could have whipped out a knife and sliced it into dainty little pieces fit for a royal tea.

The lot of them were waiting, waiting for the signal before they converged on the bottleneck and trapped themselves and the Bourjons in the bay—for better or for worse.

Her dual pistols were loaded and ready, her cutlass and dagger were sharpened and strapped at her hip and thigh, her resolve hardened. *There is no room or time for doubt and fear, now,* she chided herself.

An hour passed again before the signal sounded. Five shots in a row, quick and loud from the manor, then another three from the fort as the trap sprung shut on the Bourjons. Mayhem ensued on the ships of the enemy as their captains sought to retreat, only to find chaos all around them. The Caelish ships converged full-speed into the bottleneck, gun crews at the ready, and sharpshooters high in the riggings.

As they rounded the cliffs, Ash counted at least seven Bourjon war frigates. Their masts were tall, and their gun ports were many. The cannon fire was deafening, and splinters and shrapnel fell like summer rain as the ships began blowing each other to bits.

The fort had managed to sink one of the smaller Bourjon ships—it listed precariously to the side as it took on water through a gaping hole by its starboard stern, and sailors were hurling themselves off its rails.

"Get into position!" Neb cried from below, her voice barely audible over the din as all hands rushed to stations. The wind was on their side as they bore down on the enemy ships through the narrow entrance to the bay. Ash watched the ships as they came closer and closer, and she loaded Rorin's second gun as he took his first shot at the captain of the nearest Bourjon ship.

"Fuck!" he shouted when it missed.

"Again!" she screamed at him, slamming the second rifle into his arms.

Rorin took the shot, this time at the gunman in the riggings across from them. The Bourjon sharpshooter gave a cry and tumbled out of the crow's nest onto the deck below.

"Yes," Ash whispered with relief. She handed Rorin the third gun and set about reloading the first rifle.

Rhi just made it to the armory as they were handing out the last few rifles.

"Get to your unit," one of the gruff attendants barked at him. He didn't waste any more time, jogging down to the fork in the road where he quickly found Lachlan among the mottled mass of soldiers.

"Where have you been?" Lachlan hissed.

"Got caught up," he hissed back. "I'll explain later, but we know which way they're coming from now—the western road."

Lachlan looked at him with curiosity, waiting for more.

"I'll explain later," Rhi repeated. "It's a bit of a long story."

Lachlan returned his attention to the officer announcing the next move.

"Who is that?"

"Captain Morgaine," Lachlan said. "She was in intelligence for the Lindbarrian crown, but she turned a few years back, is what I heard."

"The tree cover is thicker the further into Taroch you go," Morgaine announced, her upscale accent reminding Rhi of some of his father's courtiers. "That's where we want to choke them off—make it harder for them to get to the clearings and the open field, and we'll stop them from hitting the city in full."

Beside him, Lachlan was so taut he looked like he was close to snapping.

"Hey," Rhi nudged him with his shoulder.

Lachlan shook his head, jaw set. "If they breach our lines, it'll be a bloodbath."

"I thought the townsfolk were all relocated to the manor?"

"Most of them were," Lachlan said under his breath. "Some refused. And even then, the manor is only fit to guard against attacks from the sea with its long-guns. It isn't fit for a full-on siege."

"It may not come to that. My source says there are a few hundred soldiers only."

Lachlan looked at him again for some explanation. "Your source?"

"I told you, it really is a long story," Rhi said. "But in short, someone's arrived with the information the scouts were meant to find. Presumably, the scouts are all dead. He says that a strange woman rides with the troops, cloaked in gray with white hair."

"I do not like the sound of that."

"Nor do I," Rhi admitted. "I have my suspicions about what she is."

"As do I," Lachlan said ominously. "The question is, what will her power be?"

Rhi shook his head. "Do you suppose when they create these magic-soldiers they have any control over what sort of magic they end up with?"

Lachlan contemplated the concept. "I'd think it has to do with what lays dormant in the host. But who's to say the stolen life-force can't influence the outcome?"

Rhi hadn't considered that. "Good point."

Captain Morgaine finished what she was saying, and began calling out instructions for each unit. Rhi, having received his approval for transfer, was now a part of the twelfth—meaning he'd be with Lachlan and the rest of his unit for what was to come.

*   *   *

Lukas and the rest of the Last-Minute-Militia, as they'd been jokingly named, had been marched down to the edge of the wood. From other more official units, gunners were being assigned trees. Sharpshooters, Lukas assumed.

The instructions his group had been given were to muck-up every movement possible that the enemy tried to make, and to generally just be in their way. He hoped the other units would be operating under a better strategy.

The army was already a hodge-podge of Caelish militia, defected Lindbarrian soldiers, previously-undercover officers whose loyalties were now public, and a mix of random volunteers. A torrent of turncoats and rebels. This unit was hardly any different.

When they reached the forest and took the correct amount of paces in, the rest of the units carried on, heading to their own stations for the oncoming invasion. When the group of thirty or so with Lukas had dispersed enough, they all began to climb.

He was secretly thankful that the air here was cooler. That there were trees and shade and a distant river, not an inch of gold sand in sight. The sun was not so harsh, the air not so dry. If it were, he didn't think he could bear it. He'd barely been holding himself together for the last few months. Now, more than ever, he realized it. For far too long, he'd tried to press every ghost haunting him down into the dark where they couldn't be seen; but they were still there, and they'd come back hungry.

If he made it out of this alive, he promised himself he would go south and return home. He needed to see this made right somehow. He didn't know what that would entail, but seeing his mother seemed like a good enough place to start.

He had other ideas about what he could find in the south, and what good it could do for the resistance. If he remembered correctly, Akhata's young royals would have come of age recently. That meant no more manipulative regents. That meant he could go to them and ask for alliance on behalf of the Caels. A country that had so recently seen the terrors of an occupation might have sympathy for them.

He would do this. A purpose would give him direction and direction would give him something to fight for. He raised his rifle to his shoulder as he prepared for the first of the vanguard to break through the thick tree line.

Fighting was what he did best.

The fort and manor had still only managed to fully sink one Bourjon ship, and set another on fire.

Ash's heart sunk, viewing the other six war-ships that crowded the bay, dozens and dozens of guns alight as they shot on the town. The houses and buildings might be empty of people, but it would be costly and time-consuming to repair. Townsfolk would be displaced for weeks, maybe longer.

And this was only a fraction of Bourjony's forces.

"Get into position!" she cried over the din, as all hands rushed to stations. The wind was on their side—for now—as they ran further into the harbor, sails at full volume and pushing them downwind past the promontory at great speed. Ash watched the ships coming closer as she reloaded one of Rorin's guns while he used another to take a risky shot at the captain of the nearest Bourjon ship.

It went slightly wide as they careened closer and closer, and Ash had only just swapped guns with Rorin when a bullet whizzed past her ear and embedded itself in the mast behind her with a loud *crack!* Her eyes popped wide as she stilled momentarily. With a quick survey of the encroaching masts, she could make out the outline of a gunman perched in the crow's nest some fifty paces away on one of the ships in the harbor.

"Rorin, look out!" she cried. "There's a gunman across the way—there!"

They both ducked as another bullet flew overhead.

"Not for long there isn't. Gun!"

She pressed the next rifle into his waiting palms and began reloading again. He aimed ahead and pulled the trigger.

"Yes!" Ash cried as the figure crumpled and rolled off the platform, careening to the chaotic deck below.

"Take that, you grimy bastards!"

Below, something caught her eye. The sea was changing, something bright and pearlescent shone beneath the roiling surface, among the blooms of blood and patches of debris.

"What is *that*?" Ash squinted and tried to focus her eyes on the strange shimmering blur, bubbling blue and white at the center of the mass of ships.

Rorin lowered his gun, ready to change targets. "What? Where?"

"*Shit*," Ash hissed as the figure came into view, surfacing with a burst of water, arm extended and pulling the sea along behind him.

He crested out of the harbor like a rogue wave, and lifted his chin as the sea below him coiled and moved. The arm he'd extended to pull water now pointed, and shot a wave of pure ice at the deck below Ash. The ship lurched and tipped, the rigid ice tilting the deck as it formed a berg around part of the hull.

"He's using magic," Ash gasped. "He's one of the ones from the lab!"

Rorin took aim and fired, but not fast enough.

"Get him by any means necessary, I have to go!" Ash barked, taking hold of a rope to drop down to the deck below.

Rorin didn't question her as she backed to the side of the platform. He spared her a glance and a nod, and she was off, rappelling down to the deck.

Ash's heart raced as the nearest Bourjon ship loomed closer. With her feet now firmly on the slanting deck, she was well within the way of enemy cannon fire. They were so close, she could see the whites of the Bourjon sailors' eyes. They were going to collide.

"Prepare for boarding!" Ash shouted, drawing her cutlass as she signaled to the flag-bearers to let the fort know they were going to board the enemy ship so they'd ease off. The last thing she needed was a friendly cannon ball to the back.

There was a bone-jolting crash as they rammed bow-first into the Bourjon ship. The iceberg attached to their side cracked and lobbed off, back into the sea. Ash had to brace a hand on a rail to remain on her feet. And then, the tell-tale thud of planks being thrown against the gunwale, bridging the gap as the boarding parties readied.

There was one split second of stillness, and then, chaos. Everyone screaming, moving, slashing.

She was across the boards, the noise of the sea and the battle around her warped into a roar in her ears as she forged ahead. A man jumped in her path and raised an axe, she swung her blade and gashed his throat. Blood sprayed onto her face in a violent arc of crimson as he crumpled, and she moved, slashing anyone who came at her, barely registering friend from foe. She pushed toward the helm.

She had seen what these people were capable of, the perversion of nature, the twisting and corrupting of human flesh in the pursuit of something stronger, *more powerful*. Rage coursed through her veins as she struck down enemies left, right, and center. What she'd seen in Danvery, what she'd been subjected to, couldn't stand.

When she came to the opposite gunwale, and set eyes on the figure in the water, the fire in her belly stoked even hotter. There he was, some soldier who was willing to let a dozen prisoners die, have their life-force torn out of them and given over to him in pursuit of stolen power.

As she closed in, she could make out his golden hair, his straight teeth.

With a grunt of fury she climbed up onto the rail of the ship, sheathing her sword and pulling one of her flintlocks.

She took aim at the maelstrom and shot.

Nothing happened. The bullet was sucked into the swirling vortex of storm and sea, and again he emerged from the waves like a furious, avenging spirit. A tendril of water shot out and hit her square in the shoulder, knocking her back off the rail. He rose from the sea and towered over her, his skin wet and glistening in the high noon light, a pillar of water bolstering him above the rail of the ship.

"Stay down," he seethed, voice as cold and unforgiving as the deep.

"No," she grunted as she rose onto her knees. She got one foot under her before the puddle of water at her feet went slick and turned to ice, trapping one foot to the deck. Even through her boot, the cold was intense to the point of pain.

"How can you do this?" she gasped. "How can you let them give you this stolen power?"

"I know what this power cost." His voice was stone and sea-ice.

With a decisive *thwack*, she cracked the ice encasing her foot with the hilt of her knife, and wiggled loose. She dove to the side and rolled out of the way just as a sharp spear of ice collided with the deck where she'd been standing moments before.

She let out a raw cry as she landed wrong on her right wrist and felt something crack and twist. Pain lanced up her arm and out through her hand as she scrambled to her feet.

Bullets sang overhead as the sharpshooters in the masts closed in on the soldier in the waves.

"Have your superiors call off this pathetic defense," he purred as he loomed toward her, still propelled by the swirling column of seawater. Below his feet, a confused fish darted back and forth. "The sea is my domain, and I am only the beginning. By years end, there will be an army of us."

"Then what's the point of this?" she screamed. "Why not give it a few months and wipe us out completely if you're so powerful?"

He let out a merciless laugh, like waves crashing against rock at the peak of storm season. Cold, black, unforgiving water.

"You understand so little of what this war truly is. You think we fight you over this strip of land?"

Ash frowned.

Wood and water exploded ten feet to her right, and the pressure of the blast sent her sprawling. By the time she dug herself out of the debris, ears ringing and vision blurry, the ocean-soldier was gone. Not dead - she doubted something as mundane as a cannon blast could take him out.

She gasped down air as her organs slowly stopped vibrating, and looked around. The enemy ship she stood on was sinking, and the ship she'd just come from had disentangled itself and retreated.

Gods dammit.

The fort was supposed to have held off on firing once the signal was given, for this *very* reason. She and anyone else still aboard were taking friendly fire.

With a deep breath, she rolled over the side of the sinking ship and swam away beneath the waves.

She had only made it a few strokes underwater before she realized her mistake. Perhaps taking her chances on the burning, sinking ship would have been the lesser of two evils, she realized, as a hand shot out and grabbed her ankle from below. A soundless scream left her mouth in an o-shaped bubble as she was pulled down, down, down, into the deep of the harbor.

She kicked and struggled as the ocean-soldier dragged her further and further below the surface, her heart racing and eating up precious air as she strived not to panic. The water was cold and crushing around her, and the face of the soldier was wicked and blue tinted as he flashed his white teeth at her, unbothered by her struggling.

Far above, cannon fire flashed across the waves, and bodies hit the water as often as debris and timber from the ships as they blew each other apart.

No one was coming after her. No one had *seen* her.

She relaxed her muscles and gave up struggling, letting him drag her further and further despite the crushing in her ears, her nose, her face. The pressure was unbearable, her eyes were about to explode in their sockets, when she finally saw her opportunity. The cracked end of a broken mast on a long-ago sunken ship jutted up from the bottom of the harbor. As she drifted past it, she reached out and grabbed a hold of the rotting, algae-encrusted wood, pulling herself back at the same time as she delivered a kick to her captor's face. Barnacles bit into her palms, and her injured wrist cried out in agony.

He jerked back, golden hair green in the deep, swishing around his face. His grasp loosened just a touch, and she didn't hesitate to draw her last knife from its place at the top of her boot.

Under the sea, her movements were slowed and silent, but she slashed out with her blade regardless. He dodged her, his shirt and hair a plume of ghostly white, green, and gold. A snarl appeared on his lips, his throat rippling with the movement, and she realized he had *gills* flaring at the sides of his neck.

Her own lungs had begun burning what felt like ages ago. She kicked for the surface, refusing to let go of her last knife. She made it a few feet before he was on her again, clawing for her in the deep. She swept out with her blade again, this time catching his shoulder. He bared his teeth at her as blood bloomed black in the water around them.

She was running out of time—stars swam in her vision as she fought towards the surface.

You can't kill me, little girl, his voice floated through the water.

How was he doing that?

But I can kill you.

She forced herself not to open her mouth, to not suck in water, no matter how starving and desperate for breath she was.

The surface was getting closer, but not fast enough, not *nearly* fast enough. Blackness was bleeding into the edges of her vision. He came at her again, this time with the speed of a shark on the hunt. Ash lurched to the side, barely missing the tackle that would have doubtless had her sucking water into her lungs.

He turned, moving with the grace of an ocean predator. His gaze latched onto her, his pupils going wide until his eyes were fully black like a shark's, boring into her with wrathful intent.

It was only when his voice reverberated through the water again that she realized what had given him pause.

I know you have what my masters seek.

Her last coherent thought drifted to the pendant around her neck, the one with the blue-green stone set in its dull metal. The cetamaris. She'd hardly remembered she was still wearing it.

No. She could not let him have it.

I will keep you alive if you show me where it hides.

Ash shook her head and squeezed her burning eyes shut.

It is only a silly thing, what need do you have of a dusty old cup?

Her arms and legs seemed far away, numb and slack. She was not registering the things he was saying. The surface may as well have been miles overhead, too far for her to reach before she blacked out.

As she let go, her fingers uncurling from her knife's hilt, her mouth drifting open, the last bubble of spent air slipping through her lips, she began to sink, and the pendant floated from beneath the neck of her shirt. Cold water flooded into her chest. There was a flash of green, burning light, from somewhere around her chest, and a garbled howl of pain from the soldier. Something solid wrapped around Ash's shoulders and pulled. She broke through the surface to the bright light and the deafening noise of the battle all around her. Someone dragged her bodily onto something solid and dry.

With a body-wracking cough, she turned over and expelled a lungful of water, and then—blackness.

CHAPTER FORTY

They'd waited minutes that felt like years when they first heard the sound. The troops from the south had come. It was not gunfire that alerted Rhi of their approach, nor drums, nor cannon blasts.

It was a high, faint, keening sound that drew his attention skyward just in time to see a blazing ball of bright fire sing by, a tail of hot smoke trailing in its wake as it careened to the earth.

Fire erupted on the road behind them, sealing them off from retreat. Yelps of surprise and fear went up as the flames sparked and spread, growing as they licked up the trees.

"I guess that answers that question," Lachlan grunted, adjusting his perch in the canopy.

Rhi turned back to the source of the fire. The enemy troops weren't in view yet, but the fireball could not have come from natural sources, not blazing pure red like that.

The woods were thick here in the north; he remembered how easy it had been to get lost among the twisting groves when he'd come here to hunt. If you weren't careful, you could lose your party altogether. Trees this thick could muffle sound, block bodies from view, swallow a person whole.

A whistle from further up told them that the vanguard had them in sight. A second later, a series of shots popped off, echoing through the thick woods. The sharpshooters trying to take out officers and, hopefully the source of the fireball.

Rhi's heart was pounding in his ears. He didn't know what to expect—no amount of study on military strategy and tactics, nor hours spent in the training room with Guntar for all his years in the capital could prepare him for a real battle. Try as he might, he couldn't ignore his fear. He'd have to try and master it.

He could hear the thump of their feet now—heard a distant shout as the approaching vanguard recognized the ambush and commanded them to spread out. A minute later, they were charging through the trees.

Rhi tucked the butt of his rifle into his shoulder to take aim. He waited until his target—an officer with a blond mustache, mounted on the back of a silver horse—was in close range. He fired.

He hit his shoulder, and the man fell off the horse.

With a sharp and anxious inhale, Rhi reloaded, his hands shaking with nerves. On the branch above him, Lachlan was doing the same. To his left, Orlah Mardoln was preparing one of the jars of liquid that an army inventor had manufactured.

An explosive.

Rhi took his shot, and missed, the soldier leaping to the side at the last second. *Damn.*

He watched as Orlah screwed the metal lid onto the glass jar and began furiously shaking it with one arm. She froze with the jar held it in her hand, poised to throw. He could see her lips moving as she silently counted.

She hurled it. Her entire body winding up to put as much distance between the explosive and their position. Even her long black braid snapped to the side as she curled into the release.

Rhi watched the jar fly through the air, turning end over end as it sailed away until it was only a tiny speck. Orlah covered her ears with her hands. A moment later, a thunderous boom rocked the world, and a chemical fire of orange and green engulfed the distant grove.

A cacophony of screams and caterwauling erupted from the explosion. Rhi winced. The sounds were ugly and painful.

The second whistle—meant to imitate the call of a jay—went up, and Rhi took his cue to get to the ground. The second line had been breached, and it was time to join the fight in earnest. Out of the corner of his eye he could just make out Orlah securing her sack of explosives before she, too, began her descent. Lachlan was already halfway down the tree, a knife clutched in his teeth as he climbed.

Rhi dropped from the tree.

The heat of the fire was impossible to ignore as Lukas focused on picking off the soldiers who'd broken through the previous lines of defense. He was up a tree, about thirty feet from the conflagration at the edge of the woods. He had two rifles now, his own, and the one from the man beside him who'd taken one look at the fireball as it sailed overhead, shoved his rifle into Lukas's arms, jumped from the tree, and ran. Along with his own two pistols, he was better-armed than most of the people he'd been sent out with.

He took a shot at the soldier running towards his tree. He hit, and the man went down, a bloody hole crumpling the side of his face. Lukas took up his second rifle and aimed for another of the enemy vanguard. They were spread out enough that it was easier to focus on individual soldiers as they came through the lines, which meant that in some sense, the plan was working.

The heat at his back grew more and more insistent. He spared a glance over his shoulder to see that the flames were closer, tongues of red and orange and gold licking up tree trunks and devouring the branches. The smell of smoke and burning wood was overwhelming, and he was one turn of breeze away from choking.

He quickly whipped the linen wrap from his neck and wet it with the small water flask at his hip, tying it over his face as a precaution. He heard the signal for the second line to drop from the trees, and cast a glance back at the fire. He wasn't so sure his own unit would be able to wait for their signal before they had to abandon their treetop posts.

The next soldier who came through was fast. Her hair was cropped short, and she moved like a gazelle, darting around the trees with graceful speed on long legs. He took aim, and missed.

He aimed again, and missed.

"*Shit*," he muttered, twisting behind him to see if anyone else had gotten her. He watched her dodge every gunner, and approach the wall of flame. She took something, a stone, a pouch, he couldn't tell, out of her pocket and tossed it in—a second later, a gap opened in the flame, and she darted through.

"She's getting through!" he shouted. No one was listening, though, not with those flames getting closer.

With a curse, Lukas shouldered his rifle strap and swung down from the tree, branch by branch, and sprinted after the soldier. His eyes stung and went dry as he neared the wall of fire, and he hoped it would not close around him as he hurled himself through the gap.

Rhi hit the ground running, his rifle grasped firmly in front of him with both hands as he made for the boulder perched at the foot of a tree twenty feet ahead. It was big enough to take cover behind, and he reached it just as a flood of uniformed soldiers materialized out of the trees ahead, surging towards them like a rising tide.

The boulder was large enough for three to take cover behind, and he found himself crowded in next to Orlah and Lachlan. He peeped his head above the cover just in time to

see a Bourjon soldier aim at his face. He ducked just as he
heard the shot ringing through the air.

"How many?" Orlah asked.

"In range?" Rhi asked, risking another peak over the edge.
"Two, three dozen."

"Cover me," she said, pulling another jar out of her sack.

On her count, Rhi and Lachlan pulled up in unison, rifles
aimed at the onslaught, as Orlah popped up and heaved the
sealed jar into the distance. The sound of the explosion
shattered the air as the three of them ducked back into cover.

When they came up again, there was a gaping hole in the
middle of the enemy horde, and the remaining troops were
forced to scatter away from the patches of flame, giving the
trio a moment to re-position.

One of the closer soldiers came at Rhi, they both fired and
both missed. The fight went to bayonets and butts—a mess of
slamming hard wood and swiping with the metal spears. Rhi
caught the blunt end of his enemy's gun in the side and felt the
air stutter in his lungs. Desperate for breath, he managed to
swing a fist at his opponent. There was a satisfying crack as he
caught him in the jaw, the Bourjon man's face snapping to the
side. Rhi's knuckles were split, but the man had gone down.
He sucked in a breath with the effort of a drowned man,
though it felt like nothing was getting into his lungs.

The next opponent was there in a heartbeat, eyes ablaze in
the surrounding fires, brow lowered in furious determination.
She moved faster than the last one, her attacks more precise to
make up for her smaller size. He managed to get her rifle away
from her, but that was all. He was still fighting for air, and his
side was throbbing something fierce.

She got in a series of quick jabs with Rhi still on the
defensive, trying to get his breath back. He blocked her with
his forearms twice, missed once, and then pulled out the knife
at his hip and swung with it. He missed once, then sliced her

arm as she spun out of the way. A surprised expression crossed her face and she seemed to go slack as she realized how much she was bleeding, a deep cut in the right place. Bright red blood was pulsing out of her like lava. Rhi felt distantly sick at the sight, but turned his focus back to his surroundings. The heat from the fires radiated all around him, and he coughed once as a bit of smoke was carried on the breeze toward him.

The soldier thumped to the ground, unconscious or dead. He didn't dwell on the distinction as another soldier came through the line. He could finally breathe again, and his heart was pumping as he met each opponent blow for blow on all sides. Things moved fast, and he didn't have much presence of mind as his instincts took over. Lachlan had been right, it was strange and horrifying and disorienting all at once.

The heat all around had blended into the background… until *she* came.

It began with a prickling, boiling sensation on his forearms, the sense that he'd opened the door to an oven, and hot, scalding steam and air was blasting him. He lifted his arm to shield his eyes as he staggered around to face the source of the heat.

There, in the middle of the clearing, stood a fire-bright core of heat in the guise of a young woman, her shape silhouetted in sharp light against the burning forest. She raised a hand and the thicket beside him leapt aflame, giving him half a second to jump clear of the fire's path.

A bullet flew past. Another flew *into* her. She didn't seem to notice as the lead ball passed through her and melted to the ground.

He couldn't make out any kind of expression on her face, for all she was was light and heat, a figure burning, a living flame. How could they fight such a force? What would injure, let alone kill, such a being?

Across the clearing, the fire maid raised her hand again, and a beam of white-hot light shot forth, piercing into the sky, raining ash down upon the world.

CHAPTER FORTY-ONE

The first flood of wounded arrived on a milk cart.

It was so remarkably similar to the milk cart on which Soviel had snuck into Everness that she had to choke back her surprised, inappropriate laugh.

"Alright, let's divide them up. Healers, you know what to do," the lead healer announced to the triage team. "Red, yellow and green."

There were buckets of ribbons of each color by each station. Red was for those who needed serious and immediate help, someone bleeding out with a bullet stuck in their gut. Yellow were those who were not in immediate danger, but would need help *today*. Green was for those with less pressing wounds, a twisted ankle or a shallow cut.

"Right," Soviel nodded, swallowing her nerves as an unconscious woman marked with a red ribbon was plopped before her with what looked like half of a tree lodged into her ribs. She was peppered in tiny cuts and minor burns. Soviel's proximity to the cannon fire of the fort had made it hard to tell, but she thought she'd heard a loud *boom* indicative of an explosion come from the woods before. "I need two sets of extra hands over here!" she called out as she reached for her pre-mixed bowl of disinfecting herbs.

"Hold fast here," she directed. "We pull it out on three, then compress. She's going to start bleeding *very quickly*."

"Ready when you are, mum," the assisting soldier said with a nod.

"One, two, *three!*" she urged, jaw clenched to the point of pain as they pulled the jagged limb from the woman's body as evenly and smoothly as they could. Red flooded out in violent pulses. "Cotton and gauze, now!" The blood was coming fast, so, so fast.

She grunted as she quickly pressed down on the wound, red gushing and soaking the padding almost immediately. "Hand me that mixture in the silver tin."

The assisting soldier obliged, unscrewing the lid and holding it up for Soviel to access. She smeared a bit of the yellow-white paste onto her fingers and quickly removed the gauze padding to swipe the mix onto the wound. The blood slowed to a still-dangerous ebb as she flowed her power into the flesh.

"Come on, come on, please," she muttered to herself as she pressed down on the wound. "Fresh bandage." She held out an expectant palm to the assistant, still maintaining pressure with her other hand.

She swapped the bandage, applying one more dose of the anti-hemorrhage mixture. With the influx of wounded only growing, she couldn't spend too much of her time and resources on one patient, if this didn't work—

The bleeding subsided to a slow trickle.

"Tie this off," Soviel said, gesturing to the bandage. "Move her to recovery. Next?"

All afternoon, carts arrived from the woods. So many burned, howling and screaming with pain. Those worse off made no sound at all, only shook in maddening agony. Blisters peeling and bubbling, blackened patches of skin that were past saving. Eyes that would never see again. Lungs that were spent raw from the smoke. Most of these people would never be the same again, some wouldn't make it through the night.

* * *

Rhi threw his hand up to shield his eyes at the brightness of her. Heat seared his skin where it was bare, and currents of hot air lifted his hair and brushed at his clothes as soldiers abandoned their post and ran in terror from the fire.

He threw himself back behind the cover of the rock as she released another wave of flame. He could feel his skin blistering as the blast of heat spread through the air with deadly speed. He looked to his right and saw that Lachlan had managed to get behind the trunk of a wide oak some ten yards away.

Orlah had not been so lucky. She let out one sharp scream as the fire engulfed her. Then she fell, silent. Nothing but a charred husk hit the ground.

Rhi squeezed his eyes shut as screams all around went quiet. He looked at Lachlan again and met his eye. *What do we do?*

Lachlan shook his head. *I don't know.*

He didn't know how they were going to survive the next five minutes, let alone come up with a plan to incapacitate her. He hoped the soldiers in the frontmost lines had spread out, had evaded her impenetrable flames.

Someone still above in the trees fired at her. Their aim was true, but the bullet passed into her glowing body and vanished. She took another step, unaffected.

"Come forward! Surrender yourselves!" a deep voice called. "Any who throw down their arms now will be given shelter from the flame!"

Rhi peaked over the rock again, the hot air still prickling his skin, and saw that a soldier had ridden out beside the fire maid, who, for the time being, had cooled considerably. Her figure was once again flesh and bone, though an aura of heat glowed red around her. He glanced back at Lachlan, who mouthed. *He's lying.*

Why would he lie? This woman could incinerate them all with a snap of her fingers, it seemed. So what was the point of this offer?

Unless she tired quickly; all that magic couldn't be easy. Perhaps it drained her, the way Soviel sometimes passed out after using too much magic. And no energy source could survive such heat.

They needed to wear her down.

Rhi closed his eyes and leaned his head back against the rock, trying to think past the pounding in his chest. He did *not* want to be burned alive. Perhaps it was vain, but he rather liked the way he looked. Liked what his looks had become for him. It was a part of who he was, and the idea of dying a broken pile of char horrified him.

The sound of footsteps on the crunching, dry earth had him drawing in a sharp gasp. *Right.*

He needed to stall, to draw her power to a false target until she was exhausted, however long that took.

He looked back to Lachlan, who was making some kind of hand signal at him. He had no idea what that was supposed to mean. The trees to the south were all on fire, or completely burnt, and the air was fouling by the second. A memory crept back to him unbidden, a cold night in early summer. He and Lachlan on the run through the foothills as the border patrol party hunted them down with flaming arrows, and they escaped to the river…

Rhi snapped his eyes back open. *The river.*

The Rhainor had a tributary not far from here. Too far to run, but not too far to ride.

He turned back to Lachlan and signaled at him, motioning to the horse. Then he pointed at himself.

Lachlan cocked his head to the side, confused.

We need the horse.

Lachlan shook his head, not understanding the why of it, but popped up and took a shot at the soldier nonetheless.

The horse reared, but the man stayed on. The fire maid snapped her head to the source of the shot, eyes glowing in her head like hot coals as her white hair lifted around her like a halo. She stepped forward once more, and before she could roast Lachlan alive, Rhi stood from his hiding place and whipped a fist-sized stone at her.

It hit, smacking her square in the chest instead of the head, but it *did* hit. When she wasn't aglow, she was corporeal.

She staggered back a step and stared down at her chest, stunned. He'd knocked the breath out of her.

"Go, go, go!" Rhi hedged as he leapt over the rock and ran at the soldier. The man took aim, but Lachlan had gotten there faster. He fired his pistol into the man's head and tore him off the horse.

"Come on, come on!"

They both mounted the massive white horse and Rhi spurred towards the stream.

Lukas chased the runner through the limits of Taroch, past the fires and into the marsh. He gained on her as she navigated the narrow path, not used to the sinking mud waiting to suck in a foot should she step astray.

He couldn't tell if she was carrying anything—an explosive being his first thought.

His lungs burned from smoke and effort as he followed on her heels through town and towards the manor. With one final burst of strength, he launched himself at her, flying through the air in a dive to tackle her around the waist.

They both crashed to the ground in a heap. She kneed him in the shoulder and began wriggling away. With a grunt, he caught her by the knee, and dragged her back, aiming a punch at her head.

A whistle of steel through air. A sharp pain at his left arm. He jerked back, losing his grip. She started to scramble away, the glint of her knife catching in the overcast light.

He reached and caught her ankle, pulling her closer. Her eyes were a wild blue, bright as the sky, and bloodshot from the smoke. She fixed him with a frenzied glare as he pinned her arms down.

"What did they send you for?" he snarled, gripping her wrist and slamming her hand into the hard-packed sand until she released the knife.

She let out a smoky, raspy laugh. "Where I have failed, another will succeed," she said. And before he understood what was happening, she opened her mouth wide, moved her jaw to the side, and crunched down on something at the back of her mouth. The fight went out of her seconds later, eyes drifting to the side and focusing on nothing.

Lukas frowned. Checked her pulse. Dead. He stood off her, breathing hard as he looked around.

Where I have failed, another will succeed.

There would be more runners heading to the manor. Why? What was the point?

He knelt beside her to check over what she carried. Rifling through a dead woman's pockets was a new low for him, but she had tried to kill him, so he decided it balanced out.

She'd been carrying precious little. Two knives, a side-holstered pistol, a few rounds of spare ammunition. There was no grenade, no explosive, no chemicals to mix such a thing, or at least as far as he could determine. Her unearthly wide eyes still stared blankly, offering no answers.

He stood and looked down at her, puzzling at what she could possibly have been trying to accomplish.

He turned back to the forest across the marsh. It was burning in earnest now, and the sky had glutted itself with smoke. He coughed and wheezed. The sun had begun a premature display of its dusk colors as the haze in the air painted it red and pink.

He raised a hand to block out the glare as he stared at the forest, hoping for some sign of life, some sign that Rhi wasn't in there burning to death, that he and Lachlan had gotten free of the fire before it consumed the woods.

The smell of burning wood and flesh and overpowering smoke had begun forcing itself up Rhi's nose as they rode into the forest. Flame was all around, in the crowns of the trees, in the scrub, in the bushes. Animals fled, or had been caught in the fire. He could feel the horse beneath him taking shuddering, raspy breaths as he pushed it to move faster.

They had to be nearing the stream by now.

Lachlan's arms were tight around his hips. He'd been coughing more and more as they pushed through the dark smoke.

"This is far enough," Rhi said, halting the horse. They jumped down, and he gave the steed a right slap to its flank, sending it free, hopefully to safety.

As the horse galloped off, they exchanged a look.

"I hope you're right about this," Lachlan said hoarsely.

Me too, Rhi thought as he nodded silently.

They picked their way down the slope to the small river. It was nothing compared to the wide rush of the Rhainor, but it was *water*. As they spilled into the gulley, the air cleared, letting him take a few precious breaths of clean air before he waded into the river fully clothed.

Rhi cupped his hands over his mouth and bellowed, "Hello!" The word came out cracked and grainy, his throat raw and burned.

No answer came.

"Hello!" he screamed again. "River-woman!"

Lachlan stood on the shore behind him. "What if she only watches over the main river, and not this creek?"

"No. No. I refuse to accept that," Rhi muttered. "Help us! The forest is burning!"

The only sounds were the distant crackling of destruction, and the rushing of the current.

Rhi waded in further, up to his chest. The current plucked at his clothes and pushed at his knees, trying to drag him under. Drowning didn't sound like the worst thing, not if it would quench this filthy burning in his lungs, his throat, his eyes.

"*Please,*" he begged, the word tearing from his throat.

Something plunked to the ground on the bank, a cascade of tiny stones.

Rhi felt the ambient heat on his face before he turned and saw its cause. The fire maid stood at the top of the bank, her molten skin aglow once again.

No, no, no, Rhi pleaded.

"Even if you put out my fires, more will come. The flame is ever-devouring." She raised one hand, palm up, a supplicant priestess beseeching the river.

"Rhi. She's going to boil you. Get out of the water," Lachlan said, his voice straining.

Rhi looked at Lachlan, looked at the fire maid, and then submerged himself in the river. A second later, he lost his footing. He waited for the current to steal him away. A scream tore from his lips as he fought to get his footing back. He couldn't leave Lachlan on the banks—

But it never came. He stayed right in place as the reeds and fish flew by. Then, he was rising out of the water. No—not out of the water, the water was rising with him *in* it. Like the sturgeon they'd seen swim through the river-woman that night, Rhi was trapped inside her form as she towered up from the creek bed.

He caught sight of the fire maid looking up, following the growing, towering form of water as it loomed above her.

Lachlan waded into the creek, staring up at Rhi. He was yelling something, eyes wild, but Rhi couldn't hear him, couldn't hear anything other than the current. He could feel the vibrations of the river-woman's words, ancient, deep and rumbling. A hiss of violent steam arced up in a wide column as she quenched the fire maid. A violent scream tore through the figure as she stayed under, assaulted by the endless barrage of river water.

Rhi was losing time. He needed air. He kicked to the side, trying every way he could to get his head outside, to the air, but she was moving and he was disoriented. There was a sudden tumble of water and fast, violent movement as he found himself tossed above the riverbank, rolled like a barrel over the rapids, and out into the forest. Steam rose all around him, more overpowering than the smoke had been. It was impossibly hot. Heat that seemed to seep to the core of his being, pressing into him. He was still rolling with the water as it went up in steam. He couldn't get his feet under him, couldn't tell which way was up, couldn't think past the pain and the movement as he was battered by the forest and river.

He slammed into a tree, feeling something in his side crack on impact. At last, he stopped moving. Above him, steam, and smoke, and dying embers of red and gold eddied around the blackened treetops. He blinked slowly, hyperaware of the rawness in every inch of his exposed skin. His eyes burned. His mouth was dry and rough like he'd eaten sand. His chest ached.

Slowly, and then all at once, he let the exhaustion drag him under.

CHAPTER FORTY-TWO

A sh woke up some time later, the world still loud and angry all around, to Neb dragging her by her shoulders and propping her against the mast of a small ship.

"Thought we'd lost you for a minute there, kid," the harbormaster said with a grunt as she tied off a splint around Ash's wrist, which had swollen to double its size. "You look like shit."

"Thanks," Ash rasped, her voice barely audible.

Her chest ached. Her limbs ached. Her head and eyes ached. She was *freezing*.

"Drink up, you're on the next launch ashore." Neb passed her a leather flask of something nasty, but warm.

"Launch?" she asked, sitting up to get a view of what was happening beyond the ship. Everything was fuzzy and woozy and dull, as if she was still underwater.

"Things are winding down. You need a real healer to look at you."

"Winding… what?" How long had she been out? "How? The soldier in the ocean—"

"We figured you gutted him under water…" Neb said, sitting back on her heels. "No one's seen him since the two of you went under."

"No, I—" she broke off, coughing up the dregs of ocean water from her lungs. "I don't know what happened, I only grazed him with my knife. He was," she shook her head, squinting as she tried to piece those final moments together. "He was looking for something."

"What?"

"Not sure," Ash said, the pendant in her shirt was still a secret to everyone except a choice few people. "I don't know if I'm remembering…"

"Alright, that's fine," Neb said rubbing her shoulder. Ash hadn't noticed the dry wool blanket that had been wrapped around her. "What matters is he's gone. They had us for a while there. But we gained an advantage, somehow." She shook her head, perplexed.

"What is it?" Ash asked, seeing the skeptical confusion in Neb's expression.

"I just can't figure what turned the battle so quickly. For a little while, it looked right like we were finished."

"How long was I out?"

"Half an hour or so," Neb said.

"It turned *that* quickly?" Ash sat forward, the blanket dropping from her shoulders. "That doesn't—" she broke off coughing again. "That doesn't make any sense."

Neb shook her head. "Could be a signal from their troops on land. We don't yet know how they fared in the woods."

"But—" Ash shook her head. Her tongue felt enormous. "The fort fired *on us*. *After* I gave the signal that we were boarding the enemy ships. I thought—" she tried to stifle the coughing. "I thought the fort had been taken."

"I don't think so. Probably just a mistake among all the chaos. It does happen. We'll get it sorted at the meeting later." Neb shoved her gently but firmly back into a seated position, her face still pinched with worry like a grumpy mother hen.

A cheer went up a moment later, and Ash shook Neb off to clamber to her feet, nearly falling in the process. Neb clucked her tongue as she helped Ash lean against the mainmast to see what all the fuss was about.

The last of the in-tact Bourjon ships had turned tail, retreating to the harbor mouth.

Cannon fire and loud, whooping cheers filled the air. Ash squinted as a shimmer appeared from around the bend.

"Neb, give me your scope!"

Neb pressed the cool metal into Ash's hand. She lifted it to her eye and squinted, hoping she was wrong about what she was seeing.

"No…"

With his hair slicked to his skull and his shirt plastered to his body, he was there. The ocean-soldier. It was too far away to see much detail, but Ash didn't know of any other men able to propel themselves on tendrils of swirling sea water. He passed something dark and bulky, about the size of a house cat, to a soldier aboard the ship, who nodded in response.

"The soldier, the one who could control the ocean. He's there."

"How? The both of you were under water so long—"

"He had *gills*, Neb," Ash explained, the chilling image of the man's cold gaze as he tried to drown her still fresh in her thoughts.

Neb grimaced, the brown skin around her eyes and mouth wrinkling. "Whatever magic they have unlocked, I fear it is something fouler than anything we could have imagined."

"He's passed a bag to the captain of the retreating ship… I can't make out what it is, though. Here," she said as she passed the scope back to Neb.

The older woman took a gander at the ship as it slipped from the harbor. "He's gone now, only uniformed soldiers above decks, as far as I can see. Come on, let's get you to the healers."

Lukas was hurrying back from his own fight on the marsh with the runner when it happened, screams rising from the woods as a rush of water and steam and smoke filled the air.

He pulled up short, horrified. What was happening to the soldiers left in the woods? How had the fire spread so rapidly?

He ran like hell towards the smoke, unsure of what he could even *do*. He had to see what was happening, had to know if fate had once again spared him from certain death for no discernible reason.

He staggered into the fog, squinting against the hot air, only to see Lachlan frantically rushing through the steam bed of the forest, his eyes were wide and crazed as he searched the smoking ruin of forest for something. He kept cupping his hands around his mouth as he shouted something between coughing fits

Then, he heard it. Lachlan was calling out for *Rhi*. Lukas's heart kicked into a gallop.

"Where is he?" Lukas asked, approaching Lachlan.

"I don't know," Lachlan said hoarsely. "I don't know, the river had him, and when she flooded the banks, he was swept away and I can't find him, I can't—"

"I'll help you look," Lukas interjected with a confidence he didn't feel. "We'll find him."

The two of them searched the area, fanning out until Lukas heard Lachlan's strained voice call out. Lukas ran in the direction of his voice, ignoring the pain in his chest.

Lachlan had found Rhi, crumpled up on his side at the base of a wide, charred tree.

Immediately, Lukas assumed the worst. His stomach lurched into his chest, and he froze, watching from ten paces as Lachlan fell to his knees and shook Rhi by the shoulders. His head lolled to the side, unresponsive, and Lachlan shouted his name again.

"Wake up, you stupid fool!"

Lukas couldn't move.

Lachlan pressed two fingers under Rhi's slack jaw and stilled, waiting to feel something.

He gasped and sat up straight. "He's alive. He's alive."

Lukas watched, still completely stunned as Lachlan hauled Rhi's unconscious body up into his arms.

"Well, give me a hand!" Lachlan barked, jarring Lukas back into himself.

He started forward and took Rhi by the feet. Distantly, he wondered if carrying him like this could further injure him, but what choice was there?

They hauled Rhi back to the infirmary with great difficulty, between the heat, the bad air, and the general awkwardness of carrying an unconscious person.

When they deposited him at Soviel's station, they lingered.

"I cannot *work* with the two of you breathing down my neck! Hand me that cloth. No, the one next to it. Thank you," she huffed. "One of you may stay and help. I *need* space though."

"I'm not leaving," Lukas said in unison with Lachlan.

Soviel looked back and forth between the two of them before continuing her work. "Lukas, there is someone here for you," she began. "A Ryder Berry rode in from the woods just ahead of the battle. Rhi and I spoke with him," she continued as she cut open Rhi's shirt with calm, fast strokes of the shears in her hand. "He was brought in to the fort earlier, but he was in Alemont's custody, so it's hard to say where he is now. Likely in the manor, in holding."

Lukas slowly turned to look at her. "Ryder is here?"

She nodded without looking up from her task. "Go on," she said. "We will manage here."

Soviel, in her years of healing, had gained a certain awareness of her power, an ability to gauge how much of it there was available to be used at any given time. She often thought of it as if it were a flagon of ale, or a basket of fruit.

464

By her reckoning, she *should* have about a quarter of her reserve left. She'd been at it for hours, setting bones, growing flesh, slowing bleeds, easing things back into place.

She knew her power had been growing, but she hadn't realized to what extent.

It was as if she'd taken only one glorious sip of that flagon of ale. One small bite of the plump, abundant fruits in the basket, the juice running down her chin and throat. Much was left unexplored.

It thrilled her, feeling the bottomless pit opening up beneath her. And, yes, it scared her a little, too. Ever since she'd used her power on the creature in the cliffs, it was like she'd tapped into this entire hidden reserve she'd never known was there.

She moved from patient to patient, addressing their needs with the efficiency she had learned from Madame Leone, applying the knowledge of the body and its needs as she went.

After an hour, she was losing herself in it. In a way, the work made her feel more at home in herself, more anchored than she had in weeks.

She hadn't realized what a mental toll her undercover work was taking on her.

Time must have been flying by, because suddenly, she looked up and found Ash sitting in the next chair.

"Ash—" her voice came out hoarse. She realized hadn't had a sip of water in hours.

Ash's smile was faint. The whites of her eyes were completely bloodshot, her skin was pale, and her arm was in a poorly tied sling.

"*Sweet Lalana*, what's happened to you?" Soviel gasped before she could temper her tone.

"Nice to see you, too," Ash said, her voice cracked and weak, but wry nonetheless. "Some jackass tried to drown me… Why, do I look bad?"

"Well, you don't look *great*," Soviel said lightly as she dropped into the seat across from Ash. She took Ash's head in her hands and turned her face toward her own. Her skin was clammy and cold, her bloodshot eyes still lovely and golden-brown. "Petechial hemorrhage, that's when—"

"When your eyes bleed in themselves from someone trying to prevent you from breathing? I remember."

"Right, sorry. That and the pressure. How do your eyes and head feel?" she asked as she gently rotated Ash's face from side to side, examining her. "Were you hit in the head at all?"

"Not hard, I don't think…" Ash said, her voice muffled from Soviel's palms squishing her cheeks.

"Alright…" Soviel frowned for a split second, then relinquished Ash's face, turning to grab some herbs and jot a few notes in the book at the edge of the cot. She turned back and squeezed the herb into her palm. "This will just take a second. I'm going to take the swelling down in your eyes and make sure there isn't any residual harbor water in your lungs."

"Oh, well, alright," Ash said hesitantly, as Soviel braced her hands on her shoulders.

Soviel sent out a rush of power, coursing through Ash's chest-cavity. Her face twisted in a restrained grimace as Soviel's power brushed up against the residual water lodged in her lungs.

"Deep breath," she commanded, *feeling* the crackle of water in Ash's chest as she drew in air. "And on three, breathe out. One, two, three…"

Ash doubled over, a wet, rattling cough sounding from her lungs as she divested herself of the remaining seawater, right onto the floor.

"Oh, yep… there it is," Soviel said gently, still bracing Ash's shoulders. "Get it all out."

"*Euch*," Ash groaned, sitting up. "That felt worse than it did going down."

"Somehow, I doubt that," Soviel quipped. "Now, let me look at your wrist."

"It's really fine," Ash protested.

Soviel scoffed as she unwound the sling and splint from Ash's wrist.

"Someone needs to teach you lot some basic med training." She tsked as she removed the last of the linen stripping from Ash's wrist. She took a moment to examine it with both her eyes and with that sixth sense that she could reach only with her magic. "You've broken one of the small bones in your wrist by twisting it. Here—"

Before Ash could protest, she sent a wave of warm rose and gold power out through the joint, coaxing the tissue back together.

"Whoa—" Ash's eyes widened. "Oh, that feels *strange*."

"A bit different than the little micro-fractures from the boxing ring, yeah?" Soviel gave a half-smile.

"Oh, shut up," Ash grunted. This was usually the point where the odd, itchy warm feeling arced into a dull pain before subsiding.

"Alright then, soldier. You're all done. Unless there's something else you need?"

Ash swung off the cot and flexed her hand, wiggling her fingers. "No, actually… that feels fine."

"Good. Try not to drown again, please," Soviel said lightly.

"I'll do my best," Ash said, tossing a mock salute in Soviel's direction.

Soviel narrowed her eyes. "I'll believe it when I see it."

Ash snorted. "Well, I guess I'd better go and see what kind of help they need down at the docks. I'll see you later, yeah?"

"Yes," Soviel said. "Go on, then."

Feeling like a newly-made woman, Ash strode down the path from the manor to the beach, rubbing her wrist.

It was strange, Soviel's power - how it seemed to fix anew everything that had ever felt amiss. Her middle finger, which had been stiff since she'd punched a rival diver at age twelve in Khalim harbor no longer ached.

She made her way down the path until she reached the second pier, where launches full of wounded were being unloaded. She caught sight of Helene's ginger hair and approached her.

"Major Wilcoe," Ash said, halting just to the side.

"Mazrihn," she nodded, a heavy length of rope coiled over her shoulder. "Nice work today."

"Thank you, ma'am," Ash nodded.

"Have you spoken with General Ashwife?"

"No, ma'am, I was only just discharged from the infirmary."

"I see. Well, he's impressed with your work these last months," she explained as she began coiling another length of heavy rope around her forearm. "He wants to bring you to the Caprianth Sea with the northern fleet."

"What? But I thought—"

"It's a promotion," was all Wilcoe would say. "Please, do not ask me about it right now," she added in a far more snappish tone than Ash was used to hearing from her.

"Yes, Major," Ash nodded. "Understood."

Her anxiety level rose. The northern fleet was meant to defend the passages around Lindbarrow between Njorske, and Bourjony, and Efel, and up into the Imbaelic sea.

That was nowhere near where she'd planned to go. Nowhere near the other half of the cetamaris. Nowhere near where she needed to be.

Shit.

"And you can't circumnavigate this?" she asked lightly. "I just thought I'd be sailing south…"

"I know, Mazrihn," Helene said a bit curtly. "I know that was what you were planning on, but the army works on a needs-basis, and as far as I'm aware, Ashwife needs your skills up north. I can't do anything about it. It is far above my pay grade. The only one who could divert your assignment is another general, and I wouldn't count on Alemont to do it for you."

"Oh, right…" Ash nodded, her mind beginning to spin. What were they to do? Ferrin and Rhi were both counting on her to go south, not north, to carry out the secret search for the sea gem and its mysteries. What was she meant to do up here, guard profits of the likes of Kenrose?

She shook her head, and then froze.

General Kenrose.

The only one who could divert your assignment is another general.

Ash forced her features into the most neutral expression she could muster.

General Kenrose.

General Kenrose, whose official seal ring she had a copy of in her room, tucked inside a pair of borrowed, moth-bitten socks—

She cut off the thought before she could finish it. Lying was *always* a bad idea. Wasn't it?

He'd made it out of the battle unscathed, only a few minor burns, bruises and scrapes. He knew he was lucky, but that didn't stop the waves of dread from rolling over Lukas. The fighting had finished hours ago, and yet his heart kept pounding.

The battle had ended so quickly, it was making his head spin. Had the fort and the naval effort managed to decimate their ships so quickly? The fight in the woods had seemed far from over, until the flood of water had come out of nowhere and swept them into a hissing cloud of steam.

The land around Galan was in shambles. Char from the woods had seeped into the ground and dirtied the marsh, cannon blasts had peppered the stone walls of the fort and manor, the harbor and beach were littered with timber, shrapnel and debris. After picking his way down from the fort's precarious perch on the rocks, and across the beach and the marsh, the hike up into the cliffs to reach the manor had taken him over an hour as he navigated around new rockslides and pitfalls.

When he at last reached the administrative level of the manor, it was a matter of finding where Alemont's office was located. Of course once he'd found the office, he found it locked and apparently empty. He let out an exasperated sigh. This day was never-ending. He stalked back down the hall, looking for someone, *anyone* who might have some answers.

At last he found a few official-looking fellows deep in hushed conversation about the days events.

"The harbor was nearly lost, then the second we started gaining ground on them, they turned tail! This reeks of a plot!"

"I wouldn't be so sure," the second one replied. "The naval effort sunk some of their ships."

"You didn't see what I saw, the soldier they brought with them, he could have sunk a fleet with a wave of his hand!"

The first one scoffed.

"Excuse me. I'm looking for someone, he was taken into Alemont's custody this morning?"

The first soldier, presumably an administrative officer of some kind, looked him up and down. His wire-framed glasses caught the light as he did. "Who?"

"Uh, his name is Ryder? He would've arrived early this morning? I'm told he was able to warn of the approaching army?"

"*Oh.*" The second one clapped a hand on the first officer's shoulder. "I know who you mean. Big fellow, right? Neck tattoos?"

"That's the one." Lukas nodded.

"He's down in the lower levels helping in the kitchens."

Lukas raised his eyebrows in surprise. "I see, thank you gentlemen."

His legs were aching and sore as he descended the many sets of stairs back to the lower levels of the manor where the kitchens and scullery were.

By the time he reached the bottom, he was well aware of the pang in his right knee. He must have twisted it chasing after the runner.

The kitchens were abuzz and chaotic as all hands readied food for the weary survivors of the battle.

He slipped into the din unnoticed and made his way around the aisles. He'd begun to lose hope when he saw a tall, familiar figure, with a head of cropped dark brown brown hair, calling out requests for what needed to be added to the enormous pot of soup he stirred over the fire.

"Well, well, well," Lukas said, exhaling in relief. "Look who decided to finally turn up."

Ryder halted in his task, and turned around slowly. "Lukas," he said with a grin. His beard had grown in thick and dark, but his smile was visible nonetheless. "I heard you were worried sick about me."

"Well, the last time I saw you you were riding like hell for Avaree with a load of stolen treasure, so…" he trailed off with a shrug. "Not to mention, all hell broke loose after you left."

"That does not surprise me," he laughed. "Come here." He opened his arms and wrapped Lukas in a bear hug. When they broke apart, he sighed. "Well, I hope Tolline wasn't too mean about it all."

"Of course she was." Lukas smirked.

"Ah, that's what I like about her," Ryder joked. "Speaking of, do you think you can get me into the upper levels? I'm told that's where the people who didn't fight are holed up."

"Once they've determined everything is truly over, I'm sure they'll let them all out."

"Strange, isn't it?" Ryder asked solemnly.

"What?"

"How quickly it ended."

"That seems to be the topic of the hour," Lukas said, crossing his arms as he looked out at the kitchen. "What was the real purpose of this attack?"

"I *saw* them marching here," Ryder said insistently. "They were a force, ready to decimate anything in their way."

Lukas shook his head. "I don't know what happened. The forest… Things turned quickly. I missed a lot of it. They sent runners in, what their purpose was, I couldn't say. I chased one down and she swallowed poison before I could get any answers out of her. Then on my way back to the forest, there were more. I fought as many as I could, but some slipped by. The forest was on fire, and then it flooded. I still don't know how it all happened."

Ryder looked astonished. "And to think I missed all that just to cut vegetables."

Lukas cut him an unamused look, to which Ryder responded with a sheepish grin.

"No matter. I'm glad you're alive and here, really," Lukas said emphatically.

CHAPTER FORTY-THREE

There was something so unsettling about Everness's streets in the hour before dawn. It wasn't night anymore, but was it really morning yet, either? Rhi wasn't sure. He paced down the street leading back to the wealthy districts and away from the Pit, adjusting his coat into place so as not to look like a complete ragamuffin. He needed to get back to the castle before anyone important marked that he'd been gone the entire night.

The sun was on its way up, the barest trace of light just peeping over the treetops in the distance. Silver fading into gold, and suddenly growing incredibly bright, blinding—

Rhi came to, his eyes peeling open. Someone hovered over him, and white light filtered in from all angles. He squeezed his eyes shut again.

"Rhiach, open your eyes," a soft but commanding voice shattered the quiet, impossible to ignore.

"No, thank you," he groaned. Everything was fuzzy and bright and too much.

"Rhi." Soviel. It was Soviel speaking.

He cracked open one reluctant eye. "Where am I?"

"Infirmary," she said, coming into focus. Her pale golden hair was pinned back with a few pieces escaping and curling with the heat. She was sweaty and flushed as if she'd been hard at work all day.

"How?" he asked, his throat still raw.

She looked to her right. Rhi craned his neck to see what she was gesturing to.

"Lukas and I carried you after we found you halfway to the marsh." Lachlan said stonily, for once his face betraying little emotion.

"Thanks," he croaked.

Lachlan set his jaw. He looked pale and exhausted.

"What's going on?"

Soviel wordlessly reached into her pocket and pulled out something. Two chips of stone.

"Do you know what this is?" she asked, holding up the broken rock. One of the halves was still tied to a bit of leather cord.

"That's my necklace. The one you gave me," he said, nodding at the gray stone.

"It's broken. Means it's spent. Do you know what that means?"

"No, but it seems you're about to tell me."

"It means it used all of its magic protecting you from the extent of your injuries."

"Oh." He snuck a peak at Lachlan, who was no longer unreadable. Barely-restrained anger distorted his features. "How long ago was that?"

"Two hours, maybe. The fighting has more or less died down. Reinforcements from Avaree are beating back the stragglers."

Rhi swallowed, the sensation of hot sand and ash in his throat still insistent.

"What did you do?"

"I told her, she didn't believe it," Lachlan shared.

"The river-woman—" Rhi began, his throat unbearably dry.

Soviel passed him a cup of water. He took it gratefully and continued. "The fire maid. She was invincible when she was alight. I remembered how the river-woman had flooded the banks when the border party chased us with flaming arrows. It was just a hunch. But it must have worked."

"Yeah, and it almost killed you," Lachlan said. "What the hell were you thinking throwing yourself in the river like that?"

"From what I'm hearing, and from the residual damage, it looks like you could have drowned, been bludgeoned by a tree, boiled, or choked on smoke."

"Well then," Rhi said with a choked laugh, gesturing to the stone necklace, "thank goodness for that."

"I've checked you over and done a bit to speed along the process of healing, but you need to be careful for a few days," Soviel advised.

Rhi nodded. His head was pounding. He said as much.

"I can give you a draught to help with pain, but I've held off thus far because it is mainly comprised of a *popava* extract."

"Thank you, I'll just suffer," Rhi sighed, closing his eyes again.

"I assumed as much."

"Is everyone else back and accounted for?" he asked. "Ash and Lukas? And did you tell Lukas about Ryder?"

"Yes, I sent him to the manor to find him. Ash is slightly better off than you. Someone tried to drown her."

"A harrowing day indeed," Rhi exhaled. "I could sleep for a week."

"You should. You need rest. Try to get some. I'll be back to check on you periodically," Soviel said, standing. Rhi could just make out her words to Lachlan. "You need the rest, too. Your lungs need to recover from that smoke."

Then he fell back into oblivion.

With her clothes finally dry, Ash limped into Wilcoe's office. The faces around her were beaten, all cracked resolve and stitched skin and wavering confidence.

It had been hours since Soviel had taken the bleeding from her eyes and mended the bones in her wrist, though the feeling of it lingered.

General Alemont was still unaccounted for, and Ashwife was laid up in the infirmary with a nasty break in his leg and a lump on his head. Grey leaned heavy on a crutch, Darius sported a nasty, jagged cut across his cheek, Lachlan had a black eye beginning to bloom, Morgaine was nursing a thickly bandaged wound on her side.

"Well," Helene began, her voice wavering. "We've fought them off for now. The harbor is secure, and the land army is nearly through securing a perimeter around the city."

"Then what the hell was the point of all that?" It was Grey, who broke the brief silence after Helene's statement.

"They *had* us. There was no reason for that retreat. They had us. They were hours, maybe *minutes* from taking out the fort, from overwhelming our ships and our forces in the woods, then out of nowhere they turn tail? I don't believe it, not for one second," Grey spat in a show of emotion Ash had not expected from him.

She frowned. Perhaps the battle in the woods had been going worse than the one on the harbor. "Only three of their ships escaped our trap. Three of seven."

"Yeah, and those numbers would be good, had they not destroyed or damaged so much of our fleet," Grey shot back.

Toscan, sitting to Ash's left, didn't seem to be paying much attention to the meeting. This was the first time she'd seen him leave his workshop in weeks. He'd been withdrawn and hyper-focused on his own studies since Col's death. A deep, stabbing pang of guilt ripped through Ash at the reminder. Though she'd never been blinded by romantic love for Zare, it was partially her fault he'd been given rein to operate here. A flash of anger pulsed through her. Helene should have listened to her and Ferrin, should have trusted their experience rather than the allure of Zare's offer. Who knew *what* he'd said to her when he was first captured.

She pushed down her rage, vowing not to let it influence her decisions now.

"It doesn't make sense," Toscan's voice was soft and low, yet it cut through the room like tempered steel.

"No," Grey cleared his throat. "If their objective was standard—take the fort, infiltrate the manor, decimate the town, then they gave up far too easily. And for what reason? Even with their fire-soldier down, they outnumbered and outgunned us."

"That's what we're trying to figure out here." Neb narrowed her kohl-lined eyes.

"Could they have been trying to kidnap someone? For ransom, or for information? General Alemont is yet to be accounted for."

"Perhaps," Helene mused, sounding thoroughly unconvinced. "What about those, ah, those things," she snapped her fingers as she tried to recall the name. "Those things. Like the one in the cliff, with the storm. The destroyer of the lands."

"*Rasernemaud*?" Ash asked.

"*Yes*. That." Helene nodded sharply.

"Why bother?" Grey shook his head. "They were close enough to taking the city that using an asset like that would have been pure waste. Why scorch the earth when you can simply reach out and take it?"

"Nonetheless, we will still send out search parties at first light to scour the cliffs and forest—we cannot afford another surprise from one of those."

Soviel cleared her throat. Ash hadn't realized she'd come in; she stood at the war tent's entrance, framed by cold white light. She shook her head. "If there was a *Ras* nearby, we would know," she said, flicking a quick, sidelong glance to both Ash and Grey, her words, *I'd be able to feel it*, hidden in her expression. "Nonetheless, I will head out with the search parties in the morning."

Helene nodded resignedly and closed the meeting. "Well, until the rest of my superiors are ready to address you, you're all dismissed. Stay close, and stay safe."

At last, the final wounded filtered out after being tended to, and the days of sleeplessness began to wear on Soviel. How long had it been since she'd laid down, sat, let alone slept? The hours of slowly expending her power were beginning to weigh heavily on her as she meandered from the manor into the encampment to Helene's command tent, her eyelids heavy with exhaustion.

"Sit." Helene gestured to the chair across the desk from her.

Soviel settled quietly into the wooden, stiff-backed chair.

"I would like your full report. Now that the Bramblehall mission is complete."

Soviel looked perplexed. "It is not complete."

"I understand you have not had time to write your full, formal report—"

"No, Helene," Soviel said, forgetting formalities. "The mission is not complete."

Helene bristled, her dark eyebrows drawing up in surprise. "You fled immediately preceding a pivotal battle. You're compromised. There is no way you can go back."

Soviel took a deep breath. "Not exactly." She crossed her arms. "I took precautions before leaving. I laid a cover. Now…

there might be some damage control to manage when I return, but I have a *plan* for that."

"I'm sorry. *When* you return?" Helene scoffed. "Larksen, your commanding officer has given you an order. Admittedly, I allow you a certain amount of lenience out of respect for your position as a healer, but you'd do best to adhere to the chain of command in this army."

"Major," Soviel replied evenly, "if today has shown us anything, it's how desperately we need eyes on their side of things. We were blind to enemy territory before, and we cannot afford to be so again, not when I have this opportunity."

Helene set her jaw and stared at Soviel with a look somewhere between disapproving-mother and concerned-older-sister.

"We don't know *anything* about Bourjony," Soviel continued, "or their leadership. The king of Bourjony might as well be some dreadful storybook villain with no goal other than to terrorize kittens and thwart true love and *be evil* for all that we know of him. We had inside information to the Lundi regime, but we always knew Bourjony would be a threat, regardless of where we stood with our southern neighbors. All I ask is that you let me find out who they truly are. Who calls the shots? *Why* are they so interested in Lindbarrow? We don't know *anything*—it puts us in a dangerous position.

"And that…" Soviel explained, "is why I am going to Larais with the Hadringstons. I have been unofficially invited to accompany her Grace Samia of Bramblehall this autumn as a lady in wait to Bourjony's season in the royal court of Larais. If the invitation stands when I return, I will go."

Helene sighed and squeezed her eyes shut for a moment. "Any information," she began slowly, "will be *useless* if you are too dead to report it."

"I'm not going to be!" Soviel threw up her hands in frustration. "Major, the duchess considers me her closest confidant. The duke is about three drinks shy of inviting me to be his mistress, and the rest of the staff think me a vapid, well-groomed upstart looking to make the best of my family's sinking reputation! I could not be in a better position for this. I have not worked this hard to come home just before making a tide-changing discovery," she said, her words tinged with desperation. "It is a risk, Major, but that's war," she said, stating what they both knew to be true.

"This is insubordination," she said, without any of the conviction it required to have the intended effect.

"Then *let* me go. Give me permission."

"We cannot set up a courier system that reaches that wide," she said.

"Then don't," Soviel said. "Send someone over the Efelian border once a month to collect intel and return here. I'll write to my family in Njorske with instructions to forward to you. Encoded."

"That is *incredibly* slow," Helene said in a strained voice.

"It is better than doing nothing," Soviel reminded her, her tone far more sour than she'd intended.

Helene was silent for a long moment, then, with a pained and resigned sigh, said, "Fine. I cannot give you clearance for this, but I cannot stop you either. Do as you will but at first whiff of trouble, the first *inkling* of something going wrong, you are to *flee*. I don't care how, or what the cost is. *Run.*"

"I will, Major, I promise," Soviel agreed.

CHAPTER FORTY-FOUR

Ferrin awoke again with the dawn, and trudged her way up the cliff to the main level after dressing and splashing her face with water.

The main level was bustling with movement and energy as the islanders went about their morning tasks. Lusia, who had an armload of books that looked like they were half her weight, jogged up to her with a grin. "Come on, you're with me this morning!"

Ferrin nodded and did her best to seem awake. How the girl was so energetic this close to dawn was a mystery to her. Perhaps it was part of the island's strange relationship with time.

"There's some re-shelving and copy work that needs to be done today," Lusia told her as she led Ferrin to the library, which was perched on the next level up.

"Lead the way," Ferrin responded.

They arrived outside the building, which looked like little more than a shack leaned up against the side of the cliff. Ferrin peered around the side, as if there were some hidden entrance to be found behind it.

"This is the library?"

"It extends way back into the side of the cliff," Lusia explained as she pulled open the rust-painted door.

The entryway was illuminated by a small glass oculus, the daylight blue and bright against the warm torchlight of the library's interior, which did in fact extend far back into the cavern.

Ferrin's jaw hung open. "This place is *huge*."

"It goes up onto a second level as well," Lusia grinned. "Come on, I'll show you the work we have to do today."

The library turned out to be even stranger and dustier than the one at Everness, though Ferrin supposed that shouldn't surprise her.

Crumbling scrolls were shelved beside luxuriously bound tomes of supple leather and flattest paper. There were even a few stone tablets engraved in a language that, to Ferrin's eyes, hardly looked like a language at all. She blinked, and they were perfectly legible, if archaically worded.

Very strange indeed, she thought.

Lusia led her to a table stacked with books of all kinds, and explained that they were to be categorized and input into a list she had rolled out onto the table between them. At the other tables, a few acolytes and attendants were doing their own research. Ferrin wondered if any of them were wasting their efforts, poring over tomes of undiscovered subjects from *their* time, while possibly researching a topic people from her time had already discovered and knew all about, like the edge of the map, or simple physics, or poisons.

"So, you see here," Lusia tapped her finger gently on an embossed *D* on the spine of the book she held, "this volume is only a copy of an existing book. We *have* the original as well. When you fill it in on the list, make sure you mark that it is a 'duplicate'."

"Right, got it," Ferrin nodded, glad for the distraction from her impending task. She picked up the nearest tome. "This one has two authors. Does it matter how they're listed?"

"We put them in order of the authors' respective heights," Lusia said matter-of-factly.

Ferrin frowned, confused. "But how am I to know which of… *Hamfell Rodinstrod and Gerriana Strupwald* is taller?"

Lusia cracked a grin. "I'm only jesting, it's by alphabetical order of their last name."

Ferrin expelled a relieved laugh through her nose at that. "Oh. Alright then."

She obliged, briefly thumbing through the pages of each one before she set it aside and moved on to the next.

There were books on *everything*. Instructional volumes on poisoning, blacksmithing, sewing. There were lengthy, rhythmic chronicles of kings and queens from times long past, from places she'd never even heard of. There were tales of long journeys across continents. There were even some dramatic romance novels that she wouldn't have minded spending an afternoon with, curled up in a corner.

They'd been at it for an hour when her thumb snagged over the embossed letters of a familiar name.

A familiar author.

H.G. Serengath.

Though the title was one she'd never seen, and the binding was far older than any of their other works she had seen, the author was the same.

The Power of the Gods read the title.

"I know this one. This writer, they…" she shook her head. "I've never heard of this title, though."

"Oh!" Lusia chirped. "I checked that one out. It's rather a topic of interest to me."

"Really? Is it a—" Ferrin squinted at the book's cover and then back to Lusia. "A religious text?"

"Well, no, not exactly," Lusia said. "It's a translation and annotation from a very old manuscript. Serengath spent some time here, many, many years ago. Before my time."

Ferrin smiled at the aged phrase coming from such a young person. "Well, what's it about?" She looked back to the book and flipped it open, her eyes catching on an image of a man transforming into a swirling mass of aether.

"Oh, mostly old, dated theories about magic and what they thought of it back then. Where it comes from, how the gods gifted it to us and why, wellsprings of magic, what the source of those wells might be."

"You seem to know an awful lot about all this," Ferrin noted, raising one curious eyebrow.

"Well, my research pertains to magical objects and how they're created, to the idea of this one, big, unified source, and how it could be universal, how it could be borrowed or stored —"

"Lulu, are you on about this again?" one of the nearby attendants asked with a sigh. "That theory had been disproven a dozen times over in the last millennia. You should drop it, put your studious efforts elsewhere."

Lusia frowned at the attendant and opened her mouth to speak, but before she could, another of the senior attendants rolled his eyes with a snort. "*Accolytes,*" he said derisively.

The girl's frown deepened and she turned back to the worktable. "Well, as I said, it is a translated version of an ancient scroll. Very outdated."

Ferrin nodded in understanding. She scanned the pages of the book once more. *Godhood. Elixir of divinity. Ascension.* She closed the book, a little uneasy, and set it aside with a sigh, picking up the quill to write down the title and author on the list.

"Oh, this one is rather good," Lusia handed her a slimmer, sleeker tome, a simple line drawing embossed on its cover of a woman in a *very* tight set of stays, her bosom all but erupting from its confines. Beside her was a similarly drawn shirtless man, with more abdominal muscles than there were books in the library.

"Aren't you a little young to be reading such things?" Ferrin teased.

"I am *not*," Lusia scoffed in indignation. "I'm fourteen! Or possibly, fourteen hundred!"

Ferrin squinted skeptically but did not argue. "If you say so. Does Nesseen know you dally your time away reading such material?"

Lusia clapped her hand over her mouth, smothering a boisterous laugh. "It's none of her business."

"I won't say a word." Ferrin pledged, raising a hand.

"Well, good." Lusia was blushing now. "It's really more of a plot-heavy read, anyway. The characters have a lot of depth and—"

"I'll take your word for it," Ferrin chuckled, her eyes scrolling down the title *The Fruits of Desire* by one L. R. Tanwirth. "I'm not so sure I'll have the time for any leisure reading while I'm here."

Lusia looked momentarily sad as she acknowledged the truth of Ferrin's words. "Right. Well, are you ready for tonight?" Her voice had fallen into a whisper.

"I hope so… from what I've gathered the first test is one of strength. That seems very straightforward, no? I either have it, or I don't." Her heart dropped to her stomach as the very real possibility of failure taunted her. She kicked away from it.

Lusia nodded serenely. "You'll be alright. Here," she handed her a stack of five matching volumes. "Sort these out, will you? They're a set but they're out of order."

Night was taking an eternity to arrive. She wanted to do it, get it done, be finished.

But time crawled slow for Ferrin on Vaiorka, it seemed. The pit in her stomach grew with every second, and her hands were shaking by the time one hour before midnight rolled around. She adjusted her clothes and hair and made for the path up the cliff—it was well lit with candles upon each step, illuminating the dark with their warm magic. The orange glow almost made her feel excited as she glanced out at the cliffs. It reminded her of the bonfire night.

The day had gone by at a snail's pace after her chores were finished. Night had fallen silver, then deep turquoise, then star-studded midnight-blue as she had never seen. She'd dawdled an hour on the cliff's edge just watching the sky and trying not to dwell too hard on the upcoming trial. She tried not to run through every gap in the training she'd received at the hands of different teachers—be it from Zare, from another of the *Gravedigger*'s crew, from Alick, from Helene, even Lukas…

She pushed those thoughts from her head and focused on honing the strategies she knew best—evasion, surefootedness, quick thinking and quicker movements.

Ugh, she chided herself. *Perhaps I should have filched one of those romance novels from the library.*

A knock on the door roused her from the edge of the spiral she'd been poised to swan dive into, brain first.

"Ferrin, it's time for the night to begin. Are you ready?" It was Galina, one of the younger—younger-looking, anyway—high priestesses.

"Yes," she said, jumping up, both nervous to begin and happy to finally get the night over with.

Unsure of what to expect, she'd buckled on the baldric they'd provided her over her tunic, the weight of it familiar, and yet altogether foreign in this strange place as she fastened it at her hips.

She followed Galina out the door after a moment of gathering herself, and found the priestess standing with her arms crossed, hip popped and head tilted questioningly.

"Well?" she asked sharply. "Everything fit alright?"

"Perfectly, actually," Ferrin answered, smoothing her hands over the front of her tunic and leggings. There had to be some magic at play, because they'd gotten her measurements *perfectly*. The fabric even stretched and moved with her, fitting without so much as a bag or wrinkle.

"Good," Galina said without real interest before turning to lead the way up the hill. Her white-blonde braids swished behind her.

"Is this a midsummer celebration?" Ferrin asked, hiking behind Galina.

"No," said Galina.

When it was clear she wasn't going to elaborate unprompted, Ferrin asked, not caring if she was being annoying. "What, then?"

"The beginning of the sacred trials. Regardless of whether you succeed, the ritual of the trials is extremely important to our way of life. We are celebrating that."

"Oh, that's nice, I suppose," Ferrin said, unsure whether to be honored or unsettled.

"Your trial will commence at midnight. Until then… do as you wish," she instructed, raising her hands in a sweeping gesture of the bonfires.

People were gathered around the fires, sipping honey wine from wooden cups while meat smoked over the flames. With a pang, she recalled the midsummer bonfire celebration back in Galan. How Rhi had smiled, a true smile, as if some of those invisible burdens he always carried had fallen away. How Lukas had somehow tracked down a bottle of Meroyan rum for her, despite the relative impossibility of trading with the far south.

She bit her lip against the memory of their fight. She wished her friends were here. She wished Ash could have come through the door with her so she wasn't alone amongst strangers.

There was still nearly an hour until midnight, so Ferrin carved herself a small helping of the roasted meat, nibbling a bit at a time despite her complete lack of appetite.

At last, midnight struck upon the ancient stone star-wheel clock embedded at the center of the garden. Ferrin stood, feeling her face drain of color as Nesseen approached her.

Nesseen offered a brief greeting before leading her a ways up the path. "Are you ready?"

"I think so." Ferrin didn't really know, but would never admit as much.

Nesseen nodded without giving away a speck of emotion. "The thing you seek…"

They rounded a corner of stone and something came into view as they cleared the next level of the island—it was massive.

Before her was a huge contraption of wood, rope and chain. There were levers, wheels, ladders, spikes. Other objects that Ferrin could not identify. Some of it was free-standing, and some of it was built into the island itself, jutting from the stone cliffs.

"What… is it?" Ferrin asked, her eyes darting from corner to angle to rotisserie.

"It is an obstacle course," Nesseen said evenly. "Galina?" she signaled.

Well, she supposed it seemed simple enough.

Galina nodded, a pale braid sliding over her shoulder. She yanked down on a smoothed wooden lever, and the thing creaked to life. Every bit of the machine moved in a different way.

Parts slashed left and right, sections swirled to-and-fro, bits swayed back and forth. Wheels spun, gears turned, spikes slashed, ladders twisted, poles turned.

Ferrin's eyes bulged. She was to make it through *that*?

"It will test you," Nesseen explained, "in more ways than just strength and agility. There is more than one way across, more than one way to reach the end."

Ferrin nodded slowly as she watched the machine in silence.

"The thing which you seek can *only* be handled by someone who is powerful in constitution *and* strength of body. This will be your first test."

"Alright," Ferrin said, mustering every bit of self-belief she could.

"You will have three tries to make it—if you cannot make it through by the third time, you cannot be found worthy."

That seemed straightforward. "Alright," she said again, her heart racing.

"If you're ready, you may begin your first attempt."

She took a deep breath, examined the course as closely as she could and nodded with resolve.

There was no use putting it off, time could already be running out. She ascended the set of steps to the start of the course and halted, steadying her breath.

She missed the feeling of flying. It had been only a few days since she had arrived on this island, feet planted firmly on the ground, and still it felt a part of her had been wrenched out of her body. There was an absence, an absence of the wind and storm within her veins. It felt flat and dead and wholly terrifying.

The crowd of celebrating Vaiorkans had begun cheering as she reached the top of the steep steps. All of the voices faded to a dull blur as one small voice in her own head drowned them all out.

What if you can't do this without your gift?

She swallowed, unable to shake that particular fear.

She stepped onto the platform, and her heart began pounding. Four rotating blades of leather-over-wood, each on a separate axis spun at different angles, waiting to smack her off the platform if she made one misstep. She took another deep breath, and launched herself onto it. She made it past the first wheel, and halted just before the second whacked her in the abdomen. Panting, she ducked around it—just as the third wheel whipped around and clocked her in the side of the head.

Everything went black before she could even hit the ground.

CHAPTER FORTY-FIVE

The next morning, Soviel took a fresh horse back down the coast road. The day's ride was slow and easy, and she was eventually able to swap back to her original horse, doubling back to the coast as if she'd been abroad all along, before meeting up with the pre-arranged escort from Bramblehall.

With the items she'd gathered, she hoped it would be plausible that she'd made a quick, week-and-a-half journey to her homeland, complete with a small gift for Samia's collection.

She had carefully memorized the story she'd told Bessa, so there would be no suspicious deviation. Her very-pregnant sister had been on bedrest after taking a fall down a set of stairs. The midwife was worried, but in the end both baby and mother were fine. She'd arrived just before the birth, and her eldest sister was now the mother of a healthy baby boy named Oskaar.

It was half-true, aside from the accident bit. She felt a pang of guilt, knowing she really should go home and visit her family. Callia and she had never gotten along. It was part of the reason she'd elected to come and live in Lindbarrow at a young age, and since her sister was the heir, it was perfectly fine for her to further her studies and her socializing in another court.

She shook her head, readying for the possibility of being discovered as Bramblehall's tall, gleaming walls and gables came into view. After dismounting her horse, she smoothed her cloak over her beautiful riding habit and approached the gate.

"Lady Soviel," greeted Anders, one of the guards, with surprise when he recognized her. "You're back!"

"Hello, Lieutenant Anders," she responded with a shy smile and a dip of her chin. "Yes, I'm back, and I am *very* ready for a hot bath." She let exhaustion and travel-weariness seep into her voice.

"Her Grace will be thrilled. Shall I alert the maid staff?"

"Yes, thank you. And could you ask for Bessa to bring that peppermint oil she has? My stomach is still churning from the sea-journey."

"I'll tell her to send it to your room."

"Thank you," she said, and passed through the gates as easily as a spring breeze.

She returned to her room with no resistance, and took her bath in peace. She dressed herself in a soft pink day-frock and went to go find Samia, her little gift in hand.

According to the guards on duty in the great room, Samia was busy with the other ladies, welcoming the new serving staff at the main dining room. It sounded as if there were quite a few of them.

When Soviel entered the platform from the side door, she noticed that Samia and her husband stood close together, clad in complementary attire of spring green and pale lilac. Samia was lifting a chalice in celebratory toast as she welcomed the newcomers. Beside her, the duke appeared to be tolerating the affair, though his jaw was clenched and he looked about ready to stalk from the room and return to whatever horrid task he was focusing his energy on that day.

When Soviel approached Samia, the duchess turned and clapped her hands to her face.

"Soviel! You're back!"

"We'd feared you wouldn't return for weeks on end," Erina drawled.

"No, no, I didn't stay long," she said with a smile. "I just wanted to see my new nephew and be sure my sister was well." She carefully pushed away the pang of guilt. "I had no wish to linger. I think I was starting to drive poor Callia mad."

Samia clucked her tongue.

"Such is the way of things," Soviel shrugged sadly. "By the by," she said conspiratorially, taking Samia by the elbow as they stepped off the dais. "How did it go the other night? Did His Grace react… appropriately?" She arched an eyebrow.

A rosy blush crept up Samia's cheeks. "Oh, he did."

Soviel plastered on a cheeky grin. "Excellent."

"He does work so hard," Samia cooed, eyeing her husband from afar. "I think he has trouble tearing himself from his duties."

"Honorable men are often like that," Soviel agreed, swallowing her gag at the idea of Hadringston being honorable.

"Come on, let's go have tea in the garden while we pick out the flower arrangements for the Summer Feast."

Soviel was nestled on a tiny cushioned chair between Samia and Tavara on the patio in the rose garden. Laid before them on the table were a stack of cards, each with a rendering of a floral bouquet on the front and centerpiece on the back, done in colorful pencil drawings.

The day was turning out to be quite hot, and Samia had rung for a servant, insisting that the climate called for iced sweet tea.

Soviel had never heard of such a thing, but the fact that it was cold sounded refreshing enough to her.

"Don't you think this one is a bit too wintry for the event?" Tavara frowned, working the folding lace fan she was attempting to cool herself with. "It has something in it called 'snow-breath'."

"The colors are a bit drab," Soviel agreed, peering at the card Tavara was examining.

"Perhaps we should switch out these hydrangeas for something… like this," Tavara said, pointing to the peach-hued peonies detailed on the next page.

"Hmm," Samia breathed through her nose. "I think not. Something more subtle."

"Well, what about if you balanced the peonies out with some more greenery? There're lovely little ferns, juniper boughs," Soviel said as she turned over the next card.

"I do like the ferns," Samia conceded. "A few peonies with the ferns will do."

Soviel was pleased to see Tavara beaming at that. It was important to keep on the other ladies' good sides. Any of them could make a useful ally should she find herself in dire straits in the future.

"What else is there to decide on for the feast? I fear I've missed most of the planning," Soviel said mournfully, leaning back in her patio chair.

"Oh, wouldn't you like to know," Samia said coyly. "You'll have to be surprised with the rest of the guests."

Soviel pouted.

"Sweet tea, Your Grace?"

The familiarity of the voice hit Soviel first like a trickle of ice water, and then like a brick to the face. She froze.

The new servants.

As the maid came around the table, any shred of doubt that she'd simply misheard evaporated from Soviel's mind.

Her red hair was tied back and secured under a lacey little day-cap. A delicate fichu was tucked into the top of her apron,

494

and her green maid's dress was far more plain than anything she'd worn as a lady-in-waiting. But still, she was unmistakably Nimhe.

"Oh, finally," Samia clapped. "We've been sweating like *piglets* out here. Just set it down there."

"Yes, Your Grace," Nimhe said with a curtsy and a dip of her chin.

As she straightened, her eyes locked on Soviel. The flicker of recognition was instant, but fleeting, as she maintained her neutral expression. If Nimhe planned to say anything, she wasn't going to do it right then.

"Is there anything else you require, Your Grace?" Nimhe once again directed her attention to Samia.

The duchess pondered for a moment before dismissing her. "That will be all, thank you, dear."

Soviel swallowed her nerves as Nimhe departed. Were it freezing outside, she'd have still been sweating. Her heart raced, and her tongue felt thick in her mouth as her throat went tight. If there was one person in all the world who was a threat to her cover, it was Nimhe. Nimhe, who was willing to sell her soul and her fellow compatriots out to see her own desires met. Nimhe, who had poisoned a neighborhood of people in Everness, had poisoned Rhi. Nimhe, who had held a gun to Soviel's own head.

She needed to fix this before it got out of hand, find a way to discredit her, or better yet, blackmail her into staying quiet. No, into *leaving*.

CHAPTER FORTY-SIX

Soviel shut her bedroom door behind her and pressed her back against it, sliding down to the floor as she let her composure crack. Just for a moment, just for a moment. She took a deep, trembling breath as her heart fluttered like a trapped rabbit. Nimhe was here. In Bramblehall.

The recognition had been unmistakeable, and Soviel might only have *hours* until the girl sold her out to her hosts.

Then, everything she'd worked for these past weeks would be swept away. The hope she'd be invited to Larais Court, the rapport she'd built, the reputation she'd shoved herself into a box for, all of it, gone.

She squeezed her eyes shut and counted her breaths for a minute, then two.

She exhaled, resolving to pull herself together. There was no other alternative. She pushed off the floor and went to the mirror.

After quickly smoothing her hair and applying a touch of fresh rouge to her cheeks, she squared her shoulders and went back out into the hallway, ready for dinner. She could outmaneuver Nimhe. She could take control of the narrative.

Samia favored her, trusted her above the other ladies—save Jorde, perhaps—though she'd only been in her service a few weeks. Even if Nimhe blabbed, it was unlikely Samia would take her side.

The duke, on the other hand—was a different story. She still couldn't quite get a read on him.

"Lady Soviel, are you feeling better?" Bessa asked as she ushered Soviel into the dining room.

"Yes, Bessa, thank you. Just a bit of belly pain from my monthlies, along with the journey," she explained.

"Shall I send up a soothing tea for you after dinner?"

"Please," she said gratefully.

"I'll tell the kitchen. Here you are," she said, seating her beside Samia. Across from her, Jorde smiled mildly.

"Soviel!" Samia greeted her. "Feeling better?"

"Yes," Soviel said, forcing a soft smile to her face. "Much better."

"Excellent," Samia said. "We were just discussing my husband's newest trade venture."

"Oh?" Soviel said, painting coy interest on her features.

"Yes, I think you'll find it rather intriguing. He has just acquired a portion of land on the island of Galus," Samia recounted. "Although, where is Galus? It's… south? Where they grow all the *arimopo* and the *pop*?"

Soviel swallowed her disgust. If Hadringston had acquired land there, he was likely exploiting more workers, growing more *popava* to be altered and used in the experiments.

"Yes, Your Grace," Lucelle confirmed. "It is far south, even further than Calixta *or* Corsovena."

"Hm, I have always wanted to visit the colonies…" Samia pondered absently as she examined her nails.

"I'm told Galus is a lovely archipelago," Soviel added. "Though, there are many small bugs at this time of year. From what I've been told."

Samia pulled a sour face. "I *detest* bugs."

Soviel nodded sympathetically. "You and I are suited to the colder climes, I think," she said with a conspiratorial smirk. "Which reminds me, I brought you something from home. It's nothing much," she said sheepishly as she fished the little thing out of her pocket. The red fabric and delicate white, green and yellow stitching was spare and beaded with silver and gold.

"Oh, Sov! You *didn't*," Samia gushed as she beheld the traditional scarf.

In Njorske, because the winters were so cold, women would tuck decorative chest-scarves into their necklines to cover their décolletage in the winter to keep warm without breaking the fashionable silhouette.

"I bought it in the village by my family's estate. It was just too lovely not to," she explained. In truth, it had been crafted five years ago by Callia and had been sitting unused in Soviel's old room at Port Galan.

"It's lovely," Samia gushed, pulling Soviel into a warm embrace. "I'm sorry such unfortunate circumstances brought you home, but thank you for this lovely thing."

"It all worked out well."

"Yes, tell us how your new nephew is?" Tavara asked.

"He's beautiful," Soviel smiled with pride. "Round pink cheeks and a tiny wisp of golden hair atop his head."

"Oh, I *love* babies," Erina sighed with a hand over her heart. "I can't wait to have six of my own."

Samia's smile faltered for the briefest second, nearly undetectable.

"*Six*?" Lucelle squawked.

"Well, still, I am glad you've returned," the duchess said.

"As am I," Soviel replied, drawing a deep breath through her nose. "I love my sister dearly, but we often don't get on well," she divulged.

"*Och*," Samia waved her hand. "You should see me and my brothers. We are a *mess* when we're all together."

Jorde giggled. "And me and mine. We were at each others' throats growing up."

"Really?" asked Soviel.

"Oh, gods, yes," Samia laughed. "Every single thing turned into a competition. Down to who could finish their porridge faster in the morning. We were so childish."

"My sister and I are exact opposites," Jorde snorted. "I'd die for her, but we get along best when we are an ocean apart and communicate only by letter."

Soviel grinned. "It's the same with Callia and I," she admitted with a smirk.

"Families," Erina rolled her eyes.

INTERLUDE

Long ago…

The sea was crashing against the rocks, always crashing, always angry. It was an especially stormy spring.

The sky was somehow blue and gray and green all at once as she waited on the cliffs, the wind whipping her hair and clothes around and against her in a frenzy. What was she waiting for?

She couldn't quite remember.

Night was falling.

She couldn't remember anything, other than that she was *angry*.

The beginnings of a storm were shoring up around where she stood on the bluff, the waves crashing into the cliffs and shattering any unlucky debris on the rocks below.

The hole in her chest was ripping, tearing, gnawing at her that day.

He had left her—no, *abandoned* her—pregnant, disgraced and alone in the harsh, unforgiving town she'd lived in all her life.

They had spurned her, humiliated her, left her for dead at the edge of the woods, but it was *he* who truly was the target of her ire.

He had told her he loved her and taken everything from her before disappearing south, and leaving her to weather the consequences alone.

And now she was here with the beginnings of their child, no money and no home. All on her own.

So she had turned to the magic inside her to help her climb from this bottomless pit.

A bargain with sea and storm, that was what she had made the day her father had cast her out amid the angry winter winds.

She'd never imagined how great the cost would be.

Her family had spurned her. *Live or die,* they'd said. *We care not.*

She swallowed down the lump in her throat and blinked against the rain, the lightning, the wind. The storm and sky were hers to command. She needed only give up one precious thing, and how easy it had been, or so she had thought.

"Take him from me," she'd said in a low and broken voice. "Take away this pain."

And so the storm had taken the payment and made her strong and powerful as a tempest in her own right.

She howled into the wind.

CHAPTER FORTY-SEVEN

Ferrin awoke slowly, consciousness oozing back to her as she stirred in her cot, impossibly bright and loud light seeping in through the windows.

Her head throbbed where it had smacked the ground, her body ached all over and her joints were stiff with misuse. How long had she been out?

She sat up in bed, blinking sleep out of her eyes. Immediately, she regretted the quick movement—her muscles tensed and a flash of pain had her doubling over. Water—she needed water.

There was a cup beside her bed, kindly left by whomever had deposited her back here after she'd so miserably failed her first trial. She drained the small glass in two gulps before slamming it back down, her arms no longer able to fight gravity. She grunted with effort as she stood, bracing a hand against the cold wall to balance herself on weak knees.

She needed more water, then she could sit back down, rest for a little while.

Resolving that this was the proper order of events, she made her way to the door and pushed it open; immediately the sound and smell of the violent sea assaulted her senses. The gulls cried above as they hung in the breeze, and she envied them their weightlessness. It took her a few minutes to make her way over to the well around the bend, where she brought up a bucket of fresh water and plunged her face into it, drinking her fill.

Finally, Ferrin felt awake, alive. She turned back to the well and replaced the bucket on the hook, her eyes catching on the dark innards of the well. How deep did it run, that long and unrelenting darkness? She paused, eyes trained on the bottomless pit of black below. Would it swallow her completely if she fell in?

A far off rumble of thunder shook her from her trance, and she stood, unsure of how long she had lingered there, ready to begin her climb up to the island's main level.

Covered in sweat and with her heart thumping, Ferrin reached the top of the cliff path and found everyone already busy with their daily tasks. She tried not to let her shame show on her face. The previous night's failure was raw as a wound in her mind, and she wondered what they all thought of it. Had previous candidates had such dismal starts to their trials?

She came to the main square and tried not to appear too downcast as she searched for Nesseen or Lusia.

Unfortunately, it was instead Galina who waited, leaning against the barn door, arms crossed and eyebrows arched.

"You look like hell."

Ferrin couldn't muster the will for a snappy retort. "How long was I out?"

"Two days, about," Galina said, flicking a blonde braid over her shoulder. "But don't worry. Your brains weren't scrambled about. Nesseen saw to that."

"Great."

"I bet you're having a fair bit of doubt in yourself right now," Galina said, falling into step beside her. "That's fair, of course. What makes you special? Why *should* you be deemed worthy? Your mother wasn't."

"What do you *want*, Galina?" Ferrin snapped, turning on the other girl, her teeth bared as she got right up in her face.

Galina shared many traits with Soviel: the pale white skin, thin platinum hair, the heart-shape of her face. The similarities were completely irrelevant in the face of Galina's expression and demeanor. Unlike Soviel, she did not possess a shred of softness or warmth.

"An answer." She narrowed her slate-gray eyes. "I'm just looking out for the best interests of everyone on this island," she claimed.

"Well, do yourself a favor and don't bring up my mother again," Ferrin snarled.

"A sore spot, then." Galina laughed softly. She flicked her finger and a shimmer of warm silver flickered through the air and popped the barn door open. "Nesseen is out that way."

Ferrin stalked off toward the barn.

"It takes more than assumed destiny, you know," Galina called after her, but Ferrin had already spotted Nesseen by the goat paddocks.

Nesseen was crouching, tending a pregnant goat, feeding the creature handfuls of grain pellets from her palm as she patted circles on the goat's back.

"Good. You're awake," Nesseen said.

"I want to try again."

Nesseen stood from her crouch. "I assumed that was implied," she said as she dusted off her hands. "You can make another attempt at the end of the week."

"No." The blood was still rushing in her ears. "Tomorrow."

Nesseen raised one stern eyebrow. "You hit your head, you were unconscious for days."

"Exactly, I can't afford to waste more time."

Nesseen laughed, as if she knew some secret Ferrin didn't. "You still don't understand, do you? Time works differently here. You can't rush the trials. If you do, you *will* fail them."

"What does that *mean*?"

Nesseen casually lifted a shoulder. "It means what it means. This island is separate from your world, from its time. We don't age here, we don't see too much change. I promise you, an acceptable amount of time will have passed when you leave."

That did nothing to quiet the frantic chorus of *move forward, move forward, move forward* that Ferrin felt in her blood and bones. She sighed with frustration.

"When did you arrive, then? I mean, when did you come to Vaiorka?"

Nesseen chewed her lip, as if calculating a difficult math problem and turned to scoop a few handfuls of feed into the goat's bucket. "I came here from a war-torn country. I believe it is part of what you are now calling *Veira*. I lived there while King Orman reigned.

Considering the Veiran Empire had come into being some five-hundred years ago, Ferrin could assume that Nesseen was indeed very old.

"Regardless," Ferrin said, "time is of the essence, and I need to get *back* to Galan with whatever it is I'm supposed to be after. My people, my *friends* are in danger."

Nesseen gave her a sympathetic look. "I suppose you should be glad there is no trial of *patience*," she said. "Very well. *Two* nights from now, you can attempt the trial again. I hope you will be better prepared this time."

The next two days passed in a blur. Ferrin completed her chores with minimal talk, ate her lunch and dinner alone in her hut, and spent her free time climbing up to the upper level, to study the contraption of wheels and wood and spikes and spokes.

Two more chances. She could *not* afford to fail.

As she observed the thing from afar, she could see where she'd failed on her first try, and why. The third wheel was at a slightly offset angle, just by a few degrees, and its spokes were longer than those of the first and second.

Beyond the initial wheels, there was a series of suspended stairs, each hung individually from two chains, built into the overhang of the cliff. They were at least a dozen feet off the ground, and would swing with her momentum when she leapt onto them. She'd have to be careful, and grab for the chains suspending them.

After the steps, there was a log. About twenty feet long, and narrow. If she remembered from her glimpse at it last time, it rotated on an axis. She was supposed to make it across that, and onto the long pike that rose far, far into the sky with tiny handholds. It rose at least thirty feet in the air and connected to a Jacob's ladder twenty feet long. From there, there was a wide gap till the next piece of the course, filled only by a trapeze bar, which would swing to a platform on the cliff wall. Then there was the climb to the platform far above on the rock spire.

Her anxiety spiked as she took it all in. Yes, this would be difficult. But it wasn't impossible. She'd spent plenty of time climbing ropes and balancing on the boom trying to secure the riggings back on the *Gravedigger*.

I can manage this, she thought, denying herself even an inch of doubt.

The day of her next trial, night came fast. More fires were lit, and Ferrin trudged up the cliff, ready and abuzz with nerves and anticipation.

Not today, she said to the nagging voice in the back of her mind. *Not today.*

Nesseen eyed her coolly, expression unreadable on the opposite side of the contraption. Lusia gave her a toothy grin and a thumbs-up for good luck. Galina gave her one, single nod as she pulled the lever to start the contraption moving.

The death machine whirred to life.

Ferrin squared her shoulders and climbed the ladder up to the starting platform.

She ducked the first wheel and dodged the second, before leaning far out of the way of the third, unlike last time. She leaned so far, she *nearly* tumbled over the side.

She ducked the final wheel and moved to the stairs. She gained speed, not letting her momentum topple her as she sprinted up the steps, only halting at the top one, her hands wrapped around the cold chains that suspended the step above the ground. With a deep breath, she launched onto the log, running across as it spun beneath her. If she let her feet touch it for too long, it would roll her off.

She reached the end and leapt onto the pole, climbing as best she could. The higher she got, the further apart the little notches meant for her hands and feet were. By the time she was twenty feet up, she could barely reach the next hand hold without stretching to her tip toes. Her fingers screamed. When she reached thirty feet, she had to jump and throw her weight up, completely untethered for a moment as she reached for the next notch.

She missed, and began skidding down the pole, her hands scraping raw on the splintering wood.

She cried out in pain as she caught herself ten feet down. Her shoulders jolted with the sharp stop, and her palms started to bleed as she gritted her teeth, eyes fixed on the pinnacle of the pole. Letting out a sharp, growling scream, she dug her feet into the notches and pushed. It took her a minute to make it back up to the point from where she'd slipped, and when she reached it, she tried again. She planted her feet into the notches and leapt for the last handhold. She was so close, could almost touch it, and—

She'd overshot it. She went sliding past, and when her momentum failed her and she began to fall again, she bumped the side of the pole and knocked outwards, tumbling, spinning, careening down the side of the wooden pole, likely to her death. How horribly ironic it was, descendant of Gwelie the Stormrider, plummeting to her death on a magical island.

Something slowed her fall, and she landed much more gently than she had the first time. Nesseen appeared out of the corner of her eye, her hand raised.

She sat up and bent over her knees, shame curdling her blood. She squeezed her eyes shut. She had failed. This thing she was meant to do, had been *made* to do, she was failing at it.

Her chest went tight, and it felt like her lungs were shrinking around the little bit of air she managed to inhale. She was on the verge of losing it - she had to get out of there.

She pushed up from the ground and stormed out of the clearing. She ran all the way down to the little hut two levels down, the lump in her throat building to the point of pain. It wasn't until the door slammed behind her that she let out the breath she'd been holding. It caught in her throat, and came out in a wretched, broken gasp.

*   *   *

The next morning came, dawn bleeding in red and dark.

She closed her eyes against the lightening sky.

Her mother had been wrong. She had put up with Henrik all those years for *nothing*, had endured it all on some false hope that Ferrin would be able to achieve something here.

She never should have come.

She was never going to make it through this.

She was going to fail.

CHAPTER FORTY-EIGHT

"Y ou have magic," Ferrin said as she slid into the seat across from Nesseen at breakfast that morning.

"Yes," Nesseen replied matter-of-factly, taking a sip of tea.

"I was told this island blocked magic."

"The island blocks any magic that is not its own," she explained, setting her mug down. "Our magic is tied directly to the energy of this place, to nature. Your ring, there, is something else."

"Where then on this scale would old magic users fall? Stormriders and water witches and the like."

"Somewhere in between."

Ferrin sat back with a sigh. This was decidedly unhelpful.

"When you say *the energy of this island*, is that what's in the wellsprings?"

Nesseen's nose twitched. She hid it well, but it was a flinch nonetheless. Ferrin tucked away that reaction to think on later.

"It's getting close to afternoon, you'd better begin bringing water up for the goats." She stood and disappeared out the hut door.

"Very curious," Ferrin narrowed her eyes. "Very curious, indeed."

There was something Nesseen wasn't allowed to tell her, something important about the wells she'd been seeing in her strange dreams. Whatever they were, she was certain about one thing.

It was a big part of whatever it was she was working towards here.

She dreamed again that night, but this time it was her mother's face she was watching.

She stood high upon the cliffs at the island's pinnacle. In all directions, there was sea and sky, and sea and sky. The sunrise splashed its usual strange colors over the Vaiorkan sky, a dark spot above the horizon puckered against the purple and orange haze. At the very center of the knoll there stood two stones. Impossibly tall, looming, crudely hewn. One slightly taller than the other, the shorter one curved and convex, bellied-out towards the bottom.

"My people *need* me to succeed at this," Arabella argued as she followed behind Nesseen. While Arabella herself was at least twenty years younger here, Nesseen appeared to be the same age as she was in the present, down to the day. "The Lundis are poised to wipe us from the face of the earth, Nesseen. They've taken our land, our forts. For centuries we've been at this with them, but these last few decades they have burned our villages and forced people from their homes more quickly than ever. They're aided by something beyond human force, I know it."

Nesseen sighed sympathetically.

"The only way to ensure they don't eradicate my people is with a weapon of magical proportions," Arabella insisted.

"I'm sorry, child," Nesseen said, the slump of her shoulders betraying her weariness. As the voice of Vaiorka, how many desperate folk had she been responsible for turning away? "What you seek here, it is not some weapon that can be aimed at all of one's enemies. To complete these trials and rituals is to take on an immense power. A level of power you can never undo."

"I don't care," Arabella said bitterly. "I will do *anything* to save my people."

"I understand that, Ara," Nesseen said sadly, "but it is not the right time."

"Not the *right time*?" Arabella snapped. "What the hell can that mean? Will it be the right time when my people are all dead? The Lundis have already killed my brother in battle. Who next, my baby sister? My mother?"

Ferrin winced from where she floated out of corporeality. She had never even known her mother had other siblings. She knew of one younger brother who'd died of sickness at age fourteen.

"I cannot give this to you, Ara. No matter how sympathetic to your plight I may be. Time is a delicate thing. You are… a generation too early."

Arabella's frustration was tangible. "What?"

"You are young. Full of ambition and life. Another, like you, will be ready for this in time, and likewise will it be ready for them, should they complete the trials."

"You're telling me I went and nearly splattered myself on the rocks for *nothing* then? Why wouldn't you have said so sooner?" Arabella asked, voice raised.

"I understand your anger," Nesseen's agelessness showed then. Someone who had seen countless heroes rise and fall, who had stayed the same while everyone came and went, striking out on their own quests and carrying a piece of Nesseen with them always. Never to return. "That's all I can offer you. I'm sorry."

Arabella huffed and turned on her heel, stomping down the cliff-stairs. Nesseen dropped her shoulders and shook her head, a strange, familiar sadness enveloping her.

And that's when Ferrin realized: this was not her mother's memory, but *Nesseen's*.

CHAPTER FORTY-NINE

When Ferrin awoke, she couldn't help but feel like she'd invaded some kind of personal space, crossed a boundary.

Nesseen didn't seem to realize what had transpired, that or she didn't care, which had Ferrin wondering if she'd imagined the whole thing.

Seeing her mother here, on Vaiorka, had been jarring. To hear her say such similar things to what had been running through Ferrin's own mind since she'd arrived was unsettling, to say the least.

And of course, there was the other bit.

Nesseen had been the one to first plant the idea of Ferrin's very birth in Arabella's head. That was why the Unification had taken place, why Arabella had put up with the absorbing of her homeland into the Lundi occupation, why she and Alick had made their pact to infiltrate the capital, bide their time, and further the Caelish cause by any means necessary, starting with the creation of her and Rhi.

She forced herself to gulp down another spoonful of warm oats as her mind spun.

"You're quieter than usual this morning," Nesseen observed.

"Just trying to focus," Ferrin said, scraping the oats around her bowl.

"Is eating oatmeal a particularly perilous task in the outside world these days?"

Ferrin smirked. "You know what I meant."

"You were much closer this time," Nesseen reassured her. "You'll make it."

"That a guarantee?"

Nesseen rolled her eyes good-naturedly, but with a hint of that same weary sadness Ferrin had glimpsed in the dream.

"You're off balance, though. You're still coming at it like someone who can't fall."

Ferrin frowned. If anything, she'd felt the opposite. "It's difficult to adjust to… the absence of the ring's gift," she said carefully.

Nesseen nodded. "I'm sure it is. The gift of flight is truly something to behold. I'm told it is a rarity in the outside world, now."

"Did you see Stormriders in your time?" Ferrin asked.

"Of course," Nesseen said. "Long ago, I trained and fought alongside them in a long-forgotten war."

"In your home country? I thought—"

"What, that the elements of magic were restricted by geography and fleeting political borders? No, child. You have so much to unlearn," she sighed.

Ferrin blinked.

"It's true, magic is largely borne of necessity. Fire in the cold and icy tundras of the northern reaches, water in the arid deserts of the south, and so on, but that is a massive over-simplification. We knew that in my time, and that's why people with magic were trained and educated on all kinds. After all, is there not an overlap? Fire requires fuel to burn, whether it be air, or earthen matter. Plants are full of water, and yet they grow from the ground. The air we breathe is made up of many things, and carries water within it. The very storms that crash upon your homeland - tell me, would you call them a product of the sea or the sky?"

Ferrin listened, rapt.

"Is there not necessity for fire in the desert? And in the midlands where they claim their gifts of healing and farming to be gods-appointed? And water? Earth and air, too?" Nesseen asked rhetorically.

"I suppose," Ferrin acknowledged. "I never thought of it quite like that."

"These boundaries that have been drawn and assumed over the last few centuries are far more arbitrary than you think."

"My friend, she's a healer, with plant magic, but she's primarily of Njorski descent."

"Precisely. And plant magic, when it's in its highest practice is *midaeri*. Creation."

"*Midaeri?*" Ferrin cocked her head. "I've never heard of such a thing."

"It is magic in its earliest, purest form. Undefined and unhindered. And also, the form of magic capable of greatest horrors."

"Really? How?" She thought of Soviel tending the little plants that seemed to glow in her presence, of the variety of woodland creatures that sought her out.

"To wield too much power over life and death is to play at being a God, and one cannot be a person and a god." Nesseen stated, a cold authority seeping into her eyes.

Ferrin wondered exactly what Nesseen meant by that but decided not to probe further. She searched the woman's face, as if she might find an answer there. And then she recalled a story—one she'd heard half-asleep in the temple one morning when Rhi had dragged her there, hungover from an Efelian wine-tasting the previous night. A story about a mother who walked through Nothing, and created a trail of stars and planets in her path and eventually a son, who ruled the land and created Gods of his own out of nature spirits, humans, wisps, sprites and beasts alike.

She studied Nesseen for a beat longer, wondering how much she knew.

"The *Dionas*. Who are they?" she blurted, immediately preparing for a defensive, closed-ended response like Madame Leone's had been.

Nesseen set her spoon down in her bowl and leaned back in her chair. "Who do you think created this place?"

"Wait, what?" Ferrin sat to attention.

"The *Dionas* are an ancient, secret society. They are from all sects, all nations, all lands and countries. Once, they were many. Sworn to protect the world from the corruption that could spread from a malicious, ancient magic that was buried by the first of them, thousands of years ago, when humans first walked this land."

Another memory flashed through Ferrin's mind. This time, symbols she'd seen carved on a sea-worn cave wall.

"What is it? This… ancient magic?" Ferrin asked.

Nesseen tilted her head thoughtfully. "There are special wards in place… wards that keep me from speaking this truth to anyone who has not passed the tests. What I can tell you is that not every god is merciful and kind. Not all creation is good. There is a horrid sort of vengeance in having made all that is. And it does not look kindly on those who would diverge from its will."

The words, for whatever reason, chilled Ferrin to her core. She couldn't parse a coherent or familiar meaning from them for the life of her, but somehow she knew that they meant something *bad*.

*   *   *

The day had come.

Ferrin woke, well aware that this was the day her fate would be decided. Her final attempt to make it through the stupid obstacle course. If she didn't make it, she would be done.

This was her last chance.

She didn't know what she would do, no longer of any use to the resistance, to her people. She didn't want to think about it. It wasn't an option.

When she reached the top level, the fires were blazing again. She muttered a few hellos and returned various smiles with the island's inhabitants she'd come to know these last weeks. Tension hung in the air—they could read it in her eyes as she ascended the stone steps.

A few words were said, and she tried to shake the tension out of her limbs. No athletic feat would be successful if she was stiff as a board.

Nesseen braced a hand on her shoulder, looking into Ferrin's eyes with a mixture of concern and like she was holding something back, but all she said was, "Are you ready?"

Ferrin nodded briskly, trying for confidence and falling short.

"Well, up you go then. Remember—move like someone who gravity holds power over."

"Right," Ferrin said, recalling their conversation the previous day.

She climbed up the ladder to the starting platform, catching an odd and intense look from Galina as she did. The blonde woman's usual stony glare was tinged by something else today, something sad and wistful. She pulled the lever, and the beast of wood, metal, and leather sprung to life beside the cliff.

With one final deep breath, Ferrin squared her shoulders and stepped onto the first beam.

She twisted past the four spinning wheels in a blur, not letting a single spoke so much as graze her. Then she was off, darting over the hanging stairs as quickly as she dared. Beneath her weight, they creaked and swung. She nearly overshot the last one and found it swinging perilously fast, nearly taking her feet out from under her. She pinwheeled her arms and grabbed the chain. With a blind leap, she jumped onto the rotating log and darted across it, not letting her mind slow her down.

When she reached the vertical pole, she leapt onto it with a grace she hadn't known she possessed. Hand and foot, hand and foot, she clambered her way up, the holds becoming fewer and farther apart as she ascended. She gasped when her toes missed one and she slipped a few feet, catching herself by bear-hugging the wide pole. She exhaled shakily and regained her footing, palms blistering with her death-grip on the wooden surface. Up, up, up she went, the ground far below her as she climbed.

The next handhold towered above, she could see it, perhaps four feet out of her reach. How on earth was she to make it there?

She sucked in a breath, eyes locked on the notch in the wood, and lunged with all her might—

and missed.

The world tumbled beneath her and she gripped at the pole, sliding down, splinters ripping into her hands as she tried to slow her descent.

She caught herself halfway down.

Try again, she commanded herself, gritting her teeth. It took her a minute to get back to where she had been, and her hands were bleeding. She lunged again, waiting for the second where her momentum passed her by and gravity took hold again as she stretched towards the notch.

It never came.

But something else did.

It was faint, but there nonetheless. As she let go of the pole to jump, she felt a little flutter in the air just below her, and caught sight of a faint, silver shimmer beneath her palm.

She caught the handhold, the jolt of it jarring her shoulder as she hoisted herself further up. From there, she reached the minuscule platform at the top of the pole. As she stood, the height of it dizzied her. Below, the ground seemed to curve. She hurried to the swing that would take her across to the rock wall, her head spinning with what had just happened. She launched onto the platform and began climbing up the face of the cliff. With trembling arms and a thumping heart, she reached the top, stunned. The idol perched on the ledge stared knowingly at her. She grabbed ahold of its golden surface.

A mystical stirring went through her like a phantom storm, a distant wind, and she was whisked away to the ground in a flash.

Upon appearing on the solid ground, a pair of skinny arms were thrown around her as Lusia jumped for joy. "You did it! I knew you could!"

"Thanks," Ferrin said breathlessly with a half-smile of disbelief. A mixture of triumph and fresh doubt swirled and eddied in her gut as she thought of the silver shimmer and the warm updraft.

She had done it, yes.

But someone had helped her. That silvery magic wasn't hers, and never would be.

It was Galina's.

CHAPTER FIFTY

Nearly a week had passed since Soviel and Nimhe had laid eyes on each other in the tea garden.

A week of walking on eggshells. A week of trying to come up with something to get rid of her without implicating herself.

Soviel was *exhausted*.

In that last week, she'd found almost nothing of use for her purposes. The new obstacle of Nimhe's presence had landed her squarely at a dead end. She'd learned nothing useful, and was no closer to figuring out what Hadringston was up to in the locked room of his offices, what he was planning for the parcel of land he'd acquired on Galus.

But she *had* to get that information, and get it up north before Ash left for the Meddemara. It was information Ash needed.

But how in the name of the gods was she meant to find her way in there when Nimhe was on her tail most hours, and Samia needed something from her the rest?

She'd had a half-baked idea to accuse Nimhe of stealing from Samia, or helping herself to the manor's wine cellars, but it would be moot without proof. She'd have to plant evidence somehow, which was not something she had the time to do, between attending to Samia and watching Hadringston.

Wilcoe was right, being this deep under cover was exhausting.

Dinner rolled around, and her opportunity to slip away finally came. Nimhe was stationed in the corner, part of the dinner service. She wouldn't be allowed to leave for *hours*.

This was her chance.

"Samia, I'm still feeling a bit ill," she said delicately, placing a hand on her belly.

The duchess looked her up and down before grimacing. "You look positively green."

"I'm sorry," Soviel winced. "Might I be excused?"

"Go lay down, we will manage without you," Samia fluttered a wrist.

"Thank you," Soviel bowed her head before folding her napkin and excusing herself from the dinner table.

She walked to her room and slipped her copy of the stolen key from the slit within her mattress, and dropped it into her pocket. The clock struck eight, and she slipped out the door. He usually left dinner at eight - where was it he went?

She trod carefully down to his office, lest it turn out that that was where he spent this time of evening, but as he strode into her view of the office door, he just kept walking.

She frowned, watching him continue down the hallway.

She squeezed her hand into a fist. What was worth more, seeing where he was going, or finally getting into his desk?

She bit her lip as she watched him disappear into the hallway, and tore her gaze from his retreating figure. *No.* She had a plan here. It had taken her weeks to get this key. She needed to stick to her original plan.

Once she was sure the hallway was empty, she crept from her hiding place and unlocked the office door. Without making a sound, she slipped into the dark room. She continued deeper into the sanctum, until she reached his small, private office, to which she'd only recently acquired the key. She'd managed to get imprints of his keys when his personal assistant had visited a brothel in town earlier that week—a task that had deprived her of an entire night of sleep between following him, printing the keys, and bringing them to a locksmith, whom she'd had to pay a hefty fee to keep from asking too many questions.

The door unlocked and opened with a click, and she stepped inside. It was a small space compared to the rest of the rooms, most of the space taken up by the big desk full of drawers in the center. It had no opening windows, only a tiny square of glass, very high on the wall, to let in a speck of light from the outside world.

She fetched the second key from her dress and knelt by the desk, cracking open the first drawer. She went through the folders and files and folios, finding little of interest. Mostly numbers and money stuffs. The duke's holdings in different areas of the continent and the Meddemara.

Things she already knew.

Making quick and tidy work, she slid the papers back into place and worked on the next drawer. There, she found what she was looking for.

It was the recent deed and information about the wide parcel of land he'd bought on Galus, as well as several dozen indentures for miners and farmers. Several acres of farmland, for popava, presumably.

Spicerock mineral deposits found on Galus. Indicative of possible Aesterium ore veins.

She frowned, skimming the paper. Spicerock wasn't the most valuable stone out there. Not even the most valuable thing on Galus, if she was right.

What could he be using it for, in such huge quantities? She hadn't ever heard of Aesterium before.

She began copying down what she was seeing, careful to code it without losing the information.

After that, she began reading over the other details on the page. There was already an existing mine on the island but it had been shut down seventy years ago. It was being re-opened and updated by Hadringston.

The mine was deep into the lava fields, and was also prone to spouts of a strange natural gas that could cause anything from a painful rash to psychedelic hallucinations. Expensive precautions were needed to protect the workers.

She copied it all down, and moved on to the next sheet.

Finally, when she had as much as she could copy down and had stayed as long as she could risk, she shuffled everything back into order and locked the drawers, careful to be tidy and quiet as she retreated from the office.

The door locked behind her and she smoothed the fabric of her dress over her full pockets as she made her way out of the sanctum.

She had just stepped cautiously out the door and was about to turn to lock it when Nimhe appeared around the corner.

"Hello, Soviel."

For a second that felt like years, Soviel said nothing. She was still as a doe in the woods after hearing a branch snap, still as stone.

What do I do? The question ran on a loop over and over and over and over in her mind.

"I don't know why I'm surprised," Nimhe continued, crossing her arms over the deep blue maid's frock. "You're always cropping up exactly where I don't want you to be."

"The feeling is mutual," Soviel said, inhaling slowly through her nose as she glared at Nimhe.

"So, what's in your pockets there?" Nimhe waved a hand a Soviel's skirts. "Stolen maps of encampments? Soldier counts? Locations of the naval bases?"

Soviel shook her head, slow and silent. "I'll be gone at first light, please. If our friendship ever meant anything—"

Nimhe scoffed derisively. "Oh, please. Don't play the guileless girl to me. You might have everyone else fooled with your gentle dove routine, but you and I both know what a duplicitous little snake you really are. I'm not letting you get in my way again."

"Why are you here?" Soviel swallowed. Her heart hammered in her throat. Nimhe had everything to gain and very little to lose. If she was turned out of Bramblehall, she'd just slink back to whoever was pulling her strings, whether that was Nerena or one of the officers in Everness. Another thing Soviel had been hoping to learn.

It was Soviel who had *everything* to lose here, should Nimhe take action.

Nimhe ignored her question. "I mentioned to Bessa that you were looking peaked. She said she would check in on you after the evening meals are over. How do you imagine it will look when she finds you gone, and I confirm you were here, wandering around His Grace's things, in perfect health, no less?"

Soviel was silent.

"They'll search your rooms, of course," Nimhe continued. "I doubt they'll find silly trinkets."

Soviel looked at her. "Why, Nimhe? Our stories… they're similar. Both of our families were exiled, both of us are only a generation removed from total ruin. Why would you choose their side?"

Nimhe snorted. "You stupid fool." As she uncrossed her arms, Soviel saw the flash of metal, indicating a knife sheathed at her hip, partially hidden by the folds of her skirts. "You and I are nothing alike. Your parents fell back on a handsome estate. My parents live in a tiny flat in Kiarlgard. This was my best option, she offered me ev—" she cut off, cursing. "Never mind that. Just turn yourself over, make it easier on all of us. They'll catch you if you don't."

"*Who* offered you?" Soviel asked. "What do you want from me?"

"It doesn't matter! You can't win, you're completely surrounded here!" she snapped, drawing the knife from her hip with surprising alacrity. "Now put your hands—"

Soviel launched herself at her.

She was no fighter, but she took Nimhe by surprise, and they both went down. Rolling on the plush carpet, clawing at each other's faces, they scrapped.

Nimhe wasn't much bigger, but she was stronger. She flipped Soviel, and drew out her knife.

"Just *give up!*" Nimhe hissed. "Don't make me do—"

Nimhe didn't finish her thought, because Soviel lashed out with her power faster than she knew possible. She took ahold of the muscles in Nimhe's shoulders, arms, neck.

"You're not pulling a weapon on me again, Nimhe," she said softly as she began to very slightly, gently, restrict Nimhe's airway. Just enough to make her dizzy.

The girl made a few gasping sounds, straining and reddening as she surely grew lightheaded. She sat back on her heels, clambering up away from Soviel. Her eyes were wide with shock and betrayal, as if she hadn't been the one to draw a weapon first.

"You're right," Soviel said softly, standing up. She was breathing hard now. "I may not be a gentle dove. But you forget that some snakes asphyxiate their prey."

Nimhe's face was blushing pink, then red.

"I'm sorry it's come to this, but you chose wrong," she said. "*You* are the traitor."

Nimhe managed to regain control of her muscles for just long enough to raise her knife again. She lunged in closer, her knife now an inch from Soviel's bare throat. Everything slowed and Soviel could sense the paths of Nimhe's body relaying the message. *One flick of her wrist—*

Nimhe was fast.

Soviel was faster.

She felt the steel just nick the skin of her neck. With a twist of her hand, a horrible crack sounded and Nimhe's face went slack.

A second later, she dropped like a stone, falling to the ground in a heap.

Soviel clapped her hands over her mouth.

She dropped to her knees, hands shaking as she shook the girl's shoulder. Her neck was bent at an odd angle, her eyes fixed on something distant, open and unseeing.

"Nimhe—Nimhe—Wake up!"

There was no taking this back. No fixing her.

"Oh, gods, oh gods," Soviel wrung her hands together. She wasn't a killer. Not like this. That wasn't how her magic *worked*.

Blood roared in her ears as she stared wide-eyed at Nimhe. At Nimhe's *body*. Her heart was racing.

What have you done?

Everything blurred around her.

Nimhe was cold, unblinking, accusing.

Dead.

How on earth was she to frame this?

She'd *killed* her. Not some cruel soldier, not an assassin, not a suffering prisoner.

Nimhe.

The knife she'd been holding had clattered to the floor and skidded some feet away.

Get rid of the evidence.

Her hands continued shaking as she patted Nimhe down.

There was indeed a second steel dagger sheathed at her hip and a pistol at the other, accessible through slits in her folded skirts.

She needed to move her. But where? And how? How could she do it without being spotted?

Her breaths were coming fast, verging on panic, and only her years of training as a healer and a spy kept her from completely crumbling. She looked around, desperate for something that could help her move Nimhe's body, and found nothing.

"*Damn it!*" she whisper-screamed into her hands.

She could plant things in her room to make it look like she was a thief. But how to explain her absence? How to get rid of the body?

She could clear out all her things. Burn them. Rip apart her room so it looked like she'd left in the night. Plant one of her own stolen keys to sew suspicion. Perhaps make a few expensive trinkets go missing around the house.

Right. Right. A plan was forming.

She just needed to take her away before anyone found her and Nimhe's body outside of Hadringston's private offices. That was her priority. She just had to move her *for now*. Then, when all was quiet, she would sneak back out and figure out the rest. She could do that.

She took a deep breath and hoisted Nimhe over her shoulder. She only made it a few steps before her knees and back began to give out. A sob was lodged in her throat, threatening to break out and send her tumbling over the edge.

She tried again, and found it completely useless. Though Nimhe was no giant, Soviel couldn't carry her. She wasn't strong like Ash, couldn't hoist the girl like she was a sack of grain over her shoulder.

Finally, *desperately*, she settled for dragging Nimhe feet first across the floor. Every thud and scrape sent her stomach churning with revulsion. After a harrowing half-hour, she managed to pop out a side door onto the dim grounds, exhaling in relief when night air touched her face. Mercifully, she hadn't been spotted by any of the manor's staff or inhabitants. She dragged Nimhe behind the wood pile and fell to her knees a few feet away to heave up her guts. It was violent and painful, and her whole body shook.

She was sobbing by the time she found a spare horse blanket by the barn, wrapping it beneath the body as her chest constricted, her hands still trembling.

She found a shovel and dug a wide, shallow hole. She had twenty, maybe thirty minutes before Bessa came to check on her. She patted the dirt down over Nimhe's wrapped body and bowed over her knees, pleading and praying in apology to Lalana, squeezing her swollen eyes shut.

The moon was high over head when she stood and staggered back into the manor, eyes bleary and mind untethered. She wandered like a ghost to her room, silent and unseen.

She sunk into cold bathwater, not really feeling it, and scrubbed and scrubbed and scrubbed, begging the feeling of grime and oil and death to lift from her skin, from her soul.

But it wasn't enough.

It wasn't enough.

CHAPTER FIFTY-ONE

Ferrin sat at breakfast on the island's main level the morning following her successful trial. She was spooning porridge into her mouth, hardly tasting the stuff as she peered suspiciously across the room at Galina.

Why had she helped her?

Ferrin knew that she would have fallen to the rocks below had that little updraft of Galina's magic not buoyed her leap. That she would have failed.

What was she to do with this information?

No one else had seemed to notice, no one had batted an eye that she had… cheated. However unintentionally.

"Your second trial will happen in the next few days," Nesseen said, pulling Ferrin out of her thoughts.

"What is it?"

Nesseen just smiled.

"Fine then, keep your secrets," Ferrin griped, turning back to her porridge. "Has anyone, I mean anyone who's been initiated, like you, ever left the island before?"

Nesseen bristled at the sharp change in subject. "Only once."

"What happened? With the strange time-thing, how did that work?"

"It didn't, really," Nesseen said wearily, as if the question had sapped her energy. "When we swear ourselves to Vaiorka, we are binding our life force to the island. We sustain it, it sustains us. We cannot just leave once we go through initiation. We all chose this, as a permanent place. Typically, to leave would be to accept death. There are occasional exceptions, where an initiated can venture out to complete a task for the good of the island, but it is rare and controlled."

"Oh," said Ferrin.

"But a long time ago, there was one. A woman a little older than you. She came in the same time as Galina, and they were close friends. Sisters, if not by blood then by every other way that mattered. But she… she coveted power in a way I have never seen before. Not the power of throne rooms or battlefields or high temples. She sought knowledge of things long buried, the power of something forgotten deep inside the earth.

"She soaked up those dark magics from our oldest books, and found herself looking toward the horizon, to what she might achieve out there with the power she'd acquired in here," Nesseen said, glancing towards the horizon through the window overlooking the cliff.

"What happened? When she left?"

Nesseen turned her gaze back to Ferrin. "She performed an ancient ritual, one that severed her tie with the island without giving back the power and longevity it gave her. She *stole* it. When she left, it ripped a hole in the island's wards and nearly sent us into the void."

"And she just left?"

"She vanished out the hole in the sky. And it took all of us nearly entirely depleting our power to patch the rift. Some days, when the sun is very low, you can see the scar on the sky, just above the horizon to the north."

"Why? Why would she do something so disastrous?"

"No one knows," she shrugged. "And we don't know what she went on to do with her stolen power, either. If you really want to know more, you'd be much better off asking Galina."

Ferrin frowned. *Galina.* She'd have to add it to the list.

When Ferrin finally tracked her down, Galina was hauling hay into the goat barn, her long blonde braids were secured in a loop at the nape of her neck and tied with a leather cord to keep them out of the way. She must have been working hard, since she was sweating through her gray tunic and her sleeves were rolled up to her elbows.

Ferrin leaned on the frame of the barn door, perched on the threshold.

"Why did you do it?" she asked without preamble.

Galina straightened, her back still to Ferrin as she caught her breath. She dusted her hands off on the front of her trousers and turned around. "I haven't the slightest idea what you're on about."

"I've only seen *you* use that kind of magic."

Her brows knitted downward. "I don't know what you're talking about."

Ferrin pushed off the doorframe and walked into the room. "You've made it perfectly clear that you don't much like me." Her voice fell to a harsh whisper. "So why would you help me on my trial?"

Galina glanced to the side, as if scanning for lookers-on, before meeting Ferrin's eye. "I may not particularly like you, but if you do not succeed, it will be a long time until another comes along."

Ferrin frowned, taken aback at the sudden and sharp candor.

"But I won't be able to do it again. So don't get complacent," she added gruffly.

Ferrin considered. "Is it because you feel partly responsible for," she paused, realizing she had no idea what the woman's name was in Nesseen's story, "the one who left this place?"

Anger flashed hot and blazing in Galina's eyes. It was replaced quickly by hurt, guilt.

"Nesseen said you were close. Like sisters."

Galina sighed and sat down on the nearest hay bale. "You're not going to leave me alone until I tell you, are you?"

Ferrin shot her a faint smirk. "I have little else to do until someone assigns me a new chore. You could distract me from my next task of impending doom."

Galina rolled her eyes and snapped her fingers as she pointed at another bale of hay. "Sit."

Ferrin obliged, half-expecting to have needed to argue further.

"Lada and I arrived here at the same time, from the same place, about…" she counted arbitrarily on her fingers. "Four hundred years ago in your time, I would think.

"We were both young, and came from small villages in Southern Njorske. She had power beyond her years, incredible life magic. *Midaeri.* She could change a plant from seed to blossom with a twitch of her finger, even, at her strongest, revive dead animals. I myself was a wielder of fire, mostly specializing in heat currents."

Ferrin nodded, recalling the strong, warm updraft that had saved her from tumbling to the ground.

"We were both recruited by the Dionas and initiated. For years we trained and studied on the mainland. We were dedicated to the sacred duty. When she found out about this place," she gestured up and around them, "she was intrigued. And so was I.

"So, we found our way here with the guidance of one of the Elders. We took the tour. But, you see, you don't get access to the power, the knowledge, all of it, until you're initiated," Galina laughed hollowly. "I didn't much care for the idea of having to stay here forever, but Lada talked me into it. We underwent initiation here, and we were sworn in together. In the initiation, you are tethered to the island, you share your life force with it."

"Right."

"For a long time, she studied and practiced and learned, and even helped a few hopeful travelers like yourself when they strove for the answers to all of their worldly problems." She waved a flippant hand. "But Lada… she grew restless. She'd always had an ambitious streak far greater than anyone I ever knew. She wanted to see what she could do with this power in the outside world.

"She began spending hours and hours, days at a time, deep in the library, reading about the wards. She said she was researching the Doors, the portals across the world. But she became obsessed. She wanted to learn how to *make* Doors."

"And did she?"

Galina sighed and leaned back on her palms. "She wanted to create a Door in the island's wards, so she could come and go as she pleased. You see, Lada and I, though we were dear friends, we came from very different backgrounds. I was raised on a farm, a successful one," she added, picking at her nails. "But, a farm nonetheless. Lada grew up in a vast and opulent compound. I knew this from the beginning. What I did not know until later, was that she was raised in a family of zealots, devout followers of an ancient god."

"What god?" Ferrin asked, tensing.

"He is so old, even I do not know his name, nor did Nesseen."

"And what was he the god of?" Ferrin asked, picturing some earlier, primitive version of *Saolath* the trickster or *Bastara* the overseer of hell.

Galina gave a joyless, wry smile. "Everything."

"*Everything*?" Ferrin repeated. "What does that mean?"

"From what we've gathered, this cult followed only the First God. He who walked this land long before any of our other deities. He who created our gods," Galina explained, drawing one knee up to her chest. She linked her arms around it, cradling her shin and resting her chin atop her knee. "I never knew this about Lada's past until it began *consuming* her. Something she learned, some connection she made…" she shook her head. "It sparked this will in her, this hunger to go back to the outside world and raise glory in his name."

"Well… whatever this nameless god was, she couldn't have been successful, because no one out there is worshipping him," Ferrin said, kicking her legs lazily against the side of the hay bale.

"Maybe," Galina agreed. "But when Lada left, she tore a hole in our wards so deep it nearly sucked this whole island into oblivion. I don't know what her plan was, really, or where she sought to end up. Just that she had this look of crazed determination on her face as she completed the final ritual and disappeared from the top level of the island. Then the sky started bleeding. *Bleeding.* It was years ago, but I remember it like it was yesterday. She stole something, too—Nesseen wouldn't tell me at the time, but later I found out, it was an ancient chalice. Enchanted."

The haunting image formed in Ferrin's mind, this faceless girl tearing a hole through the world in a rage of self-righteous fury.

Again, she thought back to the story of the woman who walked through the void and made a son, and gave her son the world.

CHAPTER FIFTY-TWO

S oviel did not sleep a single minute that night. She'd spent half the night clearing out Nimhe's small room, and the other half she'd spent going mad. She paced her floor until the light of dawn came creeping in, stark and menacing as it slowly illuminated her room.

Her eyes were swollen and sore, her skin was dry and raw from being scrubbed and soaped over and over and over. She'd cut her nails short to the point of bleeding because she *knew* there was still dirt and death beneath them.

She had to act this morning, before anyone else noticed Nimhe's absence. She had to get rid of her things, plant the evidence. Then she had to write out her findings and leave her letter in the drop spot for whenever Ash or Eiran could next fetch it.

There was too much to do. She had to keep it together. After today, she could relax a bit. She just had to *fix* everything first. She couldn't unravel.

"Lady Soviel," the voice came accompanied by a soft knock on the door. It was Bessa. "Are you feeling any better? Shall I tell Her Grace you won't be able to attend her today?"

"No, Bessa, I'm almost ready!" she called. She flung on the rest of her clothing and pulled her hair into a simple bun. Samia might notice and comment on her tired appearance, so she borrowed a bit of energy from the small tea-tree she kept by the window before walking out the door.

Running through exactly how she was going to make it out to the woods unseen to do all she needed to, she walked to the duchess's rooms, barely paying attention to the hallway before her. She'd need to maintain her appearances around the manor all day, and still make time to go out to the woods and find a more permanent solution for Nimhe's body and her things. She cringed at the idea. She wasn't a killer. Not like this.

She knew Nimhe would have killed *her*, would have exposed her and had her jailed, or worse. But couldn't she have incapacitated her some other way? Knocked her out, or frozen her movements?

She'd never so horribly misused her power. She hated it. Hated how it felt. Hated *herself* for it. No amount of bathing and scrubbing could take the crawling sensation from her skin. It wasn't supposed to be like this.

Dressing Samia was an event that occurred in a blur. She didn't feel the fabric that skimmed over her palms, or smell the perfume spritzed liberally onto the duchess's skin, and she hardly took notice of the cloud of white that sprung to the air when she accidentally dropped the tin of hair powder.

"You're clumsy today," Lucelle noted lazily.

"Didn't sleep well," Soviel said apologetically.

When breakfast was through, she tore off to the servant's lodging, and crept back into Nimhe's room and got to work. The minutes she had to get it done were precious few, as it was a markedly busy day for the duchess and her entourage.

She tore open the dresser she'd emptied the night before, and scattered a few coins, a broach she'd swiped from Erina a few days ago, one of her own pearl hairpins, and a pendant of Tavara's she'd found between the worn cobblestones of the promenade some weeks ago and never gotten around to giving back to her. Then, she slit the mattress and shoved the stolen keys inside, pulling the sheet halfway over the cut.

Her hands were shaking yet again. Nimhe was not dead a full day, and Soviel was already rifling through her drawers and framing her for petty crimes. She felt sick, thinking of the bag of Nimhe's belongings currently shoved under her own bed, waiting to be disposed of after dark.

When she was finished, she ran all the way to the kitchen, and rattled off Samia's specific demands to the cook before swiping a strong cup of coffee for herself and heading back to the duchess's chambers. Thinking through what was on the agenda for the day, a pit of dread opened inside her. There was so much to do. She wouldn't be able to start her task in the woods until long after dark.

It seemed tonight would be another sleepless night.

The day passed quickly. Servants whispered about the maid who hadn't shown up for morning roll. Lucelle complained of her missing earrings. An assistant chef barked at the kitchen maids over the incorrect quantity of expensive Bourjon wines in the cellar.

Though her plan was working, Soviel didn't feel triumphant.

Dinner finished and the housekeeper went to look in on Nimhe's rooms. Soviel didn't wait around to hear what they said. Her time was limited.

It was nearly eleven o'clock by the time Samia dismissed the lot of them for the evening. She'd had them select her another pair of lacy underpinnings to impress Hadringston, and shooed them all away once she was dressed.

Soviel wasted no time in fetching the bag of Nimhe's things, as well as the rest of the pilfered items, and hiking far into the woods with them. She spent time gathering kindling and lighting a fire, dreading the task that came next: digging up Nimhe's body from the shallow grave and finding a more permanent resting place.

Most of the items burned, and the pieces that didn't, she buried, kicking dirt and leaves over the black stain on the ground.

First light wasn't far off when she finally set about digging up Nimhe. Soviel left her wrapped, knowing that seeing her face would be more than she could handle, especially on two nights without sleep. She had only dug a few scoops of dirt when a rustle in the bushes caught her off guard.

She spun, wide-eyed, shovel raised and on the verge of full-blown panic, when she found Ash staring back at her. Soviel blinked, unsure if what she was seeing was real, or if she had suffered some sort of mental break.

"Ash?" She lowered the shovel slowly, still breathing as hard as a rabbit caught in a snare.

"Hey, are you alright?" Ash asked apprehensively as she looked from Soviel's face to the shovel and back again.

"What are you doing here?" Soviel asked, trying to calm her shaking hands.

"It's the end of the week. I'm already a day late in fetching your correspondence."

"Oh. *Oh*." Soviel nodded repeatedly, dropping the shovel and reaching into her pocket for the letter.

"Helene says I'm to extract you, that Alemont has called for your return… what are you doing out here?"

Soviel shook her head. "No. No. I can't."

If she left now, if she cut her losses, then Nimhe was cooling in the ground for *nothing*. She wouldn't let that happen.

Ash stared at her with bewilderment. "Why not?"

"I need your help with something," Soviel whispered, squeezing her eyes shut.

"What is it?"

"I need you to drop… *her*… over the side of your boat when you reach deep water," she said, something fracturing deep inside her chest.

Ash's eyes widened, clearly not expecting this. "Soviel, wait. What happened?"

Soviel bit down on her bottom lip, frozen as it all replayed in her mind. She shook her head and squeezed her eyes shut again. The tears she'd been holding back for two days finally burned their way out.

"I was almost compromised. I don't know how I did it. She's dead. I killed her. She pulled out a knife and I don't know, I just—she just dropped. She's dead. She's dead."

Ash looked past her at the partially buried, wrapped figure.

"Oh. Alright," Ash said in a slow, gentle tone, as if she was calming a frightened child. "We can deal with this. Do you have something to weigh down the body?"

Soviel shook her head.

"That's fine, we can find something. Just take a deep breath."

Soviel nodded, swallowing and clasping her hands together.

"Here. I have some ropes, we'll tie a few rocks into the blanket with… her."

Soviel nodded again, feeling as if she was unable to do anything else with herself.

"We have to move her down to the ship. Can you help me do that?"

With some effort, Soviel and Ash were able to carry Nimhe's body down the hill to the beach. When they set her into the boat, Soviel visibly flinched at the *thud* her body made.

"Alright. Go and bring me some stones from the tide-line," Ash instructed.

Stiff as an automaton, Soviel went to fetch some stones.

Ash took a deep breath, steeling herself for whatever horror lay under the woolen horse blanket. She reached down and unbuckled the fabric, peeling it back.

She didn't recognize the girl. She had red hair, freckles aplenty. She looked close to Ash's age. Young. Some dirt had fallen into the blanket and smudged on her pale skin, which looked devoid of wounds. Her neck was clean *snapped*.

Ash covered the girl back over. She pulled out the sail-repair kit she had stowed in her satchel as Soviel returned, holding a pile of stones in the fabric of her skirts.

"Perfect," she said evenly. "Leave those and bring back some more, I'll sew them in with her."

"Where's your crew?" asked Soviel.

"Came alone. Toscan's been holed up and Rorin had other duties to attend to."

"Is that safe?"

Ash lifted a shoulder as she threaded the needle. "Go on, we'll need more stones if this is going to work."

Ash began the task of distributing stones throughout the blanket, placing some in the girl's pockets as well. Soviel returned with some more stones and watched with hollow eyes as Ash finished the task and sewed them in.

It wasn't the first time she'd done this.

Once, in the early months of her tenure on the *Gravedigger*, Zare had tasked her with removing the evidence of the beginnings of an attempted mutiny. Three men had questioned his leadership, enough that they were willing to call in a vote. He'd invited them into his quarters for tea, and then dispatched them. Ash had stumbled upon it, and he'd simply told her to fetch a few cannonballs from the battery and to get to work on the one closest to the door.

She'd never said a word of it to anyone. The next day, when people questioned the mens' absence and Zare spun some silver-barbed lie about desertion, she'd corroborated his story, the look on his face telling her she'd better if she didn't want to be next.

She finished the seam and tied off the thick sail thread, looking up at Soviel, who seemed far away and unreachable in her shock.

"Pass me some rope?" she said, hoping the task would help ground her.

Soviel obliged. She seemed frantic in a way Ash had never seen her. Rattled.

She tied the rope snug around the shroud, holding everything in place. "Right, let's get her up into the boat," Ash instructed. "Sun'll be up soon."

Finally, it was done. Ash perched at the side of the boat, boots in the damp sand of the shoreline. "Please come back with me."

Soviel shook her head, her face taut and drawn.

"This is killing you. You look like you haven't slept in days. Just… You've done enough here. You've helped *so* much."

"And that's why I have to stay. I am *this* close to being formally invited to go to Larais with them, Ash. Bourjony's Royal Court."

"Major Wilcoe said—"

"Helene will not stop me."

"Sov," Ash scolded. "It's dangerous."

"We're in a *war*. And we have been blind to our enemy for years now. Someone has to do it."

But why does it have to be you? Ash didn't say. "How will you even communicate what you learn?"

"I'll find a way. I won't be gone long, just a few weeks. Until I find what I need."

"Which is?"

"Anything about their king. We know nothing about him, and it's cost us greatly. And besides… if I quit now, I killed Nimhe for nothing."

Ash could see the tempest of guilt roiling inside her.

"Soviel…"

"Just… give Wilcoe my correspondence and tell her I'll be back soon, alright?"

Ash squeezed her eyes shut. "Fine. But be. Careful."

"I will," Soviel nodded. "I swear."

The two girls embraced and Ash shoved her boat out into the sea. When she was far beyond the shallows, she heaved the dead girl over the side, and watched her disappear into the dark waters below.

Soviel managed to rest for two hours that morning before rising to attend Samia. It had taken two knuckles of whiskey to calm herself down enough to sleep, along with drawing a bit more energy from her succulents.

She awoke feeling worse than she'd felt in years, as if the two sleepless nights were finally catching up with her. She dressed and powdered her face, dabbing a bit of rouge on her lips and cheeks in the hopes that it would keep her from looking too ghastly. She fluffed her hair and arranged it in a braided pattern with a few wayward strands left artfully astray to frame her face. Finally, she completed her appearance with a pair of pearl earrings and a lace ribbon tied around her throat.

Samia was already up for the day when Soviel arrived. She was flitting about the room in her shift, stays and stockings, searching for some specific hat she *must* wear that day.

"It's much too hot out today," Lucelle said from where she lounged on the chais. "We should have the servants fan us in the garden with fronds all day."

"That is why I am looking for my damned sun hat!" Samia clenched her fists. "Jorde, have you seen my linen chemise dress?"

"You sent it for Theo to alter last week. To take the sleeves up. Remember?" Jorde said gently.

"I wanted to wear it today," Samia whined.

"Shall I have a servant go down to his shop and fetch it?" Soviel asked.

"I suppose," Samia shrugged. "And my sapphire broach?"

"I don't see it," Erina said from the jewelry box. "Did you have it sent out?"

"No, I hardly ever wear the damn thing," Samia sniped. "It should *be* there."

"It's missing?" Soviel asked, false concern in her voice.

"Now that you mention it, I've had a few jewels go missing as well," Erina said.

"Same here," Soviel said.

"Actually, so have I," Jorde scrunched her nose in thought. "That's odd."

"What kind of things?"

"Just a pair of gold earrings," Jorde said. "Thought I had misplaced them, but it's been days. I've gone through everything, and they're nowhere."

"Perhaps we have a little thief somewhere in the estate," Lucelle drawled. "One of those new servants maybe."

Soviel's heart began racing. If she'd set everything up properly, they'd reach the conclusion on their own, without her prodding them further.

"I heard one of them eloped with a priest from town," Lucelle continued, picking her nails.

"Really?" Jorde gasped. "That red-headed one? I heard she packed and left and no one knows why."

"A servant left?" Soviel asked, keeping her tone cool.

"I will have Bessa look into it," Samia said. "If some little ungrateful brat stole my broach, I shall be very vexed."

Soviel's stomach churned.

Half the items in question were hidden inside Nimhe's old room. The other half were sewn into her shroud, waiting to be forgotten at the bottom of the cold sea.

She would have seen me hanged, Soviel reminded herself. It didn't help much.

That afternoon, Bessa and the head butler approached Samia in the garden and whispered in her ear something Soviel couldn't make out. When they left, Jorde asked Samia about it.

"The missing maid, they said they searched her rooms. They found a few pieces of jewelry and two keys she had stolen. They're finding out what they go to now," Samia informed them all.

"How dreadful," Erina said, sounding only slightly less bored than usual.

"I suppose some people are just greedy like that," Samia huffed.

Soviel had to keep herself from clenching her fists.

"Well, since you are all here, I suppose there is much for us to discuss," Samia said, setting down her tea. "In a week's time, His Grace and I will be moving to our new townhouse in Larais for the fall and winter. He has business there, and I am personally looking forward to a change of scenery. As I have discussed before, you've all been invited, but I know some of you have prior engagements." She cut a glance to Jorde.

"Yes, Samia," Jorde nodded. "I'm pleased to announce that I've been invited to continue my studies at the University of Khalim. I begin my research term next month."

"Congratulations," Erina said, squeezing Jorde's shoulder. "That's amazing."

"Hmph," grunted Samia, who didn't seem nearly as pleased. "I suppose that is impressive, though I'll miss you, Jorde."

"Thank you, all of you. It's been such a pleasure to live and work with you all," she said, and it sounded like she actually meant it.

"And I," Lucelle said, drawing a soft hand from her pocket, "will be coming with you only a short way. I'm engaged to marry Lord Major Haldeaz of Ravenne. I'll be moving to his countryside estate along the riviera."

"Oh, how lovely!" Samia clapped. "I hear his estate is one of the most beautiful. He presides over a vineyard, no?"

"That is correct," Lucelle said with a proud smile.

"Congratulations," Tavara grinned.

"And the rest of you?" Samia asked hopefully.

"I'll be there," Erina said, her enthusiasm all but negligible.

"I do love Bourjony's climate," Tavara flicked a lock of glossy black hair over her shoulder.

"Splendid!" Samia threw one arm around Tavara's shoulders and turned to Soviel. "And you, Soviel?"

Soviel let a bright smile spread over her face, slow as the rising sun. "I would love to come to Larais."

Samia threw her other arm around Soviel's shoulder. "Oh, we're going to have a wonderful time in the city."

Soviel beamed as she nodded along to ideas of complementary outfits, teas on the royal green, balls and parties and luncheons among the nobility, all the while planning out just how she was going to work her way into the Bourjon court and learn each and every secret so she could destroy them.

CHAPTER FIFTY-THREE

Still rattled by her conversation with Galina, Ferrin went about her days waiting for her next challenge to be issued. Though Vaiorka was timeless, it certainly seemed like it was moving into the wet season. That morning was the fourth in a row that she awoke to insistent rain and a gray sky.

She climbed out of bed and dressed for the day, pulling a kidskin cloak over her head to ward off some of the cold rain. The trek up the cliff took her twice as long, and by the time she reached the top, her boots were soaked through, leaving her stockings wet around her toes.

"Yuck," she complained, kicking her feet.

She looked around and found the top level to be completely empty. Unless she had mistakenly risen early because of the lack of sun today, it looked like everyone had shirked their morning duties.

"Nesseen?" Ferrin knocked on the doorframe of the barn, poking her head in. No sign of anyone.

One of the goats bleated at her.

"That's enough out of you," she said, shooting a stern look at the goat.

She withdrew from the barn and surveyed the land, searching for some sign of human activity.

"Hello?"

The rain was coming down even harder now, and lightning cracked in the distance. She saw no one anywhere.

"What in the hell…" she muttered to herself as she set off toward the other end of the level. Was there something going on today she wasn't aware of? It wasn't as if she'd been given a

Vaiorkan Calendar of Events for the year of Never and the time of Always. *This place is stranger and stranger every day*, she thought.

She continued her search, her feeling of foreboding growing stronger and stronger.

"Galina?" she called. "Lusia?"

Nothing.

She stood still, unsure of what exactly she was meant to do in a situation like this.

"Might as well look up top," she sighed to herself, resolving to climb to the next level.

She'd never been to the fourth tier, but when she reached it, she recognized it from one of her dreams. The two pillars of stone that stood tall and uneven in its center, the spiral of tiles.

But again, there was no one here. No one worshipping, no one sweeping the floors or polishing the stones, or doing whatever it was they did at the island's peak. Something about the place emitted an eery, quiet energy despite the pattering of the rain. She was about to return to the lower levels when she heard a crash.

She whipped around, expecting to find one of the Vaiorkans had knocked over a rack of brooms or something, but there was nothing.

"Hello?" she called, her anxiety growing. "Who's there?"

It was then that a horrible, shrieking roar pierced the air.

It came from the sky—far off, but close enough that she could make out the shape of a great, winged *something* coming toward her, tearing through the sky, wingbeats loud as thunderclaps.

"Ferrin! Look out!" Lusia's voice came from behind her just as the beast made landfall, its feathered body blue-gray, the color of storms.

Ferrin ducked behind one of the stone pillars and picked up the first thing her hand found—a discarded sword, heavy and old, and about the length of her leg. She hoped it was still sharp.

"Lusia, get behind me!" she shouted when she saw the younger girl, small and wet and unarmed, shivering in the rain. Her eyes, wide with terror, were fixed on the creature.

"It's happening again," Lusia said in a small voice as she fell in behind Ferrin in the shadow of the stone pillar.

"What? Where is everyone?"

"Down on the beach, repairing the wards."

"Well, I *don't* think it's working!" Ferrin yelled sardonically over the storm. "What is that?"

"Another creature. From the Nothing. Sometimes the bandage over the sky-scar weakens, and they slip through. Just be glad it isn't one of the fire ones," Lusia said with a shudder. "Look out, it's coming back!"

The creature had indeed circled around, and Ferrin saw that its eyes were crackling with blue sparks. Lightning.

"You said it's not a 'fire one', is it related to the weather?"

"Yes!"

"What did you do to get rid of it last time?" Ferrin shouted, white-knuckling the sword she'd picked up.

"We hid! It burned down one of the barns. And finally when the ward was repaired, it was pulled back through the sky!"

Ferrin shook her head. How long would it take to repair the failing ward?

As it circled back toward them, the creature dove, its bull-shaped head wide and horned as it swooped low. Lower than their level—down to the barn. It soared up a second later, the bleating goat caught in its sharp talons.

"Oh, no, no, no," Lusia moaned, squeezing her eyes shut in horror. "Poor Lassie."

Ferrin clenched her jaw as the creature circled around. It seemed to have lost interest in them for now; it had landed across the level, and was ripping apart poor Lassie for its meal.

"Poor thing," Ferrin gulped as she caught sight of its razor-sharp beak. "We need to get out of here."

"Yes," Lusia nodded emphatically. "But, it's blocking us from the stairs."

"Damnit."

"We could climb—" Just then, the thing took off again, blood coating its beak and sharp talons as its wings beat a heavy, thunderous rhythm.

"Go, go, go!" Ferrin urged Lusia ahead of her, glancing frantically over her shoulder as the beast circled around, letting out a hideous, piercing cry.

They made it down to the next level on shaky legs. Ferrin's heart was in her throat, beating wildly, the muscles of her thighs tingling with urgency as they scanned the area. It hadn't landed there.

A cry from below went up.

The rest of the Vaiorkans were halfway up the stair between the lowest levels. The creature had spotted them.

"Oh, shit," Ferrin swore, clutching her sword. "Hey! Go back down!" she belted out over the wind.

They couldn't hear her over the building storm.

"Run!" she shouted again with all of her strength.

"They won't make it on time," Lusia said, terror on her face. "Not in this storm."

"We need to distract it, come on." Ferrin grabbed Lusia's hand and led her to the barn.

She ripped open the office drawers and cabinets, searching. "What are you looking for?"

"This!" She plucked up the bottle of spare lamp oil and shook it. "Find me something to make fire with."

Lusia pulled a very old-fashioned looking contraption from the desktop, a little metal box with two rocks. Ferrin had seen such contraptions before, albeit much newer, sleeker ones.

"I have *no* idea how to use that, do you?" Ferrin asked.

"Yes, what should I light?"

"Uh—" she looked around, scouring the room for something dry and flammable. She settled on a sheet of crumpled paper and handed it to Lusia. "Here. Roll it up and set the end alight. Protect it from the wind and follow me."

They got the flame going and Ferrin uncorked the lamp oil.

"Here!" Lusia said, thrusting the flaming paper in her direction.

She took it gingerly, stuffed the un-burning end in the bottle neck and took aim.

She hurled the bottle at the creature. It twisted in the air, end over end before shattering against its chest, exploding and spreading in an angry, blazing conflagration.

The creature was unharmed—and angry. It turned and roared, taking its glowering eyes off the stair and turning to Ferrin.

"Get back inside, Lus."

"What? No—"

"Get inside!"

The girl obeyed. Ferrin steadied herself, facing off as the beast closed in impossibly fast. As it dove for her, she could see the sparking energy in its eyes, smell the death on its horrible breath. She hurled out of the way at the last second, swiping out with her blade as she did. It connected with a hard, impervious surface. Her hand and wrist stung from the fruitless impact.

"Shit." She clutched her throbbing arm as the creature soared off, waiting for it to rebound. "It's armored," she said to herself.

"Ferrin!" Lusia called.

Ferrin whipped around to look at where Lusia was pointing. The creature's horns had become wreathed in lightning—the crackling strands of it like angry, vibrant brambles as it perched atop the library, the stone roof cracking beneath its weight.

"Oh, no," she mumbled, readying her sword again.

What would happen if she *did* manage to stab it? Would it electrify her? Would she be burned the way lightning strike victims were?

It dove for her again, claws outstretched and charged with lightning.

She screamed as it arced over her, a pillar of blue lightning skimming off its talons and connecting with her sword.

She could feel it, the power of that crackling lightning, of a thousand storms pouring into the metal of the sword. She could feel the metal of her ring warming. The hair on her arms and the back of her neck stood to attention, even her skin buzzed in response to the pure energy. She did not let go as it crackled through her veins, not burning, but certainly not without pain. She held the sword still, clutched above her head and extended toward the creature, groaning with the determination and exertion.

The connection broke, but the sword crackled and sparked, as if the creature's blast had managed to somehow invigorate it with the essence of a storm.

"Get off! Of this! Island!" Ferrin yelled, her voice straining with the effort as she thrust the sword up and out toward the creature. A bolt of lightning stabbed beyond the blade's reach, straight to the creature's heart.

There was a mind-bending howl followed by a deafening crash. The entire sky went blindingly white, impossibly bright for a split second.

When it cleared, the storm was gone, and so was the creature. Below, a cheer went up from the beach, distant but clear. They must have fixed the wards.

Ferrin dropped the sword, which was still crackling with energy. She sank to the ground, gasping for breath.

Tentatively, Lusia crept out of the barn. "Ferrin? Are you alright?"

"I—yeah," she said, sitting back on her heels as she looked from the sword to Lusia. "Did you see that?"

The girl nodded, the strands of her curly black hair sticking to her forehead.

"I'm not certain, but I think that might have been your second trial."

By the time the elder Vaiorkans made it up the cliff, Ferrin's heartbeat had returned to an almost normal pace. She knelt down to pick up the discarded sword, and examined the blade. It was somewhat charred, but when she wiped at the blackened dust, the blade underneath gleamed. Where her ring brushed the metal, it sparked weakly.

"That was *astounding*," Lusia said. "How did you know to do that?"

Ferrin shook her head, mystified. "I don't know how that just happened," she admitted.

Galina was frowning beside Nesseen as the two of them approached the charred ground where Ferrin and Lusia stood.

"You called it away from us," Nesseen said. "Thank you."

"It would have picked you off the cliff one by one," Ferrin said.

"These things slip through the gap in the wards every once in a while," Nesseen explained.

"You say that like it's a mouse who found its way into a drafty pantry," Galina snapped. "Let me see that." She reached for Ferrin's sword.

Ferrin handed it over, but Galina immediately winced and dropped it. *"OW!"*

"What is it?"

"The sword shocked me!" She showed them her palm, red and raw as if burned on a hot stove.

"That's odd," Ferrin frowned.

Nesseen stooped to pick up the blade and halted with her hand an inch from its hilt.

"Ferrin, would you please pick up the sword?"

"What? Why?"

"I want to see something."

Ferrin obliged and bent to retrieve the sword. She felt the crackle of energy in her hand, but it did not burn her.

"Interesting." Nesseen nodded.

"I don't understand."

"Me either," Lusia chimed in.

"Gregor would know more about this, with all of his studies on object linking," Galina suggested.

"He would indeed," Nesseen agreed. "You'll have to chat with him after your next trial."

"My next—when?"

"Soon."

As if this day hasn't been cryptic enough, Ferrin thought. She stuck the sword into the ground and as she did, she caught Lusia gazing intently at it, a calculating, curious expression contorting her young face.

CHAPTER FIFTY-FOUR

Ash returned to Port Galan just before noon and tied off her borrowed boat. She trudged straight through the encampment to Major Wilcoe's office, where the major appeared to have fallen asleep with her head on her desk.

"Where is she?" Helene asked, stifling a yawn as she leaned to the side to look into the hallway, as if Soviel might just be hiding behind Ash.

"She refused to come," Ash reported.

"And you *let* her?" Wilcoe shot out of her chair.

"There were… complications."

"What *sort* of complications?"

"I'll put it all in my report," she said, turning to leave.

"You are not dismissed yet," Wilcoe snapped.

Ash paused in the doorway and turned to face the major.

"Sit," the major ordered, gesturing to the chair before her desk as she sat back down. "I have a few things to go over with you before you ship out."

Ash nodded, too exhausted to argue, and slid into the chair.

"General Ashwife has officially requested you go south with the army, and provide naval support and scouting runs in Kalassa."

Ash stiffened.

"I know you had planned to head further south and harass Bourjony's southern fleet, among other things, but unfortunately, he far outranks me, and there's nothing I can do to change his mind."

"What about Neb? She signed off on my original mission." Ash was angry and frustrated. So much was riding on her completing this part of the plan, if she *couldn't* get permission…

"Unfortunately, Neb's jurisdiction is limited to harbor patrol and the fort's defense. Another general would have to put in a request for you."

Ash sat quietly for a moment, then said, "Kenrose signed off on it, too."

Helene looked at her with surprise. "General Kenrose, of Avaree?"

"Yeah," Ash replied casually, her heart racing. "He signed off on it weeks ago; I thought he'd sent you something about it."

"I'll have to check with the post. I've had so many reports coming in, it's been a veritable storm of paperwork," she said.

"It should have arrived by now," Ash frowned, heat creeping into her face.

"Well, I'll keep my eye out for it. Either way, prepare to move out soon."

"Yes, ma'am. I also wanted to ask about the possibility of loading *The Brisk II* into a larger vessel as a launch, so it could be used for side-missions when the main ship is too big for certain things."

"If I am not mistaken, Toscan has been working on just such a thing. You ought to check in with him, he's been hiding out in his workshop ever since… well." Wilcoe shrugged sympathetically.

Ash winced. However indirectly, she felt at least partly at fault for Toscan's brother's death at Zare's hands. "I will."

*   *   *

Ferrin tossed and turned fitfully that night, unable to get the shriek of the creature out of her head. She couldn't stop seeing it's huge talons coming at her, couldn't stop feeling the crackling lightning arcing off its body into her sword, into her hand.

When she did at last drift off, she jerked awake only to find herself in a familiar dream. She was not in Gwelie's windswept village, nor in memories of Vaiorka. Ferrin found herself laying on a puffy cloud once again, with Arabella sitting before her, clad in the same plain, gray clothing as the first time she'd met her here.

"Mum?" She sat up, rubbing the sleep from her eyes.

"Hello, Ferrin," Arabella said, uncrossing her legs and stretching one of them out in front of her.

"Are you really here?" she asked.

"Yes, my little bird. I'm really here," she said with a sad smile.

"What is it?"

Arabella released some of the tension in her face and blew out a breath. "I've been trying to reach you, but the island makes it quite difficult."

"Yeah, the ring doesn't work here, either," Ferrin said glumly.

Her mother laughed. "No, it might have made climbing that ladder up the cliffs much easier if it did."

"Ladder?" Ferrin frowned.

"The first challenge, the physical one."

Ferrin groaned. "You call that death trap a *ladder*?"

"A few different ladders. The tests, I'm told, are all a little different for everyone. I did not have the years of experience climbing riggings that you do. Perhaps the island adjusted accordingly."

"My first trial would have killed me if Nesseen hadn't slowed my fall and then healed my head."

Arabella reached out a hand and stroked the side of her daughter's head. "But you were able to complete it?"

Ferrin swallowed and nodded, choosing not to tell her about Galina's unsolicited aid.

"I did. And my second one just today."

Arabella's face broke out into a beaming grin. "That's wonderful. You're almost done then?"

"I don't know," she said, crossing her arms. "It isn't so easily laid out. Who knows what will come next?"

"You'll complete them. I know you will."

Ferrin crossed her arms. "How did you know I spent all those years with the pirates?"

Her mother dropped her hand. "I've kept watch over both you and Rhi. From a distance"

"How distant?"

Arabella pursed her lips. "You know Henrik was trying to have me killed. I had to disappear."

"Too distant to step in when Rhi was slowly poisoning himself? Or when your husband started tearing apart the country?"

Ferrin's temper grew as Arabella fixed her with a patient, patronizing expression, as if she were a child throwing a fit.

"I couldn't risk revealing myself."

Ferrin laughed. "But you could've done something." She gestured at the dreamscape around them. "Couldn't you have contacted Alick? I'm sure the two of you were close enough for you to get his attention in here," she snapped.

Arabella didn't flinch.

"I know you're upset about finding out everything this way. But it was too important to risk."

"Don't talk to me like I'm being irrational." She clenched her hands into fists at her sides.

"We don't have a lot of time. Your third trial is going to be the hardest. I never made it that far. But it will test you in every way possible. Are you prepared for that?"

Ferrin's temper iced over. She didn't even know who this woman was anymore. Maybe that's what all those years of being married to someone she hated did to her. Sanded off all the caring, human parts until she was driven by one goal and one goal only.

"Mum," Ferrin sighed.

"Are you prepared?" Arabella repeated.

She squeezed her eyes shut, trying to force back the tears that threatened to spill. "I hope so."

"I believe in you. All those years I spent with Henrik, I knew it was going to be alright because my children were destined for greatness." Arabella leaned in and wrapped Ferrin in her arms. "Everything is depending on you, my little bird. I know you will succeed."

*   *   *

After catching an hour of sleep, loading up on the remnants of the communal breakfast (eggs and bread, cold by the time she got there), Ash headed down to Toscan's workshop deep in the manor basement. She took with her a thermos of coffee, and the ring she'd stolen from General Kenrose almost two months before.

She knocked on the door for a solid minute before he opened it, looking tired and thinner than usual. His glasses slid down his nose and his hair was a mess. Stubble clung to his chin. There was steam in the air and tar stains on his hands.

"Ash," he said. "What is it?"

"Can I come in?" she asked, holding up the coffee thermos in offering.

"By all means," he stepped aside. "What brings you here?"

"I did something bad," she blurted as soon as the door shut. "But I'm about to do something worse."

He frowned. "Bad as in, insulted a relative, or bad as in *can you help me hide the body*?"

"What? Neither," Ash said, almost too quickly as she recalled the recent incident with Soviel. "Do you remember the flighty general from Avaree?"

"Of course," Toscan said slowly, accepting the thermos.

"I stole his seal ring."

"*What*?"

"Well, one of them. He had copies made, which is *illegal*, mind you, and I pocketed one. Weeks ago. And just now, Wilcoe told me General Ashwife was changing my mission, and I told her Kenrose's request had overruled it, and now I have to forge a letter and sneak it into Helene's mailbox."

"Oh. That is complicated," Toscan said matter-of-factly, sipping the lukewarm coffee. He scrubbed his fingers through his hair and set down the thermos. "You're still heading south, going after the cetamaris?"

"Yes."

"Bring me," he said.

"Write yourself into Kenrose's request letter, and you're in."

"Done," Toscan agreed.

"And… Major said she thought you were working on a mechanism to load and unload *The Brisk II* onto a larger vessel, so it could be used in tandem?"

"Yes, I am, actually." He picked up the coffee again and turned. "Follow me."

He led her down a long hall that cut in between piles of lumber, odd metal gears, a wire basket full of raw ore glinting a dim gold.

"I had no idea this was all down here," Ash mused aloud.

"It used to be storage and coffers under Lundi rule," Toscan explained. "But when we took this place over we moved all the gold out and used half of it for feeding the army, since it grew so quickly, and the other half was locked up in the vaults in town."

"Huh. I didn't realize."

"Lucky for *you*, I already have a sample of Kenrose's writing somewhere around here. He keeps bugging me for another high speed vessel but with cargo-carrying capacity. I don't think he understands the physics of it at all," he grumbled.

"That does not surprise me," Ash said. "So. What do you need to make this letter believable?"

"Just tell me what it should say. You're the one who has to sell the lie."

They rounded a corner, and Ash came to the slate drawing board. There were lots of technical sketches, numbers, angles and math that she did not understand.

"Wow," she breathed. "And when will all this," she gestured to the figures on the wall, "be ready?"

"Soon. I just need to get a good clear day to dismantle the ship we're installing the mechanism into. It's quite the process, you can come down to the docks and watch them do it," he offered excitedly.

Ash nodded, not overly interested in watching a bunch of sweaty men pry up timber from the deck of a ship. "What vessel is it going on?"

"*The Vengeful*."

"Oh, I do hope that was intentional," Ash said wickedly. "I suspect there is a long line of us with a score to settle down south."

"Of course it was," Toscan said, affronted. "I don't do things unintentionally."

"Well, I didn't know you had a flair for the dramatic, either," Ash countered.

Toscan narrowed his eyes at her.

"Right then. We need to get that letter into Helene's hands before nightfall. Can you write it?"

"Yeah, yeah, I can," he waved her away. "You have the ring?"

"Yes."

"And you're absolutely sure it's his."

"Yes, Tosc."

"Just checking. The last thing we want is to stamp it with some random mark and wind up getting caught. You know how serious this is—"

"I *know*," Ash said, trying not to sound impatient. "No one is going to find out. And besides… if they do, we'll already be hundreds of miles away with a continent and a sea between us and trouble."

"Fine, then. Let's get to work. Sit."

Ash had taken a very roundabout route to sneak the parcel of mail into Helene's mailbox, and was finally letting herself breathe again as she exited the camp and went in search of Lukas.

She knew he wasn't faring well.

When she found him, he was perched at the end of the docks, where commerce seemed to be petering off for the evening.

"Hey," she said casually, easing down beside him.

He turned his head to look at her. "How are you?"

"A little rattled," she admitted.

"What's happened?" he asked, concern spreading across his face.

"Lower your hackles, Luk, nothing yet. I've just set something in motion that… if it goes awry, may very well be considered treasonous."

He blinked.

"It's a long story, but the short of it is that I expect to be back on assignment to go south. Do not ask how I managed to persuade them."

"Not treason if there's a good reason," he said with a wry twist of his lips.

Ash barked out a laugh. "No, I suppose not. Though I wouldn't repeat that to the higher-ups."

"So, you're going to be heading south, to Tunis?" he asked.

She was thankful that he seemed clear-headed, present. Fewer ghosts in his eyes.

"Yes. Yes. And I wanted to ask you to join me. You're a shit sailor, but there's no one I'd rather have guarding my back."

"Liar, you'd pick Ferrin or Soviel over me any day." His grin made his eyes twinkle in a way she hadn't seen in a while.

"That's not true! Soviel cannot tie a knot to save her life, trust me." She shuddered as her thoughts shifted unbidden to the girl wrapped in the horse blanket, rope twisted around her dead body. "Think about it. The two of us out there, gun-slinging, harassing Bourjony's southern fleet."

His smile faded just slightly. "Ash, I would really love to do that, but…" he trailed off.

"What, what is it?"

"I've got to go south. Back to Khalim. Just for a little while, to take care of a few things. I can't go on with this… wound in my chest. It will never heal if I keep pretending it isn't there."

"You think that will help?" she asked, not following.

He expelled a long, ragged sigh. "I need to see who I can track down from the rebellion. Check in on them. Find Damijan's mother and beg her forgiveness."

"Lukas." Ash turned to face him, her knees bumping him. "It wasn't your fault."

"Then why do I feel like this?" he asked in a voice so quiet, she almost couldn't hear him over the waves.

"I saw his face, when they drugged me last spring. I heard his voice. Ever since then, it's been eating at me. I thought I could leave it all behind, but I'm not sure that's possible."

Ash nodded somberly, taking a deep breath. "I will drop you off anywhere you'd like. In Khalim, off the coast closer to Eman's estate, wherever. But I need you to promise me you'll be all right."

He met her gaze. His eyes were sleepless and red-rimmed. "I will be."

"I mean it. I don't want to leave you far away when you're like this."

"Ash."

"I'm worried about your well-being."

"I promise not to do anything self-destructive. Besides, I have another motive for returning to Khalim."

"And what might that be?"

"Ealiyah and Amar have come of age since we left. They were able to drive out most of the Veiran forces. I want to bargain with them and get them on our side. Khalim will always be a gem desired by foreign empires. I do not doubt that Bourjony is sizing them up for the taking."

"They're of age now?" Ash slumped her shoulders incredulously and swore. "When I left Khalim they were silly little children in their regent's shadow."

"That is how time works, Asha."

She snorted. "Alright then, smart-ass."

Lukas rolled his eyes and popped the cork back into his bottle. "I would appreciate it if I could hitch a ride on whatever fine vessel you'll be captaining. Just past Khalim harbor would be ideal."

She laughed. "Very well, Lukas. I'll detour to Khalim for you. I have one favor to ask, though."

"Name it."

"When you pass through Eman's estate, I need you to give a letter to her and Mama."

CHAPTER FIFTY-FIVE

A few days passed, and Ferrin was awakened before dawn by a loud banging on her door.

"Wake up!"

She jumped out of her little cot and stumbled to the door, shivering. It was Lusia and Tommen, another of the young acolytes.

"What is it?" she asked, alarmed.

"Get dressed, it's time for your next trial."

"Before dawn?" she groaned, rubbing a hand over her face.

"You leave in an hour, come on!" Lusia said, frantically tossing Ferrin's tunic to her from where it had been drying by the fireplace.

"Alright, alright! I'm getting dressed, shoo!"

The children hurried out the door, Tommen closing it behind him. Ferrin sighed and set about changing, tying her hair up and washing her face. *Honestly, everything about this place is just bizarre*, she thought.

"Where exactly is this happening? And what is it anyway?" she asked as she stepped outside. The first traces of light were gathering at the horizon far across the nameless sea.

"Down on the beach," Tommen explained in an earnest tone.

"You *just* have to make it back," Lusia said emphatically.

"*What*? From where?"

"They're going to send you somewhere, to retrieve something. Making it back is key."

Was she still dreaming?

"Lusia, you are being incredibly suspicious. Is this a prank?"

"What? No!"

"We would *never*."

Ferrin squinted and looked back and forth between the potential co-conspirators.

"If I find out you dragged me out of bed for your own amusement before the sun was even up, I'll tell Nesseen all about how you sneak books out of the library and bring them to the beach—"

"We haven't! I promise," Lusia said, raising her palm in a pledge.

"Fine, then," Ferrin said, not fully convinced. "Lead the way."

They led her all the way down to the beach where she had first washed up.

"Good morning, child," Nesseen greeted. "Are you ready?"

Ferrin looked past her and saw a small skiff with a single sail flapping in the wind, the sun bleeding over the horizon in the distance, and choppy water devoid of color as the sky broke into the silver of first light.

No, she thought.

"Yes," she said.

"Beyond the horizon, there is a tiny island of rocks. You will sail to it and find the magical item that is hidden there."

Seemed relatively simple.

"You will come back here and climb to the island's highest level, from where the item was taken. Then you will have completed your trials."

"I—really?"

"We have all agreed that you can manage it. This will be your final, most difficult test."

Ferrin swallowed and turned to the horizon. There was a storm rolling in.

"And if I fail?"

"Then I was wrong," Nesseen said simply.

Then that was that. Just do this one thing.

Ferrin had launched the skiff an hour ago. She was repeating the entire conversation with Nesseen in her head, over and over, trying to figure out what the catch was.

The task, as it had been laid out, seemed far too easy. She was taut with anxiety as she waited for the hidden meaning to be revealed, for an unknown obstacle to throw her off course.

It was just about straight upwind from the shore of Vaiorka to the distant island. She'd been tacking back and forth, close to the wind for what felt like ages, the strong breeze doing little in the way of speed, somehow.

The storm she had seen lurking in the distance was looming even closer now, too close.

She was losing her nerve.

What if the creature from beyond the sky-tear came back with the storm? She would be helpless.

The island itself wasn't getting any closer, and yet Vaiorka had shrunk to a dot in the distance at her back. The sun was arcing overhead, slowly making its way toward noon. She wondered what day it was in the outside world, what her friends were doing, how the army was faring.

She was so close, so damn close to being finished here and going home.

Wasn't she?

Unless it had all been some terrible fluke. She had, intentionally or not, cheated her way to victory on the first trial, after all. A pit opened in her stomach. *Oh gods.*

The storm loomed closer and closer, the wind had picked up and was beginning to heel her skiff to the side.

"Shit." She lunged for the main sheet and undid it from its cleat, giving the sail some slack before hiking her weight over the side of the rail. The boat flattened out, but the chop was still bad enough to rattle her as she cut through the waves.

"Come on, come on," she urged.

Finally, the little rock-pile of an island came into view. Minutes later, she dropped sail and landed. She jumped out of the boat, onto a sandbar, and made her way toward the glorified rock-pile Nesseen had referred to as an island. There, unceremonious and shining atop a flat gray rock, sat a golden key. It was simple, really. No bigger than her smallest finger. She plucked it up and strung it onto a strip of hide.

With the key secured on the cord around her neck, she climbed back into the boat and shoved away from the sandbars surrounding the rocky islet.

There was no way it was going to be this easy.

The tempest crashed through the sky, cutting over the horizon in a rolling, raging fury. Ferrin had hardly made it back into deep water when the waves began crashing and roaring at heights far greater than she. She could hardly keep the bow pointed into the waves, could hardly keep from capsizing the tiny skiff as the wind urged her outward.

In the last twenty minutes, the sky had darkened to a shade past twilight, despite it being midday.

They'd given her no compass, no map. She had no idea if she was even facing the right direction to find her way back.

The storm was violent and cruel, testing her will at every opportunity. Her hair was slick with sea-water, her eyes burning with brine. The waves seemed to crest higher and higher.

Lightning came down on the horizon to her right, violent and sharp. It brightened the world around her, blazing white.

The thunder that followed shook her to her core. She thought again of the beast that had come soaring through the tear in the world.

The storm had to be supernatural in origin. The sky had grown impossibly dark, and the water viciously rough in the span of an hour. *This* must be what made the task as difficult as Nesseen had implied.

Out of nowhere, a rogue wave swelled to her right, the boat listing to the side as she tried to head up, into the wave. The cleat tore out of the centerboard, and her eyes went wide as the main sheet bit into her hand. "No!" she cried out as she fought against the pull of the sail with her bare hands.

The ship pointed into the wave head on, and went up, up, up, climbing the behemoth with all the might the wind could lend it. The wave seemed to grow, towering around her as it crested.

"Shit!" she yelled, feeling the rudder leave the water. She threw her weight forward, praying the wave wouldn't topple the skiff.

Lightning crashed again, and in the flash of light, she caught sight of a dark shape looming within the wave, watching her, waiting.

She gasped and jolted back in surprise.

The movement cost her.

Before she knew it, she was careening down the face of the forty foot wave, the boat tumbling after her, its mast broken, sail torn.

She hit the water with a *smack*. It felt like she'd fallen on hard, cold rock. The ocean pulled at her, sucking her down into the trough of the next wave as she fought against the current. She kicked and pulled, trying to get back to the half-wrecked boat, praying she could right it.

"No!" she grunted, nearly swallowing water. Another wave lifted the boat out of sight, threatening to crash down on her.

At the last second, she dove. Underwater, the crash was so loud she felt it reverberate through her bones.

The water was frigid and unforgiving as she kicked for the surface, her lungs burning. The boat was further away now, even more wrecked. She felt desperation engulf her as she swam her heart out to get to it. It was little more than a floating bit of detritus now. But at least it was floating. She threw her arms over the biggest piece she could reach, and coughed up the water she had swallowed.

She had only just caught her ragged breath when another crack of lightning lit the sky, illuminating the huge wave, just as it came down on her, crushing and smashing the rest of the boat beneath its weight.

She scrambled, and something wooden cracked her in the back of the head. Her grip went slack on the boat, and the cold ocean claimed her.

ELSEWHERE...

In the clean, sunlit office overlooking Larais' glittering harbor, the General approached the desk where the Regent sat.

"I hope you're bringing me good news this time, General," she said, not turning from the wide window.

"The attack on the rebel stronghold was not as successful as we had hoped," he reported. "It seems someone was there to warn them of our coming. Fortunately, while the rest of Galan was distracted, our runners were able to scour the caves you spoke of." He dug into his satchel and removed the pouch, no longer than his forearm, and no wider than his head. "We cut our losses once we found this."

"You found it?" she turned from the window, her ice-blue eyes alight with hope and hunger.

"Yes," he replied grimly. He tossed the sack onto her desk.

She took the pouch in her pale, slender hands, undoing the drawstrings, finally removing the odd little cup.

"Oh, it's *perfect*. Just as I remembered it."

"If I may ask, Your Excellency," he cleared his throat. "What is its significance?"

The Regent smiled fondly. "It is something very old, General. Something very old, and very powerful. I have not seen it in many, many years." She turned the cup in her hands, examining the metallic surface.

He'd noted the old-fashioned carvings on its surface when he'd first seen it, after one of the runners had turned it in with a proud smile. He didn't know what they meant, and they weren't in any language he recognized—he wasn't sure those were even *words* decorating the exterior.

"I know it must seem a strange trinket to risk so many men and resources on, but it *will* be integral to the next movement of our plans. Your patience and efforts will be rewarded," she assured him, her smile slick. "Though, it is a shame we weren't able to capture the remaining cities on the isle."

"We have our spies, they must surely have their own," he said.

"Yes, those spies… I have my suspicions about the lynch-pin in this particular leak."

"Shall we put in for a bounty?"

"No, General. I hate to deprive you of the opportunity, but I have far bigger plans for our duplicitous friend," she said, taking a leaf of blank paper from the pile beside her. She scrawled out a quick message, and folded it into neat thirds. "I'd like you to deliver this to Duke Hadringston's new townhouse in the Garden District. He and his wife will be arriving within the week, and I have much to discuss with him."

"Very well, Your Excellency." He bowed, and took the letter. "Before I go, there's something else."

"Oh?"

"In searching the caves outside of Galan, we encountered something else that I found strange." He clasped his hands together and walked back towards the door of the Regent's office. "I recalled one of the legends you'd mentioned when last we discussed the importance of the Barrian Isle."

"Well, General, don't keep me in suspense," she said coyly, her eyes glittering with a half-playful malice.

He retreated a step to the door of the Regent's office and whistled to the three of his men who waited in the hall. After a few muffled curses and thumps, they wrestled in the prisoner.

The Regent sat straighter, looking both curious and concerned about the new development.

"What's this?"

"Your Excellency," began the general, gesturing grandly to the prisoner and nodding for his men to remove the bag.

With a growl, her head was bared. She was gagged and bound, her dark hair a tangled mess, green eyes feral and wild. Her too-pale, ageless face was smudged with dirt from all those years in the caves. Her frantic gaze darted left and right as she took in the brightness of the office. There was murder in her eyes when they landed on the General. Unsurprisingly so, given that he was the one who had bound her, immobilizing her hands so she could not claw his face off.

He let the corner of his mouth draw up in a slow, victorious smirk as he looked from the prisoner to the Regent. For once, the Regent looked surprised.

"I present to you… the Witch of Galan."

Books in the Divine Corruption Pentalogy:

Wayward as the Wind

Summer of Storm & Strife

ACKNOWLEDGEMENTS

Wow! Two books. That's two more than I had at this time last year.

I'd like to start by thanking Teresa from Westjet for helping me make my plane yesterday when I almost missed it due to getting stuck at the border on the way to Calgary from Montana, to then fly back to Boston. Yeah. Poor planning on my part.

The last six months of working full time again, actually sticking to this deadline, and still saying yes to just about everything else has been exhausting but gratifying! Nothing like girl-bossing too close to the sun to keep you on your toes, am I right, ladies?

To my parents, thank you for being there every step of the way, I could never have gotten this done without your support and example. Thank you for encouraging me to build my own life. And also… please skip page 274.

A huge, huge thank you to Sam for zipping through a previous draft of SOSAS while on your VACATION(!!). Your live comments and feedback via text helped bring the story to the next level. You're always the one who makes it start to feel like a real book. Love you girlie.

Mer, for the nudge out of my comfort zone whenever I need it. Thank you for that. I hope the rental car company sees this.

Annie, for the head-canon castings. You have no idea how much joy it fills me with when you send me your mental castings for the characters in these books.

Sarah C, thank you for reading and giving me feedback on the semi-semi-final draft, it was so helpful.

Em, thanks for listening to my deranged spirals over breakfast, and commiserating with me about the ol' business struggles. Let's get donuts soon.

Nicole, I know you didn't get around to finishing that early draft just yet, so you can go ahead and DNF that one and just read this copy. Thank you for always being willing to go on weird little adventures with me, rain or shine. I miss you in the northeast, but I can't wait to come visit you in Virginia.

Katie, for somehow always pulling something real out of me, whether it's at a poolside bar mid afternoon on a Monday, or on a work zoom for an article about book one being partly inspired by NP. Thanks for that, by the way.

Jane, a raft-load of gratitude for your wisdom and your answers to my midnight texts about how to use tik tok and wondering if a word sounds too modern for this world. I'm glad you're always down to go on a fully unhinged expedition in the middle of the week, and I can't wait to read Tāvo.

To everyone who's read this far, (through almost 1100 pages!!) I can't thank you enough for supporting me. This is truly my dream, and every person who reads my books is helping me accomplish that. I hope you'll stick with me, and with this story, through the end. Thank you.

ABOUT THE AUTHOR

Whitney Knowlton-Wardle was born and raised on Cape Cod, the flexed-arm shaped peninsula that makes up much of Massachusetts's Eastern coast. She studied Visual Arts at SUNY New Paltz from 2015-2019, and spent a lot of time in the pool as a competitive middle-distance swimmer.

From a young age, she has loved to read and write fantastical stories full of long lost princesses, forgotten evils and anything with dragons and swords.

Whitney now lives in Boston with her two cats, Hector and Cassie, and loves to travel and spend time in the mountains.

9 798986 976433